THE
DAY O
THE
ROARING

Nina Bhadreshwar grew up in Barnsley, South Yorkshire. She set up her own magazine in the UK before relocating to the US, where she became the press officer and biographer at Death Row Records. She returned to the UK in her mid-twenties and retrained as a teacher. Now, Nina is doing a PhD at Dundee University while writing her second novel. She is a graduate of the University of East Anglia's Crime Fiction MA. *The Day of the Roaring* won Little Brown's UEA Crime Fiction Award and is her first novel.

@ninabhadreshwar

THE DAY OF THE ROARING

NINA BHADRESHWAR

HEMLOCK
PRESS

Hemlock Press,
An imprint of HarperCollins*Publishers*
1 London Bridge Street,
London SE1 9GF

www.harpercollins.co.uk

HarperCollins*Publishers*
Macken House, 39/40 Mayor Street Upper,
Dublin 1, D01 C9W8, Ireland

Published by HarperCollins*Publishers* Ltd 2025
1

ISBN: 9780008645687 (HB)
ISBN: 9780008645694 (TPB)

Typeset in Sabon LT Std by HarperCollins*Publishers* India

Printed and bound in Australia by McPherson's Printing Group

Dedicated to my parents, Kathleen and Dhiru,
for making the Peak District our Africa and for
living under a different Sovereignty.

Prologue

QUARTER-MOON,
APRIL, 1955 – KENYA

Njambi

Cicadas crack the silence in the limp-leaved forest. River water a black Kenyan tea – not English, no milk. *Moja, mbili, tatu, nne.* I am escorted by four of the loyalists. They are not loyal; they are traitors. They betray the land and their blood. Boys half my age, some from the Catholic mission, carrying long sticks to look like rifles in the dark. Only one has an over-sized rifle. He looks ridiculous. I can see through this blindfold. These boys cannot catch a fish or a goat, but they think they have power. Insects screech and throb through layers of leaves. I hear the rush of whispers, the crack of footsteps over dry straw.

A dry, calloused palm on my wrist.

'*Jambo ... aberighani?*'

He speaks like I have just come on a visit. He takes me by the hand and leads me into an airless place, the kusi monsoon pattering on corrugated iron roof. Daylight is thin.

'A chair. On your right. Sit.'

I stumble into a tea chest, feeling my hip hit a sharp metal corner. I grab the rough wooden rim for balance. He pushes me

1

towards an empty oil drum, rough with rust. This is not a chair. There is a waxed cloth folded on top. The rim of the drum cuts into my thighs.

I try to take the blindfold off.

'No. Leave it. We see you; you do not see us.'

But I do see him because I can hear him. He is Atu, the sergeant who came to Miss Hulda's place, who took the body. His face is round and shiny, the whites of his eyes yellow. He is not Kikuyu. And there are others here, confused men-boys, standing around with their sticks. They do not know they will come for them too.

'You need to tell us where he is – Ebu.'

'I have not seen my husband for many moons. I do not know where he is.'

He moves closer, circling me.

'You do.'

The low whine of a mosquito, like a dying saw, circles with him, undulating over the rank air. Two shadows enter with kerosene lamps. I see silhouettes and hollows, distorted shapes. I cannot see the blood on their linen, but I smell it. Atu cricks his neck from side to side.

Fear like blood rises in my veins. The shadows get closer.

'Maybe you need help remembering.'

'I cannot remember what I do not know.'

He laughs. It sounds like mud in his throat. Over it, the monotonous moan of the mosquito.

'Do you remember your son?'

My face is stone.

'Ah, yes. Indeed.'

This is an English voice, out of the dark. I see the milky outlines, hear the hard consonants.

'They cannot remember what they do not know. If you cannot freely tell us what we need, there are other ways we can get at it. You do not want those.'

I stand mute. A sarcophagus. They will not know my child.

'Your children have no land. Your treachery has robbed them.'

My treachery? This is Atu, for whose family my father gave goat milk when they had nothing.

The milky man stands in front of me. I can smell his stale breath like mould on bread.

'You are a traitor to Kenya. You are hiding the Mau Mau.'

'I am no traitor.' There is a babbling behind me. Atu steps forward.

'The men here, some Kikuyu, tell me you are *iruga*. We shall soon see.'

The fear rises to my ears. I feel him take my arms, pin them back. Someone lifts my skirt, another knee levering my legs apart, pushing me back on the drum.

'Eww.' The boys giggle like idiots.

'She is iruga. Even the Kikuyu men would not touch that.'

'What?' This is English man.

Atu says, 'She was raised by the Stumpf woman, sir. She wouldn't let the elders perform the cleansing ceremony.'

I won't let. I won't let. I want to scream. *This is my body. My land. I won't let. This is not yours.*

'Yet you still protect these men? Your husband is no friend of Kikuyu if he marries *iruga*.'

I spit between teeth. 'I know nothing.'

I feel the weight of wood on my cheek, through my jaw. As the black flashes light, I see the English man lift his hand dismissively, muttering to Atu. I cannot hear what.

'Your husband is Kikuyu and he married *iruga*? Well, he must know you can enjoy with others. Traitor one way, traitor all ways.'

They just beat me last time. Beat me worse the second time. I know what happens the third time. Milky man returns with a glowing ember. I see it. I scream. They grunt.

They leave me dumped by the oil drum on the soiled waxed cloth, bleeding, burning. They took my son. I know he is dead. I smell his blood in the earth. But my comfort is my other child will never know this. I swallowed my seed, spit my truth far, far from here. She is safely hidden in the dark.

Here is the list of my three main issues: Land. Justice. My Seed. I forget freedom: I just want my seed to survive.

3

Chapter 1

Tuesday 14th September, 2010 – Dewbow, Derbyshire

A loud primal bellow. A living chainsaw rips through the forest. Diana opens her blackout blinds, squinting at the horizon. She starts her morning run at 5.30 a.m. when mists rise off stones and bracken. Up here on the banks by the woodland, where the moor edge pushes over, autumn's shoving in its shoulder. The lone oak stands at the door to the wild moor, arms outstretched to the elements.

She can smell the rut already.

The deer start their serious business here every September. The sweetness of a rising late summer breeze is now darker and riper: a pungent, ancient smell. She can't escape the earth.

Bang! As if to a starting pistol, the air splits, trees shudder. Silence for two seconds. Then ravens squawk, wood pigeons flutter, ground trembles as the giant stag leaps over bracken hedge, diving deeper into the woodland.

She clutches the damp, cold stone wall before vaulting, entering the Bronze Age, bracken raised like spears, the rutting season when stags stalk does, does bolt, hunters stalk stags. Predators hover. No matter how knackered, even after pulling an all-nighter, Diana is drawn by the sirens of nature, through the roots, ferns and jagged boulders. The deer dip beyond the gorse breaks, deep wooded dells, ribboned by tinkling rivulets.

Over the field, Diana swipes at unruly black Afro curls bouncing into her eyes. *Mental note: haircut asap.* Diana's work hours and personality mean she's made few acquaintances in her neighbourhood. She really should get out more – or something. In twenty minutes, she will be in south-west Sheffield and her workday will swallow her whole. But here, in the fierce elements, nature stamps its morality.

BANG!

The blast behind her rips through her eardrums, her bones. Reverbs in her head. The branch in front of her shatters, falls. She jumps to the side, all reflex now, all doe. Heart banging, she bolts across the path, the brook, stumbling on stones, her breath in hard cold knots. Don't look back. Vault the stile.

She arrives at her narrow box of a cottage, heart pumping and not because she can't run. She leans over the rose bush knowing she should stretch but she's going to retch. Her ears are ringing, her head is ringing. The shot's still ringing. No – she can hear real ringing. Still retching, she turns the key in the kitchen door, hurls herself over the sofa, reaching for her BlackBerry.

'Hello?' she pants.

''Kin 'ell, lass. Who's the lucky guy?'

'Who is this?' she snaps.

'Who is this, *sir*.'

Seriously.

'Sorry, sir. Just been out …'

'Filing cabinet on the Legley Road High School site. Flies. Smells bad. Got DS Robertson going down there. Blokes can't shift the thing. The developer Geoff Thomlins' having kittens. Get down and see what's what, Walker.'

'I'm on it, sir.'

'So I gather,' he chuckles and hangs up.

Driving over the edge of the Pennines, everything reminds Diana of what she's entering: the craggy boulders the broken crowns of a certain defendant, untameable yellow gorse the hair of a veteran shoplifter. The desolate Mothermoor, the loneliness of the sociopath. And the fraying heather hemming in the Victorian sprawl of Sheffield's south-west, the city's proud corner of opulence. She's seen it happen to the sharpest: that insidious blunting that immersion brings. The ten miles distance into Derbyshire gives her a perspective she can't afford to lose – even if her terraced cottage can get bleak in the winter. There's still a strange comfort in returning at the end of each shift to the horizon of criminal teeth boulders, the familiar silhouette of the lone oak snag, raised like a middle finger to the sky.

The first chill of the coming winter mists up her windscreen. Sky's a darkening grey. Two hawks circle patiently.

They know.

Outside the demolished Legley Road High School, DI Diana Walker opens the car door to the sheepish grin of Major Crimes' DS Carl Robertson, a tall, bulky man in his late twenties with serious blue-grey eyes and a Tintin quiff.

'It may be nowt, Boss. Just a locked filing cabinet.'

Diana frowns.

'Why didn't they open it?'

'Workmen only noticed today as they have to clear the site. Said it's been vandalised since Bank Holiday but just left it. They're a bit spooked out.'

Slamming the door, she marches next to Robertson, cold hands thrust deep in her pockets, eyes on the yellow tape manned by two uniforms. While they check her through, she pulls on latex gloves, frowning at the barely cleared approach path.

'It doesn't smell good, Boss.'

Diana looks up at the giant skeleton of a half-demolished 1960s relic. In the middle of the taped clearing, incongruous as a lost Dalek, a grey filing cabinet, a 1970s menhir tagged in orange paint with a splattery daub: 'Merka' in mushroom bubble-letters. Over it, a cloud of flies hovers.

She walks over rubble, scattered concrete islands. Robertson scrambles after her.

'Probably a dead dog in there. Bored kids in summer holidays.'

Diana does a one-eighty. A group of workmen huddle around a van on the other side of the tape.

'When was this place demolished?' she asks.

'Twenty-eighth July, Boss.'

'That filing cabinet should be in a museum.'

'The workmen say it was in one of the mobile classrooms and dumped here when they took them away,' says Robertson.

'But it was empty then?'

'Yes – the supervisor said they checked that no paperwork was left around. Data security or something. Auditors had been in and all keys were handed in months ago. That's what alerted them. It's heavy now and drawers are jammed.'

Diana ducks under the tape despite the uniform's yelp. One of the workmen, clearly the youngest, stands apart, nervously stubbing out a roll-up. An older, bald one nods towards him.

'It's Sean, detective. I think he's paranoid of filing cabinets. You can use our bradawl though.'

He holds out the tool. Diana ignores it but Robertson takes it with a nod.

The men chuckle but Diana knows it's nerves. Sean, the young kid, scowls. He's built like a bull, brown-bronzed skin stretched smooth over muscles better fitted for stadiums. His trembling hands open another Rizla.

Diana walks back over to the filing cabinet, followed by Robertson, holding the bradawl like a redundant limb. She looks closely at the lock at the top, peering in. She runs her gloved hand down the drawers and tries to open the top one. It doesn't shift.

'Think it's jammed, Boss. Here.' Robertson holds out the bradawl, but Diana's eyes are fixed on the lock.

'No – the pin's across. It's been locked.'

Robertson looks on the ground.

'Maybe key dropped out …'

Diana rummages in her pocket and pulls out a paperclip. She straightens it out, picking it into the lock like a key. The top drawer ricochets open with a clean snap. Nothing inside but dust and dead flies. As she tries the second drawer, a black cloud of flies bursts out.

Squatting down, she yanks at the bottom drawer. It slides open with the buzz of wings. Diana falls back into the swarm of flies, back of wrist to nose.

Gasping for air, she stands up, eyes fixed down. Nestling in an open black bin liner, a mass of white maggots feasts on half a fist, bust at its grey seams. Further back, eyes bubbling with larvae, the grimace of a startled head grins back.

CSI Tom Marks emerges from the tent that now covers the filing cabinet. Beyond it, a huddle of irritated workmen slouch, squinting into the sun. They answer a volley of questions from two uniforms.

Diana walks back over the rubble to Marks.

'How long?'

He shrugs.

'The foreman says place was demolished in July, but this is fresh meat. Maggots still. In this heat and a metal filing cabinet, it's like being in an oven on Gas Mark two. Not enough blow flies yet. I'll need to get it to the lab to be sure but ...'

'Roughly?'

'Two weeks max.'

Diana looks around, scrutinising the wreckage: turquoise painted drainpipes and chipped rusty frames.

'No CCTV?'

'Just over there, Boss, over the whole site. It's turned off though,' Robertson says.

'Why?'

The workmen shrug en masse.

'Boss said company was being audited for compliance with building regs and that.'

Diana frowns.

'Get details from Thomlins,' she calls over to Robertson.

'Nobody else on site?'

'No. There were a few bods with clipboards, vests and hardhats in July, early August. From council or auditors,' bald head says. 'Thomlins int pleased. Wants to get cracking on the development.'

'Tough. He'll have to wait while we're done.' Diana turns to walk across the rubble. Robertson catches up with her. 'And find out who last had the keys to the old school and is responsible for all the ...'

She waves her arm over the rubble of the school.

'Leftover objects.'

Robertson nods and swallows.

'Boss …'

Diana stops, turns.

'I used to work here.'

Diana stares at him, incredulous.

'When?'

'2005–2006. I was a teaching assistant. It's what made me want to go into policing.'

Diana sighs, surveying the wreckage from the 1960s behemoth: rusty turquoise piping, shards of grey, frosted glass, splintered yellow desk wood, etched with decades of teenage rage and obsession – all piled on top of a pyre of concrete rubble.

'Smashing. I'll have to run it past the super. School closed officially July, right?'

'All the years under Year 11 left in summer 2008 and just Year 11s in for the next year. Then it all closed after their GCSEs in July 2009. They were moving the mobile units off and out earlier.'

Diana peers down the road. A black-windowed Jeep cruises past, blasting out Dizzee Rascal.

'Bit weird, eh?' remarks Robertson. 'Just doesn't look right.'

'Not what you'd expect to find in a filing cabinet, no. And most filing cabinets aren't left out in the middle of a demolition site.' Diana looks up at the tree line. 'House-to-house for anything unusual the past month. I need to get an ID as soon as possible. So, give me a list of school employees, students, parents. Trawl missing persons.' She pauses, frowning. 'And I want everything about the history of this building and planning permissions.'

Diana looks at the filing cabinet's back, tagged with bright orange spray paint in huge letters, filling the entire length and breadth. 'Merka'.

'Find the tagger. Any tags around the city. Any unlikely lads or lasses about. Marks, how old is this paint?'

Marks approaches, bends, scrapes with a small tool. 'Recent – within a couple of weeks.'

'Filing cabinet's been here at least as long because the drips are on the rubble around it.' Diana's eyes root through the surrounding detritus. She nods at something five yards away.

Marks goes over, picks up a battered spray-can, rattles it.

'Empty. I'll check for fingerprints though. Nozzle's still here.'

She wanders over the gnarled teeth of a ravaged school, shards of concrete, spears of rust-crusted pipe.

'Moving a filing cabinet is noisy business. Even in the mud. How come no one heard this? What other noises were going on?' Diana asks the air. Robertson looks around.

'Noisier during peak times and there's been the roadworks, Boss.'

'Find out the dates of those. And if they worked overnight. And we need to find that filing cabinet key.'

As she walks back and forth, trying to outline the drag-route of the filing cabinet by the ruts in the mud, she sees something glisten against concrete crumbs. Not like the dirty bits of window in the main yard. Stooping, in gloved hands she picks up a smooth clear acrylic nail, shining like a shell on the pebbled shore of the wrecked ship of Legley Road High. White tipped, glistening like a transparent pearl. Diana calls over to Marks. He approaches with a plastic evidence bag.

She holds out the nail. 'Bit boujee for a builder.'

Marks frowns, pulls out tweezers, bags the nail.

'Indeed.'

Chapter 2

Monday 30th August, 2010 – Creamfields, Halton, Cheshire

Bruno

Creamfields catering. Nowt down for it. No change off a fiver for two coffees and queuing for twenty minutes. I walk back to her. Two days flat-out raving, Charlotte can still look lush next to a burger van.

'Here you go.'

'Cheers, babe.' She stares about with that same spaced-out look she had when I first saw her at Impy's.

'You seen Amy, Bruno? I'm getting a ride back with her.'

I shake my head. She looks at me over her rim of froth.

'How you getting back?'

'A mate,' I say.

'Can I get a ride with you?'

I look at her: peachy skin, ash-blonde hair, wispy curls, pinked-up lips sucking on overpriced coffee with a wince, blue eyes on me but wandering off. Firefox hoodie, skinny jeans, hundred-quid trainers scuffed up in mud and festival shit because she knows Daddy can get another pair just like that. Pandora charm bracelet. I imagine her stuffed in back of a Mondeo estate with greasy youts running county for Ryan, shaking blades in pocket, stuffed socks, bloodied knuckles, mouths and arseholes full of rock and H pellets. Imagine her finding it a thrill. Imagine her in a train, strung out, in a trap house. Imagine the other life she could have had with those private school A level results, uni, driving licence, laughing free, buzzing on someone else's shoulders. Kissing someone who can give her that life.

In ten seconds, I know.

'Na. Got to chip, Charlotte.'

Her face falls into the coffee. Cold, grey sludge. She tips it out on the ground.

'Text me, yeah?' she says.

I look her up and down. Leave no room for hope. Push it out at ten thousand feet.

She's doesn't get it, goes in for the hug. I just give her the shoulder stroke, my eyes already on Ryan's van at the far end. I move between the clutter of bodies and litter through to the arse end of summer.

Chapter 3

Wednesday 15th September, 2010 – Sheffield Police HQ

Diana can never find a parking spot in the rammed HQ police car park. In ten years, she's yet to find out what game she has to play in order to secure one. Getting back to Major Crimes HQ involves finding a side street without double yellows within a five-minute walking distance to Merrick Street.

Robertson is already stationed at his desk, scrolling through a list of names on an old monitor.

'Nice one, Robertson,' says Diana. 'Staff and students, yes?' She peers over his shoulder. Robertson's desk is renowned for being orderly – unlike Diana's own, which is a jumble of notepads, plastic coffee cups, bulging beige files and Post-it notes stuck on any and every surface. Robertson, on the other hand, has a potted aloe vera plant, a pen tidy, a labelled stapler and a personalised coffee mug, a gift from his fiancée, Daphne. He's immune to the piss-take.

'Made some calls, Boss. Most of them out of work, on supply or at school. There's a couple who didn't appear at start of term for their new roles …'

'Oh?' Diana frowns, sitting on the corner of her desk.

'The head of PE and Gifted and Talented – or rather ex. Leroy Young. He never showed up to his temporary contract post at High Peak. His wife says she hasn't seen him since Bank Holiday weekend.'

'And that's not odd?'

Robertson shrugs. 'They're separated. Said he'll be off with some new tart. Just mad because he was a no-show to the kid's birthday party.'

'Okayyy. And?'

'John Daniels, the Head of School. Still not showed up to his new post as deputy head at Pitsmoor High. Divorced before the summer. Ex-wife says she's no idea.'

'Any recent photos?'

Robertson clicks, bringing up an image of an athletic black man.

'Leroy Young.'

'OK … not him for sure. Let's see the head.'

Robertson clicks on another link. Diana squints, head on one side.

'Next of kin?'

'Not sure. There's the ex I just spoke with. His dad lives in a care home in Birmingham. Mum died last year of ovarian cancer.'

Diana inhales.

'Bring the ex in.'

Diana walks into the Chief Medical Officer's office. Will Gorman's long, lean fingers scroll through images on a 1990s monitor.

'Not seen anything like this in three decades. Even on conferences.'

'Pre-planned?'

'Well, he was killed before he was butchered. Look here …'

Diana moves around to where he's pointing at the screen. There's a clear, large bullet hole at the base of the neck.

'He was shot. I'd say from at least thirty yards. With a rifle.'

'A rifle?'

'Yeah. You won't find that bore from a handgun. And those fern spores. They're from the Peak District. I don't think he was murdered in town.'

'Any chance though?'

Gorman shakes his head. 'Not really. A bore like that requires a gun with a big bang. Unless you use a silencer.'

Diana purses her lips.

'What about the weapon for butchering?'

'Butcher knives. Cleaver. A hacksaw on some of the bones.'

'A butcher?'

Gorman taps the screen with his pencil, shrugs. 'Or a surgeon. They knew what they were doing, that's for sure. And that mole on his cheek …'

The intercom buzzes. 'DI Walker, Mrs Daniels is in reception.'

'Rock and roll. Let's go.'

Diana meets Mrs Joy Daniels in the foyer, looking as if she might be late for a train or forgot to switch the iron off despite her well-groomed appearance. Magenta nails, highlighted hair. Forties. Simple white shirt, jeans and platform sandals, clasping and unclasping the clip on her shoulder bag. Marks and Sparks class.

She frowns. 'Do I really have to do this? I mean his dad's—'

'In a nursing home in Birmingham. With Alzheimer's.'

Mrs Daniels sits back in a sulk. 'There's his sister in Australia. Our decree absolute came through in May.'

'We just need a positive ID.'

Mrs Daniels sighs. 'Well, I know he's been out and about this summer. A mate of mine saw him at some charity party in Derbyshire. Just because he's not answering my calls means nothing – we're divorced.'

'His neighbours haven't seen him since the Bank Holiday weekend,' states Diana, checking through her notepad, although she knows it for a fact. 'He was last seen leaving his flat with a black man on the morning of Saturday 28th August in a silver car.'

Mrs Daniels raises her eyebrows.

'He doesn't drive a silver car. He drives a …'

'Black Lexus. Which is still parked up outside his flat.'

Mrs Daniels shrugs.

'Ducking and diving his debts. As per usual.'

Mrs Daniels' lips set in a firm line of exasperation.

Diana looks at her. 'Are you alright?'

She sighs. 'Can't believe I'm doing this after everything he's put me through.'

Which is …?

15

Instead: 'This way. The Chief Medical Examiner will talk you through.'

The room's cosy: purple curtains, green houseplants, cream cushions, an oak coffee table. Two glasses of water. A tape recorder whirs. Mrs Daniels sits on an armchair facing Diana. Gorman, tall, straight-jawed, broad shouldered, in wire-framed spectacles, enters, holding a large envelope. Brief introductions are made. He sits down, pulling his immaculately creased trousers up an inch from the knee.

'We're going to see just the picture of a head, no body, Mrs Daniels. As I think DI Walker explained ...'

Mrs Daniels slowly closes her eyes and ejects an angry sigh. She opens her eyes and looks directly at Gorman, poker-faced.

'The remains were found in a black bin liner in a filing cabinet. There was obvious decomposition. You mentioned he has a scar in his cleft chin ...'

He places a photo face down on the table. Mrs Daniels' perfectly manicured hand reaches out, flicks it over, like a card in a game of rummy. She breathes in fast, blinks. Flicks the photo back down. Her fingers tremble and she clutches her bag as if for support.

'He don't have a mole on his left cheek but ... That's him. That's John.'

Gorman turns towards the tape recorder: 'For the record, Mrs Daniels, ex-wife, formally identifies the head as being that of John Daniels ... Thank you, Mrs Daniels. DI Walker will take you through to the grief counsellor.'

Mrs Daniels shakes her head, standing up. 'I'm OK.'

Takes two steps towards the door, stumbles, falling against the sofa. Diana catches her but she's out cold.

'She said he didn't have a mole though ...'

Gorman stands up.

'That's no mole. It fell off in the bag. It was a bloated tick.'

'Walker! In here.'

A shiny foreheaded wedge of pink flesh framed with wisps of auburn wire appears in the glass-officed doorway.

'Wish me luck with the super!' Diana hisses to Robertson, sliding off her desk.

Entering Superintendent Marchant's office is like entering the Tardis. Medals, certificates, trophies, press clippings, a glass-fronted cabinet, the huge mahogany desk with a massive blotter and several beige files piled up in a neat stack. Marchant's a six-foot bulk of a man with receding auburn hair and an indelible history in South Yorkshire Police. A beat officer during the miners' strike, he's now on the threshold of a well-paid retirement. His father led the policing of the miners' strike and Hillsborough. Retired to Spain now. Marchant's old school, with all the heritage of the nefarious East and West Ridings. Diana knows he expects her to bail or ask for a transfer, that he hasn't a clue how to deal with her. The lads resent her status, but he's under pressure from national legislature to show a more 'diverse' task force. Nothing too serious; in fourteen more months, he'll be on the golf course every morning – not glaring from his chair at gormless policemen and pigeons.

She stands at the door. Marchant motions her to sit on the well-worn leather chair in front of his desk.

'Well?'

'Sir, it's the Head of Legley Road High School. John Daniels.'

Marchant groans, picking up the handset. 'Which line?'

'Sir. The filing cabinet.'

He frowns at her. Drops the handset. Knuckles on forehead.

'Mutilation?'

No, sir, he did a Houdini in the bottom drawer.

'Yes, sir. We're missing the torso and legs.'

Marchant sighs. 'Smashing.'

He picks up a paperclip from his desk, looking at it as if it's an oracle.

'I need you to close this, Walker. Asap. Whatever's required. What do you know about the school?'

'We're just working through employees prior to its demolition.'

'Anything?'

'Two male members of staff missing.'

Marchant raises red wiry eyebrows.

'The ex-headmaster and ex-head of PE,' says Diana.

'Well, we know where *one* is.'

Marchant scrutinises the solicitors' rooftop opposite as if

17

expecting to find the PE teacher among the pigeons that shit on his car. He leans forward, fingers pressed together.

'Walker, we both know the row around closure of Legley Road High. Parents, students *and* staff were fuming. Don't want Mayor on me back again. Press'll have a picnic.'

Diana catches her breath. 'Sir. I'll get this sorted.'

'You better. DS Neville and DI Lawton are chomping at the bit for this murder case. Any fk-ups or delays and it's theirs. Got that?'

'Yes, sir.'

'I guess we'll be needing a press conference later,' he groans.

Diana swallows.

He looks at her. 'What?'

'I don't think we should release the ID yet, sir.'

'Of course we're releasing the ID! This is a high-profile murder investigation …'

'Exactly, sir, and with due respect, that's *exactly* what the murderer wants. He goes to the trouble of killing Daniels out of Sheff, chopping him up and lugging the body back to the site of Legley Road where he knows it'll be found. In a filing cabinet. By Geoff Thomlins & Co—'

'What? Geoff? Geoff Thomlins, the builder who owns …?'

Diana nods impatiently. '… or some random kids. This is a curated crime scene, sir. Totally premeditated. That filing cabinet's only recently been moved; we had rain over the weekend so I can see the drag marks to the middle of the site. We were meant to discover it this week before full decomposition. We were *meant* to be able to identify the victim. And it was locked. With a key.'

Marchant looks at her as if she's just swallowed his car keys. He turns to scowl at the pigeons scavenging in the gutter.

'Just saying, sir – they may drop a few more clues.'

Marchant glares at her. 'Or another body.'

'And we need to find Leroy Young as a matter of urgency, as he was the last person seen with Daniels. Just a couple more days, sir.'

'Walker, in a couple of days I want the bastard charged and locked up.'

Diana nods, heads for the door.

He groans. 'OK, but I'm saying it's Legley Road staff. And tomorrow I'm letting them know it's Daniels.'

One day. It's a compromise, but it's as good as she'll get.

'Thank you, sir.'

Opening the door, she catches sight of Robertson at his desk. Her heart sinks.

'Oh, sir. There's an issue.'

'What sort of issue, Walker?'

'DS Carl Robertson, he used to work at the school. Only for a year. As a teaching assistant.'

'Sake, Walker!'

'I know, sir. But I really need him on this with me.'

'When did he leave?'

'2006.'

Marchant closes his eyes. 'Four year since. OK, let me do some paperwork. Send him in for ten minutes. He could be helpful. We'll need a formal statement though.'

'Yes, sir. I'll send him in now.'

The usual curse is muttered as she leaves.

The allotments are stacked in lush, ordered rows along the side of the hill. It's peak harvesting time so there are several bent backs rummaging in Broomgrove greenery, cutting, pruning, collecting in barrows and buckets. Diana finds her mum's easily: the only one with the huge bean-leaved forest caged in by bamboo, the sixty-two-year-old's dark, shiny skin weaving in and out, long fingers snapping, tenderly pulling through the foliage. On the path beside the shed is a large colander of cherry tomatoes, greens and sweetcorn. A swollen butternut squash.

'What's in the pot tonight?' Diana says, peeping through the canes.

Her mum's round face peers over the heart-shaped leaves. A sunshine grin.

'Diana! Githeri tonight. You want a plate?'

Diana inspects the colander. 'Got a late one.'

'You can carry this lot to the house then.'

The house is a mere three hundred yards away, so Diana nods, hoping the veg won't dust up her black blazer and trousers. Her mum follows her out, twill garden shirt, loose floral smock and clogs, her greying hair braided tight to her scalp. Diana knows her mum wishes she wasn't police, but she's come to accept it as inevitable, growing up in Sheffield with Diana's outsider problem-solving nature, her dyslexic lateral-thinking. They walk together down the path.

A long-limbed bronze-skinned man in worn overalls and green wellies strides towards them, pushing a barrow full of garden tools. His shoulder length black twists are tied off his face with a green bandana, yellow T-shirt grimy with sweat, a huge grin splitting his face.

'Thanks for these, Rehema!'

'No worries, Michael. I can't be hoeing every day!' Rehema cackles at her own joke. Michael looks at an invisible earthworm on his shoe. Diana shuts her eyes.

'Just put them in the shed, Michael. Thanks.' Rehema chuckles.

'OK. And there's some green beans at the end of the path for you.'

'Wonderful! Oh, this is my daughter, Diana.'

Diana gives her mother a side glance. Michael nods briefly, turning and pushing the barrow towards the small shed.

'What? You don't want to stay and chat?'

'I'm working, I told you …'

'Work, work. I've got to get back anyway. It's book club later and a potluck. You can't come, I guess?'

'No, Ma. I'm …'

'Working.' They say in unison.

'It's a murder case, and …'

'People get murdered every day, Diana.'

'Can't catch a killer if I'm out at book clubs.'

Rehema pushes out her bottom lip. 'Debatable.'

It's pointless arguing with her mum. 'I got five okra coming, you know.'

'Really? You feeding them like I say?'

'Of course. Give me a year or two, I'll beat your wee forest, see.'

'Hmmph!' Rehema laughs. They are ambling up the path, Diana in front.

'What book you reading?'

'We're just finishing this new one, *The Book of Night Women*. Then we're starting *Kindred* by Octavia Butler. You should come along one evening. Help you get some perspective.'

'Ma, my whole life is perspective. I don't read books – I read crime scenes.'

Rehema reaches out and rubs her daughter's slender shoulders.

'See – that's why you need perspective.'

They are at the door to the tall, terraced Edwardian house.

'OK, Ma. Gonna get off. I'll call for a plate later.'

Rehema half-smiles at the path, but her eyes are elsewhere.

'MaMa's deposition is needed for the Mau Mau Uprising Commission. I don't want her stuck in some random hostel in London.'

'What? Aw, wicked! And it's not Mau Mau, Ma. It's the Kenyan Human Rights Commission. Is the case really happening?'

Diana puts down the colander of vegetables. Rehema inspects them.

'I think so. I'm converting my study into a bedsit for MaMa.'

'MaMa.' Diana exhales. 'Is she OK about this?'

'She needs to know she has done everything she can to get justice for Pa … and herself. But you know MaMa – a law unto herself.'

Pa. Another person neither of them know. Knew.

'When's she coming?'

'Next week. And I'll need you to help me out with her even if you have a murderer on the loose.'

A cold breeze blows down Diana's neck. Rehema's chuckling, but the air sticks in Diana's throat.

Michael walks back down the path, the setting sun radiating behind him.

'All good, Michael?'

He nods. 'Thanks again, Rehema. You have a good evening.'

'I will. You too.'

He smiles, nodding at Diana, and strides across to his patch. Rehema looks after him with a smile. Diana pecks her mother's neck.

'See you later. Love you, Ma!'

Rehema hugs her tightly. Diana trots back down the path, just as she has since she was ten.

Diana puts her key in the ignition, but has a moment to smile in wonder. MaMa is her favourite person in the whole world, her mother's biological mother. Her one real link to her family's unproven past. Her own father was a visiting Glaswegian professor with whom Rehema had a brief affair during her postgrad years. During a lecture on plant microbes, he suffered a very convenient heart attack, two weeks after Rehema told him she was pregnant. Professor John Carmichaels from Glasgow University. An expert on plant microbes. Published lots of papers on antinomycetes and algae, a couple on fungi and microbial ecosystems. Diana isn't sure what that tells her exactly. She *is* growing some black mould in her bathroom, however. Although Rehema was raised by Scottish ex-missionaries in Edinburgh, she sought out her birth mother after having Diana and finding herself a single mum in Sheffield trying to finish an MSc in nutrition. Diana's childhood summers were spent with MaMa in Bagamoyo. While MaMa and Rehema's relationship is formal and strained, MaMa's always warm and free with Diana. Still, it was Rehema who had urged MaMa to get justice. Justice for everything that started The Great Separation between MaMa and Rehema. Between the unknown and what is. MaMa is the key to that hope.

Diana starts the car.

Chapter 4

WEDNESDAY 15TH SEPTEMBER, 2010 – THE RYANO HUT, SHEFFIELD

Bruno

Man, Wednesday night queue's started rate early. Gicky gelled heads leaning on windows, hands on phones, spit on sidewalk. My clothes stink of chicken grease and Ryan's dirty roll-ups. Can't even read me own writing on this poxy notepad. Should get me eyes tested. Ms Calley used to go on about it. Don't matter now. Not like I'm studying or owt.

Tasha screeching: 'Dark chic-ken. Steamed veg. Fried dumplen!'

Usman, flashing his Nike Air Max, starts his mardy moan: 'Chips! Oi. I won me chips.'

Into kitchen where Tasha's sweating like some short treacle jug, ladling brown chicken. She's gonna kick off when I ask for chips. Watch. Number 6, I say. She's like, 'He wan chips? *And* dumplen?' Tasha can do fifty words in one eye-cut. She scoops chips onto a tray so here we go. Tasha – Usman, thank you. Rate. Next.

That's when I see her. The light green-eyed, flat-iron-haired tan lady what drives an Audi TT cuz she's a top auditor – not cuz she's some dealer's gal which makes her the ultimate baller. *Plus* she eats Jamaican food twice a week. And all I can run on her is, 'Hiya Maya.'

That's how I feel when I see her: *High on Maya*.

'Same as usual please,' she says. 'Plus a serving of fried plantain. And make that two. I've brought Mr Samuels along for him to see you butcher.'

Next to her, a tall ginger with a square chin and a large, hooked nose. Bare forest sprouting out on it. Looks like CID in his plaid shirt and corduroys. Man's nodding at me. I'm not sure about this – not on a Wednesday night. Ryan'll kick off. But chance of an apprenticeship outside of Sheff's too rare to pass up. What I really want to be is a paramedic. But nice one, Legley Road, you fked that up for me so beggars can't be choosers.

Ryan come in, trying to make out he's a boss. He's a twat. I wish he wasn't my dad, wish he'd cover his tattoos, wish he'd stop the medallion man shit. I reckon he fancies her. Holding out his hand. What's she want to shake your greasy hand for? I'm not a business transaction, knobhead.

'I'm Ryan, his dad. And his boss.'

Not for long if I can get this.

Nasal Hair: 'Rob Samuels, Exclusive Game Butcher.'

I know Ryan's got his schemes and reasons for getting me into Dewbow, but he can do one if he thinks I'm having owt to do with his county enterprising. I keep my eyes down and lead Maya and butcher through.

Back kitchen's cold, dark. Two large fridges against one wall, two chest freezers against other. A large metal table in the middle. One frosted window with a crack in one corner. A sink. Two plastic bowls. Three butcher's knives and a pair of poultry scissors resting on the draining rack. Half a bottle of cheap blue washing-up liquid and a scrubber. A roll of paper towel. Nasal Hair Samuels, sweating in his plaid shirt, leans against the chest freezer. He looks a bit nervous. Maya looks cool as fk, like it's normal behaviour to spend Wednesday night carving chickens.

No one can style a chicken quart like me.

'Maybe talk us through what you're doing, Bruno.' I love her voice. Just posh enough. I put on clean apron and take a plastic chopping board from behind the draining rack and sharpest butcher knife. Pick up the sharpening block, run the blade once, twice, thrice along its flat edge. Fridge is packed with six chickens. I get out the biggest, carefully placing it in middle of the board, plastic mixing bowl to one side. Don't want her thinking I'm some savage. Wash me hands 'n' all. Twice. Dry on the clean tea towel. Pick up knife.

'First I quart it.'

'You what it?'

'Quart it, cut in smaller pieces and then remove the skin. So.' I lift the legs. 'Find the joint, break it back.' Snap. 'And cut it.' I do same on other side. 'Then remove the wings. Find the joint. Then cut, snap it back and cut again. Then … separate the breasts from the back and again.'

I lift the bony pink mass. 'Find the joint and cut through. Separate the chicken wings.'

My fingers prise and then tug at the limbs, cut through the bone, smooth and easy like Nana showed me.

'That's a chicken quartered.' I toss the parts in the bowl. 'Then remove the skin from the legs.'

I peel off the skin with the paper towel like Nana taught me and leave skin to one side. 'Separate the thigh from the drumstick with the poultry scissor. Now there's two halves of breast. Each half cut into three pieces. So.' I crunch through bone with each cut from the blades. Their eyes never leave the carcass.

'That's your chicken, good to go, for brown stew, curry, jerk, wings. Next you just wash it through in lemon juice water.'

'He's got his food hygiene certificate,' Maya says.

Samuels nods slowly. 'Great. Some lovely butchery there. Well done, Bruno. Can you get to Dewbow for 8 a.m. every Saturday?'

I'm nodding. I don't know how, but I'll get there. Man looking me up and down.

'You strong enough for game?'

What's he mean, game? Blood rush to me head. Ohhh – deer and pheasant and that. Still, Maya best not be fixing me up with no batty man. Heard about these sheep shaggers and gay farmers. Maya laughs like she's reading my mind.

'It's hard work sometimes, Bruno.'

I shrug. 'Be a change from here.'

'Great. Seventy for the day plus bus fare? I'll get the paper-work together and expect you Saturday at eight.'

Almost what I get for a week at Ryan's chicken shit-shed.

Speak of the devil, he stomps in, phone in hand. 'Hurry up, son. There's a queue all the way down to the offy.'

He's looking at Maya weird. Red-eye wasteman.

'Sorry but Wednesday's a busy night for us.'

'It's fine. We'll get our chicken and go.'

Chicken and go. *Go go go.* She hands over a twenty-pound note to Ryan, snatches the white carrier bag off the counter as she strides out, hips swivelling in her tight navy pencil skirt and stilettos, that awesome ass on stallion pins. Rubber-necking men parting like the Red Sea before her. She turns as she gets to the car.

'See you later, Bruno!' she calls.

Sake. The grease and steam in this place. Can't even get a grip on pencil.

Chapter 5

Thursday 16th September, 2010 – HQ, Sheffield

Diana squints at the autopsy report in front of her.

'Anything?' asks Robertson, approaching her desk with two mugs of steaming coffee. He tries to find a space amidst the piles of files, paper and Post-it note arrangements, gives up and just holds out Diana's mug. She takes it without looking up from the report.

'Thanks.'

Robertson sits down on the swivel chair by his well-ordered desk and slurps. 'Brutal stuff.'

'Shot in the neck in such a way back of his head wasn't blown off. Takes some skill. Dismembered. Placed in a filing cabinet.' She flattens the report on her desk. 'Where's rest on 'im?'

She flicks through the photos the CS photographer left on her desk. She needs to go back up there.

Robertson frowns. 'A deer tick?'

'A *dead* deer tick. It fell off. That's the mark left,' corrects Diana.

Robertson continues to scrutinise the report. 'Aren't ticks parasites? What's he doing with a tick on his face?'

Diana shrugs. 'Ticks latch onto fern from animals like sheep and deer. Most likely he wasn't killed in Sheff.'

Diana hands the report to Robertson in a manilla folder.

'You checked on Daniels' social and financial situation?'

'He wasn't popular. Got the impression he was a bully, not particularly supportive of staff. I trawled through the *Sheffield Star* and the *Telegraph* too. A lot of staff and parents blamed him for the school closure.'

Diana sighs. 'Narrows it down.'

Robertson flicks through his notes.

'Divorced in May. His ex claims he repeatedly got in debt. Gambling.'

Diana picks up another file from her desk. 'Tasty.'

'Yup. Didn't sound too fond of him. But that divorce just about cleaned him out. Plus she just lost out on the pension.'

'Check her out all the same.'

Robertson shoots her a quick look. 'Daniels had no luck since Legley Road closure. His new job was as a deputy at a Manor school in Special Measures.'

Lawton, a meaty sour-faced man in his late thirties with a bushy moustache, walks over, scooping over Robertson to read the report. 'My money's on an OCG. Bloke got himself in too deep. This is an execution to send a very clear message.'

Diana takes hold of the report. 'Get me the facts, the info, even if it doesn't fit our hypotheses.'

Lawton raises an eyebrow and turns away with a shrug. 'Rate. But trust me …'

'Trust the intel. Lawton, you and Neville get his bank details. Also, interview Geoff Thomlins. Find out a bit more about the site, the sale, and tell him zero activity on there until this is wrapped. It's a crime scene.'

Neville and Lawton look at each other and nod – but not at Diana.

'Who was the colleague he worked closest with when at Legley Road?' she muses.

'Looks like Leroy Young.'

'What's the love life like for Daniels and Young? Were they an item? Or about to be?'

'Not Leroy Young. He was a right player, Boss. If there was a student teacher, he'd be sidling up to her, asking her to come out for Friday drinks after work with the rest of them, trying to get her number. Even the kids joked about it.'

'So. Doesn't mean to say he wasn't interested in male encounters. Leroy Young …' Diana looks at her screen. 'Also missing since August Bank Holiday weekend. Didn't turn up for work. Ex-wife thinks he's just dodging his debts or shacked up with someone else. And find out who could have access to filing cabinet keys.'

Diana picks up the file and heads towards Marchant's office.

'Where you going, Boss?' Robertson hates feeling he's missed a beat, his face post-penalty-kick flop.

'To tell the super we need to bring Young in for questioning pronto. Meanwhile, put him down as an official MisPer, unofficially a Person of Interest.'

The briefing room is like an unplugged fridge, smelling of mould and out-of-date meat with an underlayer of stale police fart. A clutter of tables is parked at the far end, back-ending a battered corkboard upon which Diana pierces a photo of the filing cabinet. DS Neville, DI Lawton and two other officers slouch against the back wall, DC Khan and DC O'Malley bums-on-desk. This airless box is the official incident room for Operation Kestrel – Diana's name for the homicide investigation – hoping for a kestrel's vantage. One of the room's walls is devoted to pockmarked busted corkboard, the other three to peeling paint that last saw a brush three decades ago. The carpet's worn to string in places, dried food rubbed into parts of it, cigarette ash and other unmentionables. Worn vinyl chairs are scattered around. DS Robertson pins some school photos to the corkboard. Leanna, the blonde office clerk, brings in a stack of plastic cups. Neville studies the back seam of her pencil skirt as she bends over to plug in the urn. Gorman and his crew from CSI stand in the far corner, sipping beige grey liquid out of the flimsy plastic cups. Marchant hovers around the door, nodding briefly at DS Neville and DI Lawton who give the slightest of nods back.

Diana faces the cluttered space, impatiently pushing back her wiry locks, wrenching a black band off her wrist before snapping it around the unruly curls. Robertson hands her a pointer, which she passes between both hands.

'Right, we know the basics. Gorman, can you update us on new revelations from the CSI and autopsy?'

Gorman weaves through the chairs, holding some stapled papers, pushing his wire-framed specs up his nose.

'The dismembered head, left arm and neck were in a black sealed bin bag. Entomology of maggot larvae and flies revealed two weeks of decay. The neck had been severed using professional meat-cutting surgical or butchery tools in a methodical manner. Death occurred prior to mutilation and a large bullet hole in the cervical spine section revealed entry of a bullet possibly from a rifle or large bore gun. Fern spores and a deer tick on the body suggest the murder took place in woodland. The body was alive while in woodland else the tick would not have stuck.'

'We are liaising with Greater Manchester and Derbyshire police forces as fern spores are usually found in the Peak District.' Diana looks towards Robertson, who steps forward, hands in pockets.

'Unfortunately, CCTV was taken off the site a couple of weeks before the end of August.' He hesitates, looking towards Diana and then at the large brown envelope on the table. Diana opens the envelope, pulling out a photograph which she pins in the centre of the corkboard. A grinning, round-faced, balding man with blue eyes, a wonky nose, and big ears stares back at the room. Short gasp and murmur.

'The former head of the former headmaster of Legley Road High School, John Daniels. Neville, Lawton, I want everything you can pull on this guy: his past, his future, his bank account, his relationships, his habits, how often he brushed his teeth, any parents he particularly infuriated, who he last kissed. As Gorman just told you, it would seem the body was brought back to Sheffield, having been killed elsewhere, and was purposefully parked in a filing cabinet on the same school site as his last place of employment. The murderer seems to want to make a point.'

Diana moves around the room, thinking aloud, pirouetting to face the corkboard herself. 'What is that point? Why not make Daniels a MisPer, put him in a shallow grave? Why a filing cabinet? On a site where building work is soon to start? And who was the last person to see John Daniels?'

Robertson clears his throat. 'Two different neighbours saw him get in a silver car with a tall black man on Saturday 28th August.

Neighbours put time around eleven a.m. They can't confirm the car model or plate. No CCTV. Seemed surprised to learn he was a headmaster. No one saw him return. His own car, the Lexus, has not moved. Was the tall black man Leroy Young? If not, who was he? Where is he? No sounds from flat and bins not put out. Just seemed to disappear from there. According to phone records, he's not made a text or call since then, although we still haven't recovered his phone or clothes. There's been no cash withdrawals, card payments on Daniels' bank account since Friday 27th August. His mum's dead, father in a home with Alzheimer's, siblings over in Australia. I think folk just assumed he was on holiday or busy preparing for school, a new life as a single man.'

'Leroy Young. Another missing mystery. On the run or another victim?'

She nods at Robertson.

He looks at his notes. 'Leroy sent his last text Saturday 28th August at twelve noon to his missus, Julie Young, saying he'd see her in a couple of hours. She's not seen or heard from him since. There's been movement on his joint account as Mrs Young's been using it, but nothing on his own personal account since Bank Holiday. His mum, Mrs Young Senior, came in to report him missing on Monday 13th September, but it wasn't put on the list till now. He's gone off-radar before, usually when in debt.

'Also, some gym gear for a male much taller than Daniels was found at Daniels' flat. The sofa looked like someone had been sleeping on it and there was a rolled-up sleeping bag behind it. There's some official mail for Leroy Young care of Daniels' address.'

Lawton rocks on heels, suddenly interested. 'So, these two just go AWOL?' he says.

Diana shrugs. 'Let's double-check DNA. If Young has a key, why hasn't he been back? Or asked after Daniels? And why sofa-surf at Daniels' instead of his own home? So far no indications they were an item, so what's going on?'

Scribblings and scratchings of heads, legs, elbows.

'Have we traced and interviewed all school staff?'

'In process, Boss. Several have died, or left before the closure.'

'Who?'

Robertson squints down at his list, flicking pages.

'Aaliyah Matthews, the assistant bursar left December 2007, Mr Griffiths the bursar off sick from August 2007 and then died of cancer in February 2008. Then there's Leroy Young and Daniels, obviously ...'

Diana interrupts. 'This case involves a community that feels it was betrayed by the school, the council and the Planning Commission.'

'Someone said "Heads will roll!" and meant it,' Lawton mutters.

Marchant snorts.

Diana glares at Lawton. 'Robertson used to work there, so I've asked him to provide the background context.'

Robertson end-taps his notes on the desk.

'Legley Road High School founded in 1958 as a boys' grammar school. Excellent academic reputation. It replaced Uppercliff's grammar school. In 1970, it became a mixed school and a comprehensive by joining with Uppercliff School for Girls. It's in the south-western tip of Sheffield, so focused on the diversity and excellent academics, sport and the arts.'

'It was a good school.'

'Yeah, Boss. Legley Road – split-site school as set on a very enviable green site, lots of leafy woodland, rolling grassy fields, next to the Mansley Moor Park. Old established trees. Great property round here, and it's the closest school to Derbyshire on the south-west edge.'

'What went wrong?'

'Sheffield Local Education Authority, LEA, and UK politics. At first there was a good mix of white and ethnically diverse ...'

He flicks a cautious eye at Diana, but she is staring out of the window.

'... students. But as the asylum-seeking Pakistanis, Somalis, Afghans and Syrians started to move in ...'

'The middle-class whites moved out.'

'They went to Laurendale or King Edward's, over the hill.'

'And the trauma and behavioural issues increased while the curriculum stayed the same since 1965 – right?'

'Until Mary Calley, yeah.'

'Who?'

'She was this cool English teacher. She's the one who inspired me to go into policing, seeing how she really cared for these kids, their families, where they were coming from. She used to teach in the refugee camps after uni. Spent a year in Syria or Sudan or something. She kicked out all the old books summer of 2003, when she was appointed head of English. Just ordered a skip and spent the summer hols clearing out the cupboards, ordering in books these kids could relate to. She rewrote the entire curriculum. GCSE grades went up, school attendance improved. Fewer exclusions.'

Diana raises her eyebrows.

'Yeah, anyway, Sheffield Council need to make books balance. Previously with Labour, there was a lot of funding and support for black and minority communities. The school needed a lot of EAL and SEN support. The community of South Sheffield grew poorer, lots of new incomers, less stable businesses.'

Lawton and Neville yawn, O'Malley's spacing out. *Cut to the chase, Robertson.*

'Then it goes murky. Something about the DfES five-year strategy plan, the LEA, declining rolls of kids and needing to close some schools to make bigger ones. LEA needed to amalgamate schools, making mega ones and a one-stop sixth form. After 2007, Legley Road got the worst GCSE results in the country, an inadequate Ofsted inspection. It was put in Special Measures, failed and then closed. Land sold off to a private property company.'

'Geoff Thomlins.'

'Most of the school was closed in 2009 and the Year 11s were only ones being taught while they took exams this June. Just a handful of teachers stayed. Rest were supply.'

Lawton yawns again.

'What about this English teacher's relationships with Daniels and Young?' Diana asks.

Robertson widens his eyes. 'She didn't get on with Daniels, always arguing with him about something when I was there. But she was pretty thick with Leroy Young. They had to work together on the tracking data.'

'Staff and students. I want names, dates and anything remotely and unremotely interesting on file. Including your awesome Ms Calais or whatever she's called. Let's bring her in.'

33

Robertson winces, looking down at his desk. His voice catches.
'Calley, Boss. That'll be hard.'
'But not impossible.'
'No, it will be impossible.'
Neville sniggers. The four constables turn towards the chuckling Neville and Lawton.
'Made national news in April,' states Neville.
Diana opens up her arms, shaking her head. 'What did?'
Lawton coughs. 'They found the remains of her in a Nottingham bedsit. Dental record job. Been dead two year like.'
Diana stares at him. Then at Robertson.
'Coffee, Boss?'

NOTTINGHAM STAR

Thursday 22nd April, 2010

Teacher's Body Found In Bedsit

A woman's remains were found behind a pile of unopened mail in a Beeston bedsit two years after her death, a Nottingham inquest heard.

The TV and heating were still on when bailiffs discovered the body of former Sheffield teacher, Mary Calley, 35, in the bedsitting room. On Thursday 25th March, bailiffs and housing officers had gone to the bedsit in a sheltered block for victims of domestic violence following rent arrears of thousands of pounds. Nottingham police believe she died of natural causes soon after her arrival in December 2007. The inquest recorded an open verdict.

Some of Ms Calley's former colleagues from the soon-to-be-closed Sheffield comprehensive, Legley Road High School, attended the inquest held at Nottingham Coroner's Court, held by Deputy Coroner Thomas Stevens. Ms Calley was unmarried and had no children.

Dental Records

Ms Calley's body was so decomposed that the only way to identify her was to compare dental records.

A Coroner's officer said it appeared she had been escalated to a priority case by an incident of domestic violence in Sheffield in the autumn of 2007 and placed in Nottingham's refuge accommodation as a victim of domestic violence.

When staff from the housing charity, Morningside Housing Trust, arrived at the bedsit, they drilled the double-locked door open and discovered piles of mail plus medication and food with February 2008 expiry dates, the Coroner's officer said.

Pathologist Dr Michael Evans told the inquest he had not been able to establish the cause of death because the remains were 'largely skeletal'. However, police did not regard the circumstances as suspicious. Ms Calley's previous medical records from Sheffield revealed she suffered from asthma and gastro-intestinal issues and had been referred for a suspected stomach ulcer in the late autumn of 2007.

Morningside Housing Trust issued a statement which read: 'Ms Calley moved into the property, a priority needs rented accommodation, in December 2007, shortly before Christmas. Housing benefit was in part paying Ms Calley's rent, and given her age and former professional occupation, there was no reason to suspect anything unusual had happened.

'According to our records, Morningside Housing Trust was not contacted by either neighbours or family to raise any concerns. We were only alerted when significant arrears had accrued and there had been no response to several warnings and an eviction notice. Because it is a refuge, we did ask police to accompany us when we tried to gain access.'

The bedsit is part of a sheltered housing block of flats behind a parade of shops in Beeston. Neighbours said that, because the TV was always on and no one answered, they assumed the tenant had mental health issues or preferred to be left alone.

A neighbour who moved in in July 2008 said, 'A lot of us keep to ourselves up here. I never heard anyone visit, but assumed she worked nights or liked to be left alone. It's a shock that she'd been a teacher and had some family and no one came. I don't get how her electricity wasn't cut off because her TV was on all this time.

'It did smell a bit, but they're not regular with the bins and the stairwells stink of junkies and urine. There's always flies in summer because of bins.'

Diana exhales, leans back, focusing on the photo of the vibrant woman in the pic, smiling in a school portrait photo. Her eyes flick to the photo of the book club dinner party. She jackknifes forward, black coffee flying, scalding her legs.

'Shit!' She stares at the screen.

Robertson rushes up with the kitchen roll. 'Sorry, Boss. Should've warned you. Shocking I know.'

Diana shakes her head, pointing to the photo at the bottom.

'Robertson – what's my mum doing in a photo with your Ms Calley?'

Diana pushes open the back door. Rehema's kitchen is a mess of large cast-iron pans, an assortment of jars, overspilling piles of ripening fruit, squashes. A large pot bubbles on the six-ring stove.

'Hello? Ma?'

Upstairs she hears a thump and scrape. She steals up the back stairs, careful to avoid the creak-spots. She looks at the family photos on the navy walls: African queens and chiefs, a brown, gap-toothed Diana kneeling by a billy goat, squinting against the sun. A door slams. Diana steps over the top two stairs and crouches down in the box room at the top. A door opens and Michael, face shining with sweat, steps out with a hammer. He jumps back, stumbling over his toolbox. Nails and screws fly everywhere.

Diana stands up. Michael disentangles his long limbs from the shrapnel of hardware spillage. He grins.

'You make me jump!'

He wipes his hands on his jeans, puts out a large flat palm.

'Michael. I think we met at the allotment.'

Diana looks over his shoulder. 'Where's Rehema?'

He takes the hand back and bends down to pick up his tools. 'Rehema just went out to catch the last post. I'm finishing off the shelves.'

'Oh.' Diana feels stupid. Awkward. 'I'm Diana.'

36

'Right.' Michael puts a nail between his teeth and turns to screw it in the wall.

Diana waits an awkward five beats, walks back downstairs, holding onto the banisters.

Rehema bustles into the kitchen.

'My little chief! Staying for supper?'

'Nope. Got a lot on.'

'Shame. I was hoping you'd come to The Black Sistahs Book Club with me.'

'The what?'

'We're reading a sci-fi book next month. You always used to like sci-fi comics.' Diana fiddles with some plums in a colander.

'Who goes to this book club, Ma?'

Rehema nods at a list held by a strawberry magnet on the side of the tall fridge-freezer.

'The list needs updating.'

Diana gets up to look at the curling list, handwritten in an elegant blue biro scrawl. Nine names. Diana's heart sinks.

'Mary Calley – isn't she that teacher who was found dead earlier this year?'

Diana frowns. There's another familiar name: *Aaliyah Matthews*.

Rehema fills the kettle, switches it on. It comes to the boil noisily.

'Ma?'

'We have a new member too. Can't remember her name now. Must add it.' Rehema busies herself with the tea-caddy. 'Mary's always an honorary member.'

'She used to teach at Legley Road High School, right?'

'Yes.'

She is not the one to do this. She knows, but she had to know from her mum's own mouth first.

'Someone will have to talk to you about her. Not me. Don't worry.'

Rehema snaps: 'What's poor Mary got to do with your case?'

Diana stares at the book club list, the large, scrawled handwriting.

'Dunno. Maybe nothing. Did Mary write this list?'

Rehema squints. 'No, Anoona.'

'Who?'

'Anoona. Shanda. My friend. The librarian up Pitsmoor.' Rehema turns towards her. 'You are going to meet me and MaMa on Saturday, right? Pond Street bus station. I'm taking the National Express night bus down Friday to collect her from the airport Saturday morning.'

'What time will you get back?'

'It's supposed to be five. But you know National Express.'

'Saturday afternoon – or Sunday morning?'

'Afternoon.'

'I'll be there, Ma.'

Rehema stares at her, unblinking. 'Diana, I do not care if there's a massacre, they blow up City Hall – you make sure you are there waiting for her.'

She wishes her mum wouldn't be so dramatic.

'I've said I'll be there, Ma.'

It's like she wishes them into being.

Silence holds an entire unspoken conversation. Rehema pours water into the large blue teapot. There's a sound of drilling from upstairs. Diana looks up. Then at her watch. Pushes her chair back.

'No time for a cup of tea with Michael?'

'Got to go, Ma.'

In her car, Diana punches the wheel with her forehead. Her phone rings. She looks at the unfamiliar area code.

'Hello? … Speaking … Yes, I did. It's about the bedsit case … Calley. Monday at ten? Brilliant.'

She clicks off her BlackBerry looking up at the box-room window as she starts the ignition. A glimpse of Michael's shoulder.

Back upstairs at HQ, Diana looks down the register of Year 11 students from 2009: Axmed Ahmed, Omear Masoon, Adnan Farquhar, Qasim Asman, Amal Hussein, Lee Richardson, Lori Bhartia, Sonia Kaur, Usman Clarke …

The only minority at Legley Road High School was white British. Diana runs her blue screen over the papers, meticulously scrolling through. The exams officer apparently had a bit of a meltdown in 2006, entering some students twice, some not at all.

Diana leans back, chewing her biro.

'You got anything from Sheffield LEA about the students' records or target setting? We need to find any wild cards in here. Anyone with a grudge. Staff too.'

Lawton groans. 'That'll be all of them then.'

'All?'

'Well, they all lost their jobs from a failing school. How's that look on a CV?'

Diana raises her eyebrows.

'Let's get a shortlist of the ones with above-average motivation.'

Lawton and Neville give cursory nods.

'You and me, Robertson, we'll work on the students.' Diana flicks through the papers on the curriculum award, the GCSE results for 2007. 'The ones who didn't get to take up their college place because they didn't get those results.'

Neville shrugs. 'So what? They still get into college or a job.'

'That's why they came to this country, innit? Free education, free healthcare!' shouts Lawton.

Diana narrows her eyes. 'Park your politics, Lawton, and look at the digits please. What about the kids who had their funded support pulled? That feels like someone robbing your own bank account to a kid. Check on that. Some expected As and Bs year before and they got straight Us. I want their names, numbers and traces done by end of day.'

'It's just school. Kids don't give a care.'

'It's not "just school", Lawton. It's public funds. And someone cared enough to commit murder.'

Lawton gives a weary sigh as if tolerating a teenage tantrum. 'We're not social workers.'

Diana stands up, pulls on a jacket in two fierce shrugs.

'Exactly. We're still trying to find a motive, so, unless you have eliminated before you've even investigated, crack on. As far as I can see, we've four, maybe five lines of inquiry so far: Daniels and his gambling debts – Neville you're on that. Geoff Thomlins – maybe asking Daniels to run the school into the ground for a backhander? Check on him and all the business transactions, Lawton. O'Malley and Robertson – investigate Leroy Young and Daniels' relationship. Young is a MisPer and the last person to be seen with Daniels. We have to find him.

Lawton – you seem to think it's an OCG. Follow up any reports of drug dealing at the school and Daniels' stance or connections. Robertson, check out the students – see what they know or tell. In fact, I'll come along for a couple. See if I can get a feel of what Legley Road was like under Daniels.'

Doors swing behind Diana leaving Robertson racing to catch up and Lawton scowling red.

Chapter 6

FRIDAY 17TH SEPTEMBER, 2010 – THE RYANO HUT, SHEFFIELD

Bruno

Fkn sick of this. Every time. He says 'Make sure you're at Hut for nine-sharp as I need all joints done before Tasha arrives at ten while I get in. There's a delivery at nine and you'll need to help wi unloading.' He says. He always says. And what happens? Muppet-head never turns up while eleven and I have to unload on my own and sit wi a pile of headless goose-pimply chickens, onions and taters while Tasha arrives. Then she gets face on wi *me*. Nowt to do wi *me*. Like I'm one causing her stress and inconvenience. Yeah. Tasha, sure. Nowt I like better than quarting chicken on a morning. I told Mum but she's just 'It's a job, Bruno.' I say it's slave labour. Hundred quid a week for the hours I put in? Last fella got twice my wage and worked no evenings. 'It's minimum wage, Bruno, love. It'll go up when you're eighteen.'

Well, I'll be eighteen next week. I'll be lucky if I get a card off him let alone a raise. She says he's me dad but I'm not sure. When I asked her other day, she got rate mardy like 'What you mean?

41

What you saying? I'm your mother.' I stayed over at Axmed's that night. I'm not saying she's a slag. But I know Nan always hated him. And I don't look owt like him. I wish I had a sister or brother then I'd know. Feel like getting a paternity test except it looks bad on Mum.

Meeting Gina at 4 and I'm not cancelling just cuz he's 'got to nip out, mate'. Nip out in your own time, not mine. She's gonna finish wi me I know it if I do it again. And I really like her. She's got these criss dimples. A laugh like fairy bells. She's also into Xbox. And she's going college, doing A levels. Like I should be doing – not sat on a doorstep with a box of headless chicken.

I'm a fking headless chicken. Dunt know what I'm doing here. Should just tell him where to shove his giblets. That ambulance just gone past, that should've been my job. I'd got the predicted grades, the college place. And then friggin Legley Road goes tits up.

I know Ryan wants to slide me into his shotting but he's no chance. Like I'm going to run or deal for him. Got to do something though …

That Maya Smith, classy woman who got me set up with the Dewbow Saturday butchers. I'm gonna see if I can ask her to ask him if he'd include the week too. Anything. Just get me off dirty London Road and plastic bowls of mouldy tomatoes and black bananas and A-boards telling me a head's been found in a filing cabinet. Sheff's messed up, man. I've had five different youts already approach me, give me the nod, asking if I'm serving. I'll serve an onion at your greasy head if you ask me again. Do one.

Nine fifty-three. Here comes Tasha off bus, with face on. As per. And that tosser's nowhere in sight. She's muttering and mithering like it's *my* fault. Pointless saying owt. I just nod and pull in the sacks soon as she's opened shutters and back of kitchen.

Axmed's just blanked my text. Again. Man, I think he's started running for Ryan. He best not have.

Na, Axmed's sound. He wouldn't have. Probably at mosque innit.

* * *

Diana

The Ryano Hut is at the end of a parade of shops: a hairdresser's, newsagent, a barber's and an internet café, aka community centre for unemployed men of equatorial ethnicity and little English. The takeaway is painted bright yellow in a defiant Caribbean pose against Sheffield's grubby pastels and grey, the letters painted in alternate green and red. A grease-stained front window is covered with various flyers. At seven in the evening, it's getting busy. Young males in Air Force 1 trainers, crisp dark jeans, black or white T-shirts, like a jumbled piano keyboard, bop about outside, up and down with their Nokia phones. Two in, two out carrying blue stripy carrier bags stuffed with a variety of polystyrene containers.

Diana gets out of Robertson's blue Volvo, striding towards the Ryano Hut while he checks all his doors are locked.

'Hello. Can I speak to Bruno Pierce please?'

A tall, narrow-shouldered man with a dragon neck tattoo is serving fast at the cash till. He looks up.

'Who's asking?'

Badge time. 'DI Walker, Sheffield Police.'

'What's he done?'

'We just want to talk to him. He was a student at Legley Road High School.'

The man looks Diana up and down before yelling, 'Bruno!'

Someone cough-mutters 'Feds', but when Diana turns faces are screwed to the overhead menus.

Bruno walks in, drying his long-fingered brown hands on a starched white tea towel. He wears an oversized yellow T-shirt, loose bleached jeans, Converse white high tops, Afro clipped tight to his head, a light gold chain around his long neck. His wide-spaced green hazel eyes and aquiline nose arch cat-like from full lips, a razor-sharp jaw. A faint pinky red scar from a scabbed cut above his cheekbone. The tattooed man nods toward Diana.

'Lady police needs to speak to you. Legley Road business.'

Bruno frowns. 'What for?'

'DI Walker. Hello, Bruno. We're interviewing all the past Year 11s about Legley Road.'

Bruno raises his eyebrows, folding the tea towel neatly with his hands. 'Good luck wi that. I left *last* year.'

'I know. We just want to ask you a few questions.'

'Man, I don't …'

Tattooed medallion man hisses over the counter at him.

'Oi. Stop your lip, Bruno.' He nods towards the back. 'I'm his dad, Ryan. You can use back kitchen. I've got a load of customers I'd like not to scare away, thanks very much.'

He glowers at Diana. Robertson eases his way to the front of the milling youths amidst a lot of mutterings and 'It's called a queue, mate'.

'I know you.' Bruno's eyes narrow at Robertson. Diana groans inwardly. In his starched shirt, corduroys and navy Berghaus jacket, he looks more like a PhD student.

'This is Detective Sergeant Robertson, Bruno. Would you prefer the station?'

Bruno looks him up and down. 'Na. Kitchen's good. You're not taking me in.'

Ryan lifts the Formica top and Diana and Robertson walk through.

'Hurry up wid me saltfish, mon!' shouts one impatient customer, kissing his teeth.

'Wah you let di Babylon inna fi?'

'Aks me one more time you get tuna sandwich!' retorts Ryan.

In the back, Bruno pulls up a dirty white plastic chair to the trestle table, one mist-glazed, grubby window letting in a box of light. Diana takes a chair at the side, and Robertson leans against the draining board. Bruno crosses his arms, scowling at Diana.

Name … Bruno Pierce. Age … 17. Address … 25b Park Hill, Sheffield S2 1XL. Occupation … kitchen assistant. GCSEs … Robertson scribes.

'Nada … unless you checking for Us.'

'That's strange. From the school files and forecasts it seems you were predicted straight A stars.'

'Yeah. Tons of predictions, but what they didn't predict was their own unpredictability: fking teachers leave, funding and projects pulled, school closed so they can build some luxury flats. They shoulda gid me that prediction instead.'

'Are you angry about that?'

Bruno snaps his neck around, glaring at Robertson. 'You here to wind me up, detective?'

'Your old headmaster, Mr Daniels, was found dismembered in a filing cabinet.'

'I knew I recognised your face!' He points at Diana. 'You were on TV with that fat ginger bloke.' Bruno pauses. 'Mr Daniels though … shit.'

So much for the press conference with Marchant.

Diana says: 'You don't seem upset.'

Bruno slaps the table with the folded tea towel.

'Why should I be? He wornt bothered bout us. Fkin sold us down the swanny for some poxy flats. Where's my funding gone? I had two sponsorships and study support and then everything flops. Cut back. Changed. Stopped. Bullshit excuses. Ms Calley leaves. Next ting, school's closing and they expect us to come into half-arsed lessons delivered by retired alkie supply teachers.'

Bruno looks at his fingertips. Diana waits.

He shakes his head: 'I did not kill the headmaster, detective. I just don't give a fk. Difference.'

Suddenly, he swings towards Robertson, pointing a finger.

'You're Carl, Axmed's teaching assistant.'

'He's a police officer now, Bruno.'

Bruno kisses his teeth, looks away.

Diana sighs. 'What about Mr Young?'

Bruno's eyes become slits. 'What about him? Do I need a solicitor?'

His eyes unblinking stare at Diana.

Diana groans inwardly. 'No, no. I just want to find out more about him. He was your mentor, correct? And he was close to Mr Daniels as Gifted and Talented co-ordinator, head of PE?'

Bruno shakes his head. 'Mr Young was weak, man. I knew he wor banging Ms Calley. She started acting all weird. Like my aunt used to.' Bruno's eyes grow distant.

'Weird?'

'Puffy eyes, concealer on bits of neck, nervy, mumbling not having a laugh in class any more. She used to be criss, Ms Calley. Mr Young messed with her head.' He looks to the side. 'Probably knocking her about 'n' all.'

Diana frowns.

'What makes you think that?'

Bruno shrugs. 'She just got dead nervy and moody.'

Hardly evidence.

'Do you know where Mr Young is? We need to speak to him.'

'No, I don't. Left me in the lurch. *He's* the reason I'm stuck here, chopping up onions and chicken, day in day out. Instead of on the pitch, at uni, getting on with a life.' Bruno stares at the frosted window. 'Promises but we're not a priority.'

Diana leans forward. 'Do you know why Mr Young may be missing?'

Bruno shrugs. 'Probably got with another bird. He's always cheating on his missus.'

Diana's silence grates the unspoken.

'Why? You think he killed Daniels? He fked up his career by getting school closed. That's reason enough. Just for the record or Alan Partridge back here: it all went to shit long before the school closed.'

He stares at the freezer.

'If I *was* going to kill anyone, it would be the bastard who made Ms Calley leave. Everything went pear-shaped after. But no one gives a care about *her*.'

Diana sits back. 'Ms Calley …?'

Again. Why does her name keep popping up, like a body in a river?

Bruno's eyes brim. 'Let her rot in a bin of a bedsit in a city miles away. Rot on her own for two year. *Two year*. How can you do that to your fam?'

Diana stares helplessly at Robertson, but his expression mirrors Bruno's. He's stopped writing, hand trembling.

'Daniels deserved to rot! But Ms Calley didn't. You care about some bloke with a suit, but no one looked out for Ms Calley.'

Diana puts her head to one side.

'That looks like a nasty cut you got near your eye. Been in a fight?'

Bruno lightly touches his face with a scowl.

'It's rate. Just knocked it against an open drawer.'

Diana nods slowly. 'Nearly had your eye out there.'

He whips the tea towel on the table, kicks back the chair.

'Go find your headmaster killer. I've got chicken to quart.'

Diana starts. 'You do butchery?'

Bruno frowns.

'I quart the chicken, yeah. Can fillet the fish. Got my Health and Hygiene certificate 'n' all in case you about to arrest me for that.'

'You do it here?'

'No. On the street.'

Diana deadpans, not in the mood any more.

'Yes, detective. I do it here.'

Bruno snorts, shaking his head. He gets up.

'Oh, one last thing,' Diana says.

He stops. Doesn't turn.

'Where were you this last August Bank Holiday?'

'Creamfields. Enough footage of me there.'

The door swings back and forth. Diana surveys the empty stage of the room, the demented backing vocals of refrigerators humming loudly.

'So Ms Calley's biggest fan is also a butcher …'

Chapter 7

SATURDAY 18TH SEPTEMBER, 2010 – POND STREET BUS STATION, SHEFFIELD

Pond Street bus station on a Saturday evening is a churning pot of multicolour, the pavement a shambolic wall of suitcases, boxes, blue and white nylon laundry bags stacked like breeze blocks around fidgeting would-be passengers of every size, shape and colour. The coach from London to Newcastle is late – of course. Rehema had texted Diana at four to say they had only just got to Nottingham and her battery was about to die. Diana shivers, pulling up the collar of her waxed jacket. It's damp and cold and her sweatshirt and raincoat's not giving her much comfort. She parks herself on a bench above the National Express melee, fuelling herself with vending-machine tea that tastes like reheated pond water. She's been out here for two hours now, when she could have been going through transcripts and H2Hs.

But she made a promise, and it's MaMa. Her bum's numb and cold from the bench now, so she gets up for a walk, passing the A-board outside the mini-newsagent in the foyer announcing: 'Head's head found in filing cabinet'.

Folk just walking past like it's a Sheffield Wednesday score. Diana buys a two-fingered KitKat hoping it will take the scummy pond-water taste away. And a copy of the *Star*.

The head found in a filing cabinet on the site of Legley Road High School has been identified as belonging to former headmaster, John Daniels.

The gruesome find came about when a builder noticed a distinct smell and flies around the junked filing cabinet. All building work is on hold due to it now being a crime scene.

SIO of the homicide investigation, DI Diana Walker, said: 'This is a particularly vile murder and the body part was left in a public place implying further humiliation and offence to both the victim and community. We are appealing for any witnesses of movements on or around the site between August Bank Holiday and 14th September to come forward.'

Chief Superintendent Marchant said: 'This is a brutal act and the perpetrator will be brought to a very full justice. John Daniels was a man who faithfully served the community of Sheffield and many young people.'

Then there's three or four paragraphs extolling the virtues of John Daniels, a nice shiny pic of him grinning at a school function. At least one honest statement from a parent:

'Legley Road High School shouldn't have closed like it did but he didn't deserve to die like that. It's like some horror story.'

Many folk believe his death is related to the closing of the school following an Inadequate Ofsted inspection and the council selling the land to local property developer, Geoff Thomlins.

Diana groans. Just what she didn't want: a load of opinions and conspiracy theorists. And the body part named. Who did that? The workmen? Diana snaps the last finger of her KitKat in two and scoffs it. Screwing up the wrapper into a ball, she throws it in the nearby bin, followed by the rolled-up *Star*. Leaning back on the bench, her eyes search the overcast skies for answers.

Not one witness so far. Her only leads are the silver car, the mysterious black driver, and the deer tick. Oh, and the butchery. She's got O'Malley checking on all the local butchers and sales of butcher knives. Some sour staff and students with possible grudges. Geoff Thomlins hovering like a vulture for the prime property location. And she's still waiting on the exact ballistics for the rifle shot.

The sudden roar of a bus gear change makes her sit up. The long white bullet of the bus pulls up, silhouettes of impatient passengers already standing up inside. Diana grins, despite the crowds pushing around her to get on.

MaMa's here.

Njambi

Of all the long journeys I have taken in my life, this has been the longest.

Two women sitting together on the bus with nothing to say, no common history to share but space and stale air. I just want to look at her, to see Ebu – which I do – in her deep, dark eyes, her strong jaw. She doesn't know she is the likeness of her father. I see her look for something she doesn't know in me. When she met me at the terminal, she held me so tight, I could not breathe. I see her face is tight like a drum, her voice has broken edges to it like it's grated against hard things that have refused it. Instead of love and compassion. When she talks, a mass of noise starts in my head. I don't understand her theories and rage.

When we stopped at Leicester for a toilet break, it takes me a long time. She doesn't know, not really. She asks me about the injuries like she is a lawyer, but her mouth doesn't state the question her eyes ask: *Are you mine? If you are, why did you not come for me? Why did you send me away?*

Instead, she looks at my one suitcase and says accusingly: 'You don't have much baggage, MaMa.'

Oh yes I do, I want to say. *Oh yes I do.*

I need air. I didn't eat yet. I will not break fast till I see *mwana*. Just water and this grey liquid they sell as tea.

Rehema stands up, reaching into the shelf above for her coat and bag. I look out of the window at the crowds. This is Sheffield where my seed lands. The coach, it smells like the soles of feet and onions and smoke. Meat that is too old, not safe to eat. My neck aches from looking through the side window at this green, strange land with concrete and bricks and black shiny tarmac with puddles. Puddles like there is rain to spare. You can smell the water. I follow the slow snake out of the coach.

'I'll get your case, MaMa.'

I see *mwana*'s familiar smile ahead of me. She is all grown woman now except that smile. I take the last two steps down to the street.

'MaMa!' she cries. 'Oh my days. Is it really you?'

My tears are in my throat and on her cheek.

'I seh, can you shift? There's folk trying to get off. Move, you old cow!'

I see *mwana*'s eyes turn to flint, sharp on the large blue-haired woman behind me.

'And there's elderly people trying to get off without breaking a limb. Be patient.'

'Fk off!' spits the blue-hair. 'Don't tell me what to do. I've been stuck on here seven hour.'

The woman has painted on skin the colour of weathered cowhide. She pushes us aside, reaching for her big brown case on the pavement. *Mwana* keeps a protective arm around me while saying calmly: 'Next time you use force and language like that, you can learn patience in a police cell.'

She flashes her badge.

I see her and I smile. Blue-hair scowls, moves away, dragging her bulging suitcase behind her like a dead ox.

Chapter 8

Monday, 20th September, 2010 – Nottingham

Diana looks over the balcony at the bin men dragging black bags across the car park in the September drizzle, tossing them in the filthy jaws of the crushing van. The smell is vile. She wrinkles her nose, sipping her Styrofoam cup of Americano. Footsteps on concrete steps. A beaky-nosed, brown anoraked man appears, a cig stuck on his lower lip, carrying a blue file. Behind him, a sullen-faced woman in jeans and a green parka, highlighted hair frizzing in the rain. Beaky Nose pulls the cig out like it's a rotten tooth.

'DI Walker? I'm DI Wallace.'

Diana nods. 'Thanks for meeting me here.'

'Not exactly protocol but … This is Molly Jones, the manager for the Morningside Housing Trust. She was with me that morning.'

Molly nods at Diana. 'We're redecorating later this week. Got a waiting list a mile long.' She side-nods to the faded yellow tape on the door.

'How did Mary Calley end up down here so fast?'

Molly looks at Diana guardedly. 'We have a strict code of confidentiality.'

Diana raises her eyebrows. Molly rolls her eyes.

'Some pretty nasty harassment and domestic abuse. Her life had been threatened. Wouldn't have jumped the queue as fast as she did otherwise.'

Diana waits, listening. Molly looks down.

'She was scared. Rolls up with two suitcases second Friday in December, looking like she hadn't slept all month. When I opened the door– you'd think I'd given her the keys to a palace.'

'Shame it became her tomb.'

Molly's lips snap into a line. She passes the key to Wallace. 'I'll wait out here.' Thrusting a cigarette into the line of lips, she snatches a spark from a yellow throwaway, turning her back.

Wallace takes a deep breath before opening the door of number 43 Ivy Way. Two shoulder shoves and it creaks open. 'After you.'

The smell is fetid, stale, mouldy. The corridor's dark, a grey light from the kitchen revealing chipped skirting boards, peeling paint, darkening edges of cheap beige carpet. The windowless bathroom is speckled with black mould, a dripping crusty tap with a line of brown running onto white enamel sink. Curling pink lino. The shower curtain's perished, covered in sticky webs, embroidered with flies. A 1980s veneered kitchen, adorned with dusty fungal crusts. Black pyramids of fly husks. Windows so grimy the sunlight's given up. Whole place reeks of neglect, rot. The unloved.

'Where was the … body?'

Wallace stands at the door of the bedsitting room while Diana walks across sticky carpet to the window.

'Sofabed. There. Against the wall.' Diana looks down at the windowsill. A scattered confetti of flies, the nets a hanging yellow veil, Ms Calley's great expectations to end here.

'Like I said on the phone, a very strange case.'

'Autopsy?'

'On what? Dust and bones? Heating on full whack for two years, the flies and maggots cleaned up. Dental records – best we could do for an ID.'

'Time of death accurate?'

'Stuff in the fridge, milk, state of general decay. End of January 2008. No later, no earlier.'

Diana taps on the windowsill, frowning.

'But just a month earlier she had a great job, her own two-bedroom house, a life … I don't get it. A career woman wouldn't leave all that behind.'

Wallace looks at her. 'These bedsits aren't council, detective. They belong to the Morningside Housing Trust, a charity that helps victims of domestic abuse, particularly battered women from other counties.'

Diana puts her head on one side, questioning him with one look. He shrugs, shaking his head. 'Nope. No sign of assault, violence. No blood residue. The inside chain still on the locked door.'

Diana inspects the windows.

'All sealed,' says Wallace. 'Not a window open. It was a cold December in 2007. The place was ripe when we got in. A microwave of rot. Flies got in through the vent.'

Diana shakes her head. 'You must have needed counselling after this.'

'Thought about it. Molly out there was pretty shaken up. They're keen to get it cleaned up, redecorated, rent it back out. Something like this gets under your skin – not in the Frank Sinatra way either.'

Diana nods. 'Your CSI team keep all the bags?'

He nods. 'But most of it's rotten, perished. Just paper junk. Not much for the life of a lead teacher. Think there was some smashed screen Nokia phone, couple of diaries. Seems she was planning on going back to college. Nottingham University. Social Policy. Some unopened mail.'

'She got mail?'

'Two years' worth.'

'But I thought no one would know ...'

'Well, someone did ... she had eight unopened handwritten letters in the pile inside the door, but they must have been posted after she died. That's one way we worked out the date.'

'I'd like to see those letters. Anything else?'

Wallace looks away, at a semi-peeled strip of wallpaper that requires his immediate attention. He pushes at it with a bitten nail.

'Look, it's a simple but tragic case. She had a history of asthma, anaemia, gastro-intestinal problems ...'

'The usual symptoms of a woman who's endured chronic stress ...' Diana's tone of rage makes him look up.

'I'm just saying, it was probably an asthma attack or a bleeding ulcer. Doesn't make it suspicious, just unfortunate.'

Neglect is the alias for slow murder.

'I need to find a lead, so I'd like the Key Development Log and all her items. Her phone. Her emails. Her letters. Everything you've got.'

'I already had an auditor in on this case.' He rolls his eyes as Diana stares. 'OK. I'll ship 'em off today.'

'What auditor?'

'Oh, something to do with the council and some longstanding legal case.'

Diana frowns, waiting. He sighs.

'Something between the Housing Trust, tenants and the council about the broken drains and bin men, I think. Council were counter-sueing regarding non-payment of council tax and evasion of electoral register or something. It was all in the paper.'

'I live in Sheffield, detective.'

'Yeah, but you know how these paperwork things go. Made my life even more annoying while trying to close up this case.'

'Paperwork is all our business, detective. You know that.'

DI Wallace looks surprised. 'Really?'

'Anyway, these auditors?'

'…needed proof of ID and certification of tenant's death or something. Insisted on access to the victim's unopened mail. The father of the deceased gave the company a Grant of Representation so there was nothing I could do. They were in and out in one morning.'

'This year?' Diana asks.

'Yeah. Shortly after the … remains were found.'

'You can't remember the date?'

He shakes his head. 'No. A uniform dealt with it all.'

'Who?'

Exasperated, Wallace rakes his thin hair. 'Sake, detective! I'm not a walking filing cabinet! It'll all be in the log. It was after the inquest anyway.'

He turns and moves down the passage, indicating her time's up. Diana follows slowly.

'I'd like to see that log.'

Opening the door, he stands to one side as she walks out: 'Fine. I'll send it up with the box.'

'Thanks.'

Wallace locks the door behind them, nodding at Diana to walk on.

Diana takes one last look around at the dismal bedsit. The fly-spotted windowsills, the bare light bulb, twirling in a nest of webs and dust, wallpaper curling crisply at the edges.

And the dark, indelible, long stain on the carpet.

That used to be a life.

Back up the M1. Service station cheese and onion sarnie with a shred of limp tomato. Swig of coffee. Diana stands in front of the Manse, 108 Legley Road, the end with the leafy high walls and wrought-iron gates – not the end with the chicken shops and off-licences. A hedge of rhododendrons, ivied walls, clematis crawling along the Edwardian pillars. The steps scrubbed and polished. A small congregation of terracotta pots. A bee wanders through a clump of thyme spilling over a cracked ceramic basin. To her left, the front garden is filled with neat rows of cultivated tea roses; to her right, a dense shrubbery, less well-maintained.

Diana rings the doorbell, watching DS Robertson lock his blue Volvo and struggle with his anorak zip.

'It worked this morning,' he mutters, watching forlornly as it splits all the way up. Robertson pats down his anorak, straightens his tie.

An elderly black lady, curlers in her grey black hair, opens the door. She wears a crisp floral pink pinny. Smooth skin, twinkling hazel eyes, smelling of eucalyptus.

'Good afternoon. Mrs Thompson is it?'

'It is.'

'I'm DI Walker and this is Detective Sergeant Robertson. Is Pastor Calley home?'

'He is. I told him you were coming. Come tru, come tru.'

She opens the door to a tiled hallway, ambrosia walls, huge pink cabbage roses in a silver rose bowl. Bible verses and various certificates for courses framed and displayed on the wall. Despite the smell of Brasso and floor polish, there's a mustiness in the air. Robertson clatters behind.

'How long have you been … er … keeping house for Pastor Calley?'

'Since he became Pastor, nearly forty years. I was a young girl. Sunita, his wife, she was my friend, our lead alto, and she ask Pastor. Tell him I'm a better cleaner than she. After she pass, God rest her soul, he gave me a lickle wage to look after young Mary and keep house. He so busy being Pastor wid all dem meetings and shepherding flock. My Cedric, he didn't mind. He worked at de steelworks till he died of cancer fifteen year ago now, God rest him.'

She takes them through to a large drawing room: 1980s gold flocked wallpaper, worn velvet sofas with faded gold cushions. The oppressive smell of geranium and polish. A large patio opens the south side of the room onto the garden. Robertson wanders around the room, but Diana stays behind the sofa, watching Mrs Thompson as she rearranges the cushions.

'So you knew Mary?' asks Robertson.

'Since she was born and first came home. Oh, there's Pastor in his greenhouse.'

Diana takes in the stuffy, ornate drawing room, the abundance of blousy false flowers, framed prints. Not a family photo in sight.

Mrs Thompson trots over to the patio doors.

'Pastor! Pastor!' She turns. 'He'll come. He does like to feed his plants regularly. I'll go make some tea. You like ginger cake?'

She addresses Robertson, who nods heartily.

'Tea would be lovely. Thank you, Mrs Thompson,' says Diana.

Mrs Thompson bustles out the door and Diana side-nods at Robertson, who takes the hint, trotting after her. Diana stares out at the long garden, stuffed with rockeries and awkward non-herbaceous border plants. In the far corner, a moss-roofed greenhouse from which a stooped, grey-skinned man stares, clutching open secateurs.

Pastor Calley crosses his legs, leaning back in his pink armchair, which seems to swallow his frame. He slopes to one side, or is it badly fitting clothes? Maybe he's had a stroke. His face and thick veined bony hands are mottled with brown liver spots.

'How can I help you, detective?'

'We're investigating the recent murder of John Daniels, your daughter Mary's last employer.'

He stiffens, seeming to freeze into the folds of the fabric of his shirt.

'My daughter?'

'Mary? Mary Calley?'

Pastor Calley takes a long slurp from his teacup. His eyes stay on the cup as he puts it on the saucer. 'What about her? She is dead. How does this affect your investigation?'

'Yes, I know she was found in strange circumstances earlier in the year ... or the remains of her ... in Nottingham?'

'Yes.' He reaches over stiffly to a young spider plant on the oak side table. He strokes the plant's leaves, sighs heavily.

'Mary was always a difficult child. She became ...' He looks outside, shaking his head at a fern. '... rebellious after her mother passed. Had some problems with a boyfriend or something after university. Went to work overseas, teaching refugees.'

'And then she got a job, head of English, at Legley Road. You must have been so proud of her.'

He looks back at the spider plant. 'You like plants, detective?'

'Very much so. I have my own greenhouse. Not as grand as yours.'

He pushes out a black-moled lip. 'So, you know how much attention plants need.'

'Yes.'

'And if they don't respond well, the rot gets in. The mildew, the blight. Weak root growth.'

'The consequences of a toxic environment.'

Pastor Calley's face hardens. 'Mary had a good upbringing. Didn't stop her getting with a married man though.'

'Married man. Do you know who?'

Pastor Calley sniffs, suddenly fascinated by one of the spider plant's stripy leaves.

His face goes rigid. Diana puts her cup down in the saucer, looking for a table, but the trolley's in the centre of the room.

'A married man with family. That all I know. And everyone else.'

And everyone at church.

'No name?' Diana inhales. 'You were … estranged from Mary?'

Pastor picks up his cup again, sips. 'It was amicable.'

'Amicably estranged from your own flesh and blood?'

Pastor Calley's eyes shoot fire. 'She wasn't …' He pauses. 'Obedient.'

Diana stands up, placing her cup and saucer on the trolley.

'So, you never spoke or visited your daughter for what – two years? Never thought, "I wonder what Mary's doing?"'

'She was a grown woman! She had crossed the line …' He looks out of the window. '… very much her mother's daughter.'

'Were you shocked to hear of her death, the circumstances of her death?'

Pastor Calley gets up awkwardly, shuffling to the patio doors, his broad flat back to Diana. His left shoulder is two inches lower and the left hip slightly twisted.

'Helping people deal with the inevitable – that's my job, detective. I was sad to hear how one so young as Mary had died. But surprised?' He shook his head. 'Unfortunately, no. The wages of sin is death.'

Diana stares.

'Have you any photos of Mary?'

Pastor Calley waves his hand as Mrs Thompson and Robertson enter.

'Mrs Thompson can let you have them and any other details you may need. My relationship with Mary sadly ended with her … choices. If you will excuse me, I'm in the middle of a plant feed before my visits start at two p.m.'

He leaves by the patio door, walking back to the greenhouse. Mrs Thompson picks up the tray from the trolley. 'That's Pastor for you. Everything in order and done to time, in de right way. I'll get you a photo of Mary.'

Back out on the street, Robertson zips up his anorak.

'Brrr. Turning nippy now.'

'Mrs Thompson mend your zip as well as feeding you cake?'

Robertson grins. 'Right little treasure trove, our Mrs Thompson.'

'Oh really?'

Robertson opens the passenger door and Diana gets in.

'Yeah. She knew Mary's mum, Sunita, and told me quite a bit about Mary. Said she was always getting into arguments with her dad, the pastor, but how she was a sweet, clever girl. She feels very sad about how she died, you know. Said Mary was the apple of Sunita's eye and almost a daughter to herself. She gave me these photos.'

He pulls out three: one of a gap-toothed grinning skinny kid in a navy-blue party frock, red ribbon tied around her large black ringlets, white socks, black patent shoes, holding balloons at a Christmas church party next to a proud elegantly dressed Indian woman. Another photo of Mary, taller, shapely, hair in a full Afro, graduation robe, clutching a degree outside Leeds University. And then the last one, a beaming woman holding a pile of books, wearing a huge laminate with 'Head of English, Legley Road High School'.

Diana stares at the photos. 'What father gives up on his daughter so easily?'

A cold chill runs through her suddenly. She turns the key. The car starts, but she doesn't move off.

'Just weird.'

Chapter 9

Tuesday 21st September, 2010 – Dewbow, Derbyshire

A prehistoric roar wakes her. A chainsaw? The slate grey light slides through Diana's cotton curtains before her alarm at 5.55 a.m. By 6.15 a.m., she is in her shadowed kitchen, track-suited zipped, glugging a mug of half-boiled water, grabbing keys, slamming doors, hearing the sharp '*Wawkkk!*' of the crows perched on the telephone wires. Horse chestnut leaves crunch under her feet like flattened cinder toffee. Cold, crisp air smarts her lungs with its cold, her cheeks stinging, her legs light and free. She vaults the stile into the woodland beyond Dewbright Hall.

The path is narrow, strewn with smooth boulders and thick roots. She brushes against branches that snap loudly. Fog steams off the wakening earth. Yellow, orange, red and bare, the trees stand out defiant against layers of bramble, dying bracken's skeletal broken fingers pointing to the left, to the right, to the earth.

A tawny owl blinks at her from a low branch before soundlessly swooping off, leaving a tail feather in its wake. Diana bends to pick it up, pushing it into her headband, bracing herself for the ascent. Glistening gossamer webs hang between trees. Lifting hands to untangle the sticky mesh, she plunges on, pump-pumping the hoar-hardened ground, navigating jagged rocks till she's at the crest. She pauses to wonder at the sea of white mist below, before starting the descent. She weaves, grabbing hold of branches while slipping on rocks, warm muscles commanding her: *Move on.*

Fifteen minutes from home now. Three miles covered, the sun's white gold bursts through the mist below with an eerie radiance. She's lost in the rhythm of pounding the path. The hind legs of a fleeing doe flash before her.

Her thoughts suddenly rush to MaMa. She sees her now in the backyard at Bagamoyo, the goat bucking the fence, butting the bucket, trampling the fire. Bleat of goat, hiss of broth on stone and clang of pans. MaMa – her smile. MaMa – that goat stink! Holding her nose. MaMa laughing at her. That stink of piss, earth, blood. The fight before its inevitable death. She can smell it now.

All in one primal steaming snort. In front of her. Brambles are alive. Two forked-finger antlers poke through a wreath of nettle and ivy. Goat ears, the size of shoes, flop flat to thick red neck. Heavy lidded eyes, curled lip, glistening eel of a tongue, the size of a belt. The stag, antlers thick as an ancient apple tree, glares at her. Steam from flaring nostrils, the pungent goat-stink: raw, fierce, ugly. Diana freezes, her breath suspended in the ten feet of air between them. She should have known; the dug-up muddy shallow holes, signs of the rut.

Crusted antlers rush towards her like a blade.

Earth shaking, hawk squawking.

BANG!

Black. Her cheek feels cold, fastened to the ground. A sticky warm liquid on her hand. Someone touches her, shaking her.

'You OK?'

Diana opens her eyes. Dark brown curls. A woman. Diana's head pounds. Her hand's sticky.

'What happened?'

A leather-gloved hand helps her up, one arm around her shoulders. She stares at her helper now: tall, voluptuous yet athletic, dressed in a waxed hunting jacket, boots, a rifle hanging from a belt around her shoulder. Muscled calves in jodhpur-like leggings. A symmetrical face framed by baby hairs, dark brown waves scraped into a bun. The woman nods at the huge fallen stag at Diana's feet, blood gushing from its crown and from its nostrils, another hole in its chest, hence Diana's sticky, deer-blood covered hand. The stag's antlers stick up like a demented tree branch, supporting the weight of the mighty twisted head, now broken at the neck, the massive amber shoulders now a boulder on the ground.

'*That* happened.'

'Bloody hell.'

'You'd have been a goner if I hadn't moved my morning meeting today.'

Diana's heart races. 'Thank you.'

She is shaking.

'Up you get.'

Diana allows herself to lean on the woman's athletic frame, feeling her strength and pull.

'I try to go out for a bit of practice early.'

'Practice?'

'The stags. It's the rutting season.'

Diana repeats: 'Rutting …' as she tries to orientate herself.

'Mating season. We shoot because they're at their prime.'

'I'm vegetarian.'

The woman looks Diana up and down.

'Looks like you could do with some venison. Get some iron in you.' She stares at Diana's head, puzzled. 'Or are you a hippy? Why've you got a feather in your hair?'

Diana pats the side of her head with a sticky hand, pulling out the now bloodstained feather.

The yellow gold layers of light break through the banks of fog as they move slowly back down the path towards Dewbright Hall. The woman says little, offering a hand to Diana as she tries to navigate stones and logs she leapt over ten minutes before. Diana feels cold and sick. Dizzy. Head ringing.

'Take my coat.' The woman takes off her fleece-lined waxed jacket, hanging it like a cape around Diana's goose-pimpled neck. 'I'm Maya Smith, by the way.'

'Diana Walker.'

Maya marches ahead in her gilet and cashmere turtleneck. One black leather gloved hand grips her rifle like a staff, the other pulling at her bun, freeing a cascade of irrepressible dark curls.

'I've got to get to work …' Diana stumbles on the kerb.

'Not today.'

'No. I—'

'You're in shock. You need sugar and heat pronto.'

Maya's grip of her shoulder guides Diana through the back gates of Dewbright Hall, past the outbuildings to the expanse of the back of the house and a large black pond covered with water lilies and a layer of red and gold leaf confetti. Maya unlocks the back porch, beckoning for Diana to follow. Diana stumbles, eyes glued to the mounted stag head in the hall, the antlers reaching out to the ceiling, bearing down over her. Maya laughs.

'He's not going anywhere. Get yourself into the kitchen. It's warmer there.'

Diana sits down at a large pine table, a huge vase of white lilies in its centre. The heady scent makes her head spin and, as the woodstove's warmth hits her, she collapses into a chair.

'Pull up to the woodstove.'

Diana scrapes her chair forward.

'What doctor you with? Dr Simmons?'

Diana shrugs. She's not even registered with a GP yet.

Maya drapes a soft plaid blanket around Diana's shoulders and fills a stainless steel kettle, reaching for two Cornishware mugs. She pops a teabag in each. Diana stares at her hands, as the kitchen clangs miles away. She waves her fingers in front of the stove.

A stripy cup is placed in her shaking hands, full of steaming, sweet brown liquid.

Diana sips. 'How long was I out for?'

'Just seconds. I'll call Jack. You shouldn't go to work today.'

'Jack?'

'Dr Simmons.'

Diana sips hot sweet tea, staring at the fire within the woodstove.

She is aware of Maya having a conversation on a phone, a chuckle.

'OK. Yes.' She leans on the mantelpiece, staring at Diana.

'He said he'll come through after this morning's surgery.' She smiles. 'I'll be going back for that stag.'

'Did you mean to hit it?'

Maya snorts. 'It was you or the stag. It's my land, so yes, that stag's mine.'

'Your land?'

'Yeah – that half of the woodland.'

Diana looks aghast. 'Was I trespassing? There's no sign ...'

Maya smiles, shaking her head. 'Don't worry about it. The deer don't usually go up that far.' She sips, eyeing Diana over the rim.

Diana feels like she's fallen down a rabbit hole. Maya hands her a wet flannel for her hand. Diana wipes off the brown blood, puts the flannel on the table next to the mug of swirling tea.

'You're living in deer country, my dear.'

Maya towers over her, shaking her head.

'You're in shock. Get you a hot toddy.'

Those eyes. That goat stink. 'Goat ... I smelled goat.'

Maya laughs as she fills the kettle again, nodding.

'They *do* smell like horny goats, you know. Stags' sex hormones are rank.'

Diana puts a numb finger in one ear, rattles it about. Still ringing. Tries popping them. The sound of the kettle boiling comes from underwater. Maya's green cat eyes watching her, stirring honey into a glass.

Diana says: 'You shot it.'

Maya stands incredulous, clutching a huge knife. 'You'd rather I didn't?'

'No, no. Probably saved me.'

Maya turns back, chops lemon with one fast swipe. '*Definitely* saved you.'

'You're a good shot.'

'The best. Raised shooting deer. My dad was a sportsman too. This was our main hunting lodge. Had another on the moors. Venison is prime meat around here, you know. You not been to the butcher's?'

'No. I'm a vege—'

'—tarian.' Maya chuckles, spooning in whisky, more honey, the metal clinking merging into the ringing. Another deer's head leers over the chimney. Diana eyes it suspiciously.

'Looks like it might pull that wall down.'

Maya looks up at it fondly. 'Been up there since I was six.'

Diana shudders.

'You sure you're a country girl, Diana?' Maya passes her another steaming mug. Diana grabs it – to warm her fingers if nothing else.

'I like the wild down here …'

Maya sips her own tea, leaning back on the dresser.

'Rutting starts end of August, peaking around time of first frost, early October, ending bang on the end of November. By then they're knackered, worn out.'

'Who?'

'The stags. They have to fight for the right to mate, you see. The roar—'

'I thought I was dreaming dinosaurs with chainsaws.'

Maya shakes her head.

'Nope. It's a horny stag. They're in good shape now. The louder the roar, the fitter the stag. Attracts the does. As they get tired, it moves to a clear barking sound, and then, when they're completely knackered, just this cracked broken cough. Old man sound. No use hunting that, my dad taught me. Leave 'em for the crows and foxes. You got kids?'

Diana shakes her head.

Maya sighs. 'They say teenage boys' bedrooms stink like goat too …' Maya peers out over the pond. 'It's prime land around here. I've got several glades and the does love it. They get all fat on the grass over summer for winter. The stags pick out the best in the autumn.'

Diana sips toddy. Sweet. Hot rush in her chest.

Maya is squinting out at the pond. Turns back to Diana. 'You seen those muddy patches in the second glade?'

Diana nods like a child in primary school.

'Those are wallows. They roll in the mud, kick up their stink and piss over their bodies, rub their antlers in the hedges – anything to make them terrifying to the other stags and attractive to the harem.'

'Harem?'

Maya turns, smiling. 'Yeah. The does stick to all-female groups. If they get separated, move off away from the herd or harem, they'll get jumped on by a stag of inferior quality. Or a predator. The inferior stags loiter on the edges instead of earning the right to mate.'

Maya is looking outside again, frowning. 'Is that a dead fish floating? Best get it out before it rots and poisons the rest.' She leaves the room.

Diana sips toddy, looking around her. Copies of *The Field* stacked on a nearby table. A PlayStation DualShock handset. A photo of Maya, at graduation with an elderly white couple, sits on a shelf with some onyx paperweights. Impeccably tidy. Diana curses herself. *What an idiot, going through woodland during the rutting season.* She best start running on the road. She stares out at Maya fishing something out with what looks like a long butter-fly net. Maya takes it around the back of an outhouse. She comes back in and washes her hands in the kitchen sink.

'I should get back – I'm on a case and …' Diana feels like an invalid next to Maya. She looks at her hands, barely able to grip the mug let alone a phone.

'A case? You're police?' Maya asks. Diana nods sheepishly. Maya presses her lips together, nodding as if impressed.

Diana feels awkward, exposed. She tries to get up. 'I just live down the road …'

Maya catches the vibe. Takes the empty mugs to the dishwasher.

'You shouldn't be on your own. I'm not due in the office till one. Wait until the doc arrives – just in case.'

Diana nods meekly.

'Well, I must crack on. Get Samuels to pick up that stag pronto.'

'Maya.'

Maya turns as she goes to the door.

'Thanks.'

'You're welcome.'

Maya smiles, a full bright smile.

Dr Simmons, a gangly, red-haired man with post-nasal drip, rolls up at 11.30 a.m., rattling a stethoscope in a largely empty brief-case. After prodding, pressing, listening and frowning at Diana for five minutes, he confirms she may be very slightly concussed but nothing broken and no need for X-rays.

'Just take it easy for a few days.'

Diana smiles. *Yeah right, doctor.*

'Is there anyone at home for you? You should have some supervision the first twenty-four hours.'

Supervision. Smashing.

'I can go to my mum's.'

It's closer to HQ. She wants to see MaMa anyway. She can just tell her mum the car's out of action – which it is … because she's not safe to drive it. As it is, Rehema hates her 'living all alone out in the country … how you going to meet anyone down there?'

Maya comes through into the kitchen.

'Everything OK?'

'She's fine. Just no more jogs during rutting season, eh?' laughs the doctor.

Diana gets up. 'I'll get off now, thanks.'

Chapter 10

WEDNESDAY 22ND SEPTEMBER, 2010 – REHEMA'S HOUSE, SHEFFIELD

It's after eight in the morning when Diana comes downstairs to her mum's kitchen. She plants a small cardboard box on the oak kitchen table.

Rehema is chopping kale with surgical precision, pulling out the thread of each stalk, smiling to herself. Diana had still put in a good eight hours at the station, trawled through the transcripts, CCTV footage, all the H2Hs and staff statements. She was happy to come back here last night, chatting with MaMa while Rehema cooked.

Diana lifts the lid of the cube-shaped box to reveal a squat cream candle.

She pulls it out, sniffing. 'Mmmm. Sandalwood. Can I have it, Ma?'

'Where'd you find that?'

'In the drawer in the spare room. Looking for a T-shirt this morning.'

'That's from when we launched the book club. You can take it if you come.'

Diana pulls out a cream card from the box. 'Black Sistahs Book Club Manifesto: 1. Success depends on participation – all members ask fearless questions and engage in conversation – never conflict. 2. Listen respectfully and hold space for others. 3. Critique ideas, not people.' Diana lays it down in disdain. 'Books. Why would anyone choose a book over actually *doing* something?'

Rehema side-eyes her. 'All those library visits I gave you? You a university graduate?'

Diana rolls her eyes. 'Exactly.'

'It's not the books – it's the conversation.'

'Conversation?'

Rehema blasts the kale in the blender with a ripe banana, orange juice and some dark green powder. Diana winces. The blender stops and Rehema pours its swamp-like contents into a tall glass.

'It's what the books help us to say to each other.' Rehema chuckles. 'We have conversations we'd get arrested for.'

Diana raises her eyebrows. 'Okayyyy.' Pause. *Get it out, Diana.* 'So … how come you never mentioned you knew Mary Calley? Even when she was in the papers?'

'You never asked.'

She brings over the tall glass of swamp liquid and a Habitat pasta bowl filled with her homemade granola and yogurt. Diana's head aches, ears still ringing. A wave of nausea rushes over her.

'Ma!' She needs coffee and two paracetamols – not a bush in a glass. Rehema picks out a spoon from the cutlery jar.

'You need minerals, girl.'

I need answers.

Diana takes the spoon. 'What was she like?'

Rehema stares out of the window. 'Mary? Sweet girl. A committed teacher.'

Rehema pours the remainder of her homemade granola into carefully labelled jars. Diana sips from the glass, eyes on her mother.

'I hear she got with a married man, Leroy Young. You know anything about that?'

Rehema glares at the contents of the washing-up bowl.

'How come I never met her?'

'You were …'

'Oh yeah.' *Shacking up with Phillips.* Three-point turn to: 'How long she at the book club?'

'What's with all the questions?' Rehema wipes her hands on her apron, hand on hip.

Diana shovels granola into a dry mouth. Rehema scrutinises the bowl. Diana swallows.

'You look yellow. You best drink that.' Rehema nods at the glass of green, her lips a firm line.

Why's everyone telling her to drink up?

'MaMa up yet?'

'No. She takes her time. She has … a few waterwork problems sometimes.'

Rehema runs the blender under the tap. A tidal wave of green sludge. Diana tries to drink but feels like hurling. She goes through a mental checklist of possible leads: Thomlins. A disgruntled student. Or students. Leroy Young. The OCG angle. All of them feasible, yet a vague terror grips her. Why can't she get a handle on this case?

She scrapes her bowl in the compost bin, metal spoon on ceramic adding to the ringing in her head. Takes the bowl to the sink to rinse. Picks up her car keys. Rehema stoops to put the blender base in the cupboard, wincing as she stands up.

Diana looks around and then makes her way to the fridge. She looks at the montage of photos held on with magnets, stares around the room.

'Funny. You've no photos of me downstairs.'

'Good grief, Diana. I've got a gallery of you upstairs.'

'In the spare bedroom, yeah. My graduation gown and the first day of playschool. None of me since I started at the police. I guess it might make things awkward when the book club comes round …'

Rehema vigorously shakes her head. 'Seriously, Diana. There's none of MaMa either.'

'Well, there should be. Now she's here, we'll have one done.'

Rehema's back is to her. She's snapping at magnets, shuffling the photos on the fridge.

'For goodness' sake, Diana – go and bring one down. It—'

The unfinished sentence hangs in neon over their heads. Maybe one of Diana in uniform? That '*can fit in here*'?

'Don't worry about it, Ma. It's just an observation. No need to reconfigure your fridge.'

Diana and Rehema avoid each other's eyes, staring at the photo of Rehema with Aaliyah and Mary, the unspoken admission of how the death of a stranger has exposed the strangeness between them, squatting like some venomous toad. Rehema tuts and turns back to the sink.

'If anyone needs an audit of their fridge, it's you, Diana. You look positively ill.'

Diana stares at her as if she just declared the cure for cancer.

'An *audit*! Of course! Ma, you're brilliant!'

Grabbing her waxed jacket, she slurps the dregs of the green, pecks Rehema on the cheek and is through the door, reappearing to snatch up the candle box and card.

'Tell MaMa I'll see her later!'

In her car, Diana punches digits into her phone.

'Robertson – get us the school's financial history and the bank records of Daniels, Leroy Young and the senior management team – from 2005 when Daniels started. Also, I want details about the sale of the school site to Geoff Thomlins. And the auditors' report. I'll be there in ten minutes.'

As she puts the keys in the ignition, she looks in the rear-view mirror to pull out. She's not anaemic. Just a bit pale.

I look like a ghost.

Or someone who just missed death.

Marchant stands on the threshold of his glass-cabinet-lined office. One nod at Diana. She puts down the autopsy report and walks over, aware of Lawton's eyes following.

Here goes.

'Walker, what's happening?'

Diana frowns. 'Sir, we—'

Marchant shakes his head, widening his eyes in exasperation.

'Where are your leads? Where's rest on 'im 'n' all?'

'I don't know, sir. We've got an acrylic fingernail, a filing cabinet and a graffiti tag. We're working through the house-to-house interviews, interviewing staff and students ...'

Marchant looks down at the file on his desk.

'I've got the national press, Thomlins, the mayor and every

72

paranoid teacher in Sheffield blowing up my phone. I need real critical evidence and suspects.'

He glares at the pigeons chewing plastic guttering on the neighbouring solicitors' rooftop.

'Or any reason why I shouldn't hand this over to Lawton. He's got an OCG feeling about this. I'm tending to agree.'

No chance.

'No problem, sir.'

She heads for the door, hearing him mutter: 'Fingernail!'

Downstairs, Diana taps the thin yellow file of Mary Calley's Key Development Log in front of her. She stares out of the window at a forlorn pigeon, pecking desperately in the canteen's yard, hoping a stale crust will yield up crumbs.

'You and I both, mate.' Closes her eyes. Sees the heavy-lidded glare of the stag. A door bangs. She jumps.

'Boxes here, Boss.' A sweaty Robertson stands behind her, carrying two archive boxes. 'You OK?'

'Yeah. Didn't sleep well at Ma's.'

The boxes are marked *Mary Calley 2/4/2010 Nottingham Police Department on loan for investigation. SIO DI Diana Walker, Sheffield P D, Meyrick Street, Sheffield.*

Mary's life in a couple of boxes.

'Catalogue everything, Robertson. Go through it with dental floss and a microscope. Any queries, note them, pass them over, chase them up. Anything. We need a lead. Oh, and pull out those LEA finance and performance management documents we found this morning. I've got Legley's deputy head coming in tomorrow.'

Robertson puts the boxes down. 'What you searching for, Boss?'

Diana pulls a face. 'I know it's not a lead – just … good teachers don't give up easily. There's a reason why Mary Calley walked away and no one's talking.'

Robertson fidgets.

'I forgot to tell you this morning when you called, Boss. One of the ex-IT guys at Legley Road, he used to make official videos of first staff meeting of every academic year. I asked him for the ones for 2006, 2007 …'

Diana stares at him. Robertson looks sheepish. 'You wanted some footage of Daniels.'

Diana's eyes spark. 'Where is it?'

'My desk. Second drawer. It sticks a bit …'

Diana's already at his desk.

He adds: 'Ms Calley's in it.'

Diana shoves the DVD disk into the computer drive. *Please don't be some weird software*. She double clicks. A bunch of teachers in an overcrowded staffroom, shifting uncomfortably. A healthier John Daniels, bald dome shining, stands in the centre, white shirt rolled to the elbows, stripy tie, slight paunch. He's got a booming voice, gesticulating enthusiastically.

'So, well done, everyone! And to celebrate we're going to all go out for a curry at Ramji's on Friday after the parents' meetings.'

The staff murmur with pleasure. A slight brown-skinned girl with a mass of black curls steps forward. She's wearing a vibrant red jumper and geometrical skirt, black boots. Gold bamboo hoop earrings.

Diana squints, trying to see her face, but the camera focuses on Daniels.

The slight woman, hands out at shoulder width, lean slim palms cutting like a knife through air. Her voice is nasal, incisive, like a bell.

'Mr Daniels, the timetable! These kids deserve better. They deserve integrity. Keep your word, Mr Daniels. You expect two GCSEs on three lessons a week? And where's the new budget for the curriculum I won? It's not curry I want – it's curriculum! Curriculum that meets the needs of these kids. The curriculum I won the funds for. Where is it?'

'Ms Calley, the responsibility of the school's budget lies with the head,' Daniels says calmly.

The staff around her look embarrassed. A few snigger. Daniels raises his eyebrows as the slight figure pushes through the crowd, marching past the camera, tears streaming down her face. A tall black man dressed in a tracksuit strides after her. Staff members pull faces at each other, shrugging. The film wobbles, crackling to a stop.

Diana leans back. 'Got some fire in ya belly, girl.'

A lot of passion there. May be worth interviewing the wives of Young and Daniels again …

Back in the briefing room, Diana creases her nose, making a mental note to buy a plug-in air freshener.

'Where are we with the tag, O'Malley?'

'Train stations, bus stops?' O'Malley looks through a spiral-bound scattered with doodles and random numbers.

'This Merka guy prefers private property: the sign for Fitness First on London Road, outside a solicitor's, leafy S10 shops, the wall further up beyond Hastings Road.'

'Another Fista?'

'Dint he do trains and motorway bridges? This one's just local to S10.'

'Any of your graff informers got an idea?'

'"Just a kid".'

'Narrows it down.'

Sniggers from Lawton and Neville.

Diana sighs. 'Come on, we got a full print off the can. Nothing on DNA, but must be *something* on someone's CCTV. Ask neighbours. They may not care about random filing cabinets, but damage to private property? All hell breaks loose.'

'One retired fella at number 178 said he heard rattling a couple of nights.'

'His false teeth?' Lawton laughs.

'Spray cans make that noise when they're empty,' Diana says. 'When was that?'

'He says after Bank Holiday Monday. He can't remember. He knows it was after Bank Holiday because he was waiting on the bin man to shift his extra bags. Gets paranoid about his car getting scratched.'

'So … early morning?'

'Yeah. Said it woke him. Maybe three a.m.'

'Anyone heard or seen anything else? House-to-housing?'

Heads shake.

Neville nudges Lawton who frowns back. Diana looks up. Lawton rolls his eyes.

'May have a match for DNA on that tagger.'

Diana waits.

'Small distributor for Ryan Pierce … gonna keep him in our back pocket.'

'Our?'

'DI Phillips noted the DNA. But he's gathering evidence on the county lines enterprise. Doesn't want any arrests yet.'

Diana checks her rage.

'We've got a homicide and, last I checked, you were on *this* detail – not his.'

Lawton exhales. Glares back.

'What's his name?'

'Axmed Ahmed. Went to Legley Road High 'n' all. Last intake of Year 11s.'

Diana stares at a pigeon chewing on a crisp packet in the gutter.

'Bring him in.'

Lawton nods. 'Phillips can use that as leverage …'

Diana cuts eyes at him. 'This has nothing to do with Phillips' op. Until Ahmed's eliminated, he's a POI.'

Last thing she wants is Phillips pulling rank on this one. Lawton heads towards the door.

'Today,' Diana calls after him.

Axmed leans back on the plastic chair. Red Adidas hoodie, scuffed Jordans, crumpled dark blue jeans. Gold chain. Close black crop and the skid of a moustache, a symmetrical face with narrow eyes. Diana notes his bitten nails and the scratching of his knees every time there's silence.

'Axmed, can you explain why your prints are on an empty can of orange spray paint found at the Legley Road High site?'

'No comment.'

Robertson enters the room with a manilla folder. Axmed looks up, frowns.

'What's he doing here? He wor my teaching support assistant.'

'DS Robertson should be leading this interview so he stays in. This isn't a vandalism and damage to public property charge. I don't know if DI Lawton told you, but it's a homicide case. You feel like sitting it out in a cell while we join up the dots?'

Axmed frowns.

'So … a graffiti artist?'

Axmed shrugs.

'Axmed, I have some colleagues who are not so interested in your artistic ambitions. They want to ask you about your association with Ryan Pierce.'

A faint mist appears on his brow. He wipes his sleeve over it.

'You went to Legley Road High School?'

He nods.

'Take your exams?'

He shakes his head.

'No? So what you doing now? No college for you?'

'This 'n' that. Work for my dad.'

'He's a cab driver, Axmed.' Diana looks directly at Axmed, who looks up briefly before returning to pulling at a cuff thread.

Axmed mutters: 'If you know, why you asking me?'

'I don't know everything, do I, Axmed?'

Axmed inhales. 'I was going to do graphic design.'

'So you thought you'd do a foundation course in criminal damage? Where were you this last Bank Holiday weekend? Out partying?'

Axmed scowls. 'My mates were. They were at Creamfields.'

'You didn't get a ticket?'

Another headshake.

Diana nods. 'Pricey, aren't they?'

Axmed looks to the side.

'So what *did* you do?'

'Nowt. Was going to drive round and pick up a mate from Creamfields early Monday.'

'Do you drive?'

Pause. 'A mate had a car.'

'Ah right. Another *mate*. Does the mate have a name?'

'Mohammed Mahmood.'

'Can Mohammed vouch for you?'

He nods.

'Let's hope so.'

Diana leans back, tips of fingers on the desk.

'So … the filing cabinet? When did it catch your eye?'

77

'The week before.'

'What day?'

'Wednesday. Maybe Thursday.'

'In the same place?'

'Yeah. Think so. I remember thinking that's a pukka place for a piece cuz you can see it from road.'

'Promotion and publicity.'

'Yeah.'

'When we found it, it was closer to the yard.'

He frowns. 'Someone must've moved it then.'

'You didn't move the filing cabinet?'

'Na man!'

'Had you seen it before?'

'There was lots of shit left even after the demolition. We used to go in, tag up, find old books and that before CCTV got put in and I got busted.'

'Tag up and vandalise?' Robertson pushes forward a file to Diana.

'You were cautioned previously for vandalism at the site this June.'

Axmed's eyebrows push onto his lowered kids. He glares at Robertson. Diana flicks through, eyes to the page.

'That's dealt with. Not why I'm here.'

Diana steeples her hands. 'Well – it is and it isn't. You knew the derelict site probably better than its legal owner, correct?'

Another shrug.

'You've spent more time there over the past – what, five year? So, I think you would remember where that filing cabinet used to be.'

There's a knock. Lawton enters. Axmed looks up.

'How many more of yer's needed?' Axmed scoffs. Robertson gets up, leaves, and Lawton pulls out the chair, sitting on it a yard from the desk. He folds his arms, staring at Axmed.

'Just come back from talking with the drug squad, Axmed. Seems like you're trying to move on from distribution of spray paint to distribution of something more interesting.'

'What you on about?' Axmed snaps.

Lawton pushes his jaw into Axmed's eyeline. Diana frowns but stays at the desk.

'How 'bout you help us with the filing cabinet, you little

dickhead, and we put the drugs thing down to gossip? Thing is, Axmed, our boss decides where to allocate resources. See where we're coming from? Suits another department to throw you to the wall. We're throwing you a line here, mate. If you're smart, you'll take it. Vandalism to public property – a slapped wrist, caution. Be off in a few year. The other – that's superglue, mate. You committing to a record at seventeen. Which you want?'

Axmed scrapes the chair back, forearms on thighs, hands together staring at his trainers. His feet tap a beat. Lawton looks at Diana; she lifts one finger.

Axmed exhales. 'So it'll end with the caution?'

'Unless we get evidence to the contrary. We'll have to confirm where you were Bank Holiday.'

'Plenty man see me. I weren't moving filing cabinet or offing me headmaster.'

Diana pulls into the desk, picks up the file.

'So … back to the filing cabinet?'

'That filing cabinet used to have my file in it. It was in the EAL mobile classroom. I needed extra English when I first came.'

'Well done! I couldn't speak Somali in a year. Or even four,' Diana says.

Axmed tilts his chin proudly.

'So it was in the mobile – was it empty?'

He nods.

'One day, no mobile. Filing cabinet and some old chairs by the big metal …'

'Skip.'

He frowns. Lawton repeats: 'Skip.'

'Now?' Axmed looks bewildered.

'A skip. It's what we call the big metal bin.' Diana glares at the smirking Lawton.

'How long?'

'About a week. And then week before Bank Holiday I see it pulled out facing road. I see no camera either so am like: "I'm a hit dat."'

'When *did* you "hit dat"?' asks Diana.

'Night of Bank Holiday Monday, after collecting me mate from Creamfields.'

'He with you?'

'He's watch-out.'

'What time?'

He shrugs. 'Two?'

'Tell me about it.'

'I dint have much spray left, just enough for one tag. Just tag and go, innit. Light go on, me mate whistle so I audi.'

'Who's the mate?'

'Bruno. Bruno Pierce. But he didn't do owt.'

'Was this filing cabinet locked?'

Axmed's eyes spark. 'You know what? It wasn't. I wanted to shift it round, like I said, and Bruno tried and top drawer fell out, nearly went in his eye.'

'Did he have a cut? Did he bleed?'

'A bit, yeah. He was already pissed off.'

Diana looks at Lawton, who leans back in his chair, nodding slowly.

Axmed stares at Diana, eyebrows questioning. 'Why? What's up?'

Diana steeples her hands again, pushing her first fingers together.

'DC Khan will get your fingerprints—'

'Again?'

'—check out your alibi with Pierce and Mahmood, and then off you trot for now.'

Lawton holds the door open for him.

As Axmed heads out, Diana calls: 'Axmed.'

He turns, his face full of terror.

'Stay out of trouble, yeah?'

Chapter 11

THURSDAY 23RD SEPTEMBER, 2010 – SHEFFIELD HQ

Diana is at her desk, wading through a pile of transcripts. Robertson appears beside her. She jumps, knocking her McDonald's coffee.

'Sake, Robertson! You're like frigging Mr Ben!' she growls.

Robertson looks confused.

Diana sighs. 'Has Bruno Pierce been in for his DNA swab?'

'Yeah. And Gorman checked the filing cabinet. Nothing.'

Diana stares at the corkboard.

'The deputy head, Mrs Braithwaite, is downstairs for her interview, Boss.'

Diana puts the transcripts into a deep drawer. Turns the key. Pockets it.

'Brilliant. Can you bring down copies of the two sheets I put Post-its on yesterday?'

Robertson nods. He stares at the McDonald's bag on his immaculate desk.

'Breakfast's on me.'

Diana heads to reception.

Diana faces a navy-suited, court-heeled woman across the veneered desk in a room stinking of bleach and sweat. Mrs Braithwaite's hair blow-dried Weetabix, face caked with a relentless cream

81

emulsion. Plum felt-tipped mouth. Pearl earrings. Crêpey neck beginning, but those grey eyes sharp, alert as a fox.

Diana feels she's the one being assessed, head to toe. Looks like she's a D.

'Good morning, Mrs Braithwaite. I'm Detective Inspector Diana Walker. I ...'

Mrs Braithwaite looks at her watch. 'Morning, detective inspector. I do have to be back at Manley Moor for ten-thirty.'

'I'm sure we won't keep you long. As I said on the phone, I just need to get a feel of Legley Road High School, some information about what it was like under John Daniels' leadership, what was going on with staffing, curriculum, discipline. Any other school business that could possibly help us with this investigation.'

Mrs Braithwaite inhales slowly. 'Just to clarify: I am not under caution?'

Diana points to the tape. 'No, no. This is purely part of the standard procedure of information gathering. We do obviously record and document it. For the sake of the tape, please provide positive answers. Can you just state your name, role and dates of service at Legley Road. Your current occupation?'

'Mrs Delia Braithwaite, formerly the deputy head of Legley Road High School between September 1999 and July 2009. Currently, a geography teacher and head of Year 9 at Manley Moor School.'

Diana nods. 'Age? Married, single, children?'

'Forty-nine, divorced, two children.'

Diana makes a brief note on her legal pad. 'When did you join Legley Road High School?'

'I came to Legley Road as I wanted to get into school leadership, get my NPQH.'

Diana frowns. 'NPQH?'

Mrs Braithwaite smiles condescendingly. 'The National Professional Qualification for Headship. I'd been teaching eight years, three at Shire Green, five in Rotherham. The headmaster, Mr Ratbourne, at Legley Road, was approaching retirement and said I'd be next in line if I took the deputy's post.'

Diana leans back. 'Did that happen?'

Mrs Braithwaite looks at the tabletop. 'No. Too many policy changes, the school became more ethnic each successive year. After

I was shortlisted twice for the headship that went to younger men who only stayed two years, and then to Daniels, I knew the pattern. I had two teenagers and no time to apply anywhere else, let alone finish my NPQH.'

'Can you tell me a bit about John Daniels?'

'Good at talking. Upbeat, ambitious. Milk with two sugars in his tea and coffee.'

Isn't that the truth.

'Anything about his personal life?'

Mrs Braithwaite shrugs. 'Liked the good life – drove a Lexus, the odd European weekend break. No kids. Very active socially and seemed to have VIP tickets to everything.'

'Did he have a drinking or drugs problem?'

Mrs Braithwaite crumples her foundation with a vehement frown. 'Goodness me, no. We have a very tough policy on drugs and drink.'

Try telling DI Lawton that.

'What can you tell me about Mrs Daniels, his wife?'

Mrs Braithwaite folds her hands in front of her, foundation cracking at the mouth.

'Not much.'

Diana points. 'For the tape, please.'

Mrs Braithwaite scrapes her chair forward. 'She – Mrs Daniels – came to the Christmas parties and summer social events. She worked in admin? Or was it retail? They'd been trying for kids, IVF. Very sad.' In a voice declaring it wasn't sad at all – it was just.

'Did Mr Daniels have marriage problems?'

'It was a shock when he told me she'd filed for divorce.'

Diana nods slowly, extending the silence. Mrs Braithwaite clears her throat. 'Rather spiteful, I thought.'

'You're very loyal to Mr Daniels.'

Mrs Braithwaite glows smugly. 'It's a deputy's job.'

Diana can't resist letting a bit of the gas out. 'I guess he would be writing your reference?'

Mrs Braithwaite glares. Diana points to the tape recorder.

'Well, he didn't leave after two years, unlike the others. He stayed. Appointed new staff. We got a lot more funding for initiatives to help attainment. I did the paperwork, he did the meetings.'

She fidgets. Diana waits.

'We had a few staffing issues in the last couple of years of the school.'

'Like what?'

'The head of Year 7 wasn't doing the tracking and targeting. So he was removed. Lots of long-term sickness and supply in. Staff morale was low. Mr Daniels thought providing free tea and coffee in the staffroom, an open bar last day of term, would keep folk happy. It just made it worse. I went to the strategy meetings, heard all about the five-year plan and warned him: "We'll be first to close if we don't sort our results out."'

Interesting.

'He followed up on your advice?'

Mrs Braithwaite's emulsion starts to gloss on her forehead.

'Not this time. I think that's what tipped Ms Calley, the head of English.'

Diana frowns. 'Tipped?'

Mrs Braithwaite frowns too. 'She used to be a competent head of department.'

'Are you saying that she became incompetent?'

Mrs Braithwaite flusters. Lips a thin line. 'I think that's a case for the unions, detective.'

Diana raises her eyebrows. 'We have neither Ms Calley nor the unions here. Just you.'

Mrs Braithwaite's face cracks at the edges. Robertson knocks, comes in and places two sheets of paper on the desk before Diana.

'Thanks.' She taps them into a neat oblong.

Robertson leaves, not looking at Mrs Braithwaite, who stares after him, frowning.

'Mr Leroy Young, the head of PE and the co-ordinator for Gifted and Talented and Raising Attainment in Afro-Caribbean, Bangladeshi and Pakistani boys. We haven't been able to contact him. How did he get on with the other members of staff?'

'Mr Young? Very popular with both staff and students, excellent coach. Worked very well with Ms Calley ... at first.'

'At first?'

Mrs Braithwaite wriggles. 'I don't listen to staffroom rumours, but when I'm getting staff reports and parents complaining, I have to step in.'

'What staffroom rumours?'

Mrs Braithwaite sighs. 'They had had a falling out over the summer or something. Either way, the target tracking and collaboration wasn't happening, the mentoring ...'

'So how did you step in?'

Mrs Braithwaite coughs. 'Well, I had a chat with Leroy Young. Asked him why he hadn't produced any collaborative data with Ms Calley that term.'

Diana starts scribbling. 'Which term?'

'Oh – that would be ... Autumn term 2007.'

Mrs Braithwaite swallows. 'He said Ms Calley was deluded, some fantasy that they were in a relationship and she was pestering him with emails and texts. I told him I understood he stayed at Ms Calley's over the summer. He denied this.'

Diana puts her head on one side. 'And you believed him?'

Mrs Braithwaite fixes her eyes on the sheets of paper under Diana's palms.

'He said he went over to drop off some paperwork over the summer and she'd made advances. That he was married with a one-year-old. He claimed it was bordering on harassment.'

'What was your response?'

Mrs Braithwaite, cornered. 'Well, I questioned Ms Calley, who maintained that Mr Young had moved their relationship onto an emotional and physical footing *before* the holidays. That she didn't know he had a wife and child. He moved into her place over the holidays as he said he was between places, but when Ms Calley discovered he was married and confronted him, he became hostile.'

Diana raises her eyebrows. 'What do you mean "hostile"?'

Mrs Braithwaite shrugs. 'I think it was just a turn of phrase.'

Diana holds her gaze until she looks away.

'So what did you do?'

Mrs Braithwaite looks at her watch. 'I really have to ...'

Diana's eyes don't blink. She skewers the Weetabix.

'I told her she had a job to do and to act professionally and that I would deal with Mr Young.'

Lean in for the kill.

'And how *did* you deal with Mr Young?'

Mrs Braithwaite sits upright. 'I told him I needed the data and to treat Ms Calley as a professional. That if Ms Calley was still non-compliant to let me know and I would take disciplinary action.'

NPQH my ass.

'So, you didn't support Ms Calley?'

Defiant. 'I didn't support either of them!'

Diana stares.

'I mean, I didn't take sides. They both had jobs to do.'

'But you did threaten Ms Calley with disciplinary action?'

'If she didn't produce the data, I told her I would have no option but to follow through with management protocol.'

'And how *did* you discipline Mr Young?'

'Discipline?'

'Did you also warn Young against the consequences of him not producing the collaborative data?'

'I told him we needed the data, and he said he'd get me something by Friday.'

Diana nods slowly. 'So you didn't warn him about the consequences?'

'No. I'd no need to. He said …'

Diana shakes the papers together. Taps them on the table. 'So let me get this straight: Ms Calley was warned but not Mr Young. Correct?'

Wilting. 'Yes.'

'Did they both meet and work through the data together?'

Mrs Braithwaite clears her throat. 'As I recall, three years ago, detective, I got the collaborative data from Mr Young.'

'But you had no evidence to prove Ms Calley had contributed? No sign-off?'

Mrs Braithwaite looks at the edge of the table as if it holds the answer.

Diana leans forward. 'See, Mrs Braithwaite. I have a problem. Because this …'

Diana flourishes the top sheet in front of her, pushing it across the veneer. 'For the sake of the tape, is Legley Road High School's English department's detailed grades and targets for each and every student registered in 2007, tracked and verified by individual pieces of moderated work at set times. And this …'

She pushes the second sheet across the table. Mrs Braithwaite peers at them closely. Silence. She puts them side by side, traces her fingers along lines, columns. Brow furrowed by a cracked V that won't bounce back.

'… is one with grades and attainments and dates completely different. According to this sheet, "English attainment assessment and tracking has been inconsistent, done by random isolated teachers and proves the English department's resources have not been managed to enhance the attainment of the target groups." Is that your handwriting or Daniels'?'

'Where did you get that first sheet from?'

'Whose handwriting please?' Diana says.

'Mine. Where is Sheet 1 from?'

'That document was in the English department files, emailed to the LEA and strategy development officers and Mr Leroy Young, as Ms Calley apparently did every month – according to the email trail. Have you not seen this?'

Mrs Braithwaite urgently passes both documents, as if contaminated, back to Diana: 'I don't recall …'

'So Mr Young didn't show you this or use the data in Sheet 2 – the second performance analysis? Did you discipline Ms Calley?'

'Mr Daniels said I needed to call her in for her performance management review early.'

'When?'

Mrs Braithwaite stutters: 'Friday the … the … before half-term. 2007.'

Diana nods slowly. 'Friday 19th October?'

'Yes. Mr Daniels wanted all these documents before half-term.'

'As a result, he could justify his withholding of the funding for the new curriculum Ms Calley had won for the school, correct?' Diana moves in. 'When did Mr Daniels propose his new restructuring of the budget?'

'I'm not sure …' Braithwaite's foundation-face caves in beneath the Weetabix like a soggy cardboard bowl.

Diana snaps. 'No problems. We'll check with the LEA. Can you tell me when Ms Calley handed in her resignation?'

'Just after half-term.'

Give her some breath now she's on the ropes.

'Could you tell me who had access to the filing cabinet keys?'

Mrs Braithwaite's eyes open wide. 'Filing cabinet keys? It would be the heads of department.'

'Where did all the keys go when the school closed? Could a head of department hold onto a filing cabinet key?'

'No. The closing inspection was scrupulous. Everyone had to sign in when they were given a key and sign off when they handed it back in. They all went back to the LEA. The Local Education Authority.' She pauses. 'I suppose they passed them onto the auditors or whoever bought the site? I don't rightly know, detective.'

'Fair enough. We'll check. And lastly, where were you over the August Bank Holiday this year?'

'At the caravan in Llandudno with my parents and children.'

'Thanks for your help, Mrs Braithwaite. We'll be in touch if we have any further questions.'

Ten and counting.

Chapter 12

FRIDAY 24TH SEPTEMBER, 2010 – DEWBOW

It's the first time Diana's been out since the incident with the stag. She's been making do with a brisk walk up the hill and back, but now her body's demanding a full workout. Her neck and shoulders feel wooden after a week of poring over paperwork, scrolling on monitors. Her hips are tight, her head pounding night and day.

Now, fleeced up and laced into tougher terrain-ready trainers and a luminous vest to alert any wildlife to her presence, she's ready to brace the elements again. Rising mists swirl in front of her, her breath coming out in clouds. The glowing lights from the hilltop farm are the only signs of anyone else up.

Diana plunges onto the path up the hill, arms like pistons pushing her over the one-in-six incline to the top. At the crest, she views the edges of the escarpment, its valleys and rivulets, quaint hamlets and implausible lanes stretching out before her, clothed in the glow of luminous pink. She inhales damp peat and runs through brittle bracken, filling her lungs with clean air.

Gun cracks. The forest shudders, stops. Wings rush up in an invisible mass above her. Branches snap.

BANG! Again. This time it's away from her, downwind. Diana reasons that if she runs up the back of the farm, away from the noise, she'll be safe from crusading stags and gun-toting ladies of the manor.

She carries on running, regretting stopping now as her limbs grow colder and heavier, sweat condensing to chill her back. In front of her, a stocky figure in a peaked cap stands by the gate he's just closed, as if waiting for her.

'Morning!'

Might as well be civil.

The man glares at her. 'That abandoned car yours? Only it's over your boundary line.'

Diana pants: 'Pardon?'

He looks sixtyish, wearing a bulky green anorak and muddied wellington boots, creased red face, bright blue eyes. He squints at Diana.

'Oh. You're not her.'

'Excuse me?'

'Thought you were her at Dewbright Hall …'

Diana looks around.

'Oh, Maya? No, sorry.'

The man looks surprised. 'Not seen you round here before. You local?'

'Yes. Live on Dew Lane. DI Diana Walker, South Yorkshire Police. I can call it in for you though.'

He looks her up and down. 'You police?'

Diana, not for the first time, feels she is being assessed like a sixth-form candidate. He shoots out a leathery palm. Diana tries to grasp it.

'Walter Craven. I live up top at Craven Farm. Would be grand if you could. Can't understand why it's not been claimed or reported stolen.'

Diana follows him up the lane.

'I'll get my missus to make you a strong brew – looks like you've earned it. I just want this car business shifted. Attracts gypsies and other no-gooders.'

They plod up the hill.

Make friends locally. Rehema's mantra.

'It's cold for September,' ventures Walter. 'Get you a bacon sarnie too. Keep you going.'

'I'm vege—' Diana starts, but Walter is more interested in opening the gate.

'That won't do.'

Feeling obliged to start some small neighbourly talk rather than an argument about animal welfare, Diana asks how long he's lived here.

He looks up the road. 'All me life. Me father and his father too. It took up too much time managing deer so we had a deal with the Johnsons – that's how they got the top half of woods. But this bit here – weer car is … that was nivver resolved. Not by lassie's father nor mine who had it afore me, God rest his soul. So you see it's been a dilemma. I'm not to blame and I don't want no lawyers involved – not got cash to throw away. I just don't like that car there.'

Who are the Johnsons? Previous owners, maybe. Diana approaches the silver BMW 3 Series model, parked in a narrow lay-by. A beamer whose rims hadn't been snatched. That's weird in itself. It looks abandoned, not parked, like a Sunday driver left it for a wander. On the crest of the hill, a misshapen oak tree twists to one side and bends protectively over the forlorn vehicle. Diana approaches. Blackening golden leaves lie strewn on the bonnet and roof, caught in the vents. Bird poo splatter on the roof and windscreen, grass between the wheels, a damp blackening mass of leaves collecting on the wheel arches like a slow compost. She makes a mental note of the registration number and peers through the rain-grimed windows.

'Did you see the driver?'

'No. I remember I noticed it the Sunday of the August Bank Holiday because I just thought it was a family out for the day. I didn't think none of it till I noticed it ten days later, way after holiday time. Looks like a packed lunch in there. Be full o' maggots now. Don't think anyone's been back here.'

Diana walks around clockwise, anti-clockwise, digging into her phone pouch; she's started wearing one since her incident with the stag.

'Robertson? It's me – yes. No. Look, do me a favour, will you? Run me this reg LBOY XXX … a farmer neighbour of mine's got an issue with an abandoned vehicle and boundaries … What? No, I'm fine. *Land* boundaries.'

Diana shakes her head in exasperation. The phone crackles.

Walter coming up to Diana, looking like a schoolboy who's just finished his homework: 'Tax disc ran out last week.'

Oblivious, Diana gapes at the orange sky.

'What?' She squints at the phone. 'Registered to Leroy Young? *Our* Leroy Young? OK. I'm calling the super. Get CSI and yourself down here asap …'

She rests her handset on her shoulder and looks at Walter, now bent over, peering at the car as if it's a UFO.

'Mr Craven, where is this?'

'Craven Farm, top of Top Lane, Dewbow, DE23 7PZ.'

'You heard that? Right.' Diana clicks off.

Walter stands up, rubbing the base of his spine.

'You found him?'

'I wish – but I know who the registered owner is. We're looking for him too.'

Walter grunts triumphantly. 'See. Dodgy business. You've earned a brew and a bacon sarnie …'

He strides off towards the lit windows of Craven Farm half a mile away.

'I'm a …'

Diana cups her hand around the mug of hot sugary tea and leans on the fence. This is getting to be a habit: every time she goes out for a run, it ends in drama and sugared tea.

Robertson, biting into the rejected bacon sarnie, looks like an overgrown Year 7, wrapped up in an orange-lined parka with the hood up.

'No key?'

Diana rolls her eyes. 'No Leroy?'

'No, Boss. The school hasn't seen or heard from him. They gave his job to a long-term supply. Woman at High Peak seemed very angry.'

Diana stares at a crisp packet caught in the hedge. Men in white suits buzz like alien moths around the abandoned BMW.

'Seems to have been here over two months.'

Marks pops the boot.

'Detective …'

He pulls out a brown baby doll wrapped in pink ribbon, a

pink card addressed in black capitals to MAISY. Reaching in, he pulls out a withered bunch of thorny stems, flakes of yellow petals wrapped in cellophane.

The white UPVC door opens to a harassed handsome woman, toddler on hip, blonde hair scraped into a ponytail. She runs her eyes up and down Diana.

'Mrs Young? Julie Young?'

The screeching child stutters to a snivel. Eyes unblinking, she starts sucking her thumb.

'I'm DI Walker and this is DS Robertson who spoke to you on the phone a week or so ago. We just wanted to ask some questions concerning your husband.'

Julie's even features squish into a scowl. The child stares out from piercing blue eyes under a mane of golden corkscrew curls.

'Best come in. Neighbours got enough to chat about.'

Diana and Robertson enter into the hallway. Mrs Young's dressed in red Juicy Couture joggers, electric blue Nike T-shirt, bare feet, toenails painted electric fuchsia.

She walks into the living room and they follow.

'When you find him, you can serve his divorce papers seeing as the ignorant sod's not answering my solicitor's calls.'

It's a textbook IKEA living room: scattered cream cushions, corner sofa against one wall, two-seater by the door, TV on wall. A pile of plastic toys.

'Maisy, go play with your dolls.'

'No.'

'Maisy ...' Weariness oozes out of her. 'Grown-up talk. Smarties if you help Mummy.'

Maisy trots off.

'Bribery and corruption. Never fails.'

Deadpan, Diana and Robertson sit on the edge of the two-seater.

The mother rummages in a fake Goyard handbag, pulling out a ten-pack of Lambert & Butler. She taps one out.

'Leroy's not been round some time. He's probably shacked up with some slag. Didn't even show for his own bairn's birthday. That should tell you the measure of the man.'

She goes to the patio doors looking out on a small, flagged yard with various toddler-friendly plastics. Flicks a pink throw-away lighter. Inhales. Glares at the sandpit.

'What you want from *me*? Leroy's a big boy. One thing's for sure: he always looks after Number 1 first. And apparently that's not Maisy. Or me.'

'What car does he drive?'

'A BMW 3 Series. With a personalised number plate because he's a tart.' She gives a snort, inhaling deep on the diminished cig.

'LBOY XXX?'

Her ponytailed head snaps up. Her face tightens.

'What's he done? What's happened?'

Robertson pulls out his notepad. Diana moves to the edge of the sofa. 'When did you last see your husband, Mrs Young?'

She takes two fast final draws, flicks the filter onto the step, sliding the patio door shut. Her eyes flicker as she sinks into the centre of the cream corner sofa.

'What's going on?'

'We've found his car. On farmland in Derbyshire. But no Leroy.'

She frowns, looks out at the patio. A bus lumbers past.

'Thursday 26th August. In town. He wanted us to get back together. Told me he'd got a permanent job. Head of PE or some-thing at High Peak. He wanted a brother for Maisy, for us to be a proper family.'

'Weren't you?'

'We were, and then he went with that ... slag ... teacher at school. I were barely coping, Maisy not even one. Left us rammed up to our necks in debt. Should've ended it then.'

She shakes her head. 'Silly cow. I believed him. Had him back. All sweet for a bit. Then he's at it again. Kicked him out at Easter. He's making all these promises ... I say "maybe" at end of August. He's like, "Gimme a couple of days to sort things out." I even invite him to my sister's Bank Holiday barbecue. Friday, Saturday we're texting like teenagers. He's like, "I'll take you to Sarah's Saturday four o'clock".'

Robertson scribbles rapidly.

'Did he take you?'

'Did he fk. I waited. I called. I texted. Felt a right prat going to barbecue on me tod with my sister and family giving me the "I-told-you-so" shit. My cousin reckons she saw him out with some bird. Then he misses Maisy's third birthday. Nothing. Not even a card, a text, a call. Her all "Where's Daddy?"'

Her voice catches. Diana stares at her, at the photo on the shelf of the three of them in some sunny exotic holiday location. The wife's eyes brim with rage and fear.

She pulls out her phone, scrolling. 'Saturday 28th August. Twelve noon exactly. "See you at four, babe. Need to sort summat first. Can't wait to see you both. Give a hug to Maisy. Love you loads L Kiss kiss kiss."'

Robertson's pen scratches. Julie's eyes glisten as her thumb strokes her ring finger.

'So – what's up with car? Can I have it?' Her voice brittle, she slips the phone back in her bag.

'I'm afraid not. It's been impounded until we can locate Leroy. His car's been there since August Bank Holiday so that ties in with what you said.'

The school hasn't seen or heard from him. He's not been using his bank cards, not been using his old phone.

Instead: 'Have you tried calling?'

She shakes her head, truth settling into horror. 'Just voicemail innit. Even his mum can't reach him.'

'We shall have to record him as an official Missing Person and he is also a Person of Interest to the case at Legley Road.'

'You don't think Leroy done that?'

'We don't know what to think right now, Mrs Young, which is why we need as much information as possible. Can you tell me a bit more about his work at Legley Road High School? He was there four years.'

She shakes her head. 'Right shit hole. We'd barely been married a year and he was made up to get that head of PE job. But I didn't like it. Told him not to take it.'

'Why didn't you want him to take the job?'

'Not a good school.'

'But he did well there, didn't he? Good reputation as head of PE and two promotions ...'

There's a loud pop, like a gunshot in the other room. Diana jumps.

'Old birthday balloons,' mutters Mrs Young. Another pop. 'Oh aye. Rate saint our Leroy! Pillar of society, shagging every female under fifty.' She looks down. 'Well, any road, that bitch, Mary Calley. That's karma what she got.'

'Calley. Is that the one …?'

'Found in a bedsit, yeah. Crazy that woman. Broke up my family. I'm left with a pile of credit card bills. Things were never the same after that, even when he came back, even when he paid off bills.'

'Do you have a joint bank account?'

'Yeah, but he's also got a personal one. And he's not been using our joint account for over a month so expect he's been putting his pay in his personal.'

'Well, High Peak haven't been paying him so I don't know what he would have been living off.'

Mrs Young shrugs.

Robertson clears his throat. 'Could you let me have bank statements for the past five years please?'

Mrs Young frowns. 'If I have to.'

The toddler wobbles in holding a piece of string and a deflated rag of red balloon.

'Smarties, Mummy.'

Mummy turns from her reverie gazing out of the window to Diana.

'Mrs Young, we did find a present and card wrapped up for Maisy in the boot of the car.'

The flint-like face contorts.

'… and a bunch of what would have been roses.'

'Present!' squeals Maisy while Mummy glares at Diana.

'I suppose bairn can't have it, though?'

Diana shakes her head. 'Not yet. I'm sorry.'

'Rate,' she says. 'So you've come to tell me I've a car I can't drive, presents my bairn can't open, and a husband you can't find. Basically, a mortgage I can't pay and a kid with no daddy.'

She looks into the distance. 'Have to start doing more nails. Put an ad on Facebook or summat. I'm usually elite, just low-key for the women with cash and style. I'm the only one who does the real classy stuff in Sheff. Went on a special training course down London, you know.'

She turns around, looking down at Diana's chipped cuticles and raw hands.

'Here, have a card. Treat yourself, detective.' Mrs Young passes Diana a card from a stack on the coffee table.

Diana looks at it: *Clous pour tu – Exclusive nails for Exclusive ladies*. J Young certified French manicurist 07892345616. Diana pockets it.

'I may take you up on that. You have a business premises then?'

'Used to rent a desk at a hairdresser's at Nether Edge. Just mobile bookings now though – because of Maisy, and …'

She drifts off, aware that she is alone now. Diana gets up.

'Thank you, Mrs Young. We'll be in touch in due course.'

Fixing Diana with ice-cold eyes: 'I just want papers signed. Leaving me in limbo. Nowt down for that.'

Robertson is pale as the door slams behind them.

'Woh. That's cold!'

Diana raises an eyebrow, opening the car door.

'Your missus would do the same, Robertson.'

Chapter 13

Saturday 25th September, 2010 – Sheffield

Diana buzzes the intercom at the short block of private flats. She looks over the car park to where DS Robertson is locking his car.

The intercom crackles. 'Hello?'

Diana leans into the speaker.

'Mrs Daniels? It's DI Diana Walker. We just need a few more details about your husband.'

Mrs Daniels' flat voice comes after a short pause. '*Ex*-husband. Got to go out at two-thirty.'

The door buzzes open.

When the door to Flat 4 opens, Mrs Daniels looks as grey and flat as the immaculate interior, her eyes hooded. They follow her in, down the passage to a small, blind-shaded living room, minimally furnished. They sit on slate linen sofas.

'Told you all I know.'

'I'm sorry. There's nothing easy about this, but in order to find the murderer …'

Mrs Daniels nods. Robertson pulls out his notepad.

'Had Mr Daniels got any girlfriends? Or boyfriends?'

'Not that I know of.' Mrs Daniels shrugs. 'I don't think he was that bothered about sex.'

Diana frowns.

'So he could have been gay?'

'Definitely not.' Mrs Daniels clams her mouth into a fine line of magenta.

Diana looks around the immaculate white and grey room, the succulent on the glass coffee table. A small flatscreen TV. No photos.

'You moved here after the divorce?'

Mrs Daniels nods. 'We sold the house. Neither of us had enough equity for our own, so yeah – rented this for time being.'

'What do you do again, Mrs Daniels?'

'Assistant manager at Marks & Spencer's.'

Of course.

'So why *did* you divorce? Seems like you both lost out financially …'

Mrs Daniels inhales. 'Kids. I wanted them. We tried. For years. Went for tests.' She shakes her head. 'It weren't going to happen. Ever.'

Diana wants to ask about the IVF, but holds back. 'Sorry.'

Mrs Daniels exhales, pushing her palms down her knees.

'John were all for IVF, but consultant said no point. It were John who was shooting blanks. I said I didn't mind, we could adopt. But he wouldn't accept it. He just became obsessed with proving himself. Material things, success, being seen to be this big-shot headmaster.'

'You don't think he was?'

Mrs Daniels looks at her nails. 'Don't like to speak ill of him …'

'The more honest you are, the more likely we are to catch who did this. These details help our investigation only.'

Mrs Daniels closes her eyes.

'What made you think there was no hope for the marriage?'

'I discovered the big debts. He was always out: school meetings, socialising, the gambling.'

'So it was the debts?'

'Partly.' Mrs Daniels stares at the carpet.

'But his bank statements show he paid off the debts in early 2008?'

Mrs Daniels raises her head. 'You need to keep looking then, inspector. They started up again a few months after. He was still gambling. But – it weren't that.'

Diana waits.

'After that doctor's diagnosis, he couldn't perform in the bedroom.'

She looks up, eyes bolts of fire.

'I'd had enough. The debts. Not having kids. My own clock's ticking. Nowt wrong with me. When debts started again, that clinched it. I began divorce proceedings December 2008.'

She inhales sharply, chin up defiantly. 'And I'm glad. I've got a new boyfriend. Much happier now.'

Right. Living in a rented flat. Beats being a very rich widow with a house and headmaster's pension.

And still no kids.

Bruno

Mr Samuels lets me out at three to get my lunch. I'm not fussed about snap; feel sick. Just want a juice and check me phone. Been buzzing in my back pocket for hours. Axmed goes ghost on me past week. Now he's blowing it up.

'Calm it. What's with six missed calls?'

'Alright, bro. Y'alright?'

What sort of answer is that? 'Working, innit. Down Derbyshire.'

'Oh yeah, right. Down that way myself. Want a lift back to Sheff when you're done?'

I look around, feeling watched.

'What you mean, you're "down that way"?'

'Just passing through from Derby.'

I've just necked a bottle of Lucozade but now I can feel it gassing up my throat. I want to retch. Like I want any of that shit down here. Ryan's a knob. He has to get into *everything* of mine: my mates, my plans, my teachers, my money ...

'Na. I'm sound, Axmed. I'll get bus.'

Can hear something ... people?

'Who you with?'

More muffled noise like he's in a car. Bet Ryan's with him now, telling Axmed what to say, getting in his head like the maggot he is. Mr Samuels yells me from inside.

'I'm sorted, Axmed. Got to go. Later.'

100

I hang up. Raging. He best not bring that shit round here. I put phone in my back pocket, look up just as that skinny detective comes out of shop opposite. Don't nod at me, bitch. Undercover buying eggs? You having a laugh?

Give me a carcass to chop. Now.

Diana

After a Sainsbury's shop in Sheffield, Diana heads back to Dewbow and an attempt at domesticity – not quite her style, but neither is squalor. The cramped cottage stinks of sweaty joggers, vests and a sink full of unwashed toast plates. She needs to clear her head – and do some cleaning. She has this nagging feeling she's not moving fast enough – in every way.

Eggs! Crap – I forgot.

She can't be doing with parking up, going to the overpriced Co-op. She pulls up outside the greengrocer's, opposite the butcher's. Nips into the greengrocer's. Gets a dozen. *Nice. An omelette for tea.* She's about to get back in the car when she feels the hard stare of an aproned youth from across the road.

Nodding briefly, she holds his gaze as she turns the key.

Calley. Bruno. Leroy Young. Daniels. Legley Road. The pattern is becoming regular.

If certain threads keep popping up in the pattern, it can only mean one thing: they are connected. But how does it relate to this homicide, and why are there no witnesses?

If two of them are dead, who's next?

Chapter 14

MONDAY 27TH SEPTEMBER, 2010 – REHEMA'S HOUSE, SHEFFIELD

Rehema nearly drops her cup of herbal tea when Diana taps at the kitchen window.

'Wish you'd stop doing that, Diana.'

Diana enters, stooping to kiss her mum on the cheek. She sits down opposite, picking up a thick paperback from the kitchen table, scanning the blurb on the back.

'*The Book of Night Women*.' She pulls a face. 'What is this, an A to Z of the red-light district? Something you want to tell me, Ma?'

Rehema snatches it from her with a frown. 'You should read more.'

'I'm dyslexic.'

'Dyslexic not ignorant! You did a psychology degree! You *can* read – you just don't.'

'Exactly. MaMa here?'

'Yes – she's just resting. She'll be pleased to see you. Can you help me take her to the book club tonight?'

Diana, open-mouthed. 'Ma, I'm working a murder case.'

'And so are we.'

Diana shakes her head in disbelief.

'Oh, you think what your grandparents went through a joke?'

'No, Ma.'

'I can't be twenty-four-seven chaperone.'

'MaMa doesn't need a chaperone. Anyway, what's happening about her deposition for those solicitors?'

The black hole of their history.

Rehema gets up to fill the kettle.

'She's going down to London again in a couple of weeks. Over fifty years MaMa's had to shut up, put up. The British Government needs to do the right thing. Gordon Brown promised.'

'Labour's not in government now, Ma.'

'Makes no difference.'

'Er, it kind of does,' Diana mutters.

'The government still call her a Mau Mau terrorist. Can you believe that? This test case is everything.' She turns sharply to Diana. 'You want to humiliate or support your family?' she spits.

'I totally want MaMa to get justice. I'm just – in the middle of a murder case for which I'm SIO.'

Rehema gives a short, cruel laugh. 'Fa how long? You know how it go ...'

Diana exhales.

But she loves MaMa. Her memories of her gentle ways and love of the wild, walking out in the red dirt, sitting on the steps watching the birds head out to Nakuru.

Rehema switches on the kettle. Diana stares at Rehema's back, straight, strong as a rod, yet her shoulders slump. She opens a cupboard sharply, pulls out six stacked Tupperware containers, closes the cupboard with her hip, yanks open a drawer, pulls out a large spoon, starts to ladle the cooled casserole into the containers, snapping them shut: *snap-snap-snap-snap-snap-snap*. Freezer door wrenched open. Grate of ice. *Slam, slam, slam, slam, slam, slam*. Rehema pivots, wiping hands together, looking for something to act on, contain, clean, tidy while her wild frantic eyes belie something she can't.

Diana looks at her, sees her mother spinning in the void. Wants to reach out, pull her in, hug her, but, as she moves to do so, Rehema pulls away.

'Help with MaMa. Please.'

Diana sees her hold on to that shred of dignity like its her anchor.

'OK, Ma.'

Rehema sighs. 'Thank you. I want my sisters at the book club to meet her.'

Diana has to go through the autopsy report with a toothcomb before tomorrow. Plus she's left her blue lenses at HQ. She doesn't have time for this.

The door creaks open. MaMa stands, framed by the oak doorway, a regal carving against the soft light of the hallway. Diana's face splits in a grin. She rushes over to hug her.

'MaMa! I thought you were resting?'

'With all this banging?' MaMa frowns.

Diana dissolves into MaMa's tight embrace, inhaling her body's scent of cedar and earth. Rehema smiles.

'Sorry, Ma. We're going out soon, to book club. You can meet my friends.'

MaMa pulls back, looking as though she'd rather chew rusty nails.

Diana smirks.

'You best come, MaMa. I've been drafted in too. At least I can talk to you, right?'

When MaMa smiles, these little perfect round globes appear, pushing her eyes into sparkling diamonds, her pearly grin splitting her face into joy. It's the most beautiful smile ever, a smile born from patient endurance of an unspeakable suffering and a faith refined and solid. Her face at rest always carved in sadness, but when she smiles – she shines. Diana fetches MaMa's heavy shawl from a chair, draping it over her sparrow-like shoulders.

'Come on, MaMa, we can both be initiated into—'

Biting her lip, momentarily forgetting the name.

Rehema frowns. 'The Black Sistahs Book Club. We're not a cult. We're an exclusive group.'

'You are that,' mutters Diana.

Rehema pushes in the chairs and puts her books in a large cotton bag in silence. She pulls on a red corduroy trench coat. Diana feels bad now; it's her mum's support network.

'How did this book club malarkey start anyway?'

'I met Anoona and Lubanzi at a Black Professional Women's Convention in Leeds. Anoona came up with the book club idea. 2000 I think – no, hang on, it was after Anoona started at Pitsmoor so ...'

The year she moved in with Phillips.

It's six-thirty. She'll just go for an hour, to keep MaMa company and Rehema happy. And check out this book club.

Diana shunts at the passenger door of her mother's BMW. She hates this car – always feels like she's been welded into a moving chest freezer. She looks up at Lubanzi's house as she helps MaMa out of the back seat. The house is a three-floored, red-brick, semi-detached opposite the park behind Legley Road High School. In the dusk light, the front garden's full of silver-gold honesty and blousy red dahlias.

She follows her mother up the flagged path and steps to an inset vermilion front door. Rehema raps three times and the door opens to reveal a woman draped in a gold wraparound dress, wearing a red, green and blue turban and huge blue disc earrings. Her skin's smooth bronze, her dark eyes sparkle over a welcoming smile.

'Rehema, sister! How good to see you. We thought maybe you were busy ...'

'Sorry we're late, Lubanzi. This is my daughter, Diana, and my mother, Njambi, from Kenya.'

'Welcome, Diana! And Njambi ...' She bows her head in respect and smiles gently. 'It is a privilege to meet you.'

They enter the long dark corridor. It smells of sandalwood and beeswax. Cut chrysanthemums loom out from brass vases in the shadows.

The lounge's dark walls shimmer from the lit fire. A woman with aquiline features, paper-gold skin leans over a woman with twists, hand on her knee. In the opposite corner, a curvy girl: pressed ponytail, hooped earrings, wearing a pink sweater. Next to her, an older woman, cropped hair, pendulous earlobes hung with beads, clicks on a floor lamp.

'Now we can see!'

Diana ensures MaMa's close to the fire, sitting down by her side. Rehema sits on a separate chair. Diana becomes aware of a pair of eyes fixed on her while the conversation bubbles. In the far unlit corner, under a heaving bookshelf, sits a familiar figure. Dressed in a camel cashmere sweater dress, patent boots, the cat eyes blink.

'Hello, neighbour. Met any stags lately?'

Diana feels cramped and disorientated. Maya's confidence and country pile had made her assume Maya was white, but now Diana realises Maya *could* be a sister: the symmetrical face, full lips and snub nose. Those glossy curls now straightened.

Rehema frowns. 'Stags?'

'Maya's my neighbour. She lives in Dewbow,' mutters Diana.

'Of course! You two must know each other.'

'I was on a run the other day. Maya … er …'

'Intercepted a stag.'

Chatter stops.

'A stag?'

Diana rolls her eyes. 'I was in the way of a horny male deer.'

'Deer, oh dear!' chuckles chubby girl with hoops. No one else laughs. Rehema glares at Diana.

'So *that's* why you come to my house with a headache? Concussion no doubt …' Rehema looks fit to explode.

Maya smiles. 'The doc said she was fine.'

Shut this down.

Diana turns to MaMa, who is staring intently into the fire, rubbing her thin knees.

'Warm enough, MaMa?'

Lubanzi passes a battered copy of *The Book of Night Women* over to Diana. 'My old copy. Excuse the dog ears.'

Lubanzi sits down with a flourish on a blue throne of a chair by the door.

'So, ladies. Brief introductions for the sake of our newcomers: name, job, birthplace before book-talk. Myself, Lubanzi Kuhle, your host. Obstetrician and gynaecologist. Ghana my homeland.' Rich African lady. Headwrap.

'Komal Desai. Leicester. GP.' The paper-gold sister with the twist-dread partner.

'Shola Keller. Social worker. Kingston, Jamaica.' Twist-dread. Mid-forties?

'Anoona Shanda. Head librarian at Pitsmoor library. Zimbabwe.' Bobblehead, big earlobes.

'Pauline Cuthbert. Arksillary nurse. Kingston mi yard too.' Chubby hoop sister.

'Rehema Walker, nutritionist. Kenya.' Ma.

'Maya Smith, auditor.' She shrugs. 'Sheffield.' Maya, landowner.

Diana mutters: 'Diana Walker, detective inspector. Also Sheffield.' *Po-lees*. The silence tells her.

Lubanzi smiles. 'Spot the second generationers! Anyways ...' She waves her copy of the book. 'What did you think?'

Anoona inhales, makes big eyes.

'It was hard going! No punches pulled.'

Komal, the gold-skinned woman, laughs. 'You're not joking!'

'But it also ...'

'Gets under your skin?' interjects Maya.

'Yes. I can't help siding with Lilith.'

Pauline kisses her teeth. 'She two-a-penny back home. Most Jamaican women feisty.'

Rehema turns to a page. 'I found the cellar scene one of the worst experiences. Eating from a bowl in the dark.'

'But the depiction of the men—'

Maya nods 'The Johnny Jumpers!'

Pauline sits forward. 'So many idiot come at me as Johnny Jumper man. I even called one so the other day. "Git away fa me, ya imbecilic Johnny Jumper!" Man look so alarm!'

Rehema chuckles.

Diana's utterly lost. She frowns, reading through the blurb, making some token effort to flick through the novel. The women listen and run over each other's words, repeating some with claps and snapping fingers, high fiving other comments. It's electric, full, messy. Her mum comes alive, the way she does if you ask her about the varieties of okra or some obscure African herb. Maya looks around the room a lot, makes a couple of book-related comments.

Lulled by the harmonious rush of sound around her, Diana's mind turns to the autopsy report, the orange Post-its of questions on her monitor screen, the sound of blow flies busting out of bin liners, Daniels' big fish-eye. The smell of goat ...

107

Maya's cat eyes.

The stag's stomp.

The shot in the woods.

Sparrowhawk's screech.

A shrill voice breaks into her dream: 'Wakey, wakey! Diana? Would you like to read?'

Komal with the paper-gold skin and pointy nose.

Would she fk like to read.

'Er ... no thanks.'

The room's gone from cosy to claustrophobic, cramped, smothered by the scent of sandalwood and aromatic sweat. The evening closes in on her like a coffin. MaMa's fallen into a long snooze and leans against her, so she's stapled to the sofa, sandwiched between Pauline and MaMa.

Anoona reads aloud while Pauline kisses her teeth.

After three minutes, she bolts forward. Diana winces as she is squashed back against the sofa. Pauline points at her open book.

'Lilith gyal got no morals and no ejucation. Why we reading a book about this female? She murder these men with no conscience. Johnny Jumper or who you do.'

Anoona puts down her book, faces forward on the large low mahogany table in front of her.

'But does she not have good reason to murder?'

Pauline practically jumps up off the sofa sending ripples that wake MaMa, making Diana fear she'll sit back down on her.

'Good reason to murder? This is some godless book! Lubanzi, why would anyone write such a book? Lilith – that some pagan name! These women don't know who they is.'

Rehema sips her tea too loudly.

Maya stares intently at the page, frowning. Komal grins.

'Which is why Lilith is so important.'

Diana raises her elbows to prevent a major crushing as Pauline falls back in a grump, book slammed closed on her lap.

MaMa wakes up, yawning loudly.

'What about Lilith's rape?' asks Lubanzi.

'Rape? There's no rape here,' says Shola, shaking her head.

'Of course there is, there—'

Shola pulls a poker face. 'Oh no. It's only rape if it's a white woman. Black women don't count.'

Her eyes swoop over Diana, wide awake now.

'Isn't that so, Detective Diana? Sexual assault of a black woman isn't a crime, right?'

'Bet you never worked on the rape case of a black woman,' Rehema says.

MaMa opens one eye, glares at no one in particular, closes it again.

Diana glares back at Rehema. What is this? In her mind's eye, she rapidly reels through all her cases.

Blank, blank, blank.

'See?'

'Hardly fair. I'm sure ...' Diana starts.

'Agreed. It's *not* fair.'

Pauline growls: 'I'm not here to chat about adverbs and rape.'

'To be fair, Mr James uses few adverbs ...' says Maya softly.

The women laugh, even Pauline.

They laugh hard.

The discussion returns to Johnny Jumpers. Maya, now wearing horn-rimmed tortoiseshell reading glasses, turns pages urgently with quick cat licks, flicking pages. Diana glances at her own eczema-wracked stubby fingers. Clipped spooned nails. Maya's polished boots, *tap-tap-tapping* each other, Diana in her scuffed black brogues.

A cough next to her reminds her why she's there. She looks at the clock. Quarter to nine!

'Let's split,' she whispers in MaMa's ear.

Chapter 15

Tuesday 28th September, 2010 – Sheffield

Diana won't sit on the fence any more. It has to be done.

Bite the bullet.

She slaps a list on Robertson's desk.

'Robertson, can you co-ordinate intelligence interviews with my mum's book club? I want to get as much intelligence as I can as to what was going wrong at Legley Road. Both employees Mary Calley and Aaliyah Matthews used to attend that book club and both left Legley Road before the closure was announced. Keep it low-key, casual but – you know the drill. As much info as poss.'

Robertson smiles. 'Right, Boss.'

Six hours later, as Diana is lining up a ruler over the list of keys from the LEA, Robertson returns to her desk.

'I've done Anoona Shanda, Komal Desai and Shola Keller. Pauline Cuthbert didn't want to do it at work or at her shared house, so she came in. I taped it.'

He passes a folder to her.

'Transcripts in there, Boss. DI Lawton did your mum – sorry, Rehema Walker.'

Diana stares at him, mouth open.

He blushes, looks down. 'Not transcribed the Cuthbert interview yet, but got the video.'

110

Taking her mug of tepid Nescafé into the small back room, Diana reads over the transcripts with her blue overlay. Anoona Shanda, having arrived in the UK with her doctorate in anthropology from the University of Zimbabwe, finds the only steady job she can get is librarian at Sheffield Public Library, which she's been doing since 1998. She met Lubanzi Kuhle at Legley Road Bethel Church and then at a few charity events. Some of those Black Professional token conferences, evening affairs when the library wasn't already booked out for more pressing matters like Nether Edge Hedgehog Society's AGM. Diana licks her finger, turns the page and smiles. Robertson and his details: Anoona bakes lemon semolina cake and spiced okra for this one event. Bonded with Rehema over the okra, which Rehema grew. Lubanzi asked Anoona why there was little reading material by black females. Anoona and Lubanzi resolved to set up The Black Sistahs Book Club focusing only on black – preferably female – writers. That was in July 2002. They held the first one in a disused backroom in the library, and felt like they'd sneaked into the broom cupboard to talk about Toni Morrison's *Beloved*. They were charged fifty pounds for its hire. Anoona said they were outraged when a security officer thought they were the cleaning ladies shirking from their duties. After that, Anoona proposed they held the meetings at her flat in Pitsmoor, but the other members lived on the west side. So Lubanzi asked her husband, Samuel, and he agreed. When the extension was being added, the Black Sistahs Book Club moved to Komal and Shola's. Yes, they are a couple (*squiggle here*) and now it's two a month at Lubanzi's, one a month at Komal and Shola's. And 'we have dinner parties, probably once every two or three months – usually at Maya's or Lubanzi's. But, yes, standard book club meetings are basically a discussion over the chosen monthly book selected every quarter by consensus, a mix of recent releases and old gems.'

Anoona invited Mary after they'd met at a few black book initiative groups at the library. She liked that she was the only schoolteacher who actively sought out YA novels written by black authors for her students. It was Mary who invited her friend Aaliyah to join.

Anoona's responses regarding Aaliyah are brief, monosyllabic, stating she left in the late autumn of 2007 when she moved out of Sheffield. She believes Aaliyah's now at university doing post-graduate work.

Mary's attendance of book club became more sporadic, and then she just stopped. She didn't answer her phone or emails, and when Anoona called around to her place in Heeley late December 2007 with a Christmas present, a neighbour said she'd moved out. Anoona had to assume Mary didn't want to stay in touch which made her sad.

Ms Shanda is crying.

'But not as sad as when we heard on the news how she passed … no one knew. Two years.'

Robertson's question: 'What do you think happened to Mary Calley?'

Anoona's reply: 'I think she had an asthma attack or something to do with stress. Mary was too positive to take her own life. She would never do that. But something was eating her up, I know that.'

Interview terminated 28th September 2010, 4.32 p.m.

Next, Diana watches the video of Robertson's interview with Pauline. DI Lawton enters, leaning against the wall, slurping from his polystyrene cup. The interview's long, winding, entertaining, and reveals nothing she doesn't already know. Even Pauline's bored, scraping back her chair to make the point. Robertson finishes scrawling and puts his pen down, spreading his hands wide.

'Thank you, Ms Cuthbert. Sure. You are free to go.'

Pauline's already at the door.

'Oh, Ms Cuthbert. One last thing?'

She stops, hand hovering over the handle.

'How did Ms Calley get on with her boss, John Daniels?'

As if suddenly aware of the camera, she stares straight at it.

'She hate him. Call him a liar.'

The door slams behind her. Robertson raises his eyebrows at the camera. Then the screen goes black.

Lawton tuts. 'All that and he just let her go.'

Diana glares. 'More than what you got out of Rehema Walker. Robertson and I will do the intel interview with Lubanzi Kuhle.'

Lawton shakes his head. 'All we're getting are complaints. You've no leads.'

'Best get out there then, detective.'

The glare is mutual.

Chapter 16

WEDNESDAY 29TH SEPTEMBER, NORTHERN GENERAL HOSPITAL, SHEFFIELD

Diana jogs up the stairs of Northern General Hospital. Her body's missed running the past three days. Five flights to Obstetrics and Gynaecology. Above her, the clatter of a couple of registrars chatting about a case. Robertson huffs and puffs a flight below her, grunting like a man twice his age. Diana holds the door open to Ward 8. He smiles gratefully.

'You can introduce yourself to Dr Kuhle.'

The ward is busy with nurses' brisk chat, the murmuring, pinging and beeping of machines. Diana follows Robertson, whose flat feet make a loud *squeak-plonk* on the floor. A red-haired nurse pushing the meds trolley looks accusingly at Robertson.

'Visiting is over for today.'

'We're not visiting a patient. I'm Detective Sergeant Robertson.'

'DI Walker,' Diana announces coolly, looking up and down the corridor. 'We made an appointment to get a statement from Dr Kuhle.'

'Mrs Kuhle,' corrects the red-haired nurse. 'Wait a moment.'

She bustles off around the corner. Diana looks at the ward list pinned above the nurses' station. Robertson fiddles with his anorak zip again. He feels Diana's bemused gaze.

Diana points to the list of African and Arabic names and DOBs.

'Quite a ward round.'

So many young women. Well, her age. That's young.

The nurse reappears. 'This way.'

They walk down the corridor, post up outside a door labelled 'Consultant'.

Lubanzi's soft-consonanted voice comes from within: 'Well, send up the lab results today and I'll look at them.'

The receiver clicks. Even next to a cleaner's cupboard, Diana can smell the intense musky perfume: sandalwood and lemon. Lubanzi Kuhle appears at the door. Her face drawn, stripped of make-up, braids swept up off her face into a high knot. She wears black slacks, a turquoise, tailored cotton shirt, and a large white medical housecoat, her hands buried deep in its pockets.

'Diana. Sorry, detective.' Her eyes pass over Robertson. 'You wanted a statement.'

'Just a formality. This is DS Robertson.'

'Right.'

The office is small, plainly furnished in that basic NHS way: orange plastic chairs. Chipped desk. Free-standing filing cabinet. An IBM computer. A small photo of a solemn black man, standing by a lake with two lanky laughing children and a bubble-trunked baobab tree. A stack of manilla folders and Dictaphone on the desk.

Diana walks over to stand by the window, indicating to Robertson that he sit on the one plastic orange chair. He gets out his notepad and a Bic blue biro.

'So … your name is Dr Lubanzi Kuhle?'

'*Mrs* Lubanzi Kuhle. I am a consultant.'

Robertson looks confused, Lubanzi offended.

'A consultant surgeon,' Diana states. 'Correct?'

Lubanzi stares back, nods.

'How old are you?' asks Robertson.

'I am fifty years old.' Now really offended, she scowls while giving her address.

'How long have you been consultant obstetrician at the Northern General Hospital?'

'Five years in December.'

Robertson looks over at the photo. 'Your … family?'

'My husband, Samuel, a urologist, and my two children. How does this relate to your case?'

Diana nods at Robertson.

'We're investigating the murder of John Daniels, the former boss of Mary Calley, who we believe you knew. Apparently, Mary had a few disagreements with Mr Daniels before she left the school.'

'Mary had many disagreements. She stopped being a regular at the Black Sistahs Book Club from October 2007 and was irregular in attendance over that summer.'

Robertson looks up. 'Do you know why?'

Lubanzi pulls the tape out of the Dictaphone.

'Not really.'

'How did you and Mary meet, Doc— Mrs Kuhle?'

'I met Mary – let me see.' Lubanzi sits back on her swivel chair and rubs her temples. 'Doris told me about her – after her dad …'

'Doris?'

'Doris Thompson – cleans for the pastor at the manse. I know her from Legley Road Baptist Church.'

'You were saying her dad …?'

Lubanzi's brow furrows. 'Her dad wouldn't let her come to the church because there was a rumour she was seeing a married man. I felt bad for her. Anoona invited her to book club, and she became a regular. Such an intelligent, enthusiastic young woman. A fantastic teacher. Shola is Schools Community Officer. She said the kids all loved Mary. And Mary loved them, wanted to change things to help them. Played the game, applied and won that funding. Such a committed young woman.'

Robertson scribbles. 'What do you think happened?'

Lubanzi looks down at his notepad. 'Mary did not value herself, so made bad choices often.'

'Can you be specific?'

'Bad choices in men. Her relationship with her father wasn't good.'

Lubanzi looks at her watch.

116

'I have another clinic in twenty minutes.'

Diana needs a lead today.

'Anything you can tell us to get some insight into what was really going on at Legley Road High School. Do you know of any fall-outs with colleagues or students?' she asks.

'I know she had some issues …' Lubanzi frowns, impatiently looking at her clinic list. 'She was always talking to her union rep.'

Robertson starts scribbling.

'What was the rep's name?' Robertson asks.

'Young … Young … first name Lamar. Leon?'

'Leroy?'

'Leroy! Yes. Leroy.'

Robertson drops his biro, picks it back up. 'Leroy Young?'

Lubanzi shrugs.

'So Leroy's also a union rep? He wears a lot of hats. Busy guy.'

'*Very* busy guy,' Lubanzi says with an eye roll.

Robertson looks up.

'I don't like to publish scandal.'

'This is a police investigation into a murder, Mrs Kuhle. If it can lead to an arrest, it's valid information,' Diana says.

Lubanzi edges forward on her seat.

'Gossip-mongers told Pastor that his daughter was seeing a married man from her school.'

'How did he take that?'

'He made it clear to Mary he wouldn't tolerate it. She was upset, confused. There was some issue at school, Mary said Leroy was helping her out. I told her to cut ties, that we were there for her. But she said we didn't understand.' Lubanzi shakes her head. 'I do understand. I see every day. She'd come to book club once a month but always late, distracted, checking her phone.' Pause. 'She had been threatened.'

'She told you?'

Lubanzi shakes her head. 'A book club member told me.'

Diana waits.

Lubanzi sighs heavily, closing her eyes in exasperation. 'Ally Matthews.'

Diana looks over to check Robertson is printing that, not scrawling.

'Ally? Do you mean Aaliyah?'

Lubanzi stares at her and then away.

'Do you know where she is?'

Lubanzi looks at her watch again.

'Think she's doing postgrad work somewhere. Both Mary and Ally made their choices. Ally broke off her engagement, Legley Road High School was closing. Talented, ambitious women move on.' Lubanzi stacks her manilla folders.

'Did Mary call the police about her … problem?'

Lubanzi turns her back. 'The police do nothing. Rehema and I helped her apply for sheltered accommodation.'

'But Mary was a teacher, she knew better. She'd know harassment was wrong. Surely she reported it to someone – if it really *was* happening.'

Lubanzi snaps around, a sharp fury in her voice.

'Detective, you think black women are born survivors? You want to come down to my clinic, see how death warrants are dished out in neglect and abuse? Poverty's an apocalypse in slow motion.'

Robertson's biro hovers, unsure what to write.

Lubanzi stands up. 'I need to get to my deinfibulation clinic.'

Diana frowns. Lubanzi sighs.

'To women who were sliced with a razor, sewn up with thorns, bound for days with sheet and cord as children by women they should trust.'

'Are we talking Female Genital Mutilation?'

Lubanzi's lips a thin line. 'A third of my work is dealing with complications resulting from FGM.'

Diana scowls. 'That's funny. I've never seen your name on any papers or investigations for FGM.'

Lubanzi folds her arms, forces her smile down. 'Well, detective, what's that tell you?'

Diana shrugs. 'You don't report them?'

'Report who? These women, these girls – most of them are cut when they're babies. They don't even *know* they've been cut till they get married or get problems or have a baby. Then it's like the trauma is relived plus the shame and rage. The mutilators are usually dead or in another country by then.'

118

'And you hear no names?'

'If I had even the hint of one, I'd report it. I'd lose my medical licence *and* my soul if I were to allow FGM to take place under my watch.'

'Do the women talk to you about it?'

'Sometimes. They're ashamed, angry, and in a lot of pain. Most of them are still in the communities which authorise it, so they say little. Those who do, face a far greater consequence in terms of isolation. Lack of a home, family. Sometimes worse.'

'Worse?'

Lubanzi closes up. 'I don't get paid to pry, detective. My job is to save and preserve life. These women disappear from my list and no GP refers them again.'

'But don't you—'

'Don't I what, detective? Do *your* job? No, I don't.'

'Nobody's asking you to, Lubanzi. Just any information—'

Lubanzi sighs, looks at her watch. 'I have to get to clinic. Any info, don't worry, I'll pass it on. But in the decade I've been doing obs and gynae here, I've had nothing but silence. The only evidence is in the bodies.'

Tell me about it.

Lubanzi opens the door. Robertson stands up, holding out his hand to Lubanzi. She looks at it like it's a misshapen vegetable.

'Thank you, Mrs Kuhle. You've been really helpful.'

As they leave the room, Diana throws over her shoulder, 'I really did enjoy book club.'

Lubanzi's face splits into a beam.

'Fantastic! I look forward to your comments next month when we move onto *Kindred*.'

Five yards down the corridor, Diana turns just as Lubanzi is closing her door. 'One last thing.'

Lubanzi's face clouds.

'Ally Matthews' details? She's disappeared off the radar.'

Lubanzi keeps the door half-closed.

'I can't give out personal information like that.'

Diana sighs. 'Too bad. I'll have to register her as another MisPer.'

Lubanzi locks the door behind her. 'She went to Wolverhampton University to study.'

'To study what?'

Lubanzi shrugs. 'Statistics? Computing?'

Diana is at the door, close enough to read fear in Lubanzi's eyes.

'Anything else about Ally which could help me find her?'

Lubanzi shrugs. 'Be careful, detective. If you can't find Ally, it's because she doesn't want to be found. And if Mary and Ally didn't want to be found, there would be a very good reason.'

As they walk up the stairs to HQ, Robertson says: 'Got the sense she felt you were opening a can of worms with this Aaliyah, Boss.'

Diana continues with her hasty ascent, not looking back up. 'Better a can of worms than a can of maggots. Talking of MisPers, we need to find Leroy Young. We've still nothing on him as a MisPer. And find what teachers' union he was rep for, what issue he was dealing with for Mary. Pull the school's finances and audit again.'

She slings her coat over her chair, bending over her desk to rummage through folders.

'If she was in conflict with her union rep, the union rep is now missing, the assistant bursar's left town, the head's head in a drawer, and Mary's a mark on a bedsit carpet.'

Lawton leans on the doorframe, arms akimbo, eyes dipping thirty degrees. Diana's three-sixty vision kicks in. Without turning, she says: 'Lawton, we need confirmation the black man who drove Daniels away was Leroy. Show the neighbours a pic of his car. I'm calling a briefing – let's see where we're at.'

The briefing room seems to get smaller with each day. Diana frowns at the whiteboard.

'Leroy Young is our number one suspect, but we haven't got the evidence we need to really land him. His abandoned car and the presents in the boot indicate he had every intention of returning to Sheffield. Just like Daniels, he's not been heard or seen since Saturday August 28th, August Bank Holiday weekend.

120

Where is Young and why did he not turn up for his new job or little girl's party? Where's his phone? Is he not just a MisPer but a suspect?'

O'Malley frowns, Robertson scribbles. 'Or another undiscovered victim?'

Diana nods. 'So, the next question is: who would want both Daniels and Young dead?'

Neville shrugs. 'A creditor? They both had big appetites their salaries couldn't match.'

Robertson shakes his head.

'But what would their deaths achieve? They'd get no payment then.'

'Exactly!' says Khan, a bit too emphatically. Neville turns to scowl at him.

'Scratch that line of inquiry unless you can see how the creditor would benefit.'

'Maybe they had a grudge? Something personal?' says Neville.

'Like?'

'A member of staff? There were enough pissed off. Both Young and Daniels seemed to have passed the buck.'

'How about the bursar?' says Robertson.

'He'd been dead over two years.'

'The assistant bursar?'

Diana bites her lip.

Every time she hopes this case will pull away from her mum's book club, it comes spinning back into the centre, like some cosmic centrifuge. Diana raises her eyebrows and taps the board.

'Aaliyah – or Ally – Matthews. Assistant bursar. Former member of book club—'

'And Mary Calley's emergency contact,' DC Khan says.

Diana nods approvingly. 'Interesting.'

She stands back. 'We need to find her. She's another one disappeared into the ether.'

'What about one of the school's students?' asks O'Malley.

Sold us up the swanny.

On the board she writes: 'Year 11, Year 10. Bruno Pierce – butcher. Axmed Ahmed – tagger.'

She says: 'These two were at the scene of the crime. They had

121

means, motive and unverified alibis. But, apparently, they did not have the filing cabinet key.'

Robertson says: 'And what about Mrs Young? She seems pretty pissed off still about Ms Calley and Young. Plus, she's still married, so she'd get his pension. And the car. She was asking after the car.'

Diana winces. She can't quite see Julie Young as willing to kill her daughter's father out of spite.

'Yes, but we don't know Leroy is dead yet. And why would she kill Daniels? Even if she has motive, has she means? I can't quite see how the delicate Julie could carve up a grown man over a weekend in the woodland in between a toddler's birthday party and a barbecue. Nor why.'

'No. Defo a bloke,' Neville says.

'Where we're at on the audit by Bracewell Smith?' Diana asks.

'Still awaiting the FCA's analysis, Boss,' Robertson says.

'Let's close the gaps on Ms Matthews, Bruno, Axmed. And find Leroy Young.'

Diana puts the lid on her blue marker.

Lawton tilts up his chin, hands in pockets.

'What about the OCG?'

'There's nothing to suggest it's the work of an OCG.'

'Only an execution style exhibition of a high profile murder, Ryan Pierce going over counties with his little drugs enterprise and his son being one of the key suspects. Phillips reckons it's an OCG linked to his op.'

Lawton and Diana glare at each other.

She shakes her head. 'Shifting a few ecstasy tablets and weed? Bring Pierce in then.'

'No! We brought him in a couple of years back, swabbed him and everything. Not enough evidence for a charge so he walked free. The kids wouldn't speak. Everyone loves the Ryano Hut. We know he's dealing – just can't get owt on him. And now, now he's talking to some very dangerous folk. So, Phillips' prerogative is to let him do his thing till we get enough to land not just him, but the whole OCG.'

Diana closes her eyes. This homicide is not the priority – Phillips' promotion is.

'It's an OCG, mark my words,' Lawton mutters.

'OK, well does your OCG have access to the filing cabinet keys?'

Lawton's eyes narrow.

'How'd you get into the cabinet, detective?'

'I picked it.'

'Exactly. And you don't think a professional criminal knows how to do the same?'

'It was locked with a key – not a wire. No damage.'

Lawton just shakes his head.

'Where'd you learn that skill, Detective Walker?'

Diana straightens up. 'As a WPC in Barnsley in the nineties. We had so many heroin overdoses, if we were to wait for muscle to break down a door, there'd be more deaths than there were. Our Chief actually brought in a locksmith to teach us.'

'Interesting. Well, next time we have a burglary in the area, maybe we should put your name in the frame 'n' all.'

He laughs to Neville, who gives a smirk back. Diana rolls her eyes.

'Crack on with the leads – not the jokes, folks.'

'While you—'

'—will be at City Hall double-checking some statistics.'

'Cracking doors and chasing statistics. Sounds fishy, don't you think, Nevs? Thought you'd be identifying the murder weapon or something – you know, related to a homicide.'

Diana scowls. Maybe she should do the stats hunt at night.

After an afternoon and evening of running through a list of licensed rifle owners in Sheffield, interviewing five before eliminating them all, Diana pulls into the car park at Merrick Street; the other big plus of working late – she can get a parking space. Out of habit, Diana does a quick three-sixty before exiting her Golf. Can't be too careful. Balancing the cup of McDonald's coffee on her car roof, she locks the door, looking up at the office. Back lights are on.

Walking up the stairwell, she's immersed in the smell of fresh cig on stale. Maybe Neville and Lawton are pulling overnighters too? There's plenty to do if they're pursuing this gambling gangster business. Peeking through the door window, she sees three working the graveyard shift. She shoulders open the door, jolting coffee onto her jacket.

'Not again!' she moans.

Heads turn from monitors, but her only greeting's the unique odour of sweat, cigs and Pot Noodle. Switching on her monitor, HQ's stink brings her back. She puts on her blue lenses, starts the trawl through digits, facts and reports. The autopsy report first. Pure air: not a metaphor in sight.

Or rape.

By 1.30 a.m., she needs a break from online butchery and bullets. Maybe just check on the local Rape and Serious Sexual Offences data. She's been irritated by the book club's insistence of there being no reported rapes of black women.

Bollocks.

She scrolls. No ethnic breakdowns, but 11.3 per cent of all reported offences end up with a charge or a summons. Of those convicted, it ends in a custodial sentence ranging from eighteen months to 9.8 years.

For 3 per cent of cases.

The estimation for Sheffield has applied the CSEW prevalence figures. These figures are estimates and national averages have been applied. Sheffield may or may not have a higher incident rate of sexual abuse than the England average. Again, we do not know whether Sheffield has a greater likelihood of sexual assault or if the recording of incidents in the city is more effective.

Therefore, it is estimated that in Sheffield the number of people who have been a victim of a sexual assault or attempted sexual assault since the age of 16 years old is as follows:

Sheffield population (15–60 years)	MALES	FEMALES
	173,430	176,420
Rate in the last year	3.8% 6,590	19% 33,520

Ethnicity: The ethnic group with a higher prevalence than the average for all ethnicities (2.7% women) is the mixed/multiple ethnic group (9.3% women).

The police do not record all reported sexual abuse incidents as crimes. The HMIC report of 2008 found that 36% of sexual assault reported incidents were not then recorded as a crime.'

Unreported statistics. Unreported crimes. Unreported ethnicity. Diana swigs cold coffee.

There must be something here ... the ghost of a phrase from her degree echoes in her head: *What gets measure, gets managed.*

She leans back. Frowns. She hates it when anyone's right about the police being wrong. Especially her mum.

Diana needs more stats, a log of 999 calls from 2007. She stares up at the yellowing polystyrene-tiled ceiling, at rags of Sellotape, tinsel, faded crêpe paper streamers and two broken links of a paper chain. Memories of the Christmas Party 2004 waft out, like opening a jar of mouldy jam. When Keith had grabbed her and snogged her under the plastic mistletoe hanging over the back exit. The room cheering. His tongue, beery, fresh nicotine, leathery, thrusting itself down her throat.

Well, she was a DC then ...

'Alright, stranger!'

Diana jumps. Double blinks. The same flustered embarrassment – as if she's just manifested DI Keith Phillips into the swivel chair spinning behind her, legs splayed.

'Oh ... What are you doing here?'

'About to ask you same. OCG ops. Warrants to issue.'

He rakes his hand through his sparse blond hair, leans back, making stretching noises. Filling up the corner, blocking Diana's easy exit. She came up through the ranks with this guy, but they couldn't be more different now. Fourteen years in the force have radically changed them both – but in different ways. This is the guy who'd done long duty shifts with her; they'd been road buddies, trusted each other, knew each other inside out. Became an item in 2006. But the SYPD's Boys Club mentality had got hold of him by then. He began to resent Diana's competence and moral integrity. The casual humour had turned into overt racist barbs, and he started to behave like the men he was locking up. As Diana's passion and trust diminished, he became more controlling, and Diana herself became more aware as she was dealing with the victims of coercive behaviour and probable, if unreported, domestic violence. It all went from an Arctic Monkeys meet-cute to something resembling a Def Leppard mosh pit in the space of three years. Finally, after several major rows, she'd called time. Diana moved to Dewbow, trusted her fellow officers less, her intuition more, while Phillips was now SYPD's poster boy-wonder, tipped for promotion.

'Right,' is all she can manage. She doesn't want a conversation with someone who yelled 'Black whore!' when she ended the relationship.

'You?' he asks. But it's not an ask – it's a demand.

'Just some background info.'

He stares at her.

Diana blinks away, saying: 'Best get home. I need to look at 999 logs for 2007. Can't get them while reception opens to give me keys to archives.'

Phillips jangles a set of keys in his pocket, drawing attention to his crotch.

'Well, isn't it your *lucky* night, Walker? Because I have a master key!'

The corridor smells of bleach trying to cover up mould. Diana follows Phillips down the airless warren of locked doors and curling lino'd floors, sticky under her feet.

'I can wait till the morning …'

He doesn't appear to hear her. Maybe he's busy counting doors.

'I think it's— Aha!'

She's too tired, feels sick, would rather do this tomorrow with Robertson. He jams the key into the lock, shoulders the door, which gives in with a grunt, indicates with his head for her to go in before him. Diana is unsure – it's dark. He enters, yanking on the stringed light. Nothing happens.

'Shit! Tell you what – I'll hold door open. You get up on step-stool. All the 2007 logs are on top shelf.'

'Look, it doesn't matter, I'll …'

He's already wheeled out the step-stool. Diana hesitates.

'I'd rather see what …'

'I've got you. Go on. Up you go, lass.'

He leans against the door, holding the step-stool rigid with his foot. Diana gets up, groping in the dark. She can just about see 2007 in black on several archive boxes, but can't read the contents labels.

'I can't read the …'

It's one movement, short, swift, sharp. A flip of his wrist and the flat sweaty palm around her thigh, the probing fingers on her fly. Zip, flick of the gusset and beyond, pushing his fat greasy thumb in, his fingers reaching further. Diana stranded mid-air in the dark clutching at a box of nothing she needs. She kicks out, falling off the step-stool. His hand tries to grab her crotch, but she jacks her knee against his shoulder.

He's laughing, standing back, hands up.

'Little fumble in the store cupboard for old time's sake. That's what you're missing these days, detective! You just need to ask.'

'Let me out.' She says it in a low voice, attempting to zip up her fly and grab the door handle without touching him. Cheap burger grease and *Joop!* aftershave. His filth in her skin.

His laugh like ripping card, echoing off the lino and peeling walls as Diana runs out, straight to her car.

Only as she pushes the key into the ignition does she notice her hands are shaking.

Chapter 17

Friday 1st October, 2010 – Sheffield

With one hand Diana grips a piping hot espresso in a card cup. The skies above Merrick Street are gathering weight a thuggish northerly blowing dull-anoraked shoppers across pavements. They skitter in front of honking trams, braking buses. Diana shivers. Sheffield's door to the misery of the north: greasy grit in the eye, lead heavy sky. Pulling up the collar on her black Berghaus, she jogs to the steps of HQ. Instinctively, she looks up at Marchant's office. Hands in pockets, he stares down at her. His face is never welcoming, but today he's a pug with constipation. With one hand, he beckons her.

OK.

A nod means 'Nice work'. A beckon is a summons. And a summons means words are required. Marchant puts words in the same category as cat litter.

Diana swigs her coffee dregs, throwing the cup in the bin by the door, her fingers still numb.

'Took your time.'

'Sorry, sir.' Barely five minutes to take off her jacket and go to the loo.

What's the mad rush?

'I've been looking at the Daniels' Key Development Log.'

128

That.

Marchant shakes his head. 'This is a homicide, Walker. A major homicide. Of a headmaster. A public figure.'

Diana nods.

'I've had two separate complaints from members of the public.' Marchant sighs.

Who?

'I don't know why you're gallivanting down to Nottingham on some bedsit overdose instead of presenting me with some hard evidence.' He pushes the file from him as if it's the cat's litter tray, fleshy nose wrinkling in distaste. 'And you're conducting too many interviews. You're supposed to be guiding the ship not rigging the sails! What you get those stripes for? Or do you prefer being a sergeant, Walker?'

The book club? Mrs Daniels?

Marchant goes to his door and nods at Lawton, who stands up, straightens his tie, and marches over to the office. Diana frowns.

'Sir, why did you make me SIO based on the case of a bad smell on a demolition site?'

Marchant frowns. 'There was a locked filing cabinet with a bad smell.'

'But it was based on a hunch, right? No police were there then.'

Marchant raises his eyebrows, pushes his bottom lip out. Diana presses in.

'Sir, the Ripper was caught by a regular copper following up on a hunch. Intuition is intelligence without words.'

'Walker, there's a head in a filing cabinet and your hunch is not getting us anywhere …'

'Sir, we've got four possible lines of inquiry but no real leads. I've got a lead regarding an abused teacher who later ended up in a bedsit, a teacher who reportedly caused problems for Daniels and Young.'

'What lead?' snorts Lawton.

'A former student, the deputy head … and that's why I need intelligence from the book club of which she was a member.'

Lawton looks at Marchant, who sighs heavily.

'Lawton, what did you want to mention earlier about this headmaster homicide?'

Lawton thrusts his chin up. 'Phillips says one of the POIs in this case is the SIO's own mother, sir. A member of the book club. If that's not a conflict of interest, I don't know what is.'

Diana feels her face burn. Her stomach knots with the urge to heave.'

'Actually, Robertson and Lawton have handled all those interviews, sir.'

'Hmmm.' Marchant pulls his top lip in. 'Alright, Lawton. I'll speak to you in a few minutes.'

A dismissal, but Lawton just turns, smirking at Diana as he heads back to his desk.

Diana's heart drops as Marchant closes the door behind him.

'I want Lawton to take over as SIO. Walker, you stay on the case, but don't direct.'

'But, sir, I've not—'

'No argument. I still want you on the team, but you answer to his lead now. Understand?'

It isn't a question. Nothing's ever a question with Marchant. Lines of inquiry do not exist – only hard evidence to back up rigid theories. Diana doesn't bother to flinch. She won't give him that much satisfaction. If she'd been playing the game, she'd have left the book club alone.

'You'll still be on the same pay – just not SIO,' he mutters.

'Why, sir?'

He looks up. 'You're good in the trenches, but you're not a general ... I gave you a chance.'

You gave me no chance.

But Diana just presses her lips down, shrugs. Marchant averts his eyes. 'I've passed the KDL to Lawton. Go report to him for directions.'

Diana moves towards the door.

'And don't think of going rogue, Walker. I'll have you back in uniform and shipped off to the back of some north-western cesspit before you've time to file your complaint form.'

Diana returns to her desk and her multi-coloured Post-its thinking a north-western cesspit sounds like a holiday. She picks up the autopsy report.

'You OK, Boss?'

Diana winks at Robertson. 'Sure.'

His face flashes genuine concern. He whispers: 'It's bang out of order, Boss.'

Sake. Everyone must know. She was the last.

Diana flicks through a sheaf of Post-its.

'Legley Road, Legley Road …' She pushes her chair back and calls out, loud enough for the phone-occupied Lawton to hear: 'Did our H-2-H go as far as the manse and church on Legley Road, detective?'

Lawton's brow furrows impatiently. He shoves the phone under his chin, cupping the receiver. 'Look on the transcripts, Walker.'

Diana turns back to her manilla folders.

'What you up to now, Boss?' hisses Robertson.

Diana bites her lip, picks up two paperclips, weaving them in and out of each other. Where's the bloody filing cabinet key? All this case means to Lawton is a fast promotion. Marchant won't put the funding into Domestic Violence; he's always on about more resources for his drug squad. But she knows, in her gut, it's not gang-related, not drugs-related; maybe money-related, but not money-motivated. Bruno's an angry black teenager, but that doesn't make him a murderer. And if Young's and Daniels' debts have been paid off, the question's no longer, 'Who did they owe?' but 'Who paid the debts and why?' Neither of their salaries have increased. Were they paid for a service? Or to block one? The school's now closed. The price and purchase had been made years ago in 2007, according to the paperwork.

Diana holds up the chain she's made with the paperclips.

She sits up. If the sale of the school was agreed in the summer of 2007, why had Daniels agreed that Mary's curriculum could be implemented at Legley Road High School? That wouldn't be feasible. If the award had been received, why wasn't it returned? The NCC said no funds had been returned. Diana reaches for the phone.

Teaching Unions … the NASUWT, the NEU. She calls them for Mary Calley. Expired membership for NASUWT as of December 2007, attempted membership of NEU in October 2007. Ongo-

131

ing case with NASUWT regarding intimidation, constructive dismissal, bullying and sexism. Rep's notes read that Mary Calley was suffering from mental illness. The last note in December 2007 commented that Mary Calley had tendered and served her notice at Legley Road High School and would no longer be pursuing her complaint. Diana exhales as she highlights the rep's name printed at the bottom of the page.

Leroy Young.

Diana leans back from the desk and notepad she's been curled over for the past three hours, the stack of dismembered, restructured paperclips. Massages her temples, closes her eyes. Sally Jessop, a detective in the drug squad who had come up the ranks almost parallel with her, had told her to 'kick up shit' about how Marchant was 'doing her'. It's alright for Sal; right surname, right colour, a game-player who's therefore earned the right to say the token phrases. But that's what they are – token. There's no appeasing racism, sexism. Rolling over and playing the game – police banter, shredding all dignity until she sings: 'Sorry, guys! You were right – it's all in my head!'

Unspoken traumas are in her bones.

She opens her eyes, looks at her hands, her knuckles. Red raw and rough, like those of an old woman. Mary Calley had Betnovate cream in her box of belongings; had she suffered from eczema? Diana picks up the inventory list on her desk: Gaviscon, Omeprazole ... sounds like an ulcer. She should pull her medical records. Had she moved to a Nottingham GP?

What made her body revolt, turn against her?

Diana calls NHS Medical Records.

'I need it pronto please.' She watches Neville and Lawton guffaw and idle by the kettle, hands in pockets, miming the expression of someone caught out. More laughs.

Diana's line crackles. 'Her files were moved, according to this screen ... to Nottingham. May take a few weeks.'

'A few weeks? This is a murder case. I need them now.' Diana knows she hasn't the authority to do this, but is prepared to drive down to collect them.

Should have them by tomorrow. Diana puts the receiver down.

Lawton and Neville amble back to their desks, leisurely shrugging on nylon coats, heading out. She wants to know where. It shouldn't bother her, but it does. Like they're rubbing her face in it: *Down, dog.*

The door swings open. Diana watches DI Keith Phillips enter, slap Neville on the back, a cursory glance at her and nod. She looks away, stomach knotting.

'Want a sarnie, Boss? I need some fresh air and to stretch my legs … been hunched over those figures since seven,' Robertson says.

Diana's not hungry, but she needs air. 'Sounds like a plan.' Robertson waits as she shrugs on her coat. They pass Neville's desk on the way out.

'Alright, Di?' Phillips' casual comment, eyes resting on her while Neville just smirks, looking down at his desk.

'Phillips.'

The door swings behind her.

Don't Di me, you git.

MaMa shakes her head when Diana indicates the space next to her on the makeshift bench made from an upturned wine crate. Instead, she stands next to the cornstalks, pulling her red and blue checked shawl around her, knotted on the shoulder. Diana looks along the remnants of this summer's corn and beans.

'What do you think of Ma's *shamba*?'

MaMa nods.

'She doubled her quota of maize and beans this summer because she knew you were coming. And peas and potato. She's hoping you'll make *githeri* and *mukimo* – maybe even *irio*.'

MaMa shakes her head. 'She serves up rice and meat and vegetables like she never been taught. And what is this custard business?'

Diana giggles. 'She grew up in Scotland, MaMa. Not many spices north of Edinburgh in the fifties. She does a mean mac 'n' cheese though.'

MaMa's face flickers with pain.

Diana continues: 'She learned to make *mukimo* from a book. It's not like you do. Maybe you can teach me?'

MaMa bends over, picking up a handful of soil. She holds it loosely in her cupped lean, long palm, jiggling it like gemstones.

'This soil – too wet, too heavy for growing.'

'Yeah, needs compost. It's gritty and peaty where I live. Not like the good red soil of Kenya.'

MaMa's eyes narrow.

'Ruined soil.'

The sun bleeds down the horizon, over the allotments. A lean silhouette rakes leaves against the amber sky. The hedgehog of an older man shuffles, locking up his shed. Diana watches MaMa follow him.

'What's it like, MaMa? To wait fifty years for justice?'

She can barely wait fifty minutes.

MaMa pulls at a stem of corn.

'Justice has its own time, *mwana*. I don't wait on any government or man decision. I see already. I *see* and wait – but not on them.'

'So … we'll just wait and see, hope the Commission, Leigh Day and George Morara …'

MaMa shakes her head vehemently, beads rattling around her neck.

'No, no. I no *wait* and see. Kikuyu we don't *wait* and see. That is white man way. No – me *see*. Me see already. Me see – and wait. It's coming. Our life is to wait. Wait under the tree. Wait for the rain. Wait for the crop. Wait for the locust. Wait for the storm. Wait for the dawn.'

A life of patience like a weapon, faith like a scalpel. Diana feels a gap open beneath her feet, a seismic shift. Her hands going black-blue. MaMa looks down at them.

'What is this, *mwana*? You go blue so young?'

Diana stares at her dead digits. Takes a moment to consider.

'What happens to me when I wait.' She chuckles darkly.

MaMa shakes her head. '*See* first … Then wait. The believing is the seeing.'

She takes one of Diana's hands in hers and rubs it fiercely. 'The seed's there, *mwana*. Justice *always* on time.'

Diana squints down the path. 'Fancy church this Sunday, MaMa?'

'Church? You are talking to a Kikuyu raised in a zinc-roofed mud hut chapel in Kijabe.'

Diana puts her arm around MaMa's bony shoulders.

'Come on! It'll get you out of the house, away from Ma and Radio 4.'

MaMa looks sideways at Diana. 'And you away from work?'

Diana just smiles, but nothing escapes MaMa. She raises her eyebrows.

The lean silhouette stops, waving at them across the corn row.

'Who waves?' squints MaMa.

'That's Michael, MaMa. He built your room. He has an allot—*shamba* here too.'

He emerges out of the shadows, gleaming with sweat, smelling of earth and wood.

'Hello. Is this your grandma?' he grins.

'Michael, meet MaMa, now sleeping in your creation.'

MaMa bows her head. '*Asante sana*, Michael.'

'Is the bed too hard?'

'The bed just right.'

'Good.'

MaMa looks over at Michael's allotment. 'What do you grow?'

'Pumpkin, Scotch bonnet, tomato, kale, garlic, scallion, corn, potato, beans.'

MaMa grins, a slice of sunshine that transforms her into a radiant six-year-old girl. Diana shivers. 'Best turn in. It's getting nippy.'

MaMa lifts her face to Michael. 'Good to meet you, Michael.'

MaMa walks off. Michael stares after the retreating cloaked figure. 'I'll let her out. There's little light on the path.'

Diana chuckles. 'Don't worry about MaMa. She's not scared of the dark. Or anything else.'

But Michael is already by MaMa's side, his hand steadying the trembling elbow. Diana looks at them both as they walk into the shadows. She gives one last look at the bled-out sky, standing up with a sigh.

See and wait. If only.

But right now, she can't see.

And she can't wait.

* * *

While MaMa goes upstairs, Diana loiters in the kitchen where Rehema is grinding spices in a pestle and mortar. She moves towards the fridge photos of Rehema with book club members.

Her mum's arms around these two young women. Women her age, darker-skinned, with free-flowing curls, wide grins. Together.

'You look pretty close here.' A statement but also an accusation. Rehema barely looks up.

'We're all there for each other in the book club.'

'Like a family.'

Rehema snaps around. 'What's that supposed to mean, Diana? It's not a bloody crime. Books bring you closer together for sure. That's why we started the book club!'

Diana says nothing as she takes the photo off the fridge and looks closely.

'When did you last see Mary, Ma?'

'I don't know. Maybe before Christmas. No, it was the Saturday after Ally broke off with Ryan.'

Ryan?

'Ryan? Ryan Pierce?'

Rehema fills the kettle.

'No idea. Run a chicken shop or something totally beneath Aaliyah.'

'So you saw Mary right before she left?'

Rehema's voice is weary and exasperated. 'I don't *know*, Diana! Can you even stop treating my fridge door like your murder wall? That young woman was a dear friend.'

Rehema puts the photo face down on the table.

'Boundaries, Diana. I may be your mother but I have my own life.'

Diana swivels. 'I *want* you to have friends! I just don't want you to end up in court or jail.'

Rehema snorts. 'Because it will look bad on you? Don't try to moralise me, young lady! I'm the one who taught you your right from wrong.'

'Actually, it was MaMa,' mutters Diana. 'It doesn't matter anyway. I'm already getting it in the neck at work as you're a POI and so there's a conflict of inter—'

'Wait! What? POI?'

'Person of interest.'

'What kind of euphemism is that? Interest to whom? And why?' Rehema's hand shakes on the tap. Diana looks at her.

'Robertson will pick it up. It's just procedure, Ma.'

'Procedure. POI. Police. See what a hornets' nest of trouble you've poked, Diana? No wonder I don't want a photo of you in uniform on my fridge door!'

'I just find it strange you never mentioned Mary before.'

'I find it strange you police the woman who birthed you.'

'It's not policing ...'

Her throat's tight and she turns towards the door.

'I'll pop in later this weekend.'

'Right.' The lips close tight. 'Bye.'

Chapter 18

Monday 4th October, 2010 – Legley Road Manse, Sheffield

The ambulance's blue lights flash, radio beeping, low level intermittent voices as Diana steps from her car outside the Manse on Legley Road. The CSI has already erected the white tent over the garden wall and ginnel. Neville looks harassed, having a low-level disagreement about yellow tape with a white-suited technician. There's the buzz and whirr of the CSI photographer as Diana, diverted by a hand signal from a greened-up paramedic, heads down the front garden path to where Lawton stands over a distressed Mrs Thompson. She is leaning against the door frame, fanning herself. Diana nods at Lawton, who scowls.

'You're late, Walker.'

'I came directly.'

'Yeah. Whatever. An hour ago, Pastor Calley went out to feed his plants …'

'No – fleece his plants!' interjects Mrs Thompson.

'Fleece his pants?' Lawton frowns.

Diana mutters: 'Insulate.'

'Any road, he's upset by the noise of the crows. Finds bin bag at side of greenhouse, just behind wall. Mrs Thompson swears it worn't there yesterday.'

'Bin day Friday. I brought empty bin back down ginnel,' yells Mrs Thompson, rummaging in the pocket of her blue housecoat for a crumpled pink-daisied handkerchief.

'Where is Pastor Calley?' asks Diana, although she is already looking at the ambulance.

'He collapse. I call ambulance straight. They think another stroke.'

'Paramedics won't let us near him for now. He was barely able to speak when I got here.'

'He keep saying, "Bin bag, bin bag, don't look. Police!" to me,' says Mrs Thompson.

'Walker, can you deal with her? Before you start on the house-to-houses?' Lawton is speaking *sotto voce* still, but Diana realises it is pointless; nothing is escaping Mrs Thompson's ears. Diana turns towards her.

'Good morning, Mrs Thompson. It's DI Walker. You remember me from the other week?'

Mrs Thompson is glaring at a potted geranium, wringing her trembling hands. Diana turns back to Lawton.

'Detective, can you bring Mrs Thompson a cup of tea please?'

He looks aghast. 'I'm the SIO here!'

Diana shrugs. 'I'll make tea then.'

Lawton rolls his eyes, stomps off.

'Tree sugars!' yells Mrs Thompson.

'Mrs Thompson, can you tell me in detail what happened this morning?' Diana asks.

She sighs. 'I get here at nine. I get the 8.42 bus from the hill. Pastor has been a bit shaky past two weeks so I been coming most day, check on him. I let myself in.'

'You have a key?'

Mrs Thompson nods.

'Has anyone else access to that key?'

She shakes her head. 'No. I live on my own. I call for Pastor. He no answer, so I go upstair, but he not there. But I see him from bedroom window, in garden shooing the crows.'

'How long does all this take?'

'Maybe five, ten minute. I'm not too fast at moving. I come back down. He at bin bag. Never a good idea to open full bin bag.'

139

'No.'

Mrs Thompson starts crying. 'Such wicked things.'

Diana is unsure whether she means bin bags in general, the contents, or the people who cause the contents. Lawton shoves a china cup, no saucer, filled with a swirling greyish liquid towards her. Diana looks at it incredulously.

'I have things to do!' he snaps, walking away.

Robertson emerges from the ambulance. Diana beckons him.

'Mrs Thompson, you remember DS Robertson from the other day?'

She nods.

Robertson beams at Mrs Thompson. 'Let's make you a decent brew, Mrs T.' Robertson lightly pats Mrs Thompson on the shoulder and they enter the house. Diana pours the offending grey liquid into the geranium's pot.

Around the back, the photographer takes shots of the contents of a bulging bin bag, the heavy-duty kind usually used for rubble. A jagged rip down a seam reveals something mottled. Green, black, blue. Rustling.

Gorman steps away, shaking his head. 'I think he thought it was a fly tip. Tried dragging it out himself. It ripped.'

The sickly-sweet stench, fetid and sulphurous, rotten meat and sewers, at odds with the petrichor after October rain. Diana peers in. The rustling's from maggots on maggots, a warm stench. She steps back, looking at Gorman, who shrugs.

'I won't know for definite until the lab results come back, but it's a torso, one arm and two legs. Mr Daniels was missing those bits.'

'Looks like very clean cuts, like his head and fist.'

Gorman nods.

'Time of death?'

'Can't say yet.'

'A guess?'

'No earlier than end of August,' he says, starting containment.

Diana stares at the mass. 'Over a month ago. Why's it just been dumped now? Why here at the Manse?'

Her questions hang in the foul air. Robertson appears beside her. 'Woah. Bit déjà vu.'

Diana sighs. 'We need trace investigations of the congregation of Legley Road Baptist. Check with the council and those houses over there for any CCTV of the ginnel. O'Malley can check with bin men – they took bins Friday. Any random bin bags they wouldn't take as not in wheelie bin. Lawton's got us finishing off the house-to-houses. Our Doris OK?'

'Yes, Boss. She'll live.'

'Only cuz she didn't drink Lawton's brew.'

'I think some ladies from the church are going to come round for her.'

'Not to a crime scene, they're not. Take her home, will you? I'll check out the ginnel.'

'Right you are, Boss.'

In the packed conference room, Diana watches from the side as Lawton pulls himself up to the mic. He clears his throat.

'Early this morning, police were summoned to a house on Legley Road where body parts were found in a black bin liner behind a greenhouse. It is thought they are part of the same mutilated body as found on the premises of the former Legley Road High School last month.'

She's aware of flashing cameras, spectacled eyes penetrating beyond spiralbound notepads, shiny domed journalists.

'We are following every lead in this most gruesome inquiry, and urge members of the public to come forward with any relevant information if they were around Legley Road or saw anything suspicious over the weekend or anyone carrying black bin liners, moving bins.

'The mutilated body has been identified as that of former headmaster of Legley Road High School, John Daniels, who was last seen leaving his flat in a silver BMW with a black man thought to have been former head of PE Leroy Young, also missing, on Saturday 28th August. Again, if anyone has any further information about this or knows the whereabouts of Mr Young, we would urge them to come forward. We are very keen to eliminate Mr Young from our inquiries.'

A thin-topped man with a paunch and North Face jacket: 'Detective, is it true John Daniels was assassinated by a crime syndicate for allowing drugs from another gang to be distributed in his school?'

Lawton looks at him, giving an almost imperceptible nod. Or is that just Diana's paranoia? He leaves the podium.

O'Malley mutters to Diana: 'Boss, I've already taken over a hundred calls regarding sightings of bin men moving wheelie bins.'

'Keep going.'

Chapter 19

Tuesday 5th October, 2010 – Sheffield HQ

The briefing room is cluttered with cups, chairs at odd angles, and a grubby, scribble-full whiteboard. Diana begins to believe another body is putrefying under the room's ashy, stained carpet.

'Neville spilled the milk last week, Boss,' hisses Robertson in a low whisper.

'Could've bleached it up,' returns Diana. Robertson smirks from behind his Styrofoam.

Lawton's loving this: shirt sleeves rolled up, treading a rut in the carpet, reorganising the board: OCG, Ryano Hut, Legley Road High School, Daniels. Police Jenga.

'Right. Following the discovery of Daniels' remaining body parts yesterday, it's clear it's an OCG. We've got unexplained clearance of Daniels' debts. We also have evidence from a separate investigation by the Drug Squad led by DI Keith Phillips that Ryan Pierce had Legley Road High School youths selling drugs both in and out of the school. We're looking into some connection there. Also exploring Geoff Thomlins' purchase of the property prior to its closure.'

He turns towards Diana and Robertson.

'You two, get over to Sheffield LEA offices. Go through the paper trail there. Neville, O'Malley, Khan and I will be liaising with DI Phillips' team.'

Diana frowns. 'Sorry, detective. Maybe I missed some details. What is the specific evidence that points to an OCG ...?'

Lawton puts his hands in his trouser pockets, blows out his cheeks and exhales noisily.

'Um – mutilated body in high visibility site, still identifiable to send a clear message to someone – possibly Leroy Young who's on the run? Suspicious large amounts of cash being transferred to both Young and Daniels' accounts. Silence within the community, particularly the ex-students and staff. Geoff Thomlins being able to obtain premium green land for development at low price. The death of Legley Road finance officers ...'

'Mr Griffiths, the bursar, died of cancer,' Diana says.

And Aaliyah's still alive.

Neville butts in. 'Ongoing drugs investigation since 2007.'

Diana mutters, 'Drug Squad dragging ...'

'Particularly vicious and brutal mutilation – calling card of OCGs and purpose to terrorise community into silence and compliance.'

'What about Leroy Young?'

'What about him? We haven't found him yet, but he is a suspect. So, get out looking, Walker!'

Diana keeps her eye roll internal and responds with a clipped: 'OK, detective. We'll go back through LEA documents.'

But first she needs to find and have a chat with Aaliyah Matthews. See what she's running from in Sheffield.

And if she had access to the filing cabinet keys.

Chapter 20

Wednesday 6th October, 2010 – University Of Wolverhampton, Canteen

Diana waits outside the lecture hall as the Information Engineering & Software Management second year cohort dribbles out. A mix of pastel-hoodied twenty-somethings – apart from a amber-skinned woman at the back, dressed in a parka, black hair pulled into a neat bun, clompy boots to facilitate an obvious limp. She carries a large tote bag in her arms like a shield as they enter the dining hall, heading straight for a small round table in the far corner. Diana buys a vending machine black coffee and watches parka-girl park herself at the round table, peering around nervously as she pulls out her laptop. She jumps at Diana scraping the chair back.

'Afternoon, Aaliyah.'

Diana puts down the coffee, sitting down opposite her. The hooded eyes spark up in alarm, her hands cover the laptop. One of them, a clawed paw; a stump where the ring finger should be.

'Or do you prefer Ally?'

The woman slams her laptop shut, gripping the edge of the table, glaring at Diana.

'I *prefer* not having strangers act like they know me.'

Diana sips her coffee. 'DI Walker, Sheffield Police. Won't take up much of your lunch. Thought you'd prefer a low-key visit to a trip to the station.'

She clocks a hardness in Ally's big green-brown eyes – and a scar perilously close to the left lid.

'What is this?' Ally growls.

'Just an impromptu chat.'

Diana slips her card discreetly over the crumbed tabletop. 'I'm investigating the murder of your ex-boss John Daniels, the head-master of Legley Road High School. I believe you worked there four years: 2003 to December 2007.'

'Oh, that.' Ally sighs.

'Yes, that. I understand you were Mr Griffith's assistant, in charge of all the school's book keeping. I've looked at your accounts: meticulous.' Diana nods appreciatively.

Ally watches her warily.

'Bit of a change: giving up a salaried job at thirty-eight, going back to uni … But your office was on the second floor – that must have been hard work with your leg, going up and down.' Diana sips her coffee. 'Or maybe you didn't have your disability then?'

'Piss off.'

'Look, Ally. The sooner I get the info, the sooner I can get out of your hair, the sooner I can stop digging around, trying to work out what went on at Legley Road High School. What went on that led to Mary Calley's death, two missing members of staff, and the mutilated body of a headmaster.'

Ally continues to glare. Diana drains her cup. 'Not to worry. I'll send the request for an interview through your department as I don't have your address …' Diana pushes back her chair, getting up.

'Why you mention Mary?'

Diana sits back down.

'Because I have a feeling Mary – or what happened to Mary – has something to do with this murder. I may be wrong.'

'You reckon?' Ally's scarred eyelid glistens. 'I'll need a cig and a coffee.'

She pulls out a pack of red Rizlas and a green tobacco pouch

146

tied up with yellow ribbon. A red disposable lighter. 'Not that vending machine shit. Double espresso. Three sugars.'

Diana watches as Ally inches out meagre tobacco strands onto the frail paper. Her left hand trembles. Ally catches her staring, glaring up defiantly.

'Barista's over there.'

Diana sits down with two freshly pumped espressos, one with twice the coffee, three times the sugar.

No Ally.

She looks around desperately. *Idiot*. Oldest trick in the book. She does a three-sixty and her heart stops its race when she sees the parka-d form, outside in the October wind, phone to ear, fag in the other hand on an intense phone call.

Who's she on the phone to?

Diana focuses on her mouth.

Re-

He-

Ma.

Four times now. Re-He-Ma. There's no other word similar in the English language. She's talking. Smiling! Her shoulders drop.

Diana hears her mum's voice so many miles away. Within her, an instinctive jealous yell: *She's my mum!*

As if aware of Diana's gaze, Ally nods briefly, pockets the phone and sucks the end of her homemade cig before flicking it to a puddle.

'No lunch?' Diana says as Ally sits down. 'Or is it the student lunch: caffeine, nicotine?'

'Occasionally codeine. Never morphine, case you're wondering.'

'I'm not but good to know,' says Diana.

Wincing, Ally sits down. 'What you asking?'

'I'm looking for information about John Daniels and Leroy Young. The state of the school's finances. Where Mary Calley's new curriculum money went. How you met Mary.'

Ally raises the espresso to her full, chapped lips. Then stops.

'Where's sugar?'

'Oh. I put it in.'

Ally frowns. 'That all you put in?'

'No truth serum. Promise.'

Ally sips cautiously. 'Police promise in't worth shit.'

Diana drinks her own coffee. 'OK, well, no promise then. I just put three sugars in and stirred.'

Ally continues to sip tentatively, frowning.

'Mary?'

'Mary and I met out on the back steps, having a fag. She didn't really smoke – just the odd one. Any excuse to avoid the gossipy staffroom. She stopped totally when she got her gastric reflux.'

'Ulcer?'

'Don't know about that. But she had gastric reflux for years. Heartburn and that.'

'Pretty young.'

'Stress, innit. She dint look after hersen well, either. Didn't have a GP till she were at uni, she said. Only went for her smear doing. Right martyr, our Mary.'

Diana purses her lips. *No GP till uni.* That would explain Mary's slim medical record – and also suggest childhood neglect at the very least ... She must check in with Mrs Thompson again.

'Tell me about Mary.'

Ally's face softens. 'She were right lively. Funny, sharp as a blade. That were our therapy: break, lunch, after school – out on steps. Then she got more busy with her new curriculum, I'm sorting out all this government funding coming in when it were Labour. Feels like a lifetime ago – all that dosh. Before the crash. Daniels was spending it like Brewster's Millions. Mary were going to this book club up at Carterknowle. Invited me along.'

Please don't mention my mum. Please.

'What about John Daniels?'

Ally shrugs. 'Not very good with his expenses. Spent more than he had. All in the name of the kids – except "the kids" included *him* and excluded *them*. Not a believer in hard graft was Daniels – unless someone else was doing it.'

'How did he get on with the bursar, Mr Griffiths?'

Ally nods. 'Poor sod. Just a year off retirement. But he was a yes man, Mr Griffiths. That's how he kept his job so long.'

'But you did most of the paperwork, the balancing of books? He just signed off?'

Ally stares back. 'He was ill. He knew I knew what to do.'

'I'm just trying to tally up what happened to the new curriculum funding. It came in but it never went out. And it wasn't there in January 2008.'

Ally glares. 'Well, I've not got it! I left before that.'

'How long had you been working at Legley Road?'

Ally shrugs. 'About five year. Started off as a junior clerk but Mr Griffiths taught me everything. As he got sicker, he trusted me to do more. When I told him I wanted to go back to uni, he wrote my reference. Said he was pleased I was going to do something better with my life.'

Ally stares over Diana's shoulder. 'He never even knew I got in.'

'Did he know Daniels and Young were—'

'On the fiddle?' Ally nods. 'I think so. He never said owt but he just dreaded being called into Daniels' office.'

'So, he was in a very difficult situation?'

'Well, if he whistleblew and it backfired, he'd have lost his pension. His wife doesn't work. When he found out he had the cancer, he just—'

'Shut up and put up?'

Diana looks at Ally, who stares back.

'Basically.'

'So, when Griffiths left, Daniels expected the same service from you?'

'I wouldn't go to his office – always had an excuse. He had to come to mine so I knew Lucy, the clerk, would be a witness. He was a sly one though. He'd be like, "Oh, here's an invoice for a purchase of books I made over the summer from my personal account." He'd always say it was urgent, hand me some typed-up invoice on Word. "Just write me a cheque," he'd say. "No need to put it through wages." I'd ask for a receipt or delivery note.'

'Did he ever give you one?'

Ally stares evenly. 'Kept saying it must be at home. Then he couldn't find it.' She sighs.

'Did you write the cheque?'

Ally looks out of the window. 'I had to. While Griffiths weren't there, I was the second signatory, so ...' Ally swallows. 'I need to go – I've got lectures.'

Diana leans in. 'You never got the receipts or delivery notes? Can you remember how much it was for?'

Ally shakes her head. 'No. And I handed in my notice straight after.'

'You didn't tell anyone?'

Ally snorts. 'Who? What was the crime? He'd just say he'd lost the receipt and I was being unreasonable. Bang goes my job and reference.'

Diana drains her cup.

'That sounds like how they treated Mary. You must have known the new curriculum money had come in already?'

'Yeah, but that doesn't prove owt. Daniels was within his rights to decide how to spend it.'

'On the school.'

Ally raises her eyebrows.

'But you were Mary's friend. She must have asked you?'

The table behind them erupts in loud laughter. Ally picks at her fingers.

'She told me how Leroy was doing her, and then about her performance review being moved up ... I could see their game. I may have told her before half-term.'

'May have or did?'

'I may have said summat about thinking the money had already come in.'

'She must have been very disappointed.'

Ally snorts again.

'And Daniels and Young, did they intimidate you?'

'I'd handed in my notice.'

'Not even harass you ... or anything physical?'

Ally's face closes up. 'No, detective. There was an official audit done – look at that. I've said what happened. I signed that cheque in good faith he had the receipt.'

'We'll get the cheque from the bank.'

Ally scrabbles her bag and coat together.

'Did you have access to the filing cabinet keys?'

She pulls her neck back, snorts. 'Filing cabinets? Yeah, ours. But I handed in all my keys ...' Her face freezes. 'On Friday December 21st. To Mr Daniels himself. Signed the paper 'n' all. It should be on record.'

'Could you be mistaken? Or have mislaid—'

'Most definitely not mistaken.' Her voice sharp as metal.

Diana desperate: 'Can I ask how you ... got your disability?'

'Ask owt you like, love, but I'm not giving any more answers when you're accusing me of fraud.'

'I'm not accusing you of anything. I'm asking about Daniels' intimidation of Mary. Not to worry – maybe the book club can tell me.'

Diana holds Ally's face of terror with a level stare.

Ally's eyes spit fire at her.

'Leave *them* alone. What do you need to know?' She looks at her watch.

Diana pulls into the table. 'Did Daniels have enemies? He had money problems, we know.'

'He wasn't popular.'

'No angry parent or scorned lover? You probably worked the most with him on the day-to-day.' Diana waits.

Ally sighs.

'He wasn't liked much. He did the dirty on Mary – only that weren't public knowledge as far as I know. That's one of the reasons I left.'

'"Did the dirty"?'

Ally screws up her face as if she had just bitten a rotten olive.

'He messed with the finances behind my back and then denied it. Him and Leroy. *I* knew. *Mary* knew.'

Ally focuses on the seam of her roll-up pouch, then shrugs and looks out of the window at a cleaner picking up trays after a group of students leave a table.

'It was a shit job. Hard work. Lots of responsibility for not much money. When Mary told me she was leaving, it was a definite I'd quit too.' Ally's eyes fill. 'I really got to go.'

'What about drugs in school?'

Ally deadpans. 'What about them?'

'Was Daniels aware? Was he dealing with it? Stopping it?'

'Not really. We had bobbies in and out on the regular, but nothing major. Couple of discreet exclusions.' Ally looks at the canteen clock. Diana needs a lead.

'One mo – Ryan Pierce. The guy who runs the Ryano Hut. I understand you used to be engaged?'

Ally's body stiffens. 'Who told you that?'

'I thought it was a known fact. The students, the book club—'

Ally's face darkens. 'If I was, I'm not now. And I don't need reminding, thanks.'

'Just seems a disparate coupling.'

'Definitely desperate. And dumb. I came alive at the book club though. I found myself there, felt like my brain was worth something, that *I* was worth something.'

Diana cuts in. 'Who broke off the engagement?'

'I did.'

'Can I ask why?' Diana looks at a face that really wants to spit 'No!' Instead, Ally narrows her eyes.

'He's a wasteman. Mary told me she saw him with this other gyal. Furthermore, I wasn't feeling it by then. I wanted uni.'

'Nothing to do with the drugs?'

Ally shakes her head.

'When did you break it off?'

'Before I left Legley.'

'Before Mary left?'

'I'm off to my lecture.'

Ally gathers up her parka, tote bag, avoiding Diana's eyes. Three-hour round trip on her own time. She can't let this go.

'How did Ryan Pierce get on with Daniels?'

'Parent, innit? Him and Mary clashed because she suspected he were trying to get Bruno involved in his dodginess.'

'Did Mary report that?'

Ally's hand is trembling as she hoists the tote bag up on her shoulder. *Is that a shrug?*

'So, Mr Pierce wasn't helping Daniels with his financial problems?'

Ally tugs on her parka hood-strings.

'Mr *Pierce* couldn't even afford a proper engagement ring and

152

used to buy his wholesale chicken with my credit card. Wasteman – not a gangster.'

She suddenly freezes. She's not looking at Diana, not looking anywhere.

She's somewhere else.

She hisses. 'Don't even tell that man you've seen me, you hear? I've given you more than you need. It's not *my* job to solve crimes.'

Diana gets up. 'Thank you. I'll be in touch if we need any more information.'

Ally scowls, snatching up her laptop, ramming it into the tote bag.

'I bet.'

The kissed-teeth 'bitch' rings out under her cough as Diana watches the slight parka'd frame limp out of the dining hall.

Chapter 21

Thursday 7th October, 2010 – Dewbow

MaMa hands Diana a steaming stoneware cup. She inhales the dark rich aroma, admiring the crema with a wide grin. The drive back from Wolverhampton last night had knocked her out.

MaMa smiles, sitting down opposite Diana at the small square table. Rehema had dropped off MaMa this morning as she had 'appointments' and then needed to get some fabric from Cole Brothers for MaMa's room. Diana had been asleep, so MaMa had pottered about the house, inspecting the dandelioned garden, arranging pots in the greenhouse, writing letters. On waking, Diana spent half an hour trying to find some notepaper. Now she chews her pen, writing down ten dates, five bullet points. *One name*. Chews it again. *Three sentences*. Signs it. Dates it. Rummages in every drawer looking for a pack of envelopes she knows she has. Somewhere.

At last, she sits, drinking the coffee MaMa made using the beans from Nairobi.

'Sorry, MaMa, I'm a rubbish host! I didn't know Ma was …'

MaMa screws up her face. '*Tchh!* It is wonderful to get to see your home without noise and chatter.'

'Ma does like people around, yes.'

Diana seals her letter in her own envelope, her hand hovering over the front. She puts her pen down, places the long envelope

154

behind the clock. She watches MaMa lick the pale blue airmail envelopes. Her handwriting is neat, scrolled carefully on the red pre-printed lines.

'Who you writing to?'

MaMa sways her head from side to side. 'Nyambura and Wambui. Just news about the Commission and you.' She rubs her eyes. 'My eyes hurt now … I need those glasses. Rehema took me for test in Sheffield.'

Diana nods, but she doesn't understand. She doesn't understand why MaMa has stayed in a country without family. Or why she is more bothered about reading glasses than going back. But she knows MaMa's community is important to her.

'We'll go to the Post Office. Then get back to Sheff.'

There are only three people in the Post Office. Miss Rawlins, the post mistress, is a fifty-something plain schoolmistress type, greying dark hair scraped back into a combed bun, black-rimmed glasses, plain white blouse, navy cardi. No wedding ring – she's married to the Post Office, keeping her corkboard busy with Parish notices, the Brownies, the Bakewell festival, the Dahlia Society, Sunday league football. Diana notes the clientele: the flat-capped pensioner at the glass-fronted till was pure 'heritage', as was Mrs Richardson with her basket of joints, cauliflower and worming tablets, handing over packages to be sent to Daughter Number Two at Durham University. Miss Rawlins is always courteous to Diana, efficient but not chatty. Maybe if Diana hung around for another decade. She notes Miss Rawlins' cursory glance at MaMa: the straight-backed, dark-skinned woman with a lean body denying her fourscore plus, belted in a worn gabardine mac. A woman who walks everywhere, is on no medication – even though she probably needs some. MaMa keeps her body's secrets to herself.

But right now, MaMa is acting very strangely indeed. She's staring like Miss Rawlins is some long-lost relative. 'Good morning – I mean afternoon.'

'Good afternoon. How can I help?' Miss Rawlins replies, briefly smiling.

MaMa slides the three blue envelopes under the glass.

'To Nairobi, Kenya, please.'

Miss Rawlins pushes her stringed glasses halfway down her nose, lifts a blue envelope closer.

'Kenya? Not sent anything to Africa for a while. Let's see … yes, they'll go airmail letter. Be there in two weeks. Mr Smith sent a parcel last month to his cousin in Johannesburg. He said it took ten days.'

'Thank you. How much?'

'One pound ninety-six please.'

Diana looks at her watch. Gorman's only on duty while three. Or was it three-thirty? She needs to catch him before he clocks off. Miss Rawlins is still chatting to MaMa.

Hurry up.

'You on holiday here?'

'Just visiting my granddaughter.'

Waiting for justice.

Miss Rawlins looks at Diana as if she's just appeared.

'What a long way to come. I hope you both enjoy the Peak District.'

Diana's about to say she's a Council Tax-paying local, she's come in here at least once a week for the past two years. But she doesn't.

MaMa smiles her radiant smile.

'Thank you so much. Yes. It reminds me of Kenya.'

Mrs Rawlins blushes as if it's a personal compliment. 'Isn't it very hot there? Not many giraffes in our woods.'

'Nor in ours these days.'

Miss Rawlins counts out her change backwards: 'Two pounds, nine, eight, seven. Cheerio now.'

'Thank you. Goodbye.' MaMa puts her four pennies into her small, zipped cloth purse. Diana's at the door, holding it open, desperate to get out before there's a queue. She hates herself for being embarrassed, but she is.

Outside, the autumn breeze kicks up brittle leaves that scutter across the pavement like copper shrapnel. MaMa is thoughtful, moving slowly behind Diana. Diana waits and links arms with her.

'Dewbow's not like Africa, MaMa.' Diana looks around at the pub, the bus stop, the Exclusive Butchers, estate agents.

'You don't even know Kenya, *mwana*.'

'Yes, I do. I've been to Nairobi and Bagamoyu many summers!'

'No!' MaMa's fierce reply bolts out. 'Not my Kenya. Not the highlands, Kijabe, Lake Nakuru.'

By now they're at Diana's car. She unlocks the passenger door, holds it open for MaMa. But MaMa stays on the pavement, looking up towards Curbar Edge, still frowning.

'I wish you had. Then you would know.'

'Maybe I will one day, MaMa.'

MaMa gets in the car slowly. Diana shuts the door and walks around to the driver's side. Maya's Audi zooms past blasting *Fluorescent Adolescent*. The village eccentric. Diana flattens herself against the door and makes a mental note that she's doing at least forty in a twenty mile per hour zone. She glares after the rapidly disappearing car and gets in. MaMa's still staring ahead, lost in thought as she clicks in her seatbelt.

'No, the highlands are not … it's not the same any more. That lady …'

Diana starts the car, looking at the clock. She can just make it before noon if Rehema's in. It takes twenty-three minutes in the afternoon to get in. Diana's already totting up the list of calls to make, questions to ask Gorman before he leaves.

'Miss Hulda.'

'What?'

They're stuck at the red light at The Stag and Gun pub before hitting the A621.

'Miss Hulda. That's who the Post Office lady reminded me of.'

'MaMa, who is Miss Hulda when she's at home?'

Diana glances at MaMa, who looks to her left.

'Miss Hulda is not at home. Hulda Stumpf raised me.'

Diana changes gears her gut clenching. Is this senility? Or family truth? MaMa seems to be absorbed in the sky, the moors, her mind elsewhere. Diana puts on Radio Hallam, needing white noise to work out the pattern of this murder … The radio plays the rest of the Arctic Monkeys. She remembers five years ago, policing after that crazy gig at Plug when Keith Phillips asked her out …

STOP IT.

'Hulda Stumpf? Sounds German.'

'She was American.'

Rehema's story's always been she was shipped over from Kenya with a missionary couple when one year old, MaMa was supposed to come over, but never did and Rehema only found her in 1976 after rigorous research – living in a hut in Bagamoyu. Diana moves down a gear as they hit the hill.

'Nothing about Americans. Ma told me Great Granddad died in the famine.'

'He didn't.'

'Oh.'

She needs a last-seen moment for Leroy Young.

'Your great-grandfather disappeared. There was a row about our land. Under Kikuyu law, you cannot sell outright your land. You can rent or lease out for a period while it lies fallow but it is always yours as the ancestors are buried there ... I would have been buried there ...'

And why's no one talking?

'But we were so poor, he rent it out, so he thought, to some British coffee farmers for five years, but when he come back to work the land, they chase him off with threats, say he sold it them. He not the only one. We were cheated out of our land.'

'We used to own a part of Kenya? That's incredible.'

'The forest edges and the slopes ...'

Diana gives a slow nod. 'Ahhh! That's why you think Dewbow's like Kenya!' She smiles. 'Kenya's better.'

'Not now. It's gone. That soil's not fit for purpose. The woodland, it's ...'

If she drops MaMa off at Rehema's, she can catch Gorman before he leaves. She needs more detail on the blade used.

'My father – he tried – but – I don't know where he went. He said he'd return for me so I wait. The elders took me to Kijabe Girls' Home. And Miss Hulda raised me.'

'You think he joined the Mau Maus?'

MaMa shakes her head. 'No, no. He had disputes with them too ... I think he was killed by either the settlers or the Masai. I remember when I was very young, he took me out on the ridge.'

'How old were you?'

'I don't know my day of birth.'

'I thought it was the first of January?'

158

'No, Miss Hulda gave me that as she said it was a new day. My dad told her in moons.'

'Well, I think we should celebrate all the ones you've missed, MaMa!'

Diana doesn't know what else to say. They are winding through the moors, purple skies ahead, hawks hovering, the shadows of clouds skittering across the mauve brown of the moors. Diana looks at the clock: 12.20 p.m. Rehema must surely be back from Coles by now. Some dull DJ going on about Sheffield Wednesday. She lowers the volume.

'So – this Miss Hulda. You do well to remember her, MaMa.'

'I will never forget her.' MaMa looks out at the moors.

Ravens post up on the stone wall layby. They stare directly at the car.

'I can't tell Rehema these things. She's so labile. Her generation lost their roots.'

Labile? Diana sighs. She's not going to get much thinking space today. Maybe she should just let MaMa talk. She's happy she's talking. She hasn't said much since arriving.

'Miss Hulda – she part of the African Inland Mission. Good woman. She saved my *kisimi*! Very strict. Very smart. American lady, but not like the others. Does not think like European. Even Kikuyu think she's crazy – but respect her. She keeps boundaries. Looks after the orphans.'

What's kisimi?

'I didn't think any Kikuyu respect white people.'

Diana rummages in her memories for what Rehema had told her – not much. She's not had a one-on-one grown-up conversation with MaMa since her trips to Kenya stopped with uni. Then work took up her summers.

MaMa's voice takes on a serrated, tough edge.

'See!' she hisses. 'That's your mother. Plenty good relationship. Kikuyu the best workers, East African Women's League – they love their Kikuyu. They trust Kikuyu until British Government say not to. That caused problem.'

'That makes no sense. They were the workforce, right?'

'Land, *mwana. Land.* British Government say Kenya poor quality land, not as good as Uganda, keep telling lies until Kikuyu believe them. And Kikuyu had rights. We are gentle people not fierce like Masai, not stubborn, we don't burn the cattle. Kikuyu negotiate, co-operate.'

MaMa struggles to roll down the window. Diana watches her, presses the electric button.

'Not too much ... that's fine.'

'What's *kisimi*, MaMa?'

MaMa laughs. '*Kisimi! Uke.* What make a woman feel sex is good!'

Is MaMa losing her marbles?

MaMa closes her eyes, breathes in, looking out on the cresting ridge.

'I walk on the crest of the foothills as a child. Even when the famine started. The air so pure.'

'Yeah, it's still crisp. It'll get wilder and colder soon though. I bet Africa never gets like that.'

Is a kisimi a clitoris?

MaMa kisses her teeth. '*Mwana*, African mornings, nights are cold. You don't know cold. The uplands, *mwana* – near the mountains and Lake Nakuru.'

Diana descends into Totley Brook. The only ridge she's thinking of is the border of established deciduous trees around Legley Road High School.

'This Miss Rawlins – sorry, Miss Hulda. How long you live with her?'

MaMa glares through the back of the articulated lorry in front.

'Many Kikuyu become Christian after famine come, but some half-half. Half Ngai and ancestral believers, half a bit Christian called Kikuyu Christian, and then a few bona fide full Christian. Kikuyu elders not like them.'

'Which were you?'

MaMa shoots her a sharp side glance. Even with her eyes on the snaking road, Diana feels it.

'I Kikuyu and I Christian, full real bona fide both. I will not let them mutilate me.'

'Pardon?' Diana presses on the brakes on the hairpin a bit too sharply. Down a gear. *Twelve twenty-five.*

'They are not taking my *kisimi. Majina ya labia.* Miss Hulda

160

help me stop them. Most Kikuyu tribes think no circumcision for women makes you unclean. They say take away the privates is only way to guarantee woman marriageable, of good quality. Get the payment. My father gone so I have no protection. Kikuyu women are a prize, but not made for their own personal pleasure. African Inland Mission not like female circumcision. Unbiblical. Many Kikuyu leave, start own church – Christian but with circumcision so they can keep their ties with tribes and they land. But I and we *irigu*. We trust God not tribes. Not *irua* so not allowed to be with *irua* or other Kikuyu women.'

Keep your eyes on the traffic, girl.

'Miss Hulda, she call *irua* "sexual mutilation". That when you cut the woman, you cut yourself from the land. No one like her for that. Kikuyu didn't like, but they let be as they have own church now. But white settlers they furious with Miss Hulda.'

Diana can't focus. She grasps at the threads of her case but is absorbed into the first traffic lights in Totley, traffic already beginning. Radio squawking: 'Traffic jam on the A621 between Beauchief and Totley Brook due to roadworks.'

She groans as the tail lights in front start blinking, pulling up the handbrake.

'Miss Hulda a white missionary then?'

'See?' MaMa shakes her head. 'Your mother again. White and black. She not seeing, not hearing. That's why I never tell her.'

Diana's never heard MaMa angry before.

'Miss Hulda, she different. She fierce. Raising twelve tough Kikuyu girls, fighting for us to get the calico dresses and nice things foreign church sent instead of the mission ladies taking it, saying they kids should get it first. She feed us, raise us, teach us. Respect your *kisimi*. Respect your body. Temple of God. Very smart lady. Made me learn reading and writing, arithmetic, sewing. Help her grow vegetables. She wouldn't let the Kikuyu elders take us for the ceremony. When they say, "*Irigu* forbidden to marry Kikuyu man, always be poor", she say, "*Irigu* will marry if and whoever she please and never poor."'

FGM. Female Genital Mutilation.

The penny drops. It was in the training Diana had for the Muslim communities in 2005. But MaMa's not Muslim. Here she is

161

stuck in a traffic jam with her grandma talking about the clit. This is all the Post Office's fault. Bet Miss Rawlins doesn't even know she's got one.

'I was her best girl. My dorm next door to Miss Hulda's study and the white ministers and settlers they come many time to tell Miss Hulda stop irritating the Kikuyu and all this sexual mutilation propaganda. Let them do what they want. They say it none of her business and now they start they own church, they learn they don't need white governing or religion. "Good!" Miss Hulda say, "Good. Good."'

MaMa hits the dashboard with her flat palm, fingers splayed. Diana jumps.

'"Good!" she say. "Not good!" they say. "Now all Kikuyu and Masai think they can govern themselves. Not good. This is our workforce." One minister come. He say she is destabilising country with her silly Sunday School and *kisimi* nonsense, and to shut up or they make her go back to America. Miss Hulda say, "I'm not leaving. I am charged to care for these orphan girls. I'm not leaving."'

Horns parp behind her. Diana snaps to, takes off the handbrake, inches forward. She's now absorbed in MaMa's tale, ignoring the glares and hand gestures in her rear-view and wing mirror.

'Miss Hulda sounds like a hero. She must have been so proud of you. Did she come to your wedding then?'

MaMa looks out at the upper-middle-class Edwardian terraces set far back from the road. Her hands are trembling, still on the dashboard, gripping tightly to it like she's about to fall out of the car.

'One night I hear yells, screams, mad banging. A man's voice. British. I hear him before. Minister or missionary or both. I was scared. I try to get in. Knock on door but then silence. I try and try. Fall asleep. In the morning, I go to raise our man servant, Kakoi, and tell him Miss Hulda not answering our knocks. He angry at me but he go in, come out and vomit, shaking. Won't let us in but when he go for police, I go in.'

So this is where she got it from. Her MaMa. Diana wants more traffic lights. They're all green.

Come on, be red. I need to hear this.

'Miss Hulda, she so tidy. Like your Post Office lady. Everything in order. Always. Her room, her office, smashed to pieces,

162

her bedroom, she lay bad-ways on bed, pillow on face. Curtains drawn close. Blood on thigh. Leg like so.'

MaMa moves her fingers on the dashboard so they are splayed into a V.

'She was raped?'

MaMa shakes her head. 'No rape. Killed. They did something to her privates. Not like Kikuyu do. This a chop-up job by someone who does not know a woman's sex from a cucumber. I saw. I saw. They didn't know I saw the doctor when he come because I hid under bed and police tell doctor say nothing. They say: "No one sees this." Then they arrest Kakoi. Say he smothered her. They bury Miss Hulda slapdash like a rotten dog less than two day later. No question, no ceremony. The Mission sent me to Nairobi to work there.'

Green light. MaMa nudges her. She shoots off, straight up Sharrow Vale. Has her gran just reported an uninvestigated murder from seventy years ago? Or is she going batty? It's Kenya. It's history. It's not her problem. It's …

A woman.

The radio beeps for half-hourly news. It's twelve-thirty and she's still not even at Millhouses.

'Police are still searching for the killer of Legley Road High School's headmaster, John Daniels, whose body was found butchered on the old Legley Road High School site earlier this month. They are appealing for witnesses for anyone who saw anything suspicious around the site from Bank Holiday weekend in August.'

Diana exhales. Lawton is doing this all wrong. She needs to get at this case sideways. All she needs is a break. Someone to have a Post Office lady experience. As she pulls into her mum's road, the thought arrives on time: maybe she's just had one. The silent witnesses.

She needs to get them to speak.

Diana intended on just making sure MaMa got in safely, but, as soon as she's gone upstairs, the purse-lipped Rehema pounces, closing the door.

'Who do you think you are, Diana, interrogating all my friends?' Rehema stares at Diana. 'You're certainly not the girl I raised!'

Diana smarts, her cheeks flush, but she bites back. 'You didn't

– MaMa did! You sent me off to Nairobi each summer, remember? While you did your Masters.'

Rehema's eyes widen and she slams the knife on the chopping board.

'To get a job to feed *you*! MaMa take you to the doctor's, sit with you each evening to help you through your homework, feed you …? Who do you think you're talking to?'

Diana cuts her eyes, pulls on her coat.

'A woman who has more time for her beloved book club and their secrets.'

Rehema glares. Breathes in deep. Diana knows she should stop but her mouth keeps spilling.

'This headmaster homicide investigation keeps looping back around to your book club. One member died in mysterious circumstances, the other recently disabled and terrified of returning to Sheffield. What else does your book club hide, Ma?'

Rehema shakes her head, her mouth twists in distaste as if she's just swallowed a rotten pip.

'We're having to put our own lives on the line because police does nothing. Wait till the pack turns on you, Diana – and they will. Who you going to run to then, huh?'

Diana swallows. 'Pack done turned on me years ago, Ma. Only you were too busy analysing a book or sorting out strangers' problems to notice. I'm trying to protect you – not my so-called career.'

'Stop being so melodramatic, Diana! *Your* life wasn't at risk!'

Diana just stares at her. All this time, she thought Ma knew about what happened with Phillips, that her silence was protecting her from reliving the trauma. But either she didn't know, didn't notice - or doesn't care. Diana's not sure what hurts most. Her eyes fill. She shoves her arms into the sleeves of her coat.

Rehema continues: 'Poor Mary and Ally didn't have mums who …'

'… who what?'

Diana pauses, hands on the door handle.

'Where are you going?' Rehema's anger turns to confusion.

'Obviously, I've got extra work to do.'

'Just *stop it*, Diana. Sit down. Calm—'

'Yeah, I *am* going to stop it.' She's on the doorstep. 'That's my job. DS Robertson will be in touch.'

As she walks down the path, Diana hears the key turn behind her. Feels her own heart crack.

If Ally won't speak, maybe Mary will …

She crouches over the yellowed pages of Mary Calley's rounded handwriting, scattered with inverted capitals and lower-case letters. More like a teenager's diary than a professional's. She's immersed in this spiralbound Asda jotter pad like it's a bestseller, frowning, flicking pages. A cough interrupts her and she looks up at John, the guy from tech, standing in front of her with Mary's Nokia in a clear plastic bag – along with a wad of printed transcript of the messages and emails. He has a slight squint, but, in ten years, there's not been a mobile he can't crack into.

'Here's phone, detective. Rate mission unlocking that Nokia.'

Diana looks at him in surprise.

'Was about to give up and then remembered a shortcut me mate taught me when we were at school.'

'Thanks, John. And Ms Calley's emails?'

'DI Wallace just sent them through, all they could find anyway from 2004 to 2008.'

'Great. We'll go through these. Chase up on the computer analysis on Daniels and Young. Can you make a start with the social media stuff, for what it's worth? Facebook, Myspace, Bebo. Whatever. Match dot com even. Anything that can fill some gaps or introduce some.'

'On it. Computer analysis takes ages.'

'I know. Keep at it.'

John nods, turns to leave. 'DI Wallace was a bit grumpy.'

'I bet. I don't think he investigated Calley's death as a potential crime.'

'She *was* two year dead though, ma'am.'

'Yeah, and in a preserved crime scene.'

Diana swigs cold strong black coffee from a chipped KitKat mug. She squints at Mary Calley's handwriting. Patterns. That's what's missing from this case. *Patterns*. Patterns mean truth. She

165

can't get a grip. It's like trying to contain a puddle. All murderers have patterns, so where's this one's?

Handwriting analysis was part of her first-year psychology degree. Not scientific, but weirdly prescient of character. Mary's simple typography demonstrates she's intuitive, able to get to the gist of things fast, an empathic soul who infuses harmony and balance in her environment, the slanted incline of distanced capitals indicating a protective spirit, a reflective person.

None of this admissible in court. Mary may have been a contentious bitch.

Conscious of Lawton's critical gaze, she drops the diary back in the Nottingham box, picks it up. She needs to find an empty interview room, immerse herself in Mary's chronicles and the phone and email transcripts.

Unnamed number 0039: What did u tell my bird 4, u cunt? You are just a weirdo dirty slag who can't stand the fact she can't keep a man. U best undo the damage uve done slag ur ugly enuf – don't tempt someone to give u a face lift 1 night.

LEROY: Mary, just cuz we shagged dusnt make us a couple. u need to sort your head out and stop the dramas. Leave me and my family alone!

JD: I need the appraisal before half-term. The LEA are scrutinising your department particularly prior to the Ofsted.

jdaniels@lrhs.ac.uk: Mary, these files are inadequate. Where's the five-page lesson plan and differentiation for the NQT? I need the KS3 targets and intervention program itemised. Now.

jdaniels@lrhs.ac.uk: We scraped a Satisfactory from two Inadequates. I want a Good if not an Outstanding Ofsted inspection. Do not let the school down by slipshod paperwork and inadequate lessons from your department. I need ALL books marked. If the school fails, the blame will be on you. On YOU. So stop whining on about the Award and DO YOUR JOB otherwise you may not have one! I am not going into Special Measures because of incompetency.

TEXT unnamed number 0039: 20th November 2007

Yeh nice 1 u sly little slag. u fkn blank me ? right now the games start. u watch! fkn watch now. ur a no good fkn little lying cunt. u got me down Meadowall and acting all sweet as pie while slagging me off to my bird, u little bitch! ur a fkn liar. do u know wot I mean? none of ur bizniz. U 'n' ur nasty mouth. I fkin hate u, u sour faced slag! ur mental. u need help. no 1 fks with my biznis. now my bird's gone all paranoid all down to you so u watch wot im gonna fkn do now u CUNT!!!!!!!!!!!!

Diana leans back, bones cold, head hot. Looks at her watch. Two hours later. So, Mary and Leroy Young definitely had a thing. And he dumps her for one reason or another. Diana knows she has to re-interview Mrs Young, ferret about for the cracks in that relationship.

But the texts. The emails. There's something else going on here. What is not helping is that she's got numbers but no names; it still Pay-As-You-Go in 2007. The school emails are more helpful, but still it's a muddle. Daniels' and Young's correspondence she can work out, but 0039? Who was this, freely using the c word? It was a different tone, a menace skinning her vertebrae just reading it. It doesn't fit in with her diaries either. What had Mary done to get such texts? It wasn't the vernacular of a headmaster, but then …

A call to 999 logged on 5th August 2007 but no diary entry for two days. Strange as she's pretty consistent. But 4th August spoke of her hearing a rumour that Leroy's married and has a kid. Her doubts and determination to ask him straight the next day.

Nothing then till the 7th August and the following few days. Just basic details. What she's eaten. A trip to the GP. Getting a window replaced. A row with the landlord. Getting ready for results day.

Dreading going into school now.

Why?

23rd August 2007

He wouldn't even look at me, the coward. Mrs Braithwaite can swivel if she thinks I'm going to meet with him to do data analysis and target tracking of Year 10s. I'll do it myself. He never did anything anyway. It was all me. He can't add up or deal with percentages – just promotions and bonuses. I'm shaking with rage. Daniels has pissed me off : swerving my emails and all his 'Not now, Mary's when I ask if I can start buying the books for the new curriculum. I know the Award money's come in. Ally told me. I wanted to talk to Ally but she was in a right mood. Wearing sunglasses in the office like a weirdo and long-sleeved T-shirt when it's hotter than Ibiza. She just said she was busy with a lot to sort as Griffiths off sick.

Saturday 8th 2007

He came round for his stuff. I'd put it all in a cardboard box by side of the door. Told him he was a lying slimeball and had broken my heart. Out of nowhere, he starts yelling, like proper yelling: 'You're mental. Get off me!' I hadn't even touched him. 'There's something wrong with you. Don't touch me.' I was shaking. Neighbours looking at me funny. Then tonight, someone tries my back door. I heard it. Called police. Reported an intruder. No one came or called back yet. Then at 9.35 p.m. a brick through back window. I called police again. NOTHING. I can't pay for another window. I don't want to stay here I want to go stay at Rehema's but daren't tell her as they already disapprove about Leroy and I can do without the I told you so.

According to the diary, no officer ever appeared. Or did Mary call up and take back her statements? Happens a lot in Domestic Violence. But nothing. Diana cannot shake a sense that something very serious, very threatening *was* happening, however. The texts and emails support that.

The body in a sheltered Nottingham bedsit confirms it.

Monday 24 September

I was just making a cup of tea about to start marking loud banging on front door. My nerves already on edge. Open it. Leroy, spitting mad. Hissing at me, jabbing his finger, YELL-ING 'Don't ever call my house or try to speak to my wife or kid again. This is the last time. I'm warning you. Leave us alone!' Marches off. Mr Ali, from next door staring at me like I'm the problem. Kids across the road gawping.

Diana checks the 999 call on Mary's phone: 2.53 a.m. Tuesday 25th September. Again, nothing logged on PNC.

Wednesday 17th October 2007

Performance Management Review this week. Jokes. Ofsted looming early next year. Kids acting up. The new supply is about as useful as a chocolate teapot. Still waiting on police.

Diana desperately scrolls through the police logs. Surely there's something ... there's got to be. Maybe she just didn't record it ... For a busy teacher, she writes a lot. But for a single stressed woman, probably not enough. Writes more than the police log anyway.

Diana's eyes focus on a significant event recorded on Thursday 18th October 2007 when she reports seeing Bruno's dad with a teenage girl.

I always knew he was a scuzzball but he was roped round

169

Sonia from last year's Year 11's at the chicken shop. I actually felt sick. I don't want to tell Ally but she's engaged to this hairball.

And then the 0039 texts start four days later … The journal entries, texts just suggest the average stress and chaotic life of an overstretched single professional. Yet Diana can't shake the sense that something more sinister is unravelling.

'Robertson.'

'Boss?'

'Find out who was the duty pick-up officer for these dates and times … all 2007. August … late October and November.'

'Will do, Boss.'

At the door, Diana stops. Turns. 'I'm going to call DI Wallace at Nottingham. He said Mary had received eight personal unopened letters, but I only found six – from her bank, GP, a hospital appointment and final demands. You've not seen any when going through the box?'

Robertson pushes out his bottom lip, shakes his head. Diana frowns at a piece of ancient tinsel hanging from a skylight.

'Weird.'

Diana punches in the Nottingham number.

'DI Wallace? Hi. It's DI Walker here – no, Sheffield. I came down about the Calley case? Yes, yes, we did, thanks. Just a bit concerned as you mentioned eight unopened letters but we only found six? On the Key Development Log it reads eight … Definitely eight? You don't know about the other two? Hmmm. No, we did an inventory immediately on opening. OK. One other thing – there's no mention of that auditing company here in the file … yes, I know it was after the inquest but it should still be … OK.'

She sighs, holding the receiver a couple of inches from her ear.

'Can you remember the name then? Who came down?'

Diana blows out her cheeks. 'What about the name of the constable? Yes, yes, detective. And I appreciate all you've done and know you're very busy with a murder right now and that this case has been closed but I really need—'

She holds the receiver well away from her. Finally, she pulls it in.

'You too, detective. Have a great day.'

Hanging up, Diana turns to Robertson.

'I don't think DI Wallace likes me much.'

'You reckon?' smiles Robertson. 'Can't think why.'

Diana scowls. 'You try then. I need to find this nameless Nottingham PC and this nameless auditing or legal company who got access to Mary Calley's mail and stuff after the inquest. Oh, and a copy of this so-called Grant of Representation Pastor Calley apparently gave to them.'

'Easy peasy,' winks Robertson.

'You're so annoying when you're smug, sergeant.'

In the interview room, she rummages through the box again, finding an older diary but no letters. She flicks through the curled diary, a reappropriated school jotter for July–August 2007.

Tuesday July 17th 2007

THIS HAS BEEN ONE MAD MAD DAY. Oh my dayz. I mean madddddd.

Just one and half more weeks till we break up. Woke up to a text from Leroy: HIYA BABE. COMING OVER TO STAY AT URS THIS WKND OK? X

Buzzing and nervous too. Not had time to do the washing and change my bedlinen to the grey stripes. But yeah – excited.

Had to do cover in my one free for Miss Foers. She's always pulling a sickie the week before holidays. But Leroy winked at me after assembly and also when I was on duty at break. Year 9 and 10 Somali boys had a big fight in backyard. I went to Post Office at lunch to mail Anoona's birthday card, letting her know I couldn't make it over this weekend. I know they don't approve

171

of me and Leroy. Ate my tuna bap round back with Aaliyah. She's smoking more and eating less. She wouldn't even have half my Twix. She had this bruise on her arm – a new one. She had one the other week. Says she bumped into a filing cabinet. I was going to say she should put in a complaint about filing cabinets but she wasn't in a jokey mood. Asked her if her n Ryan set a date yet. She just snaps 'No.' Think he's a knob myself.

I had to stay on after period six to finish marking Year 10's coursework. There's a knock on door and it's Aamiina. She stays on after school to do her homework in library. I tell her to come in. Such a wide sunny smile. By far, brightest student in my Year 9 top set. She'll get an 8 in her SATs. I think she's worried about her exams, but she asks if she can talk to me about something 'personal'. That dreaded word.

The words you know you need pen and paper for.

So, I do the 'Aamiina-you-can-tell-me-anything-you-like-but-I-am-duty-bound-to-share-it-with-the-DSL' spiel and her face just freezes and she makes to get up from the chair she's just sat on, wailing her family will be deported or put in jail. I'm like no, no calm down. Somehow get her to sit back down, telling her I care and nothing unfair will be done. I reckon that's a promise I can make. She sits down, muttering about it not being a Muslim thing, that Jews and Christians do it too. I have no idea what she's on about at this point. I reckon she's having some sort of breakdown so just listen. She's, twisting her scarf in her hands, holding her schoolbag against her chest like it's body armour. She keeps saying something about a ceremony and how it's not in the Holy Koran and she doesn't want to do it. I'm thinking suicide-bombing or something, way she's clutching her bag.

172

She keeps looking at the door. I ask her if she's scared of someone in the school. I've got this dread. Aamiina's a smart girl, no drama queen.

I just sit and listen to her tell me about this ceremony girls have in her culture when they're young but she didn't because they left Mogadishu in a hurry and now her mum's saying she has to have it done and her legs will be tied together and she won't be able to pee and she'll be off school and she doesn't want it because – she just doesn't want it. But her mum says she has to.

She starts crying. She says it's not doctors, it's women in the community with razors and they hold a party and then I can't hear what she's saying because her tears are angry tears so it's just a snorting mess.

That's when I feel the floor move up and that I'm going to faint. I can't do this.

I'm holding onto the desk. You can't ask leading questions, but my mind is trying to fit all this together and it won't.

I let her sob on me. My shoulder is drenched. It's just a T-shirt. I give her some of my bottled water. She's not finished, just breathing in gulps. She tells me she had a big row last night. Told her mum she wasn't having it and that she got good grades and it wasn't fair and she was going to uni and going to get a good job and her mum's saying that's not enough we won't be accepted at mosque. How her mum had called her a slut and she'd be raped and treated like a white girl. That Axmed and her dad had come in and Axmed tried to reason with them and tell them they were in the UK now, things

173

were different. But then her dad had hit Axmed and told him he was worthless and Axmed had yelled at him, run off.

She's saying more and more but my head is like wohhhh. Suddenly I know. I know why Axmed was fighting the other Somali kids at break and why Bruno stood up for him. I ask her if they all know and she nods and I ask her if she feels safe here and she nods. She tells me Axmed hates her dad and doesn't want to be part of mosque any more. He wants money.

So yeah – no year 10 marking. Two hours of Child Protection paperwork, calling the DSL, Mrs Braithwaite who was as much use as a chocolate teapot, the police and some flimsy desk sergeant who seemed as keen to help as my year 10s are to do their coursework . CSC -jokes. Bottom line: she's staying with me overnight cos they couldn't find accommodation. Police say they'll talk to the family. I can't believe this is going on right under my nose, every day in the classroom. There's nowhere for these girls to hide. I'm trying not to think. I've got to speak to Daniels about this. It's messed up, man.

I'm on the couch tonight, she's in my bed. The bed with the floral bedsheets.

Probably good job Leroy didn't show.

FGM. What had MaMa said about it? It was critical to Kikuyu culture – not to do with religion but about controlling the girls and women, the community. But why wasn't Ms Calley trained to recognise this? What had the police done? Who took her call? Did Mrs Braithwaite make it? Who was at the Strategy meeting with Children's Social Care services? *Was there even a strategy meeting?*

More importantly, *what had the community done?*

Diana takes the stairs two at a time and returns to Robertson's desk, panting.

'Robertson, find me a call log for 17th July 2007. Who was on the Child Protection calls?'

Robertson wordlessly clicks, scrolls, pushes his neck forward in disbelief. Diana nods at a glowering Marchant staring at her from his office.

'Boss, it was DS Neville.'

'What – our Neville?'

He nods. Diana groans.

'Smashing.'

'Why? What's up?'

'According to Ms Calley's diary, a pupil called Aamiina confided in her about her parents planning a cutting for her. She was terrified. Mary said she reported it and Aamiina stayed overnight at hers as Social Services couldn't find her alternative accommodation.'

'Shit.'

Diana walks over to Neville's desk where he is leaning back on his chair, guffawing at one of Lawton's jokes. They simmer down as she stands over him.

'Neville, you used to man the calls for Child Protection, right?'

'Years ago.' He reddens as if embarrassed. 'Why?'

'Remember a teacher calling up about FGM?'

'Who's FGM?'

Please don't do this. Am not in the mood.

'FGM, detective. Female Genital Mutilation. July 2017.'

He shrugs. 'Dunno. We took a lot of calls.'

'What? About FGM?'

'Possibly. Look, I don't know without the paperwork in front of me.'

'There *is* no paperwork.'

Neville sighs, shrugs. 'No case then.'

'There should *still* be paperwork. A case logged. Basic info.'

'Look, if it's Child Protection FGM or whatever, I'd have gone, checked on the family. If there's not enough evidence for a prosecution ...' He talks to her like she's some nagging kid. '... and these communities don't talk to us. We can't do owt.'

'You mean *you* don't do owt!'

Diana turns, marches out of the office, oblivious to the pulled faces, into the Ladies', kicking open the doors before launching a scream down the bowl of the furthest clean one, flushing it at the same time.

When she returns to the office, Marchant is standing at his door. He beckons her in. She stands behind the door.

'Close door, Walker.'

She does so.

Here goes.

'What's this Lawton's been telling me? You screwing poor Neville over some alleged historic FGM report? Can you please explain to me what the *fk* is going on? Why are you stressing out my officers and going down wormholes, rabbit holes, FGM holes, instead of solving this murder?'

'Sir, with due respect, I believe this is relevant.'

'Walker, it is *not* relevant! You are making *yourself* irrelevant! I'm getting tired of you dancing about this case while I have the mayor and his mother breathing down my lughole. Lawton's SIO, and we'll be liaising with DI Phillips' Major Crimes undercover op on the OCG. I do not want to hear any more of this voodoo-collective-staffroom-bookworm-FGM nonsense. Get on with your job! You're still on the team, be thankful for that. But put your nose out of line one more time and you'll be on roads policing till your pension.'

Returning to her desk, she hisses to Robertson: 'Go interview Axmed's mum and dad. Ask them about the FGM and social services in the summer of 2007. Double-check with Social Services too. I need to know if Mary's report was followed up – or if she even made one.'

Diana takes Mary Calley's box down to Evidence and clears her desk, her mind racing – in the opposite direction. There's one person they haven't interviewed yet. It's a long shot, but she may have something to say – even if it's just about the audit.

Chapter 22

Friday 8th October, 2010 – Bracewell Smith, Sheffield

Bracewell Smith's black marbled frontage is immaculate but discreet, down a quiet side street behind the solicitors' offices. Diana pushes through the revolving doors, which swoosh her into a glistening floored foyer. The suited receptionist, small gold sleepers glinting in her ears, smiles up from the well of a crescent desk, her blonde hair arranged with the same precision as the tall vase of lilies beside her.

'Good morning. Can I help you?'

There is a cream leather sofa by the floor-to-ceiling window. Robertson sits while Diana approaches the desk, looking over the fanned copies of *Accounting Today* and *Auditors' Weekly*. The receptionist's smile flattens at the sight of Diana's badge.

'Morning. DI Diana Walker and DS Carl Robertson. We're here for a statement from Ms Smith. She's expecting us.'

'Oh, right.' The receptionist blushes, her hand drifting over the switchboard. Sensing eyes on her, Diana looks up to the mezzanine glass-fronted office where a cream-co-ordinated Maya is looking down, smiling. She walks over to the intercom, which crackles.

'It's OK, Rachel. Send them up.'

Rachel flicks a half-smile. 'Up the stairs, first on the left. Would you like a drink? Coffee, tea?'

Maya's office is at least twenty feet wide, bone-white on two walls, macaroon-cream on the others, a glass-fronted bookcase filled with neatly labelled books and journals, framed certificates on the wall. Her walnut desk hosts a glass of water, a blue file and a laptop, which she clicks shut with ruby-painted nails, a heavy gold bracelet clinking on its side. Diana looks around the room. Nothing to indicate she's a country girl: no mud, no trophies. No photos. Just a well-groomed, voluptuous woman in a cashmere turtleneck. Diana thinks of her own basic desk chaos. Sniffing the sandalwood candle on the low oak table, she sits down on the sofa. Robertson takes the brown leather chair closer to Maya's desk.

'Here for the statement, I presume, detective?'

Diana nods. 'Same as the others. Nice offices. How long have you been here?'

Maya leans back on her chair, swivelling a few degrees.

'About seven years. Since I moved back up from London.'

Diana smiles patiently. 'DS Robertson's got a few questions for you to help us with the Legley Road case. You audited the school this last spring/summer?'

'I did. The Local Education Authority needed a closing audit so selected us to carry it out.'

Diana nods. 'Find anything interesting?'

'It's all in the audit. You can look at it for yourself if you go to the LEA.'

'Thank you. We have. Very thorough. And you do quite a few external independent audits, I see.'

Maya nods. 'I do, detective. Including quite a few HM Inspectorate of Constabulary audits.' Her crimson-painted lips curl. 'Yes. In fact, I have another one down in Nottingham lined up later this year.'

'You did our own South Yorkshire Police Department last year, didn't you? You made some very sharp observations.'

'That's what they pay me for, detective. I checked your file as a matter of fact.'

Diana doesn't blink.

'I bet that was riveting reading,' Diana says.

Diana smiles with her mouth, warns with her eyes. Robertson, confused by the emotional ping-pong, clears his throat.

'So … Ms Smith … it's Maya Smith, correct?'

Maya nods.

'But you were previously Maya Johnson, correct? Married, divorced, single?'

'Single. Never married. Just prefer my real birth certificate name.'

'Your real father?'

'I was adopted – is this necessary?' An edge to her voice. Diana stares coolly back. 'After my adoptive father told me my biological father's name on his deathbed, I decided to change my name by deed poll.'

'When was that?'

Maya rolls her eyes.

'Seriously? I don't know. December 2007 maybe. He died in the November. This seems really intrusive when I'm not under caution, detective.'

'No, no. Just making sure we use your correct legal name. Date of birth …?'

'Twenty-second of the third, nineteen seventy-two.' Maya yawns.

Something fizzes in Diana's brain. She tries to see the figures.

'And you live?'

Maya looks at Diana, rolls her eyes. 'Dewbright Hall, Dewbow, Derbyshire, postcode DE45 1LA.'

'Right.'

Diana looks at the bookcase.

'So how did you get involved with the Black Sistahs Book Club?'

Maya shrugs. 'I like reading. I live a pretty erratic life with my job and meetings and charity responsibilities. The book club was a way to meet regularly with other …'

She looks at Diana who stares back. *Go on. Say it.*

'… women of colour. Get some stimulation and …'

'Sisterhood?'

Maya shrugs. 'If you like.'

'So, the book club. How did you hear about it?' Robertson glances around the office.

'I met Anoona during a charity event raising funds to sponsor inner city literacy projects.'

'Oh. What's the charity?'

'The Dewbow Shining Light Trust. I'm on the board of directors, and Anoona gave a presentation about books by black authors for teenage boys. I chatted to her afterwards, interested in reading some of them.'

'Where were *you* educated, Ms Smith?'

'Sheffield Girls' High.'

'Classic – no black curriculum though?' Diana interjects.

Maya flinches slightly. 'When Anoona invited me to the book club, I was interested. I enjoy it: the books, the conversation, the food, the women. I try to make each meeting.'

'But you never met, or heard them speak of, Ms Calley?'

Maya shakes her head. 'No.'

Diana is frowning at her frizzy reflection in the spotless glass door of the bookcase.

'Are you in touch with your biological parents?'

Maya stiffens. She flicks an icy look at Diana.

'I just told you. My adoptive father didn't tell me till he was on his deathbed. Him and his wife gave me privilege, but I worked hard too. I don't owe them more than what they took ... Look, I thought you were here about the audit?'

Diana frowns. 'We are, but we need to get your details correct. How long did the audit of Legley Road High School take?'

'Three months: four weeks planning, four weeks on the job, four weeks compiling the report.'

'But the school was already closed?'

'I had to do a lot of investigation to get the information I needed.'

'Like going through filing cabinets?'

Maya sighs heavily. 'No, detective. Boxes of files taken *out* of filing cabinets.'

'Did you find any of the keys missing?'

'Pardon me?'

180

'Keys.'

Maya rolls her eyes. 'Detective, I deal with so many audits. The whole point of a detailed report is so that I don't have to carry specifics around in my head all the time. Check the report.'

Diana and Maya stare at each other evenly.

'Did you discover any evidence of fraud? We're still waiting for the full FCA analysis, but …'

Maya raises groomed eyebrows.

'There were some discrepancies which were duly highlighted. Seems to have been going on for some years, mainly to do with an outdated accounting system. But no endemic fraud.'

'What about the new curriculum award?'

Maya shrugs. 'Seemed to have been allocated for curriculum development – just not a new one. I did make some recommendations, but it's all largely hypothetical. It was a closing audit. You have the auditor's report, detective, and I have appointments …' Maya flicks up her sleeve to reveal a man's gold Rolex. '… in five minutes.'

'One last question. What were you doing Bank Holiday weekend?'

'I was at the Dewbow Summer Fete, organising, giving speeches, networking. One of the most knackering and rewarding annual events for our charity.' She smiles broadly.

'Can anyone verify that?'

Maya sighs. 'Most of Dewbow. But if you want specifics, ask Rob Samuels, the butcher, and a fellow director of the board. Plenty of pics on our Facebook page too.'

The intercom buzzes and Rachel's voice comes through. 'Ms Smith, your eleven o'clock is here.'

Diana stands. 'We appreciate your time in helping us with our inquiry.'

Maya smiles and strides over to the glass door, holding it open as a flustered Robertson gathers up his anorak, pen and pad.

'Glad to be of help, detective. Let's hope you catch this killer soon. Must be a lot of pressure on you.'

Diana nods, mumbling, 'And thanks again for …'

'No problem. But be careful: those stags mean business!'

* * *

Outside on the pavement, Robertson fumbles, putting his notepad in his inside pocket.

'Stags?'

Diana sighs. 'She's my neighbour, Robertson. Lives in the big Dewbright Hall in my village. I nearly got gored by a stag while out on a run, and she shot it.'

'You were shot at?'

'No – the stag. It was her land. Technically, I was trespassing.'

'Wow.' He looks back at the office. 'Quite an accomplished woman, Ms Smith, eh?' He points at the initials 'RI' after her accountancy accreditations on the gold plaque. 'What's the RI stand for?'

'Responsible Individual.'

'What's she responsible for?'

Diana snorts. 'Everything.'

He stares, confused.

'She's the trusted investigator.' She looks back at the office. 'Maybe she should be doing my job.'

Chapter 23

Saturday 9th October, 2010 – Dewbow

This case is taking her through files of accounts, statements, transcripts, profiles, trying to find one loose thread. Her head's in bits after Marchant pulled the plug on her – just when she's getting some traction. Lawton's trying to convince the team of his OCG theory. Diana gets back to her cold, forlorn cottage at eight forty in the morning, runs a hot bath, wakes up in a tepid one, the cold tap dripping on her left toe, skin crumpled to a prune. Towelling herself roughly, she pulls on a random oversized T-shirt and curls under the duvet, yanking down the blackout blinds with her left hand. Her last thought: *Where's that bloody filing cabinet key? Who would have one? Someone from school …*

The whoops of kids kicking leaves wake her at three-thirty. Her head's buzzing, deeper thoughts and questions having pushed their way up like plants in her sleep. Peeking out through the blinds, she realises she missed most of a brisk, bright day, the last of the sun now streaming through the beech trees. Five days since her last run. No space to think. Just Marchant's hawkish hover, the greedy eyes and sneers of Lawton and Neville. The shadow of Phillips pushing into this case. Stress may be keeping her on her feet, but not on her *toes*.

Gulping down a glass of water, she grabs her keys from the kitchen table and heads out.

183

The lane's empty apart from one pepper-haired woman ushering a toddler and squalling child into a Land Rover. Diana pounds down the main road, over the stile and up the muddy path to the steep woodland, trees lying at ridiculous angles to counter north-easterlies, their silhouettes stark against the pinking horizon. A shoal of starlings flicker and wave over the sky. Beyond them, a constant sentinel, the lone sparrowhawk circles, focusing on a space at the crest of the woodland, its random screams echoing over the skies.

The hill's hard on her calves. Her thighs tighten, head down, eyes fixed on the tracks of deer and the occasional dogwalker. Tufts of couch grass, half-filled rabbit holes in the peat, bared roots threatening to snap her ankle. Last thing she needs is crutches right now. A pheasant bolts into the scrub. Another scream from the sparrowhawk.

Diana plugs her heels in, her legs taking her onward to the granite up-thrustings, the crag, the edge, to the spot where Leroy Young's car had been found. The shadow of its presence remains in the outline of green grass and leaf banks, the tread marks of the tyres, the flat dark earth where the car had been. The CSI team plus herself and Robertson had combed the area. Yet she still feels something's missing. Why had he parked up here on the ridge? What could he see from here? Or who was he hiding from? Was Daniels with him? Did he kill him or see who did?

Where is he?

Diana peers over the stone wall where the land drops away at a ridiculously steep angle. Too steep for a casual country walk, too steep if you're thinking of walking back up again, even for a fit man like Leroy Young. She looks down at the copse. Maybe he *wasn't* thinking of walking back up. No. The presents and roses. She remembers as a detective sergeant a grim case of a dogwalker out in Stocksbridge being hit on the head by a cervical bone. That was before the skull fell. Some suicide had roped himself high up in the tall chestnut years before. It became a national forensics case, working out the guy's DNA. Turned out to be a jilted ex-con.

Scout the woodland just in case.

The whole point of living out here in the sleepy sticks is to escape the job. She moved down here after the split from Keith

184

Phillips. *Yeah right.* There's no escape. She kicks the ground savagely and a buried cig end sticks to the toe of her shoe. She uses a leaf to flick it off. It could be anyone's. And she hazards a guess that a PE teacher doesn't smoke. *But his missus does* ... She has two clear plastic bags in her pocket – a habit now. She bags the cig end, ties a knot at the top of the bag, shoves it in her tracksuit pocket and opens the gate to walk down the steep, muddy incline.

Once under the canopy of the leafless trees, she picks up her jog, stopping every hundred yards to look up. No hanging limbs. According to Robertson, Leroy Young has motive for suicide: imminent bankruptcy, wife threatening divorce, a failed affair, fraud, career down the toilet. But out here? In the woods? No suicide note? He'd have to be some angry man to do that to his wife and kid.

Above her, random squawks from the hawk, a waxing gibbous moon eager for darkness. The peaty earth treacherous, spiked with briars, broken branches. Part of a ripped antler is embedded in a Scots pine. Suddenly, the woods feel oppressive, suffocating.

Breaking out on the far side, Maya's land, there's a broad pond edging onto the back lawn. If Diana keeps within the wall bordering the woodland, she's not on private property. She keeps looking up at the trees, just in case. A squirrel darts across her path, scrabbling halfway up the trunk of an oak tree, stopping en route to glare at her.

Cheeks burning, her lungs cold and clear, her eyes focus on the impudent squirrel. She stops. The squirrel glares – but not at her; at two symmetrical holes in the trunk.

Diana prises with a stick.

A gold torpedo cartridge drops out.

Diana stares down at it. She pulls out the second plastic bag, carefully puts it in and seals it.

As soon as she gets into the house, she puts the bags on the table, snatches up her phone.

'Robertson, what you doing?'

'I'm just going through these H2H reports and ...'

'Can you get down here, take some photos? I'm not sure, but I've just found a random bullet in a tree in the woodland down

185

from where Young's car was found. I know we searched the area, but this was closer to private land. I'm going to bring it in for Marks to look at and log it up, but if you can get down here … my camera's at work. It's not necessarily suspicious as it's hunting ground, but …'

She can hear her own self-doubt crawling in as she imagines asking Lawton for a CSI team.

'Sure, Boss. Be straight down.'

'Thanks. Catch you in a bit.'

Diana holds up the plastic bags.

Out collecting random bullets and cigarette ends on her day off. Maybe she is losing the plot.

Chapter 24

SUNDAY 10TH OCTOBER, 2010 – SHEFFIELD

Legley Road Bethel Church's white building has seen better days, standing like a chipped enamel tea mug, stained with too much tea and too little care. Pouring into it, a stream of bright yellow, fuchsia, lilac hats and jackets, a shimmering prism in the last of autumn's morning sunbeams. Diana is wearing plain black slacks and a stripy shirt, a red peacoat. She's not a church-goer, but Rehema used to attend some small Baptist church in north Sheffield, and MaMa has always attended a local hut in Bagamoyu as far as Diana can recall. She's supposed to be MaMa's escort today – but really it's the other way around. Poor MaMa's been unwittingly drafted into her undercover scoping out of Legley Road Baptist. She preferred MaMa's chapel; they had drums.

She makes her way past the roadblock of bustle and greetings. A smiling round woman in a lemon suit beams at her.

'Welcome, sister! This your first time?'

'Yes.'

'Well, we hope you enjoy the service. Do sign our visitors' book.'

Diana is directed towards a large volume open on a trestle table. She'll wait on a comment. She's here to check out the Legley Road community and Mary Calley's family situation – or rather, the Pastor Calley and Doris Thompson situation. See if any familiar names or faces bob up.

Inside, the small church is full. Diana takes a back pew, as close as possible to the side exit and close to the ladies' toilets for MaMa, who sits down beside her. Diana's eyes are on the ones up and down like engine pistons, the stooped figure of Pastor Calley, assisted to the front pew. The choir bubbles away at the side with an angular man waving limbs like drumsticks in a two-size-too-big navy suit. There's a band of ragged drums, two guitarists, an electric piano, and three buxom women slamming tambourines against thighs that vibrate far louder. Mrs Thompson hobbles past, in a lilac suit. She smiles at Diana but moves on.

Thank the Lord indeed.

Diana inwardly panics. *Please do not be some wacky Pentecostal affair with all that bodies-dropping palava.* The thought of Marchant's face if she adds this to the Key Development Log makes her smile. She looks sideways down her pew: a white couple in their fifties leaning over to speak to a smartly dressed Asian couple. In front of her, a young family with three children being fed bits of apple from a Tupperware container by a woman with two Rice Krispies stuck in the back of her ponytail.

Then a tall black woman walks along a pew and up the rest of the aisle, dressed in a tangerine gown, yellow and turquoise headwrap. The crowd parts, seats are taken. The choir – and MaMa – start singing, 'Blessed be the Rock'. Despite herself, Diana's swept up by the rapid rhythm.

A wizened black man, in a bottle-green suit so old it shines, starts to speak: 'We are so glad to see our Pastor Calley recovering and able to join in worship this morning. And we are grateful to have our sister Lubanzi Kuhle to share a message from the Lord today. Parents, please take children to my left where our Sunday School teachers and crèche ladies will collect.'

A mass exodus of toddlers. Lanky teens huddle in clusters around the back doors.

Diana sneaks out to the empty foyer while the green suit prays. Flicks through the visitors' book, using her finger to train her eyes on the printed names, dates.

An old woman potters out to the toilet. Diana picks up a pen and signs off 'DW' and the date. Re-entering church while heads are bowed, she scrawls dates and names on her hand in biro.

Pastor Calley's head swerves left to right, an unwilling hostage, picking at his fingers as if there's hardened glue on them. Lubanzi beams at the elderly compère, walking regally over to the lectern with a big floppy black leather Bible, gold-edged pages. She props it on the lectern, bending to take up a glass of water. She drinks it halfway, the congregation watching in silence as if this is the full message. Then she opens up the Bible, bows her head. Looks up.

'Good morning, church. Today I have a very short message, but, I feel, it is a very important one. Let's turn to John 4.'

There's a rustling of pages.

'"Now, Jesus learned that the Pharisees had heard that he was gaining and baptising more disciples than John – although, in fact, it was not Jesus who baptised but his disciples. So he left Judea and went back once more to Galilee." That is a long walk, my friends. Fifty-five miles is hard on the feet, even for a fit man in his early thirties.

'"Now he had to go through Samaria. So he came to a town in Samaria called Sychar, near the plot of ground Jacob had given to his son, Joseph. Jacob's well was there, and Jesus, tired as he was from the journey, sat down by the well. It was about noon." (It is hot – no time to be walking and without water.)

'"When a Samaritan woman came to draw water, Jesus said to her, 'Will you give me a drink?'" (His disciples had gone into the town to buy food.) "The Samaritan woman said to him, 'You are a Jew and I am a Samaritan woman. How can you ask me for a drink?'" (For Jews do not associate with Samaritans.) "Jesus answered her, 'If you knew the gift of God and who it is that asks you for a drink, you would have asked him and he would have given you living water …'"'

Diana is still looking at the scribbled dates on her palm. She looks around the chapel, women's eyes trained on Lubanzi's every gesture, frowning, scrutinising their Bibles, reading glasses clicking on and off ears. To the far side, nods, 'Hmmmhmm's, 'Preach', gentle affirmations. Stony-faced men. Pastor Calley leaning to one side, his face distorted into a scowl. A partially bald man two rows in front is humming, just low enough to deflect Lubanzi's clear words.

'"… many of the Samaritans from that town believed him because of the woman's testimony: 'He told me everything I ever did.'"'

Lubanzi inhales deeply. Ten beats. She closes her eyes. Finally, opening them, she speaks: 'This is the first female missionary – the first evangelist, long, long before the commissioned apostles. This woman, a fallen, marginalised Palestinian woman is the first to believe Jesus Christ was the Messiah. Scripture says it.'

Lubanzi prods the black book defiantly. Diana hears gasps and grunts from pews in front of her. Pastor Calley looks catatonic, like a rigid broken coat hanger. The humming grows louder.

'It is she who immediately went and told her neighbours. She did not wait. She did not wait for the disciples to approve her. She did not wait till her bucket from the well was filled so she could go back to her normal tasks. No. This woman ran straight back to her town where she was notorious. Everyone knew she slept around.'

Shaking heads. Humming man stops to clear throat before resuming.

'Everyone knew she had had not one, not two, not three – but *five* former husbands. And the man she was currently living with was not her husband. This was long before the text message, newspaper, satellite TV, internet. There was no way, *no way*, an Israelite could know a Samaritan's business. He would not *deign* to share the same breathing space! So here was Jesus, exhausted from a hundred-mile round trip, stopping for a drink from a well – not just any well, it was *his* well – his forefather Jacob had made it. It was rightfully his, yet here was this foreigner taking water. Jesus himself when he lived on earth was a Palestinian Jew displaced from his own land. He was chased out as a baby into Egypt by a ruthless Jewish king who feared him, a baby, taking over, King Herod who massacred every firstborn male. Israel was a colony of Rome, occupied by foreigners. And the dispossessed Jesus was thirsty.'

She wishes someone would throw a book at the humming man.

'Jesus's approach to women was revolutionary. He saw them with intrinsic value equal to that of men. Notice that none of the disciples dare say, "Why are you talking to her?" so when Jesus was speaking to her it was as an *equal*, with courtesy and respect. He did not shield her from uncomfortable truths. Jesus saw her first and foremost as a human being. He considered women in terms of their relation – or lack of one – to God. He refers to women as daughters and, even when he hung on the cross, he still cared for his own mother and made sure she had a "son" who could look after her. The first person he appeared to after his resurrection was a woman. He revealed to them the truth of sin, but he cared enough to help them overcome it, to forgive and accept them. He, more than any movement on this planet, uplifted and freed women. Tell me, please, where in the Bible does it say, "What you need, sister, is a good man?" or "And Jesus said unto her: Go and get you a husband and I shall forgive you" or "Return to the man who beats and rapes you and be ye healed"?'

The pews are silent – apart from the humming man.

A woman screams out: 'Nowhere!'

'Yes, sister! Correct. Brothers and sisters, I want you to prayerfully reflect on our Bible reading today and to consider these three things: who *is* this man who owns a well yet asks for a cup of water in occupied territory? Who *is* this man who saves a village through an encounter with one outcast woman? And, lastly, do *you* know him?'

Diana scoots to the end of the pew, hissing to MaMa she's going to the loo.

Putting her key in the ignition, Diana sighs. MaMa belts up, humming to herself. Well, Pastor Calley on his last legs. There are no names she recognises in the visitors' book – although that doesn't mean Mary didn't attend. Diana had made a note of the last visitors between 2008 and August 2010: literally four. R Abdali, Georgina Hitchcock, M Johnson (three times), and a Martha Molloy.

Well, that told her not much. She could have had her lie-in.

'That was a good worship, *mwana*. The book club lady speaks well. Thank you.' MaMa nods.

191

Diana smiles. 'Glad you enjoyed it, MaMa.'

Not a wasted morning after all.

'I'll drop you off at Ma's. See you later for dinner. Need to pop into the station.'

Several hours later, Diana smells the aroma of cinnamon as she enters Rehema's kitchen, pushing the door closed with her hip. Rehema frowns at the scattering of water over the table.

'Why don't you just put your hood up?'

Diana hangs her waxed jacket on the back of a kitchen chair. Rehema turns back to where she is dishing rice onto three plates.

'Because I'm not ten? Have you made apple crumble?'

She grins at the golden crusted pie dish, but Rehema's back is to her still.

'It stop raining after you ten?'

'I think that's when it started.' She looks at the three plates. 'It's pissing—'

A steely look from Rehema over a steaming colander.

'—banging it down.'

Diana stares at Rehema's back as she ladles dahl from a steep iron pan. 'You OK, Ma?'

Rehema nods but doesn't turn.

'How was London?'

'Fine.'

Pulling teeth. What's up with her?

'How did MaMa's deposition at Leigh Day go?'

Rehema turns, avoiding Diana's eyes, bringing two plates to the table.

'She says nothing to me. You're the one who took her to church this morning. In fact, go call her for her dinner.'

Diana stands up, approaches Rehema, who turns back to the counter to fetch the last plate.

'Not until you tell me what's up.'

Rehema's dark eyes are full, fierce, ready to burst open in either fury or tears. She pulls off her striped pinny, hangs it behind the kitchen door.

'This bloody investigation! It's nothing to do with poor Mary; it's about you, Diana. Resenting my friends.'

192

'It's not resentment – it's concern. While you and your cosy book group sip wine and chat about some made-up story, I'm cheek-by-jowl with the reality each day. You all talk all night about justice, but none of you stepping up to make it happen,' Diana snaps.

Rehema slams the cutlery drawer.

'Why don't you *step up* and take some responsibility for your own family then? Like take MaMa to live with you? Your version of justice isn't doing any of the women *I* know any good.'

Diana wants to scream but instead her lungs collapse into the distance between her and Rehema – a chasm words can't cross. Half of her aches for her mother, who spins in a black hole, deprived of her history; the other rages at the woman who caught her up in this limbo.

'Go get MaMa. She needs to eat.'

MaMa appears at the door, a slight shadow that floods the space around her with a latent radiance, her face exploding into a smile on seeing Diana. She loosens her red shawl and holds out her sinewy brown arms. Diana hugs her tightly.

'MaMa, I'm getting you all wet. You're ten days early with your Manshujaa shawl!'

The embrace seems to crack some warmth into the room. Rehema sits alone at the table, pouring water into a tumbler.

'Let's eat. MaMa say grace.'

MaMa sits one side, Diana the other. MaMa bows her head.

'Thank you, Father, for this day, this family, this food. Bless us in Jesus's name.'

Family. Yeah, right. Diana opens her eyes; Rehema's glaring at the window.

'Amen.'

The silence is eaten in mouthfuls interrupted with scrapes of plates, gulps of water, appreciative mumblings. MaMa finally puts her spoon down on the plate and looks at Diana.

'*Mwana*, I would like very much to stay with you.'

Rehema stops, fork midway to mouth. She swallows. Diana looks from Rehema to MaMa.

'What's going on?'

Rehema pushes her chair back, collects plates in a snatching sweep, back turned, heading to the dishwasher.

'MaMa does not want to stay in her customised rooms.'

'Yeah. I get that. But …'

A cacophony of cutlery crashing, cupboard doors slamming, a silent scream in splinters.

'It'll be good for you both. And me.'

Diana flounders.

Her case.

'MaMa, I'd love to have you, but I'm barely home. Sometimes, I work nights …'

'I know, *mwana*,' says MaMa.

Rehema stares out of the window, breathing deeply. Finally, she turns, her face drained.

'City life's not for MaMa. She'll be happier in the country, able to get out.'

Diana looks at her mum, examining her. Then at MaMa, this solitary, worn, tired woman in the red shawl. Stranded at a table in a home she cannot connect to. In a land far from her own, distanced from her blood even after a meal. Lost. Unknown to her daughter. Unknown to her granddaughter. This wonderful triumph of humanity treated like a leftover relic instead of a woman alive. Real. *Now.*

'Pack your bag, MaMa. Let's rock and roll,' Diana says. She stoops to whisper to MaMa while winking at Rehema: 'I prefer sleeping on my sofa anyway.' Diana stands up. 'She'll soon be back here, Ma! Not many humans can cope with my mess and muddle.'

MaMa gets up. 'You not muddled, *mwana*. Straight as an arrow.'

Rehema sniggers: 'A wonky arrow.'

Diana shrugs on her coat, looking at her watch. 'I need to go to HQ. You'll have to bring MaMa down if she wants to come tonight. Put on the heating.'

Rehema approaches Diana, looking like she wants to kiss her, her eyes relieved, grateful, whispering: 'It's just till the Commission Report, Diana.'

'I don't need heating!' shouts MaMa.

Diana looks at her own dead fingers. 'Well, I do.'

* * *

194

Diana bolts for her car, jacket over her head in the drilling October rain. From inside, she stares at the front door, yellow light in MaMa's room above. These two mighty matriarchs can face anything – apart from each other.

She starts the engine, pulling off.

Chapter 25

MONDAY 11TH OCTOBER, 2010 – DEWBOW

MaMa picks up Lubanzi's copy of *The Book of Night Women* from Diana's hall table.

'You didn't give this back.'

'I know. Forgot. Can you give it to Ma?'

MaMa nods, flicking through it slowly. Diana feels bad that MaMa will still have to be shuffled back and forth like lost luggage, but she has appointments – all still based in Sheffield, and Rehema's still in charge of co-ordinating them. 'They all love stories. Especially the tall one—'

'Who? Maya?'

MaMa nods. 'Only she wants to *tell* a story.'

Diana scrolls down her phone. Two missed calls from Robertson, one from Gorman.

'Maya barely speaks, MaMa!'

MaMa shrugs, running a finger along the condensation on the windowsill. 'I don't read much now. My eyes ache.'

Diana is desperate to call. She sighs. 'But you can listen.'

'Listening is reading.'

Man. Making small talk with MaMa is nigh impossible. Nothing is ever small for MaMa.

'Thought you slept through book club? I read nothing but

196

crime reports and statistics, MaMa. And a rate comic book that is,' she mutters.

'Yes.'

I need to get on the phone.

'Well, you don't need to go if you don't like the women.'

'I didn't say I didn't like them.'

Diana squeezes her eyes tightly. A day wading through council spreadsheets suddenly seems very inviting.

MaMa sits down at the kitchen table. Diana zips up her coat.

'Can you make *githeri* today, MaMa?'

'Now?'

'No – for tea.'

'Tea?' MaMa moves to the kettle.

Diana sighs. 'To eat.'

MaMa sits back down. 'When?'

'Whenever.'

'When is that, *mwana*?'

'Your time.'

MaMa nods slowly, turning to look out of the kitchen window.

An hour later, at HQ, Diana knocks on Gorman's door.

'Come in!'

He pulls his glasses off and gives her a brief nod, half rising out of his seat.

'Morning, Will. Sorry to bother you. I just …'

She pulls out the freezer bag containing the gold torpedo.

'I found this lodged in a tree on my run on Saturday in the woodland by my place. It's within a mile of where we found Leroy Young's car. Could you check ballistics – see if it's similar to the bullet that ended our Mr Daniels?'

'Don't you live in the Peak District?'

Diana nods. Gorman frowns, takes the freezer bag, and looks at it closely, holding it lightly. It seems to have the same effect on him as it did the squirrel.

'Off the record, a point 308 Win cartridge. I don't think it's a 7.62 NATO. But I'll double-check.'

Diana bites her lip, stays standing by the door. He winks at her.

'I'll also check if any residue indicates it being shot from the same gun. Although it won't be the same bullet!'

She grins broadly. 'Just wanted to eliminate …'

'Examine every option.' He nods.

'Thanks, Will!' She practically bounces out of the office.

Stick that in your OCG, Phillips.

Sheffield Local Education Authority is housed in a multi-storey building that looms over the Bullring, an ugly, functional structure, casting a giant shadow over the subway abyss. The badge is received with cautious nods and Robertson and Diana are taken to an airless room centred by a small table, more filing cabinets, and a bulky IBM monitor. A lumpen woman in a tight mint-green blouse brings in a box of black ring binders, stuffed with invoices.

'You're welcome to look. We were audited just a year ago and passed with flying colours. I run a very tight ship here, detective.' She folds her arms, lurid lipstick lips pressed tightly together. Diana lifts a folder, looking up.

'How long have you been admin manager at the LEA, Ms Clarke?'

'Twelve year now. Worked at council since I left college. Anything else you need?'

Robertson pulls up a chair to the bench holding the IBM monitor and a battered keyboard. 'To get logged on, please.'

Ms Clarke reddens, crouches over the keyboard, tapping.

'There you go. Like I said, everything's in order.' Ms Clarke loiters by the door. 'Ladies down the corridor to the right. Gents to the left. Vending machine next to photocopier and printer.'

'Where were the keys from Legley Road kept?'

'Excuse me?'

'The keys. That were handed in.'

'Oh, they were all submitted as part of the closing audit.'

'And then returned?'

'Yes – but then they were passed on to the purchaser.'

'Mr Thomlins?'

She shrugs. 'Probably his solicitor. I'll get Victoria to email you the confirmation of receipt, if you need it.'

'Thanks.'

'My extension's 1513.'

Diana, head in a folder, nods.

Three hours, four vending Nescafés later, Robertson calls over to Diana.

'Boss.'

Diana peers over his bulky shoulder as he pulls up a receipt of the new curriculum funding.

She says: 'Print that. And the autumn term's income/expenditure spreadsheets. Spring term's too. Let's find what happened to this money.'

Robertson pushes his head closer to the screen, frowning.

'Scroll down. Maybe it's at end.'

He scrolls.

'Nothing deposited near the twenty thousand for the new curriculum. Plenty going out though.'

'Try Spring Term 2008.'

The printer starts rattling and churning next door. Footsteps on the lino outside. Muffled voices, post-weekend banter.

Diana pulls up from her stoop, stretching her back out. 'Where's it gone then?'

'There's six hundred cash withdrawal here. Not sure where it goes though ...'

She frowns. 'Twenty grand? Why's it on none of these spreadsheets?'

'Dunno, Boss.'

Diana's eyes narrow. 'Just disappeared into the carpet along with Mary Calley.'

Chapter 26

WEDNESDAY 13TH OCTOBER, 2010 – SYPD HQ, SHEFFIELD

Diana's paperclip chain is getting quite impressive. She leans back to admire the two-foot-long necklace before wrapping it around her empty desk tidy. Even her files are almost in order. She checks her drawers. Flexes her fingers, frowning at her flaky nails and raw knuckles. She must get some hand cream or something. She leans back in her chair and sighs. Robertson's spent most of the day peering at endless CCTV footage of Abbeydale Road from outside Tesco's. Diana shakes her head; he never seems to get bored of *anything*. He could watch a kettle boil with fascination – in fact, she's seen him. Which makes her even sadder: watching someone watch a kettle boil.

Two days of diddly-squat but paperwork, revisiting transcripts, trying to pace things together to fit Lawton's theory. Nothing does. They'd investigated both Geoff Thomlins and his solicitor: all the keys submitted have been put into a safe, still in the LEA sealed package. But yes, the Local Education Authority did pass them on.

Robertson comes over with a print-out and some kind of hand-drawn Venn diagram. Diana looks up.

'The filing cabinet key analysis! Awesome.'

'Victoria sent the email and I did my best – tallying up the LEA report with the auditor's and what Thomlins' solicitor gave

200

me. Most of the filing cabinets have already been taken to the scrapyard and are now sheet metal. But there were sixteen in the school ...'

'So sixteen keys?'

He nods. 'Decades ago, yes, but only three were handed in by the heads of department, nine still in the filing cabinets – taken out and added to the collection – and four missing.'

Diana inspects Robertson's intersecting circles and figures.

'Four missing keys. And both Bruno and Axmed maintain there was no key in the filing cabinet and it was unlocked on Monday 30th August.'

'I did try to find the actual keys, but—'

Diana smiles, shakes her head. 'I can't see anyone classing them as vital when the stuff's going to be scrapped.'

She sighs and leans on the desk, resting her chin in her hand and frowning at the figures.

'So, whoever placed Daniels' head in the filing cabinet must have either kept the filing cabinet key—'

'A student or staff member?'

Diana shrugs. 'Or had access to the whole collection of keys. But they would also need to know which key fitted what, and there's nothing here to identify any of these keys to specific filing cabinets.'

Lawton enters the office, closely followed by Neville. Robertson walks back to his desk and gives him a cautious nod. Diana notes it from the corner of her eye.

'What's up, Robertson? Any news regarding drug distribution at Legley Road?'

Robertson shakes his head. 'Not really.'

'So, what you doing then? Bean-counting again?'

Neville chuckles.

'Filing cabinet keys, actually,' Robertson mutters.

'Smashing. The public can rest safe in their beds tonight then.'

Lawton shakes his head, Robertson blushes, and Diana's eyes narrow.

'Stick to the brief, Robertson.'

'He is,' Diana pipes up. 'The filing cabinet is a major lead, and we need to work out who had access to keys.'

201

Lawton acts as if she never spoke, and is already on the phone.

Diana picks up her paperclip necklace. The filing cabinet key went missing at some point in the chain.

Eliminate, eliminate. She picks up Robertson's Venn diagram. There are several possible suspects, but so far no realistic motive or lead.

She bites her tongue, her gut instinct hissing: *It's not here. Go back to Mary.*

Two weeks of wondering whether she's got the bottle to report Phillips – and what would happen if she did.

That's a line of thought she does *not* want to pursue right now.

Only one option then.

She jolts upright.

Just like the murderer. *Only one option.*

Chapter 27

THURSDAY 14TH OCTOBER, 2010 – BRIEFING ROOM, SHEFFIELD

Diana winces at the murder wall, blowing on her hands. Sitting on a desk that wobbles, she opens a manilla folder. Lawton and Neville enter with brews in matching Sheffield Wednesday mugs. O'Malley, Robertson and Khan appear. Robertson carries in two Styrofoams, passing one to Diana.

'Thanks.' She attempts a sip but it's scalding.

Lawton nods at Diana. 'Give us the evidence update, Walker.'

'OK. So far: an acrylic fingernail, our tagger Axmed Ahmed, an empty spray can, one moved filing cabinet. One dysfunctional school. An abandoned car belonging to a MisPer, former head of PE, Leroy Young. The decapitated head of former headmaster John Daniels. And his left arm and fist. The rest of him found in a binbag behind a greenhouse three weeks' later. Oh, and a missing filing cabinet key.'

Lawton raises his eyebrows. 'House-to-house revealing anything? Or just an old fella hearing a rattled can? Where's the murder weapon?'

Shuffles and mumbling.

Diana coughs. 'I found a rifle bullet in a tree when out on my run …'

Lawton looks at her, incredulous. 'And I saw a dead pigeon outside the offy. Not relevant, Walker.' He shakes his head.

'Gorman seems to think it is. The ballistics …'

'Walker, it's yet another random goose chase. Please tell me any logical reason why a random rifle bullet has owt to do—'

'Robertson took photos … it's barely a mile from where we found Young's car.'

'Oh, so you've got DS Robertson chasing your goose 'n' all? Fantastic. We already searched the area round his car. Nothing.'

Robertson shrugs at Diana, who grips the edge of the desk to stop herself punching it.

'No. Leroy's done a runner. This blanket community silence indicates some intimidation. OCG tactics.'

Diana says: 'Possibly. But it was Bank Holiday weekend. Folk may have been away on holiday, or …'

'Pissed,' mutters O'Malley. Khan half smiles, nods. 'Hungover.'

Diana scrutinises the list of houses in her manilla folder.

'Some were away in September. Have we done them all now?'

Neville coughs. 'There was number 64. Old woman, Mrs Beck. On a cruise in September. Just got back. Says she remembers seeing a black jeep a couple of nights a week before she left. She was a bit concerned about being burgled while away, so asked lady next door to go in, close curtains, put on a light each neet.'

'Do we have details about this black jeep?'

Neville looks at Lawton who clears his throat, as if on cue: 'I want that jeep's model, serial number, registration plate, mileage … whatever. What time, when she saw it. There must be one house, one business between here and London Road with CCTV. A speed camera. Owt. Get it.' Lawton puts down his mug. 'Black jeep. Tagger. Possible fraud. Execution style homicide framed to send a message. It *reeks* of Ryan Pierce and his OCG. We will need to liaise with DI Phillips' undercover op regarding the OCG unit and Drugs Squad.'

Diana frowns. 'We need to find Leroy Young. It's clear there was some altercation between him and the deceased Mary Calley. Her death may not be officially suspicious but her sudden leaving of Legley Road *is*. As is Leroy Young and Daniels' resolving their debt problems straight after she left. And the fact that Young appears to have been crashing at Daniels' flat but hasn't been back nor heard of since Bank Holiday weekend.'

Lawton shakes his head.

Diana sticks the photo of Leroy Young's BMW to the right of the one of John Daniels' smiling head – before it was severed from his body. She sticks a photo of the filing cabinet underneath Young's and the orange spray can photo next to the cabinet. She picks up a blue board marker and scrawls: 'Mary Calley's national Curriculum £?'

'No photo of that,' chuckles Lawton.

'Maybe because it's missing. We went through LEA budgets, spending and income. The money was sent out by Acorn To Tree trust. The cheque was deposited but it appears Daniels "purchased the books"' – she wiggles her forefingers – 'without either a delivery note or receipt according to the assistant bursar, Aaliyah Matthews. That's effectively twenty grand AWOL.'

She swoops the zeros on the board next to a large question mark.

'Robertson?' asks Lawton.

Robertson clears his throat, shuffles his papers.

'Plus plenty of petty cash withdrawals for sports fixtures, books, various ad hoc events. From January 2008, they were labelled under LEA Bonus for Curriculum Development.'

'Nothing to the library or English budget?'

'No.'

'Or on the school's ledger? What about the accounts girl, Matthews?'

Robertson shakes his head. 'Checked all bank accounts. Plus Aaliyah Matthews left before the spreadsheet was created or cheque cashed. There was a gap of a few weeks before a new bursar was appointed. The last email to Matthews from Daniels on the school system indicated she had left without handing in the bursary keys to the office, so he said he would call round to her flat to collect them after the school staff party.'

'She could have siphoned the money first,' Neville mutters.

'I checked. The books weren't touched during the Christmas holidays and the office confirmed Daniels passed them the keys before the school was locked up at end of autumn term.'

'There's nothing there formally, but there was some email mentioning a reconfiguring of the curriculum in the light of the possible Ofsted. Different priorities required a different strategy and a different curriculum.'

'Wouldn't Ofsted have picked that up?' Lawton frowns.

Diana shrugs. 'Why? It's the head's job to reappropriate funds to meet needs of the school. And there's no fraud at LEA level. Everything above board there. The award came from an independent educational NGO.'

Neville raises his eyebrows. 'Bet they're mad. That'd be motive enough.'

Lawton yawns. 'The money was still used for curriculum. No crime.'

Robertson interrupts. 'Daniels was in debt for fourteen grand, Young for ten. And nine thousand went from Daniels' personal account to pay off his credit card debt in July 2008. Six thousand deposited in Young's account. In the school's books it's under Extra Curricular Development for Gifted and Talented. Which, apparently, isn't even a Local Education Authority scheme. He paid off various cards, mortgage arrears.'

'And the rest?'

'That does seem to be backed by appropriate invoices or delivery notes.'

'Is that even allowed?'

Robertson shrugs. 'Apparently.'

Lawton steps forward, shaking his head. 'Come on. Headmaster gets a whopping big salary. Even head of PE and all those extra titles – bet Young were on forty grand plus. Where's it all going?'

Diana sighs. 'You got a gambling debt like Daniels or stay a player like Young, it's surprising how fast it flies.'

Lawton jams his hands in his pockets, shakes his head, feet apart.

'We've got major fraud, an execution killing to send a public message, a disaffected youth tagging the cabinet who's a known county runner for Ryan Pierce … whose own son is also pretty nifty with a butcher's knife. What if Pierce or Daniels had something over each other? Or were in collusion with Thomlins?'

Diana shakes her head. 'We urgently need to bring Ryan Pierce in to eliminate—'

But Lawton motors straight over her: 'Daniels may have fed some early info to Thomlins about the school being on its way out – he made a bid in February 2008 – way before the postponed Ofsted in May.'

Robertson shuffles his papers. 'Over several months, Daniels was paying small amounts of cash into his personal account. He withdrew six grand in May.'

Diana starts. 'Where from?'

Six grand to Leroy?

'His bank on the Moor in town.'

Lawton nods. 'That could've come from Thomlins …'

'Or Pierce,' says Neville.

Robertson says: 'Either way – his debt's already paid off. No more unaccounted for cash.'

Diana looks down at a chewing gum splodge in the carpet. 'When was he divorced?'

'Mrs Daniels served him his papers for divorce in August 2008. Their divorce was finalised this May.'

Lawton puffs out his chest. 'All leads point to a cover-up regarding the drugs distribution at school. Where are we with the CCTV footage?'

Diana says: 'Robertson's covered all up to Tesco's on the Abbeydale Road. CCTV cameras were shut down during the roadworks and auditing over the summer.'

'That's the time when you need them on!'

'No one knows where the order or action came from.'

Diana glares at a cracked polystyrene ceiling tile.

'This is a homicide. Our priorities should be finding, interviewing and eliminating – or charging – Leroy Young and Ryan Pierce, otherwise we're going round in circles. A speculative OCG angle should not take precedence over risk-of-life. We're doing three times the work and criminals are just passing through the sieve.'

'There's no speculation. This is a serious OCG network, using Pierce to set up county lines. I can't share classified info, but the OCG investigation's escalating fast. We've got technical and physical surveillance on Pierce, so he's going nowhere without us knowing. Young – well, we've put it out nationwide now and in the press. And what you on about – sieve? We're not making scones, love.' Lawton snorts. Neville sniggers. O'Malley smiles but drops it when Diana glares.

'We might as well be. The system. Us. These crimes are passing through because they've not been caught – logged, entered onto the PNC.' *Like with the FGM.*

'Nothing's logged because there was *no crime*.' Lawton shuts his eyes.

'There was nothing *investigated* – difference,' Diana snaps back. 'It's on us to do the work. Last I checked, criminals don't come with a bar code.'

Lawton gives a heavy sigh.

'OK. A bit of context for you all. Illegal firearms are being trafficked into the UK from central and eastern Europe, transiting into Ireland or France via the ferries and tunnel. Usually in vehicles delivering bulk food items. This particular OCG, codename Ting X, is receiving guns from the ferries into Liverpool.'

'What guns?' Diana frowns.

'Handguns. Ninety per cent of guns are only used once and then just – vamoosh. Disappear. Not even fired – just used to intimidate, so the National Ballistics Intelligence service and the NCA have trouble tracking them.'

'Yeah, but handguns are not—'

Lawton ignores Diana's interjection.

'It usually takes a couple of weeks in Liverpool but the gangs tend to borrow or rent them from each other. They just get one from a holder—'

'A what?' asks O'Malley.

'Holder. A gun holder. They hold the guns and take them back, quick-time, so there's no connection. Just do whatever you have to do and give it back. We have reason to believe Ryan Pierce, although a low-level Class B drug dealer, is *the* main gun holder for South Yorkshire and Derbyshire.'

'No way!' says DC Khan. 'He serves chicken.'

Lawton glares back like he'd like to serve *him* as a dumpling.

'This is Phillips' case, involving covert surveillance in both

Liverpool and Manny. Recent intel update is that there's been a shipment of handguns from Albania, consolidated at Belgium, which arrived via ferry at Liverpool last month. The undy lost track of them from there, but the Manny one found some and has reason to believe that from the Cash & Carry they got into some tubs, collected by Pierce, who is delivering or holding weapons for various OCG units across this region. That enough intel for you, Walker? No more.'

Diana squints at the board. OK, she can buy Pierce as a gun holder. It would explain Bruno's dislike of his business.

But handguns?

'I don't quite see how this is a lead for our homicide though, detective. The ballistics indicate Daniels was killed by a big bore gun, a point 308 cartridge probably, not a—'

'Ting.'

Diana looks at him. 'A pardon?'

'A handgun. Ting.'

'OK.'

'Yes, but he could have been shot first by a handgun.'

'He could have gone on holiday to Ibiza, but there's no evid—'

Lawton impatiently shakes his head. 'Handgun, rifle. Look, it was a gun and, right now, we've gone through and checked the licensed gun holders of handguns or rifles in Sheffield. Traced, interviewed. And eliminated.'

'But he wasn't shot in Sheffield. The tick and spores—'

Marchant is frowning. He clears his throat. 'Walker, Neville and Lawton are part of Phillips' OCG operation too. They're handling classified information.'

'With due respect, sir, they've not been trained. And they may have intel on Pierce, but it's not logged as a crime or on the PNC. You're talking about OCG; I'm talking about cross-county homicide, and we're having to double up on trace-interview-eliminate with half the manpower. Young's not just a MisPer; he's a wanted man. Maybe a dangerous killer on the run. Classified info is neither here nor there – I'm talking about police basics.'

Neville's eyes narrow and Lawton reddens.

'I'm not having that!' says Lawton. 'I'm a trained and qualified detective. If anyone's out of rank, it's you, Walker!'

Diana glares at the corkboard. 'I believe this case hinges on perpetrators of extreme gender violence and abuse not being brought to justice, and *we*, all of us, are failing the victims.'

'How'd you work that out?' snorts Lawton. 'Guess work and random bits of rubbish on your lonesome walks?'

'The same intuition that made the super call me in on a smelly locked filing cabinet. The same boring plod police work we do each day: trace, investigate. Look at what's left. What question to ask next, what to find, what we need to eliminate. But we can't close incomplete investigations just because we can't engage well with victims or pursue cases for them.'

Marchant looks fit to explode. 'Walker! I've warned you. You're investing too much time with non-ongoing investigations and ferreting about with community groups to no effect.'

Marchant can sweep her under the carpet, but she'll kick up a stink anyway.

'Sir, I understand, but why is Ryan Pierce not on the PNC? Or Leroy Young? We've got two vulnerable young women, one of whom became a corpse, the other permanently disabled and traumatised, living in fear she might be the next. And where's Pierce? Walking free as a bird, corrupting youth, opening a line a week, apparently running guns while waiting on a new female to ruin. All because his details are not on the PNC due to Phillips' precious OCG op.'

Even Lawton's jaw drops at such irreverence. Diana carries on: 'Plus there's no specific forensic evidence that could possibly link to an OCG retaliation or an assassination of Daniels. There are more genuine leads related to Ms Calley's constructive dismissal and her claim of domestic violence and intimidation. All these women—'

'Which women? What are you even on about?' snarls Lawton. He nods at Diana but looks at Marchant. 'Going sideways all the time, sir. There's nowt on bloody system! There's *not a crime*, Walker! No FGM, no proof of a report of domestic violence. Nowt.'

'Wrong. Her deputy head, book club members, former students, all have separate tales of her domestic abuse. We also interviewed Calley's previous neighbour, Mr Khan, who said there'd been ...'

210

Ignoring Lawton's glare and Marchant's pursed lips, she looks over at Robertson, who pulls open his file.

'Er – window-smashing, cries, raised voices during the summer of 2007. He couldn't be sure about dates – said it was ages ago. But I contacted her former landlord, Peter Tarek, who said there'd been several complaints about the noise, he'd sent her a warning letter and then she'd just upped and left without notice late autumn, leaving her furniture and a right mess for him to clear up. No forwarding address or notice given, so she didn't get her deposit back. He still pursued rent arrears through the courts, but got nowhere and then he heard it on news this year. He re-let the place February 2008 anyway. Still mad, saying he's owed money and he wasn't surprised she came to a bad end.'

'Nice chap,' Diana mutters.

'See,' Lawton gloats. 'Even neighbour and the landlord say she was a liability, and there's no police report—'

'No police report but there are 999 calls – all on her phone.'

Marchant frowns. 'They weren't followed up on?'

Neville stiffens, Lawton looks sideways.

'The duty officers were notified, but, for some reason, no follow-up.'

'Bloody hell. Who was the twat? Who was the duty officer?'

Neville is tomato red.

'It were me, but I always followed up, sir.'

'So, do you remember paying Mary Calley a visit?' asks Diana.

'How do I know? Do you know how many calls I'd get?'

'According to police log, you got the call, got the details, but didn't make the visit.'

'Stay on job, Walker! Stop sneaking around—' growls Lawton.

Marchant thumps the table. 'Enough! Both of you get a grip. I'll have a word with Phillips. See if he can share—'

Diana butts in. 'Sir, this is procedure. It's what the PNC's for, and Derbyshire Police need to—'

Marchant glares at her. 'Walker! There is an ongoing major OCG op that can't be jeopardised by lower arrests unrelated to the homicide. Both of you, get on with your jobs and stop wasting time. We've got a killer out there while you squabble over intel.'

211

Diana's bristling not because *she's* been shut down but because intelligence and analysis has. She's not got a team; she's got a war. But Marchant's right about one thing: the killer's still out there.

A phlegmy cough. 'Go liaise with Phillips, Lawton,' says Marchant.

'Will do. Let's try to get a firm lead on this money movement. Robertson, bring in the LEA's accountant and check the outgoings.' Lawton romps out of the room, followed by Neville.

Diana takes a swig of tepid dishwater coffee and spits it right back out. Marchant beckons her into his office. As she closes the door, he points his pen at her from behind his desk.

'You want to burn more bridges, Walker? Stop it!'

'Sir.'

Shutting the door as she leaves: *Yeah, I ride at dawn. With a box of Cook's matches.*

Still raging hours later, Diana barges into her cottage, throwing her bag on the sofa. Stripping off while climbing the stairs, she drags her buttoned shirt over her head. Shower on full dial, hot as she can bear to warm these frozen fingers. The steam, the hiss, the grapefruit-scented soap lather over her, trying to scrub off the stink of those maggoty bags. She steps out, rubbing a rough bath towel roughly over stinging skin. Wipes mist off the mirror. In the reflection, her eyes: large, black holes. Thin lines from her nose to her mouth. They weren't there last month. Laughing too much? *Not.* A V at the top of her nose. *Thinking too much.* Stares at her fingers. Bloodless, aching. *Remembering too much.* She runs coconut oil through her black loose curls, slathers moisturiser over the creases, long wiry limbs, and a defiantly round arse, over her flat chest and blunt pointed nipples. What did he call them? Monkey's fingers. *Yeah. Like his dick.* She thrusts open the window. Must get an extractor fitted before the black mould takes over. Another mental note to be forgotten.

Diana stares down at the greenhouse, squinting at herself stooping over the dead stalks of tomatoes. She jumps. It's one thing to forget an extractor, quite another to forget your gran's living with you. MaMa, dressed in Diana's old parka, is stuffing a

212

sack with withered, decaying stems at the greenhouse door, humming to herself. Diana smiles.

After pulling on fresh clothes, she trots downstairs to the kitchen. The plughole is visible, courtesy of MaMa. Diana makes two brews.

She carries the mugs outside.

'Here you go, MaMa. Looks like you've earned a brew.'

MaMa jolts. Her round cheeks pop over her big smile.

Diana looks around the small walled yard. 'You need to be more careful. I coulda been a burglar, MaMa.'

MaMa takes the brew. 'Your house look like it already been burgled.'

Diana blushes. 'I'm not the most domesticated. Sorry. I tend to go for a run rather than do the dishes.'

MaMa raises her eyebrows. 'Won't get a husband that way.'

Diana leans on the greenhouse door. 'That's the plan.' She winks. MaMa laughs her bell-like laugh. Diana breathes it in.

'No husband. Just vermin and disease.'

'So, I'll get a cat and a bottle of bleach.'

MaMa nods at the dead stalks. 'Bad men hard to get rid of.' She ties back a clematis with twine. 'Good ones harder to find.'

Diana looks at her watch. 'Well, I'm hunting a killer not a husband right now.'

Although they are often one and the same.

She pecks MaMa on one cool, soft brown cheek. 'So glad you're here, MaMa. You OK? Not lonely?'

MaMa shakes her head. 'I'm in heaven, *mwana*. Fresh air. Peace. Being able to be useful. Your mum makes me feel like an invalid.'

Diana takes MaMa's mug. 'Aw. Mum likes to look after folk. Just roll with it. She does love you, y'know?'

MaMa looks up at the darkening sky. 'It's cold now. I'll come in. Are you back tonight?'

'I don't know, MaMa. Be very late.' Diana looks down at the mugs, tips out her dregs on the dead roses. 'I'm a disappointing granddaughter, a lousy host, a useless friend, a deviant daughter.' Mutters to herself: 'And a demoted SIO.'

MaMa's eyes pour over her. She shakes her head. 'What nonsense is this?'

'Ma doesn't like me being police, MaMa.'

MaMa snaps off rose deadheads. 'She grew up in their lies.'

Diana blows on her fingers.

MaMa frowns. 'You have no blood?'

Diana snorts. 'Tends to leave me when I have a case. Out of sympathy for the victim, I reckon.'

Although her sympathy for Daniels is growing less by the day.

Chapter 28

Friday 15th October, 2010 – Park Hill, Sheffield

Bruno

Mum stands by kitchen window, sucking life out of her cig, her coffee going cold on table.

'But why Dewbow?'

I zip up my Adidas jacket. 'Pays me better. I like the country. Gives me a break from *him*.'

I know she knows it's none of them reasons. But she raises her eyebrows anyway.

'Can't fault you for that.' She stubs cig out, coughing.

'You need to stop smoking.'

'Tell me what I need when you pay my bills.'

I laugh. 'You still wunt listen.'

She pushes out her bottom lip. 'True.' Gives me a wink. 'You're a good kid, Bruno. Enough lads round here running for him.'

I zip up my backpack.

'More fool them.'

'You could have more money than butchering.'

'You suggesting it?'

I need to know. She just stares at me. Then down at her chipped nails.

'No, love. Just admiring you.'

Nowt to admire. I just like to remind him he's no big man to me. I know he's shifting weight and he never helped me or Mum out. Hundred a month. Joker. Thinks he's Mother Teresa because he's got me slaving. One good chance 'n' I'm outta there.

She whispers: 'You're not grassing, are you? I mean, not that I blame you but ...'

'Fk off.'

'I'm sorry, love. I didn't mean ...'

'What you say it for then? I'll see you later.'

Door slam.

My stomach's still tight by time I get to the Hut. Not in the mood for shit today. I snap at everyone I serve.

'What's up with you, mardass?'

'Five fifty,' I say.

'Service with a smile, please.'

'McDonald's down road, bro,' I say.

Ryan appears. Nods sideways at me. 'Oi. Out here.'

I go into kitchen, ready for an earful. Ready to spit back.

'You want to peel onions all day?'

I shrug. He knocks me behind the ear. 'Be nice else you coming in van with me to Manchester. Not having you scare customers off.'

'Put me on onion duty.'

He looks at me. Shakes his bald head, pointing with his inky finger. He goes out front door, faffing about in his van. He's mighty precious about those tubs of onions.

I go through to serve last customer and Aamiina walks in. No make-up. Wearing a yellow hoodie, plain black headscarf. Looks about twelve. Her eyes glisten, dark shadows under them.

Tasha chirps up: 'Alright, love? What you want?'

Mina looks at me.

'It's OK, Tasha. She's a mate.'

Tasha gives me eye roll that says otherwise.

'What's up, Mina? Not got halal in today.'

'I know.' She looks around. 'It's Axmed.'

I look outside. Ryan's getting in the driver's seat, glaring at me.

'One minute.' I wait while he drives off and close the door to the kitchen.

'Me dad's going mental. They say I've got to get his mates to bring him home.'

'Mina, I told you. Not seen him for time.' It's true.

Her eyes fill.

'Aabe's gonna send him back. Me too.'

Sake. I lift up the counter lid. Give her a shoulder hug. She starts sobbing.

'It'll be alright. Look I'll find him. Have a word.'

Three youths come in and an older woman.

'Gotta go,' I hiss. She nods. Pulls back.

'Tasha!' I yell. 'Alright, mate. What you want?'

Mina leaves, head down.

I spoon jerk chicken into Styrofoam boxes, trying to work out what to do. Not sure if I can.

'She ya gyal?' Tasha gives me side eye.

'No!' I screw up my face. Maybe a bit too much as Tasha smirks.

'Right,' she says, nodding at the onions she pushes towards me, as if they told her different.

Diana

Briefing room. It smells – everything smells – of those rotten bags of maggoty limbs. No matter how much she washes, it's in her clothes, her skin, her nails, her own bones. Phillips enters. Diana picks furiously at a flaky desk veneer with her Bic biro.

No preliminaries from Phillips: 'Creamfields – Ryan defo running drugs. Contact in Manchester for pills and weed. No evidence *yet* that he's moved onto the harder stuff, but defo evidence he's holding handguns. We've got technical surveillance and trackers on some on 'em, with the aim of them coming into the warehouse and going out with Ryan's van. He's got a lot of the youngers running for him, part of a bigger network: Nottingham, Manchester, Derby. It's crucial we have no swoops on Pierce without my involvement.'

Marchant frowns. 'What's the critical evidence? How close are you to taking him in?'

Phillips looks at the beaten whiteboard, clicks on a remote control which pulls up CCTV footage on a ropey screen: 'Footage from Creamfields. Drop off of some kids. We do have technical surveillance, trackers on some of the guns. Physical surveillance too, from Manchester through Sheff and down into Derby. So it should be soon.'

'Guns?' says Diana. 'We're investigating a homicide by gun-shot and still not found the weapon. If Pierce is a gun holder, runner whatever – we at least need to bring him in for an intelligence or elimination interview.'

Phillips rolls his eyes. 'Obviously, we want to get the guns off the street – but the gangs'll just re-up with new ones unless we get the evidence.'

'You wait too long, someone'll get shot. They're not wanting guns as an ornament.'

Phillips glares at her. 'Thanks for the info, Walker. I'll bear that in mind. This is a two-year op and we're just about to close in on the big cats.'

'Technical surveillance? So you're monitoring phones?'

Phillips looks over at Marchant. 'Not yet.'

Phillips turns his back, pressing play on the screen. The grainy footage shows youths toing and froing from Ryan Pierce's van at Creamfields. Catering vans receiving tubs.

Diana screws up her face: 'One of them looks familiar – our filing cabinet artist. Axmed Ahmed. He's a POI in this case.'

Marchant says, 'I don't want you putting this OCG case in jeopardy, Walker. A lot of manpower and time across several forces gone into this. It's Phillips who holds the reins.'

'Talking about the filing cabinet, where is the missing key? Who locked it between Axmed and Bruno's vandalism and the deposit of Daniels' head?'

'I reckon they're lying …' snorts Lawton.

'Risking your eye to fake an empty filing cabinet is quite a cover-up,' Diana returns. 'That key was on the list that was given to Thomlins' solicitors, but seems they didn't check the keys against the inventory before putting it in their safe. I'm sure looking through two hundred odd keys of rooms and cabinets that no longer exist is not a priority. Anyway, it's not there now and they're both adamant they haven't touched the package. Seeing as it was still sealed in the packaging from LEA and the auditors, we've no evidence to prove they have removed any keys.'

'So, it must be …'

'Either someone at the school, auditors or LEA,' Diana says.

'Who could be working for the OCG …' smirks Phillips.

Here we go.

Phillips' phone buzzes. 'Excuse me, I have to take this now.' He holds up his hand, strides out of the room.

Diana hisses at Robertson: 'The OCG handgun case doesn't connect to our murder. They're just trying to shoehorn it into one.'

Robertson's face twists like he's got bad piles.

Phillips re-enters: 'We've evidence that Daniels knew drugs were being brought into school by kids. He reported it and we were investigating. Then suddenly school's closed, sold. Kids dispersed. Daniels said it was out of his hands, but Thomlins told us Daniels had told him council were going to sell the site.'

Diana shakes her head. 'That's because the LEA would have been on Daniels' case regarding the Ofsted report. Looks better if school closes due to a political strategy than because it's failing or a drug den. He wouldn't be sacked. Plus, he's massively in debt at that time. Can't afford to lose his job and needs to get his hands on some money.'

Lawton sniggers: 'Which is why he'll be in an OCG's back pocket.'

Diana looks at the board.

Shaking his head, Phillips turns to Marchant. 'More likely the cash came from Pierce or the OCG, and then when Daniels got greedy or threatened to blab again to us, they sent a clear message.'

'To who?' Diana focuses on three pigeons on the scaffolding opposite, pecking at a stale sausage roll left behind by a workman. Marchant pushes out his bottom lip, nodding slowly.

'The youngers. Other staff. It wouldn't have just been Daniels who knew,' states Lawton.

'Mrs Braithwaite, the deputy head, maintains that …'

Lawton shakes his head. 'She just said Daniels wasn't involved in drugs. Nowt about kids.'

They're after Axmed and Bruno wrapped up in a tight bow with Ryan Pierce.

Unless she gets the truth out of them first.

Diana stands in the kitchen with MaMa's last suitcase of clothes.

Rehema turns from the wall calendar on the side of the fridge. 'You got everything now? You can drop her off so I can take her to the optician's next week.'

'Can't she leave some stuff here? Instead of being a bag lady – going to and fro all the time? She's spent a lifetime doing that.'

Rehema glares back. 'Exactly. So, best she has most of her stuff at yours.'

Diana sighs; that doesn't actually answer her question. She nods but doesn't head out. Instead, she sits down on the edge of a chair.

'How come you never told me everything MaMa went through?'

'Pardon?'

Diana looks away from Rehema's fiery glare. 'You know – Hulda Stumpf and the FGM. Her PTSD.'

Rehema's glare turns to a baffled eye roll. 'Stump what? Not FGM, Diana? MaMa was raped, tortured and scarred for life by *British* soldiers.' Rehema shakes her head and squints at Diana. 'Are you looking after her? Is she getting confused? She could have a water infection.'

'She's not got a water infection, Ma. She's sorted out my green-house *and* my kitchen cabinets.'

So, Rehema doesn't know about Miss Hulda. Why did MaMa tell her and not her own daughter? *To protect Rehema.* Diana wants to blurt out what MaMa told her, but stops her mouth. It's MaMa's one agency – her voice, her experience, and she is aware of its impact. The question is not why she didn't tell Rehema, but why MaMa told *her*.

'Did MaMa ever tell you much about her childhood, Ma?'

Rehema fidgets with a tea towel. She speaks very slowly, eyes staring out the window. 'She did tell me about going on long treks with her father across the uplands to the north-west. To Kijabe. About a big meru oak, its broad straight trunk and starred leaves. Big steam clouds rising off the central highlands like cakes. She said that's how you knew the south-east kusi monsoon was coming. She liked the meru's white blossom with the dark mauve inside. When her father was off talking to the herdsmen, she said she'd pick up the fruits when they were half-ravaged by monkeys. She'd peel the skins off, digging with a stick in the soil, burying them in a row.' Rehema shakes her head. 'Weird thing to remember.'

'Did she ever talk about him – her father? Your grandfather?'
My great grandfather.

Rehema turns from the window, shaking her head. 'Even MaMa doesn't know where or when he died. Or how. Just that he never returned and so she was taken to the Kijabe Girls' Home.'

Rehema starts rinsing kale.

'Are you eating enough beans, Diana? You're looking very ashy these days.'

Beans?

'You don't have any early memories of Kenya, Ma?'

Rehema snaps stalks. 'You know I don't, Diana! I was taken, barely weaned, to this country. Took a lot for me to even find MaMa.'

She grabs a carton of eggs from the side.

'Do you want an omelette or scrambled eggs?'

What I want is for you to talk to me. To talk with MaMa.

To talk about all the things you've locked up because they hurt or are too messy to pull out.

Diana grabs her coat. 'I'm good. I ate a cereal bar.'

'A Nutrigrain is not a cereal bar. You need iron.'

Diana pecks her on the cheek and picks up the small, battered suitcase. Rehema's hand still hovers over the carton of eggs.

'See you later, Ma.'

Diana approaches her car just as Michael is walking up the road.

'You finished for the day?' she says, smiling at him. He nods, his eyes remaining on her. Diana looks down at the pavement.

'Sorry I was rude the other day when you were working ...'

Michael leans into the gatepost, looking at her.

'You *were* rude. But thank you for the apology.' He winks. 'Not one for holding grudges. At least you didn't arrest me!'

Diana grins. 'Not yet.'

Michael raises his eyebrows. 'So, the jury's still out? Bit prejudicial that. You haven't even examined the evidence.'

'True.' Diana's eyes meet his. Lock, spark.

'You look knackered,' he says.

'Thanks.' Diana sighs. 'I *am* knackered. Non-stop, going nowhere fast.' She exhales. Michael nods towards the suitcase.

'So, you're going on holiday?'

'Chance would be a fine thing. It's MaMa's. She's staying at mine now.'

Michael smiles, his eyes filled with compassion.

'Family, eh?' he says. 'Best go. Got to drop the boys off at their mum's.'

'Sorry – didn't want to keep you. I just wanted to apologise.'

'No, I just have to fit in with a schedule.'

Diana nods and makes to move up the path. He opens the gate.

'Were you playing some old-school jungle when you left the other day? Or some remix of General Levy?'

Diana reddens. 'Maybe. Thought I kept it low.'

Michael shrugs. 'Good taste.'

Diana beams. It's the most affirming thing anyone's said to her in … years.

'I'd put you down as Girls Aloud and Arctic Monkeys.'

Diana pushes out her bottom lip. 'I wish I was in Girls Aloud sometimes. I'm making you late.'

He smiles. 'Another time though? Stand you a drink at Henry's bar.'

Diana grins. 'Maybe.' She pulls out her phone.

'What's your number?'

As she punches in the digits, she wonders at herself.

What am I doing? He could be a serial killer.

Or he could be a decent bloke. Besides, a serial killer wouldn't make it past Rehema's front door.

Chapter 29

Saturday 16th October – Dewbow

Njambi

I wake at dawn. Big full moon still glows. I will go into the forest. I have decided. I waited for no rain and the night was dry, cold. I put on *mwana*'s green waterproof coat, her boots. It is a cool clear morning – like the mornings on the ridge with my father before he took me to the mission at Kijabe and went north to fight.

The air is welcome to my lungs. Going to London, telling my story to strangers who listened, has loosened something in my bones. Even down there and in my heels, in my fingers. I feel it. When they look at me, there is none of that fear – just compassion. The man's cheeks were wet with his tears. The woman's jaw tight. She closed her eyes. All those years. They see it for what it is, unafraid to speak it aloud.

I feel a freeing. I walk up past the stone wall, slow but steady. No one but an old man with a dog.

'Good morning.'

'Good morning,' I say back.

'Can I help you? Are you lost?'

'No. I am not lost,' I say. He looks lost now himself. Grunts. Frowns. Moves on.

The trees call me like they did in 1955, '56, '57, '58. The forest. The place Ebu and Dedan and the Mau Maus run for safety. Before the darkness creep in.

I pass through the gate, crunch bracken, listen for the call of the turaco which Ebu used to tell me it safe to walk on, the sign so the man will not mistake me for one of the traitors and hack me with machete. I still tremble, carry milk in a can, the rations of root and *githeri*, fruit. Whatever I can find without being seen from Mbasaki.

I walk up the woodland path. Every rustle on the way, I jump. Scattered leaves, claw marks on trunk. I look for the trail of a dragged carcass. My skin twitches, listening for the clink of blade on bark, blade cutting through air. I walk through leaves, stinging scratching briars, through the trees, shedding their summer in piles on the track. I smell goat. I look around, confused. The stink is real. The ground shakes, ferns part, like the grassland for the Thompson gazelle and buffalo. The briars and branches alive, red eye glaring like demon. We lock eye. I stay still. Just as Ebu teach me. Still still if the Mau Mau appear or hyena or wolf or lion. They do not know you. Stay still. Say my name. Clearly. *Ebu. Mzumara.* I say it aloud now. The head stares and then turns, flash of brown flank legs. Ground trembles. My father's mother's name still my refuge: Wamugunda. Njambi Wamugunda. *Intelligence of the land*, in my bones.

I walk on. My breath is short but my legs are long. I can breathe. I have all day. I have all time. Now my story free. I can climb. My knees feel warm. My ears hear hawk, the scream not as fierce as the vulture. The vulture would tell me shredded Kenyan lie ahead in bush.

At the top, trees part, boulders grow, sky opens. A grey-purple sky, heavy with something, a heavy day but the ridge like my father's place. The land returns to me, rolling in purple and green wild rolls below. The air purer. The sky rips and sunlight pours down through cloud, over the ridge. Like the Kenyan kopjes, one spindly one. The crag. A wind grows strong. I feel it through my bones, in my chest, taking, replacing my breath. My father's promise. My father's hope. Njambi Wamugunda. Ebu. The oak, the meru oak. He stands by the grey boulder bathed in fierce gold and orange. The heavy day breaks through.

224

This is the place, they say. *This is the place your seed will stay. This is our land we take, our air. For you, for ours. Today. This heavy day, soaked in gold and blood, is yours.* I lean back on the boulder, face to light, eyes closed. Let the warmth kiss my skin. Let the wind take my breath and give me theirs.

Chapter 30

Tuesday 19th October, 2010 – The Ryano Hut, Sheffield

Bruno

It's raining mad tings. Ryan comes into back kitchen, telling me to empty van. I'm in the middle of quarting chicken.

'It's pissing it down! I'm doing chicken.'

He gives me deadeye. 'You're doing what I say! I need van in twenty minutes. Going through on Snake Pass.'

'I can't unload van in twenty minutes!'

'Axmed'll help you.' He goes into the cook's kitchen.

I wipe down my hands, take off the apron, pull on my hoodie.

Axmed's in front seat, hood up, rubber-banding his notes. He looks up as I rap on window, like he's forgotten I work here day in, day out. He jumps out, bang into a puddle, all over his trainers.

'Naaaa!' he yells.

I laugh. 'Never wear decent trainers on London Road.'

Axmed laughs, goes for a hug.

'How you doing?'

'Oy – you two. Stop fannying about and empty that van.'

Knobhead's on his phone, pacing about the yard like he's busy and important.

'Open her up then,' I say.

Takes us about ten minutes to do two thirds of van: cans, tubs of oil, sacks of fruit, rice and veg. Meat came in this morning.

'I need a cig.' Axmed perches on the end of the van. The doors are open, blocking Knobhead's line of vision.

'Can't believe you're being a joey for Ryan.'

'Says he.' He peels the Rizla open, scattering 'bacca over it.

'I won't go jail for chopping chicken.'

'Not going jail.'

'That's what Omear said. That's what Nate said. That's what Isaiah—'

'They were daft.'

'And you're smart?'

Axmed flakes weed on the 'bacca with his long fingers. 'No – I'm desperate. Desperate can sometimes make you smart.'

'I thought desperate made you stupid.'

Axmed cups his long brown hand around his throwaway, sparking it once twice, zoot in mouth, sucking in air, head on one side against the pissing rain. His hand's too elegant for thugging.

'S'alright for you.'

This again. 'Yeah, OK.'

He inhales. 'Prenticeship or that thing you do in Derbyshire.'

'Two days a week.'

He exhales smoke away from me. 'That whole thing with Mina in Year 9 – proper mashed my head up. Been bad for Aabe's and my brothers' businesses. I'm not working in Suleman's shop any road. I'm glad Aamiina's at college.'

'Me too.' Just the thought of someone trying to cut her pussy makes me want to smash heads in.

Axmed seems to be talking to the air, the onions, not me, as he exhales smoke over his left shoulder.

'I thought we were leaving all that madness behind when we left Mogadishu. But we just brought it with us.'

'Just ignore it, bro.'

He spits on the ground. 'You don't get it. If Aamiina's not cut,

227

we don't belong, so I've *got* to get this money together. I've got to make my own world.'

Sewing up a gyal's gash seems a dickless way to control a community, but I say nowt.

'You and me should team up. You should sack this butchery off and go OT with me.'

'Axmed, I'm not getting in Ryan's schemes. Undys been all over him for time. And these tubs weigh a ton. He's got more than onions in here.'

Axmed gives me a fast look. *Yeah, you know.*

'Bro, Ryan can't show me shit I don't know already. All my family been selling khat for time back home.'

I screw up my face. 'You had a pet shop?'

He looks at me, confused. 'Khat. Q.A.T.' Showing me his tongue, the qh – not the k. Back in his throat.

I can't do it right. 'What's khhhhat?'

'A herb, dried leaves you chew, gives you a high, stops the hunger. Later drowsy and downer, gives you munchies. Everything's about khat back home. That's what I'm saying. I know what I'm doing.'

'No one's chewing leaves for highs here, bro.'

I can see Ryan pacing in the back kitchen, begging someone on the phone. A strung-out old turkey covered in ink and gold. Reckons he's still stud.

I shake my head. 'You think Ryan and those guys in Manny going to let you roll once you've stacked?'

Axmed sucks out his cig, flicking its glowing end into a puddle of engine oil, grey water and a crisp wrapper. 'I'll just bounce.'

'And do what?'

'Set up shop.'

'On your own?'

'I'll get a woman and … a gun.'

'A gun? Are you mad? No gyal worth having is going with a roadman … Why don't you just sign on for college?'

Axmed shakes his head. 'Easy for you to say, gyalis.'

I shake my head, but he is right: girls seem to like me. He pulls his cuffs over his knuckles, drops his eyes and voice. 'And even if I did get one, how do I know she'd not turn slag? Not boy me off and go with someone else?'

I frown. He turns and looks at me directly, his eyes desperate. 'What if I can't satisfy her?'

I laugh. 'Not the end of the world! It's a mutual thing, innit.'

He looks confused, turns from me and jumps into the van, hissing: 'Look, not having a job – that's normal where I come from. But not being able to … you know …'

He starts jerking with his head, pulling a face.

'What?'

'Satisfy your woman … well, you're not a man.' He shakes his head.

I laugh.

'You numpty … you get to know each other. It's not a transaction, Axmed.'

Axmed just looks blankly at me. *Sake*. He has no idea what I'm talking about. Guy's my best mate and I'm only just now seeing him.

'You've never been with a girl, have you?' I whisper.

He snarls defiantly. 'I have!'

He yanks the onions on his shoulder. 'Get my dick sucked enough times!'

I shake my head, suddenly working it all out.

'All I know is, if you can't satisfy a woman, pretty sure the answer's not cutting her clit off.'

Ryan comes to the door. 'You two finished yet?' he yells. 'I'm not paying you to smoke and have a chinwag.' His phone rings and he walks off, but I can hear him. 'Tez, I'm opening a new line every month. And the two in Derbyshire are already burning through the stuff so they need protection 'n' all. Yeah, still holding for now.'

'Shut up, knobhead,' I mutter, picking up a tub of oil.

'Your Aamiina's brave, you know,' I say loudly to Axmed.

Axmed returns to the van doors. 'I know.'

'Why don't the women stop it?'

Axmed freezes, incredulous, pulling his hood up. 'You kidding? The women are the ones who do it! It's *hooyo* who were trying to force our Mina. That's what messed my head.'

Ryan whistles at Axmed through the rain. 'What's he think you are – his dog?'

Hate the way he treats Axmed.

'You're disrespectful to your dad, you know, Bruno. Least he gives you a job.'

'A real dad wouldn't get his son's best mate to turn county.'

I'm about to kick off, but then I remember Aamiina and the promise I made her to talk to him. 'Axmed. Ryan's game is not the answer to your problem. Think of something else.'

Axmed goes to hug me. 'No choice, bro.'

Axmed slams the van doors, nodding at Ryan who is marching towards the driver's side.

'What you two talking about?'

'Eating pussy,' I say.

Ryan kisses his teeth, slams the van door. I glare at him in the wing mirror.

He blinks, looks away.

Yeah, drive off. Wanker.

Chapter 31

Thursday 21st October, 2010 – Sheffield

Diana waits for the kettle to boil, cramming handfuls of Raisin Poppets into her mouth.

'Easy there, Walker. You hungry or something?' laughs Lawton.

Not hungry. Just raging.

Robertson comes to stand next to her with his mug.

Neville leans back in his chair. 'When my missus eats a packet of custard creams in two minutes flat, I know she's pissed off. Or thinking. And neither of them's good news for me!' he laughs.

Lawton chuckles. 'I always wondered why you keep a stash in your drawer.'

'Nivver get a chance to eat one at home!'

I bet.

While they continue their custard cream behavioural analysis, the kettle boils and the Poppets packet is empty. Diana carries it forlornly back to her desk along with dishwater coffee and sits down.

The receptionist calls through the intercom: 'The press on line six, sir.'

'Rate. Give them something to tide 'em over. Don't want them broadcasting our moves on the OCG,' Lawton says.

They're going to do a fit-up. I know it.

She could care less about losing her SIO tag. What irks her is that there is a real chance the wrong guy is going to go down for this. Not that Ryan Pierce is not wrong; he's about as wrong as a person can get, but that still doesn't make him *the* person who committed this crime. And that bothers her. It bothers her because someone will genuinely get away with murder. And it bothers her because DI Phillips has always been lousy at his job, always been promoted, goes around like he's the saviour of the free world when he is a coward, a liar, doesn't do the detail, the legwork. And he's a …

Don't say it. Don't think it.

He gets away with it. He gets away with everything.

Diana breathes, leans back. She's got one shot at proving him wrong and getting this case solved. She has to find the real killer before Phillips and his minion Lawton fit this up. She is also bothered because she knows if they can't frame it on Ryan, they will fit it for Bruno, and there's no critical evidence yet. Bruno is a promising kid from a poor background who was let down by Daniels *and* Young, *and* Mary Calley was his favourite teacher so, yeah – revenge motive. Opportunity too: he knew about the filing cabinet. He was in the area. He's a butcher.

Diana needs to know for a fact it was *not* Bruno. He needs to be a suspect eliminated – or charged. Diana looks at the empty packet of Poppets like they're the criminal.

'Why are there never enough Poppets in a packet?'

Robertson looks up from his screen, unsure if she's addressing him.

'Not sure, Boss.'

She twists the wrapper into a tight knot before hurling it into the bin, picks up her coat and nods at Robertson.

'Let's pay Bruno's mum a visit.'

Jane Blake looks warily at Diana and Robertson when she opens the door, exhaustion carved into her face.

'Knew you'd be back. Bad things always come in threes, they say. Bruno's at work.'

'Actually, it's you we wanted to chat to. We're trying to get a bit more information and verify Bruno's statement.'

'Just got back off my shift so …' She shrugs, opening the door to stale squalor. Diana keeps her eyes fixed on the tired woman in front of her, a black Afro pulled into a bun, wisps of baby hair gelled to brown, strained skin. Big dark eyes and full lips just like Bruno. Must have been a looker before living-with-not-enough-for-too-long. Jane Blake taps a cig from a ten pack of Lamberts, lights it off the gas ring, cracks open a window.

'Where was Bruno this August Bank Holiday?' Robertson asks.

'Creamfields.'

'Who was he there with? Anyone to verify that?'

'I dunno. This girl. Charlotte something, he said. He was definitely there. I got him his ticket for his Christmas present.' She scowls at the scummy taps. 'I'd been saving since the year before – supposedly for his GCSEs. The exams he never took.'

'How did he get there?'

'Think his dad took him. Or he went with some mates.'

'His dad's Ryan Pierce?'

Jane drags on the cig, nodding at the window.

'Do you get on with Ryan?' Diana asks.

Jane chuckles. Robertson pulls back a chair and sits down. She stares at his notebook.

'I get on with him enough to keep him away. Let's put it like that.' She frowns. 'You're asking me about Ryan. You said you had questions about Bruno.'

'Ms Blake, to eliminate Bruno from this investigation, we need to check out where Bruno was August Bank Holiday. Can anyone verify he was at Creamfields?'

Jane sucks the last rites out of her cig before crushing it in a coffee jar lid.

'Course he wor at Creamfields. Ask any his mates. They were with him. It'll be on Facebook.'

Diana nods at Robertson, who scribbles something down.

'Can't be in two places at once,' Jane says.

'Mr Daniels was not killed in Sheffield. And Bruno was at Legley Road when another former student was spraying the filing cabinet.'

Jane hisses: 'Never liked that Axmed.'

'What makes you think it was him?'

Jane groans at her mistake. 'Bruno told me. He tells me everything. After that Axmed blabbed, your lot came tipped my house upside down, remember? Looking for a filing cabinet key and a butcher's knife, no doubt.'

She kisses her teeth.

Diana continues, unfazed. 'By Tuesday 29th August, we have it on pretty good authority that the body parts were in the locked filing cabinet. Both Bruno and the other student maintain that it was empty when they turned it around late on Bank Holiday Monday. And unlocked, as the drawers shook free.'

'Don't know about that. I know he was in a mood when he got dropped off Bank Holiday Monday. Just threw in his backpack, showered, changed his clothes, went straight out again. I remember, as we rowed about him using up hot water just before I needed to shower for work. I didn't get back till four and he was in his bed then. When I got up later, I had a go because he'd used up all milk and then the argument went onto college. He told me he'd not signed up for his second year. I kicked right off with him because that meant he wouldn't get any ELA allowance. Told him to get to his dad for a job at the Ryano Hut.'

'Why hadn't he signed on for his second year at college?'

'Didn't see the point, he said. Just stopped caring. When his sponsorship stopped, he gave up going to practice, got dropped from the team. Started raving. I was worried he was ...'

She looks down at the stained linoleum floor.

'On drugs? Or selling them?' ventures Diana in a soft voice. Jane's eyes snap back: *Not that fast, bitch.*

'Told him to get a job at his dad's takeaway.'

Diana keeps her voice low. 'But Ryan doesn't just run the Ryano Hut, does he?'

Jane stares out the window.

Diana sighs. 'We'll follow up on this Charlotte and anyone else he was with at Creamfields. How does Bruno get on with his dad?'

'Works for him, dunt he?'

'That doesn't tell me how they get on.'

'Bruno's not got much respect for him. But it's a job. Least he's not doing same shit kids round here are doing.'

'You know that for a fact?'

'I know my son, detective, a lot better than you do for all your "investigations". I know he didn't kill anyone. I know he's not taking drugs.' Her eyes narrow. Jane stops herself, watching Robertson scribble.

'Was he aware kids brought drugs into Legley High to sell?' Diana continues.

Jane slams the window shut. 'I know what I need to know. I'm not solving this crime for you or framing me own son. He's not done owt wrong. You can check CCTV of Park Hill flats if you don't believe me. I'm off out now so—'

She opens the front door. Diana raises her eyebrows to Robertson. He scrapes back the chair.

'Thank you very much, Ms Blake. You've been most ...'

The door slams behind them ...

Diana walks in silence as they make their way down the wide, litter-strewn concrete walkways. Kids staring, doors slamming, curtains being pulled to.

'You alright, Boss? That was intense in there. Ms Blake seems to know something.'

As they get into the car, she sighs.

'There is a strong circumstantial case for Phillips and Lawton saying it was Pierce – or someone he was working for – who killed Daniels. Or for saying Bruno did it for his dad.'

'You don't think so though?'

'I don't think anything without critical evidence. We need to eliminate these two or charge. And fast.'

She looks up at the looming block of concrete.

'And find that key and the cleaver.'

Charlotte James comes out of the gates of Golden Oak Girls' High School as part of a posse of girls dressed in business suits. Diana steps out of the car, flashing her badge while Robertson locks up. The giggling girls suddenly freeze.

'Hello, Charlotte. I'm DI Walker and this is DS Robertson. You got ten minutes? We just need some information.'

Charlotte's upper lip quivers.

'You can't arrest me. I'm calling my dad ...' Phone out at the ready.

'Easy! No one's arresting anyone. Just asking some questions.'

'About what?'

Charlotte waves her friends on.

'Specifically, your August Bank Holiday and your relationship with Bruno Pierce.'

'What relationship?'

'We understand you were at Creamfields together this August Bank Holiday? Let's sit down for a hot chocolate. Getting a bit nippy out here.'

Diana side-nods to cross the street into a small park. A café in the corner.

The café is boutique, trying to crush a whole personality into twenty square feet. Leggy, blonde, ponytailed schoolgirls in the corner giggle over pink and chocolate smoothies and their phones. A swollen-knuckled white-haired old lady in a swamping red anorak tries to navigate the table and crockery to get to the sugar bowl. Robertson brings over a hot chocolate, going back for Diana's black tea and his strong brew. With milk. Diana puts her hands around the steaming mug.

'Did you attend Creamfields this year?'

'Yeah. A whole load of us went. Results Day Treat.'

'Including Bruno?'

Charlotte sips her hot chocolate, winces and spoons three large teaspoons of sugar into it.

'Who told you I was with Bruno?'

'His mum.'

'His mum!' Charlotte's eyes widen. 'Wow. He told his mum about me?' She looks incredulous. Diana nods. 'Yes. I was with Bruno at Creamfields. But we all went together as a group.'

'Can you give us the names of the other people in the group, please?'

Robertson takes out his notepad, writing down the names.

'I'm guessing most of these go to your school or the boys' grammar?' Diana asks.

Charlotte nods.

'So, how did you meet Bruno?'

'We met at a club, Impy's, in Sheff, a rave for end of GCSEs.'

'Impy's? That's over eighteen ...'

Charlotte frowns. 'Hey ...'

'Don't worry. I'm after facts – not fake IDs.'

Charlotte is hammering the hot chocolate, a frothy milk moustache over thin lip-glossed lips.

'You're not telling my dad this? Or putting it on record? Tell *him* to stop writing.'

Diana nods at Robertson who puts down his Bic and sips from his mug, eyes staying on Charlotte.

'Bruno?'

'OK. So, Bruno knew a friend who knew a man about a dog.'

'Are we talking about drugs here?'

Charlotte focuses on her diminishing chocolate. 'Bruno doesn't take anything. So straight he's square. Says he hates drugs. I mean it's cool, he's still fun. Dances like he's got a demon in him.'

'So, you liked him.'

Charlotte swallows. 'We liked each other. We copped off. I got all the signs that we were an item. But Monday morning, he just goes right cold. One minute he's giving me a coffee and a snog, next minute it's "See you later." Walks off. I'm like "Okayyy." That was it. Not heard from him since.'

She looks genuinely bereft. Draining her hot chocolate, she puts the mug down.

'Why? He's not in trouble, is he? It's just that I can't have anything on my UCAS statement ...'

Diana shakes her head. 'He used to go to Legley Road High School and we're investigating some of the final students there. Bruno's just one of them.'

Charlotte's relief is immediate. 'Oh, yeah. That head in a filing cabinet. Ewww. I saw it on TV. Mad. Is Bruno mixed up with that?'

Just raised his street cred.

'No, no. Did he ever mention anything about his schoolteachers there?'

'I know he was mad about what happened, the school closing and the teachers not giving a ... care. Think he regretted not taking his GCSEs. Then next minute he'd be "Fk 'em" ...' She blushes.

'Sorry ... but I think he did care. He was smart. We wouldn't have got together if he weren't.'

You just said he was fun and could get you drugs.

'You did well in *your* GCSEs, Charlotte. Straight As I see.'

Charlotte looks shocked.

'Are you investigating me?'

'No, just trying to verify the circumstances here. You're doing A levels now? What do you want to do?'

'Be a lawyer.'

'Just like Daddy.'

Charlotte's shoulders slump. 'My dad doesn't know I'm being interviewed, does he?'

'I've told you. You're helping us eliminate Bruno from our inquiries and find out what happened.'

'Don't tell my dad about the drugs. Don't mention ...'

'Charlotte ... focus. Bruno. Anything else he mentioned? How did he get back from Creamfields? Who picked him up?'

'Bit weird, actually. He'd come up with me in the car with Molly and Cole and that's what I'm saying: we were tight, were going to travel back together. He shared my tent and that. Dad was picking us up and I presumed we were an item and, you know, he'd stay the night at mine. But he's like, "I'm getting picked up by someone else." Blew me out basically.'

'He's not contacted you? Never explained?'

'Nothing. Not about to ask him either.' Charlotte tosses back her hair.

Diana puts her empty mug to one side.

'So, did Bruno supply you with the ...?'

'No, he didn't and I'm not covering for him. He just got us a phone number. This other kid served Cole the Es.'

Immediately, she blushes. 'Or something.'

'What was *this kid's* name?'

Charlotte pulls her chair back. 'I don't grass. I don't know! Someone from Legley Road High. Everyone else was doing it.'

Diana rolls her eyes. 'OK, you don't have to tell me his name, but you can tell me if it was *not* Axmed Ahmed.'

Charlotte winces, trying to work out the double negatives.

GCSEs, but not that smart.

'Some silly name like that. They're all the same,' she spits.

Diana stares. Even Robertson momentarily stops writing.

'Well, thank you, Charlotte. You've been most helpful. Hopefully, we won't be seeing you again. Until you're in the courtroom.'

Charlotte looks aghast. Diana gets up, slowly pushing back her chair. She gives a half-smile.

'As a lawyer. Good luck with your studies.'

Diana and Robertson tuck in their chairs, nod at the café owner, and leave Charlotte biting her lip.

Njambi

The 'protected village' smells of pig oil, *manil* and blood. Groans pierce silence, sticking like glass in my brain. It's not courage or hope make me take milk, vegetable, rice and palm meat to the forest. It is fear. Fear of what I will feel if I stay still. Fear of thinking about Rehema, my child. The only one left. Ebu, my love. My father. So, every week I do the missions to the forest.

I smell my own sweat. I know men with hair in knots and yellow eye from no sleep and too much blood. I know they watch me from the leaves. They hold machete like it is friend, like a brother. When I had to chop chicken at Kijabe I learn to hold wooden handle so, to feel it in my finger and in my palm. Atu teach me how to cut and chop. Hold knife like an instrument. Cutting is an art. But these men in forest know no art. They know no friend only foe, only traitor and the machete is they arm to destroy to hack and cut. I see dried blood on leaf, grass, the path, hear the long hissing rushed wail of the vultures hovering north, south. The forest has arms to grab and embrace and hide and arms to cut, chop the enemy. The forest is my friend.

Not the camps. They call it camp, they call it 'protected village'. Protected from what? The truth of the forest. Our village is now their camp, a place to rip away our sex, to grind us every day to crawl in spaces wrapped in barbed wire and man with gun.

I see man trampled on slow-slow-slow. I hear the sounds of bones and boots and groans and screams swallowed by dust and earth and his own blood. I see the big iron pliers they turn his body over like a dead dog: one kick, rip off his groin, pull, tear off his testicles, fling them in ditch like gristle. I see the child-woman less age than me have broken soda bottle push in them, the older woman have the bigger Tusker beer bottle push up in them. The bottle scream in flesh is seared in *my* flesh, in my ear for ever. They die slow-slow, green stuff leaking. The stench of rot, the rot of these men's souls infecting their victims' wounds.

I am blessed and give thanks. My seed planted in the mission and taken to England. So they take my womb with the fire and bottle? A stranger takes me to King George Hospital. I heal. No womb but I want no womb for a land of traitors and thieves now.

I take food for my husband, Ebu. And for Dedan in the forest. Years I know how to hide and survive. I keep quiet in the camp.

The forest is my friend. The forest hides the men. In the town they call them rebels. But they are no rebels. They are defending their own land. Four years and then British Air Force they catch Dedan by treacherous men. No trial. He hang from a tree the next year, poisoned by their rot. Ebu, I never see again. I never see his body. His smile, his pain. They tell me he dead but I keep wait. Maybe he's turned into tree. His trunk of brown steel, long knotted locks, yellow eye in bark, reaching out, gripping me to hold. Hold, hold the smell of wood, blood and smoke, his heart pounding *dumdumdum* breaking through leathered skin.

I see. And wait.

I wait. Now I go to the forest again. Somewhere in the forest my seed waits, my lover waits. I spit my seed far, far from my mouth to keep it safe. Till it reclaims land and future stolen. My bones ache. My bones. I want them planted here with my seed. I want them to stay here with you, *mwana*. You are the seed I kept secret, secret even from myself.

You will be the seed to bring justice. Njeri.

Diana

Diana walks into Rehema's kitchen, shivering against the October chill.

'Nice 'n' cosy in here. Alright, Mum.'

240

Rehema's face is grey.

Diana frowns. 'What's up? You said it was urgent.'

Rehema is sitting at the kitchen table staring at a letter in front of her. 'It's from the Kenyan Human Rights Commission. About MaMa's and the others' cases. The Mau Mau case.'

Diana pulls up a chair. 'Have you opened it?'

Rehema looks up from the envelope, sighs. 'No. It's addressed to MaMa.' She gives it to Diana. 'Give it to her. Let me know what it says.'

'Do you think?'

'What I think is this new coalition government are liars. I don't want to raise her hope. But I don't want to see her despair either. MaMa's staying with us. As for the case, we'll cross that bridge when ...'

Diana picks up the letter, pushes back her chair.

'Bridge *been* crossed, Ma.'

The rain patters on the window.

'Best get home.'

As she reaches the door, Rehema stands up.

'How's – work?'

Diana turns, surprised. Rehema has never asked after her work. Diana shrugs. 'Marchant took me off as SIO. Gave it to Lawton.' She expects the 'I-told-you-so'. Instead, Rehema's eyes soften.

'Maya's having a book club Hallowe'en brunch week on Sunday. You and MaMa are invited, although it might not be ...'

'Appropriate? No offence. I'm sure I've given plenty.' Diana gives a wry smile. 'No apologies either.'

The washing machine starts beeping its end of cycle. Neither of them move.

'Our book club ... for us to trust each other, that's a big deal, you know?'

Diana does know. It stings that her own mother trusts these women more than her own daughter. Her shoulders drop.

'Look, I'm doing my best, Ma, but it's hard work fighting *for* you when you're fighting *against* me.'

Rehema wrinkles her nose. 'I'm not fighting against you. I'm defending women against ...'

Diana rolls her eyes. 'OK well, I'll leave you with the semantics, Ma. But if any of you are hiding evidence, I *will* come after you.'

Diana leans on the door. Rehema's eyes narrow. She stands bolt straight, arms folded into her chest.

'Is that a threat? If your precious police are denying a sister justice, we will do it ourselves.'

'Two wrongs don't make a right, Ma.'

'But what about *our* right to live safely? *Our* right to justice? Look at MaMa.'

'I *am* looking at MaMa, every single day. This is the last time I'll ask. If you know anything, pass it on. Here's Robertson's card.'

She slides it across the table. Rehema wrinkles her nose in distaste as if Diana has just smeared it with mud.

'You can't keep silent about crime yet claim to be standing up for human rights and justice.'

Rehema picks up a folded tea towel, her eyes scrutinising its hem. She looks up sharply.

'And *you* can't deliver justice.'

Rehema opens the back door. 'I'll let you know when MaMa's prescription glasses need collecting.'

The door clicks behind her and Diana walks back to the car slowly, despite the rain.

Proper blowing it down out here. A mad October evening. Hard hats and roadworks at Totley; an interminable wait for traffic lights. What a job flicking that Go–Stop sign. *Just like my job.* Power but no power. A guy with a clipboard – in this weather? Hard hat too. Must be another of these quality assurance audit things. Must check on that. Legley Road School site. Audit. The hardhat brigade. Bored, she looks sideways at the detached houses with long drives. Must be nice to have electric gates onto the main road and a private security camera …

A camera. A remote chance it's still got footage.

Ten minutes' later, Diana blinks into her rear-view mirror where a full beam is careering ever closer. The shape of the lights is the

242

same since Beauchief, so why the sudden aggression? Diana's never felt concerned on this long, unlit stretch of road across the moors, but suddenly she feels exposed and unsure. Her heart is thumping in her ears. No signal up here, even if she could make a call. No backup either, even if she could get through; this is the hinterland between Sheff and north Derbyshire.

The jeep gets closer yet; Diana sees the blank where a registration plate should be and the full beam blinds her. Within feet of her rear, it accelerates. She doesn't want to be pushed into a ditch out here.

The lights go out. Pitch black, leaving Diana alone at speed in the dark. Terror swarms her brain; she waits for the ram. Her foot is hard on the pedal. Five minutes. But nothing. Mentally, she tries to map out where it disappeared. Past Owler Bar, as it's moorland. The only turn off is a narrow sharp left towards Unthank. That's the only place.

Adrenaline pumps through her veins. She doesn't exhale till she gets to the Sheffield Road junction and the lights of Dewbow appear.

Should she call it in? An unmarked car heading towards Unthank? It could be halfway to Dronfield or anywhere east; there are untold little lanes and no main roads for quick access. Or just some bad boy looking for a quick scare?

Except those weren't tactics a road boy would know. *Steering sharply into the target so the fleeing vehicle's rear tyres lose traction and start to skid. The chasing car continues to turn in the same direction until clear of the target.* More of a committed lane change than an actual turn. TPAC-trained.

Diana parks up outside her cottage. She checks her rear-view.

Leave it, Diana. It's late – you're getting paranoid. This is Dewbow.

Through the pelting rain, looking over her shoulder up the empty street as she locks the car door, Diana can't shake the sense that she's being watched. She runs the gauntlet up to the cottage.

Shaking herself inside the door, she's glad she kept the letter in her inside pocket. It's slightly bent.

'Vile, vile night, MaMa!'

Diana pecks MaMa's cheek. She smiles, continuing to run rice and water through long brown fingers at the sink.

Heart still pounding, Diana throws her wet coat over the banisters to dry. 'Letter come for you, MaMa.'

Diana places it on the table. MaMa turns her head to look at it. Switches off the tap. Dries her hands on a crisp tea towel hanging from the oven door. She moves to the table. Sits down. Stares at the envelope. Picks it up. Turns it over.

Diana flops down on the sofa that's been her bed since MaMa moved in.

'Want a brew, MaMa?'

MaMa is immersed in examining the envelope, turning it over in trembling hands.

'I'm making one any road. Gasping. Mad weather out there tonight.'

Hating herself for her fear of this silence, Diana boils the kettle, rummaging for what she calls her Best Mugs – the ones not chipped or carrying memories of tense conversations. She stares at her reflection in the window. Behind her, MaMa opens the cutlery drawer, taking out a butter knife. She returns to the table. She carefully slits open the envelope.

Two teabags in the pot. Diana gets milk out of the fridge, honey from the shelf, teaspoon from the drainer.

MaMa tugs at a folded piece of heavy paper inside the envelope. The paper has been scored and folded twice. MaMa smooths it out in front of her, her long brown fingers splaying out like starfish.

Diana turns to glare at the teapot. *Come on, brew.* She pours milk into each mug. Sees MaMa look so frail – a ghost in the window outlined against the black wild wet night, the storm from outside flailing at the glass, hammering at the door. Threatening to enter, to rip this sanctuary into a sodden wild mess. MaMa holds up the paper closer to her face. Diana pours. It needs another minute. She stops. Stares out but really in, behind her to where MaMa has put the paper back down on the table.

Diana waits, finally pouring. She spoons in honey, grateful for the clink of the spoon to pierce the silence of an unspoken roar and the storm's wail.

Putting two mugs on the table, Diana pulls up a chair.

MaMa stares beyond the envelope.

'You alright, MaMa? What they say?'

MaMa looks down at the letter.

'The Home Secretary has dismissed it as a priority for consideration.'

Diana feels a tightness in her jaw.

MaMa's case is about the historic sexual violence she suffered at the hands of the British and African loyalists, the confinement camps during the so-called Mau Mau Uprising. Ma had started asking questions about why she'd been abandoned and adopted while at university, ultimately leading her to a path from Scotland to Kenya and finally to MaMa, equipped only with the sparse information her adoptive missionary parents had given her. Rehema had transferred her rage to the system that still denied her own history. MaMa's own shame is only eclipsed by gratitude for her daughter's efforts to make things right. Still, their relationship remains broken by the lasting debris of the hurricane of hate that had ripped through their lives – and still does. Diana still can't reconcile the love and joy of MaMa with such intense abuse and denial – from the country of her birth, the country she served.

The state that paid her wages.

But, right now, there's no avoiding the fact of the envelope: the raw hatred typewritten in black and white on expensive paper, signed by a fountain pen for extra authority:

It never happened.

It's not our fault.

We won't help you.

'What? But – didn't David Blunkett promise in …'

MaMa neatly re-folds the letter and puts it back in the envelope. 'Promises mean nothing if you have no power, *mwana*. Mr Morara says he is now pursuing this through the Royal Courts of Justice.'

'He's going over government?'

MaMa nods. Smiles, shrugging. She speaks slowly, carefully. 'To put a name to this would unravel history, but I will not stop trying while I breathe.' She looks up at Diana, eyes dark pools in an unsmiling face. 'I have to, *mwana*.'

Diana reaches over, grasps MaMa's trembling hands. The heat pours in from MaMa.

'Maybe it needs unravelling.'

MaMa withdraws her hands, gets up suddenly, returning to her rice at the sink.

'I went for a walk in your forest today.'

Diana sips her tea, pulling a face. She really should have let it stand. 'It's not *my* forest.'

MaMa ignores her. 'I walked almost to the top.'

'Wow! Did you not get lost? Did you wear my wellies? I'm not sure I like you walking all over on your own … There's folk out there with guns.'

MaMa shoots her a look. Diana looks down.

'I met that lady from the book club, Maya.'

That's what she means.

'I didn't know she live here too … big house. Invited me in for sandwich.'

'Nice …'

She doesn't want to talk about Maya's sandwiches.

'I would like to be buried here, *mwana*.'

Diana sees herself in the reflection, standing behind MaMa, folding her narrow shoulders in to her chest. Her bones, fragile as a bird's. Her muscles taut, the sinews of her arm carved. Diana buries her head into the back of MaMa's shoulder, feels MaMa's chest heave and sob while the cold water runs.

Chapter 32

SATURDAY 23RD OCTOBER, 2010 – SHEFFIELD

Two days later and Diana's still bugged by Rehema's taunt about her inability to deliver justice. In the airless room two at HQ, Diana goes through Mary's box again. She needs to know it inside out. There's something here. Something someone doesn't want to be known. She takes another look at the diary.

Tuesday 20th July 2007

Leroy left before me for school as he says it's best folk don't know we're together. Bit of a weird day tho. When I got into school today at 8.30, going in, there was a right ruckus behind me on the steps. Bruno's yelling at a fat woman in hijab – I think she's Nadhiya's aunt. Not sure though. Anyway, it was an aggressive rant. I know he hangs out with the Somali boys a lot but didn't know he could insult! He's yelling Ka daa or something over and over. Somali girls watching in horror, white girls laughing. Bakhad and Axmed dragged him away. Then the woman starts pointing and yelling at me in Somali. The same words: 'Ka daa!' I'm about to call the cover supervisor over. Axmed says

'Leave her, Miss.' I ask Bruno what's going on. He says 'Nowt' but the woman is still raging and pointing at me.

At break, I ask Ally what 'Ka Daa' means and she says 'leave it alone' or something like that. Leave what alone? Bruno won't talk to me and Nadhiya and Year 8 girls were naughty in class. I find two limes with a screw in in my bookbag. Some idiots playing jokes. Then there's a big fight at break between the Somali Year 9s and Year 10s and some of the Pakistani boys. Daniels has excluded Axmed, Bruno, Omear and Bakhad for five days. There's something going off but no one's telling me anything. I ask Leroy and he just says 'Usual bullshit.' Aamiina's really quiet today. She hadn't done her first draft of original writing – not like her. I ask if she's OK, how are things at home and she just says 'Fine'. I ask Mrs Braithwaite if she got my paperwork and she says yes and she'll get round to it. My reflux is bad. I need to go back to doctor but no time. Only appointments are during day. Oh Leroy's knocking.

Diana frowns, flicks through entries, one after another until she freezes:

Friday 19 NOVEMBER 2007

Year 10 Parents' evenings are always a pain but this one's really done damage. I should have left earlier. Had twenty-three parents, Mrs Khan, Miss McIntosh and James' gran in a real state. Feel like I'm a therapist, social worker, teacher and MP every parents' evening. I'm shattered, not thinking right. Should have left early.

It's my own fault. I shouldn't have got involved. I should have just let things be. I should have just let a child under my care

248

suffer? It's my own fault. Why call the police or A & E who never come and if they do it's to tell you it's your fault.

Whatever I do, it's my fault.

But, oh my dayz, did she have to punch me so hard? A grown woman, no girl. I should've done those self-defence classes. I should have left early. I should have gone out the school front door or called 999 to say I was locked in. Brown anorak, head-scarf, short and tubby, yelling at me. The only words I recog-nise: 'Ka daa!' I'm sure it's that same woman Bruno was argu-ing with at end of summer term.

My gut kills. It seriously does. I can't eat. I didn't tell Ally or the doc but I spat blood. Even sipping water hurts.

It'll go down. I'll take it easy. Take more Gaviscon. Just get rest this weekend. It'll be ok. I'll be ok. Stop being dramatic, Mary.

So Mary was assaulted by a *she*. But who is the she? If Mary's spitting blood, that's not a good sign; this woman had done some real damage to her. Why has no one mentioned this before?

Diana goes back to the main office. Neville and Lawton are out, but Robertson is still poring over the spreadsheets.

'Robertson, did you ever meet Axmed's parents?'

'A couple of times, yeah. But they don't speak much English. The teachers used an interpreter at parents' evenings.'

Diana looks at him.

'What's up, Boss?'

'Could you go interview them with an interpreter? I need to find out if this alleged FGM cutting ceremony of Aamiina Ahmed was followed up. Or even properly logged.'

She hands him her sheet of notes. He scans it quickly, his eyes widening.

249

'Oh my days.'

Diana smiles. 'That's a Daphne-ism.'

He blushes.

'Yeah. I'll get in touch with Guleed Ishmael. I think he's the interpreter we use.'

'Thanks. Could be nothing.'

'Or could be something. I'm on it.'

Diana picks up her coat.

'You off?'

'Not really. Picking MaMa up from my mum's.'

She winks and picks up her car keys.

Lubanzi's Mercedes is parked outside when Diana draws up. *Book club plotting, no doubt.*

Diana knocks at the back door but can hear laughing inside, the scraping of chairs and soft music from the radio.

'Hello? Ma?'

She opens the door to a room filled with the aroma of cinnamon and cardamom.

'Mmmm. Apple crumble?'

Lubanzi is seated at the table, a large planner open before her, a bucket of a tea mug steaming next to her. She's wearing a purple and yellow headwrap and a mustard angora polo neck. Her relaxed smiling face falls back as Diana enters. Rehema turns around from the oven.

'Oh, hi. You're early.'

'Sorry – you busy? Just come to collect MaMa. Did she get her glasses?'

'Yes – but whether she'll wear them is another thing. She's having a nap at present. Do you want a cuppa?'

Why not?

Diana pulls out a chair.

'You said you'd come to the book club,' accuses Lubanzi.

'Sorry. I did. I've just not had a spare minute with … work.'

The kettle boils. Diana checks her nails. Lubanzi turns the pages of her planner.

'Pity. We've been having a great time with *Kindred*.'

'Oh. That's good. I'd probably not have time to read it.'

'Even Ally finds time to read it, and she's doing a Masters!'

'Isn't she in Wolverhampton?'

Rehema cuts her eyes at Diana. 'Diana, you *know* she's in Wolverhampton. You've been stalking her.'

Diana's hackles rise. 'Not stalking her. Been very nice, actually. She should have been brought in for a full-on interview – not off-piste intelligence chats on my own expense.'

'Leave her alone.'

Rehema puts a swirling cup of brown liquid and a plate of cardamom cookies in front of Diana.

'Ma, it's not about me! She's a key witness from Legley Road.'

She watches an unspoken sentence pass between Lubanzi and her aproned mother. Rehema gives a slight nod.

Lubanzi sighs heavily. 'Diana, Ally suffered a terrible injury under suspicious circumstances. After Mary had been ignored by the police, we were not going to allow Ally to go through that. Besides, Ally would say nothing. We – your mother and I and Anoona – made a choice to do what we could to save our sister's life, dignity and help her build a new one.'

Rehema. Always has to be the saviour of the sisterhood.

'What are you talking about? What suspicious injury?' Diana gratefully sips the hot tea, feigning marginal interest.

Rehema unties her apron.

'Lubanzi knew of a private hospital …'

'Where?'

'None of your business.'

Diana wants to spit out, 'it is actually', but something tells her to bite her tongue.

Lubanzi closes her planner, picks up a cardamom cookie, splitting it in two.

'I have a colleague from medical school, a specialist like myself who deals with certain cases that … don't want police investigation.'

'Illegal?'

'No – not illegal! Just, for whatever reason, they do not want the stigma, the intrusion.' Lubanzi looks at Rehema. 'We had called around to give her her Christmas present. No answer but

251

lights on and she had just texted to say she was back from the staff Christmas party. So, we knew she was in. Rehema looked through the letter box—'

'I saw her leg. And the fallen fridge.'

'Staff party? Friday 21st December?'

'I don't know.'

Rehema looks down at her lap. Diana gasps.

'We went round the back, broke the window. I called Pauline and Anoona and my friend. We got her to the practice just outside Nottingham ...'

'How? If her injuries were life-threatening, she'd need—'

'Specialist care. A fridge had fallen on her.'

'Er ... call an Ambulance? 999?'

They stare at each other. Diana doesn't want to ask who drove. *Bloody hell. What madness is this?*

'She stayed at the private clinic for almost a month and moved into her accommodation in Wolverhampton in the January. Started her physiotherapy there, signed on and then started uni in the September.'

'But why didn't you call the police? The emergency services ...?'

Lubanzi looks at her.

You told them not to.

'She was attacked, wasn't she?'

'She was not attacked!' Rehema exclaims with too much vigour. Diana pauses. Her voice drops.

'She was raped, wasn't she?'

There's a beat that tells her everything before: 'Why would you even think that?' from Rehema.

'Fridges don't just fall on people, Ma. Give me a break.'

'She was moving house ...'

'At ten-thirty at night, when she knows you're coming around? After a staff party? Just stop it, Ma. I don't want to hear any more of this nonsense. You just gave a violent criminal a get-out-of-jail-free card and precluded Ally from getting any compensation or justice for her – her disabilities.'

Diana can't swallow. She puts the tea down. 'And what about her psychological injuries? The ones you can't see.'

Lubanzi is glaring at Rehema, who frowns back.

252

There are thuds on the stairs. Rehema gets up, pushes her chair in.

'Ally got counselling. The best care. She has us. Ally's a strong woman.'

Ma, Ally's broken.

The door creaks open and MaMa appears, squinting in her new glasses.

'I don't like these glasses. Nearly fell down those stairs.'

She takes them off and puts the plastic frames down on the table next to the biscuits.

'That's better. Oh, good. It's teatime.'

'Take a cookie to go, MaMa. I need to get off,' Diana announces abruptly.

She has to get out of here.

Now.

Chapter 33

SUNDAY 24TH OCTOBER, 2010 – THE FOUNTAIN, SHEFFIELD

Bruno

Aamiina is sitting here, next to me, talking about a stretching pussy.

Pinch me, please.

'Bruno, my mum went through hell with her pregnancies. When they cut you, and bind you, the scar tissue is not like vagina. It doesn't stretch.'

Aamiina stares out over the fountain outside the Crucible, sucking on her Rubicon carton. I'm still holding mine, trying to deal with the image in my head.

'When she had my older brothers, it ripped her apart. Her first child died and Usman has epilepsy because he nearly didn't make it out in time and his brain was starved of oxygen. Me and Axmed were both born by C-section because we were born in Nairobi. Mum's body is cut up and ruined, man. She has urinary infections. Kidney damage. Her womb's a rag.'

Focus, Bruno.

I try. I didn't want to meet in a caff, didn't want her thinking it's a date. I just need to know she's OK. And work out what to do about Axmed's situation.

The fountain splutters low. Baggy-bottomed junkies huddle at the other end, two of them touring steps, trying to tax off mothers with prams, old biddies with inhalers, shaky hands gripping carrier bags. Bloke in a suit smoking like his life depends on it. Three kids in High Green uniforms. Bunking.

'Why did your mum want you cut then?'

'Community, innit? Built on clans. If women not cut, you lose control of your community. Why would the older women *not* want the younger to be cut? If you free, they just alone, old, deformed and still have to take care of the men. It's community, culture.'

'That's not culture, Mina! That's barbaric! You just said yourself, Mina – it's wrong.' I sigh. 'Man, if I knew you were getting cut, I'd go and cut them! I don't care if it's a woman! I'd shank her.' I didn't mean to go there but it's making me feel sick all this. I try to change the subject. 'You still want to be a doctor?'

She nods. 'I don't want any woman to go through what my mum did. I'll run away.'

'Is that why Axmed went bonkers in Year 10?'

'It messed with Axmed's head. Now all this community stuff – he can't handle it. He doesn't even want to. Going county is the fastest way he knows to get money and get out. He won't even listen to me any more. Won't tell me anything. Says he's doing it so I don't have to go through it.' Aamiina sighs. 'He's not like that, Bruno, though. He's not good at …'

I nod. I know what she means. Us guys were doing same stuff as him but it was always Axmed who got caught.

I really wish she hadn't told me all this.

There's about a metre between Aamiina and me. She parks her big black tote bag there. It's got her phone and purse in and I put an arm over it as the stringy junkie in stained joggers approaches.

'Lend us fifty pence, love,' he drawls, lids half-closed. 'Lost me bus fare.'

'Piss off!' I spit.

He scowls at me. 'Not asking you.'

'No – I'm telling *you*. Do one.'

He does, like a rat, back to his hole.

'It used to be safe up here,' Aamiina says.

I shrug. 'Selling shite to shite is a booming trade.'

'What our Axmed's doing.'

I rip off the cellophane around the straw, stab the silver dot. Suck up sweetness.

Should have got a can.

Chapter 34

Monday 25th October, 2010 – King Edward's School, Sheffield

Diana waits in the foyer of King Edward's at the end of the school day, back turned to the throng of students pouring out. Volume way up. She waits till the mass has emptied before she turns. The receptionist is pointing at her while remonstrating with a slim Somali girl clutching a file-filled black tote bag.

Diana steps forward. 'Hello, Aamiina. I'm DI Walker. I didn't want to interrupt your classes or go to your house. It's not an interview.'

A heart-shaped face scowls back. Dimples disappear, Aamiina's lips a straight line. 'I've got homework.'

'Just a few questions.'

Aamiina's face twists to a frown. The receptionist, a plump woman with a highlighted bob, opens the side door.

'You can use one of the small interview rooms we usually keep for parental meetings.'

Small is an understatement. There's no window in here, just two chairs and a table. Aamiina sits, bag on her lap like a shield.

'I've got to get back, I've …'

'It won't take more than ten minutes.' Diana pulls her chair in. Aamiina keeps hers against the wall.

'It's about an incident that was reported the summer before you went to King Edward's. End of Year 9.'

A shadow crosses Aamiina's face.

'It's on record you reported it to Ms Calley.'

Aamiina's grip tightens.

'It's important you tell me what you know or even what you're *not* sure you know. She reported someone was going to carry out an FGM procedure on you?'

'I never said that.'

Diana waits.

'Mum and I were stressed in case I didn't get my SAT grades.'

'According to Ms Calley's diary, according to the CSC report, you stayed over at Ms Calley's house that night in July. Just before the summer holidays.'

'So?'

'Why? You're a minor.'

'I had a row with my mum and dad. I didn't want to go home that night. Social services couldn't find somewhere at such short notice so she took me in.'

'Just the night of the 17th?'

Aamiina nods. 'Yeah. I went back home after school next day.'

'Were there any consequences for you staying at Ms Calley's?'

Aamiina glances at Diana, picks at the zip on her bag. 'Consequences?'

'Did you get into trouble?'

She shakes her head. 'My parents moved me to King Edward's School.'

'Is that what you wanted?'

Aamiina looks confused. 'What?'

'Did you have to go through the cutting?'

'No.'

'And you weren't punished in any way?'

'No. Social came round and a couple of bobbies to check up, ask some questions. But me – no.'

'We asked your parents—'

Aamiina's eyes narrow. 'I know.'

'... and they denied this cutting was ever mentioned. Don't have a name for the would-be cutter. They seemed to be very distressed when my sergeant mentioned it.'

Aamiina shrugs, staring at Diana.

OK.

'Well, if you think of anything related to this or hear anything, please let me know.'

Diana passes over her card. Aamiina picks it up.

'Can I go now?'

'Yes, Aamiina.'

Five minutes later, having signed out, Diana walks down the steps outside the school. Shreds of her torn card, now confetti, scutter across the schoolyard.

Chapter 35

TUESDAY 26TH OCTOBER, 2010 – CAFÉ, WOLVERHAMPTON

Diana had spent almost an hour scouring the uni campus and nearby shops. She remembers the Italian coffee house by the bus station. Worth a shot.

Bullseye.

A familiar figure is hunched over a book titled *Data Science III* at a corner table.

'Hello, Aaliyah – sorry, Ally. Is the coffee better here?'

Ally's looks up in disbelief, face twisting into a grimace. 'I should report you for harassment.'

'And I *should* file an arrest interview.'

'For what?'

'For facilitating fraud. For concealing an FGM cutter.'

They stare across the table at each other.

'Instead, I'm buying you coffee.'

Ally blows out her cheeks. 'And the biggest slice of that carrot cake. To go.'

Diana's up ordering, watching Ally frown and fidget. Returning to the table, Diana gently pushes the tiny cup of black across the round table, a yellow polystyrene box and a plastic fork. Ally opens the box, scrapes off vanilla Philadelphia butter cream, picking at the walnuts. Diana sips an Americano.

'What's up with your fingers?' Ally asks.

'Raynaud's disease.' Diana looks at Ally's clubbed paw. 'You?'

'Got trapped behind a door.'

Yeah right.

She watches Ally spoon heaps of white sugar into her espresso. 'It would be much easier if you came up to Sheffield.'

'Easier for you, yeah.'

Diana looks out of the window at the busy street.

'What happened to you in Sheffield?'

Ally's eyes move to the cup's lip.

'You haven't a clue what you're doing here, have you? You go round, stirring things up, solving nothing. You lot just make things a bigger mess than before you started your so-called investigations.'

Diana raises her eyebrows, picking up her cup with both hands. 'Largely because folk don't report incidents when they should.'

Ally laughs a short, brittle cough. 'Like Mary, you mean? She called your lot nuff times. Reported untold shit going off at Legley Road. Where'd that get her, huh?'

Diana sighs. 'It's appalling. An apology's inadequate. But *you* kept schtum for what?' Diana looks around. 'I bet uni is actually quite lonely for you.'

Ally closes her book, picking up her bag.

Diana fastens her with a look. 'Ally, I need to know how you got your injuries. I'm not a doctor, but, at a guess I'd say: a fractured pelvis, eye injury and one brutalised hand, the loss of a finger. That's not from an RTA – nor your fear of returning to Sheffield.'

Ally's eyes grow dull. She looks sideways at a pram parked beside a nearby table.

'If you know, why you asking?' she mutters.

'Was it your fiancé, Ryan Pierce?'

'Ex-fiancé.'

'It was Ryan?'

'I never said that.'

'Didn't deny it either.'

A bus goes by. The coffee machine fizzes and spits. The toilet door opens, closes. A man coughs.

Diana pushes her empty cup to one side. Fingers on tabletop.

'Let me hypothesise: Your book club decide the police are ineffective and you're desperate to get away from Sheffield and Ryan. You break off the engagement, get an offer from uni, make plans. But then … Ryan gets wind. Or jealous. And your book club saves the day.'

Ally's eyes are narrowed, pinning her down with its green glare.

'Detective, don't go accusing *anyone* at the book club. I wouldn't be alive, let alone have a chance of rebuilding what's left of my life, without them. They did more to serve and protect than any of you lot. Fat lot of use I got out of my taxes.'

Diana lets her rage on before quietly asking: 'Has Ryan been in touch since?'

'You can stay here with your "hypothesis". I've no time for this.'

'Ally, if you don't tell me the details, I can't serve and protect, can I? Not you or some other unsuspecting young woman out there with a bright future. The Ryan Pierces of this world believe they have the right to take that – because no one stops them.'

Ally looks at the pram again.

'You don't know that. You don't know anything.'

'I wouldn't say I don't know *anything*, but yes, I don't know enough. Enlighten me.'

'Enlighten yourself!' Ally snaps back.

'Ally, if not you, he'll find someone else on whom to dump his inadequacy and rage. It was never about you, you do know that, don't you? All I need is you to be brave enough to allow me to do my job. A name, a date, a—'

Ally grips the edge of the table. 'No! Because then it'll all come out …' She breaks off suddenly, reddening, aware she's said too much already.

'Including how Lubanzi got you doctors who didn't ask questions or notify police …?'

Ally hisses: 'I am not going to court! You can't make me.' She's trembling.

In a heartbeat, Diana sees Lubanzi and her mum in the witness dock, skewered by the defence solicitor, twisted into criminals by his knowledge of the law. She takes a deep breath, closes her eyes. *Don't bottle it now, lass.*

'OK. Here's what I *think* happened, Ally. I'm probably, hopefully wrong. I often am. A gloved-up Ryan Pierce is stalking you out. His ego's a bit dented after you dumped him based on Mary telling you about the blonde.'

Ally snorts. 'A bit?'

'Well, whatever you want to call it. He sees Daniels call in to collect your keys one evening ... or, I don't know ... needed to make sure you wouldn't say anything about the school finances. According to the school's Facebook photos, you were fit and healthy at the staff Christmas do on Friday December 21st at The Bridge pub. Let's say later that evening?'

Ally blinks.

'Ryan sees Daniels call in to collect your keys ... seeing as you've now left Legley Road High. Puts two and two together and makes sixty-nine. Why doesn't he confront Daniels – or maybe he did?'

Ally gives a dramatic shrug.

'Either way, there's a knock on the door shortly after Daniels left, so you assume it's Daniels again ...'

Ally swallows.

'Only it's not, is it? And it's not Rehema or Lubanzi, who you *were* expecting as they were going to drop off your Christmas present. The person at the door is not welcome and you tell him so, which doesn't seem to go down well.'

Ally clenches her fist.

'I don't know what he said, or what you said, but at some point words ran out and the furniture moved in. A fractured pelvis – fridge freezer on top of you. Your left finger ... ring finger – I am guessing he didn't want you to get married to someone else? Or he wanted to keep it as a memento?'

'You've got some imagination, detective, I'll give you that.' But Ally's face says the opposite.

'And he left – assuming you were finished, one way or another, and that Daniels would get the blame.'

Diana's not mentioned the rape. That would be too much, but Ally's face tells it all: no longer defiant, twisted – but fragile, broken, frightened. Alone. Diana should have been there. She sees Rehema and Lubanzi knocking at the door, not giving up, looking through the letter box, seeing the ruin. Making a decision *not* to call the police. *Not* to call the ambulance.

Ally stares out of the window. Diana rattles her brain for some logic. Why had her mum and Lubanzi, two socially responsible, professional women, chosen a route that cost them, one that risked having another woman's life on their hands? Just wished the trauma away. If it's not reported, it never happened and the shame won't stick.

Why not just call the police?

Because they had seen what had happened to Mary when *she* called the police. They *thought* they were doing the best thing. They believed they were giving Ally the best chance.

While effectively giving a free pass to Ryan Pierce.

'That would make a good horror movie, detective.' Ally gives a slow hand clap. Her face has closed up. Diana gives a wry smile and a shrug.

'Maybe. But there are some things I *can* prove ... Mary writes of a safeguarding incident concerning a female student ...'

'Safeguarding?'

'Suspected FGM.'

Ally snaps back, glad to get the attention away from her. 'Mary reported anything she suspected. Mrs Braithwaite proper hated her as she was forever writing her reports.'

'You don't know any details?'

'I do not. I was assistant bursar not the Designated Person for telling that shit to.'

Diana watches Ally stab at the cake. 'Mary's diary states she stayed with you after the Year 10 parents' evening in November 2007, right?'

Ally's hand trembles as she tries to put the plastic fork down, her face screwing up. A prong snaps.

'It's all in Mary's diary, remember? And in her medical records.'

Ally's eyes close. 'Kin 'ell, Mary.'

Diana continues: 'Mary's the last to leave school. It's dark. She comes out the back as caretaker's locked front entrance. Someone punches her in the gut, kicks her on the ground. This someone is

264

a female, wearing a brown anorak and headscarf. She says "*Ka daa!*" And something harsh in Somali. Then she's gone. Mary's lying there, nine at night in the dark. In pain. Who does she call? The police?'

Ally's hand still trembles as she stabs the cake with the plastic fork.

'No. She calls you, doesn't she? What happens next?'

Ally looks around the café. Professional women in suits with briefcases, River Island carrier bags, on the phone, one mum with a baby in a pram. No one who would understand this terror. These women can sip cappuccino, eat gluten-free Bakewells, fiddle with their paninis, laugh.

'I'd just finished writing my application, was in the bath. When I go to the lounge, there's a missed call. I call back. She's panting. I'm proper scared. Like "Where are you?" She's like, "Ally, I've been hit. I can't move." Told her I wor calling the police. But she won't let me, just tells me to come. That she was on back school steps. I get a cab straight off.'

'Which cab company?'

'Usual one I use. Ahmed Taxis.'

'Go on …'

'I get there, tell him to wait for me. I go round back, scared in case they're waiting for me. She's lying doubled-up on steps. I'd have missed her if she wasn't moaning. I get her up. She's screaming in pain. I walk with her to the cab. Cab driver's freaking out a bit, but he says nothing all the way back.'

Ally's brow beads with sweat.

'She stays at mine overnight, takes a load of painkillers. I call in sick for her. She's never taken a day off and I tell her she's got to go to the doctor's. She won't eat or drink. Says it hurts. When I come back from school, I go with her to the GP's and he gives her some stronger painkillers. She says he made her an appointment with the stomach consultant.'

Diana frowns. 'Why didn't she call the police?'

Ally drains the espresso.

'Who punched her? Someone she knew? An angry parent? Pierce? Young? Daniels?'

Ally glares at Diana. 'I just told you.'

265

'No, you didn't. I gave you a description.'

'Mary's diary gave you a description.' Ally pushes her cup away.

'Ryan was sending her very menacing and threatening texts.'

Ally's face flashes pure anger. 'That prick doesn't speak Somali or wear a headscarf.'

'Why wouldn't Mary report this?'

'Why would she? Police not come to any of her calls before. Mary kept secrets.'

Diana nods. 'True. But she did tell you more than she told the GP. More than she told the school, and certainly more than she ever told the police.'

The buzz of female chatter, the radio, the hissing, spitting coffee machine.

Ally shrugs. 'I told Lubanzi after she'd been to the doctor's. Lubanzi and Rehema went round to see her. Next thing I know Mary's not at school.' She pauses. 'They got her into priority sheltered housing. Before I left Sheff, she's gone.'

'And none of you discussed it for two years?'

'Of course we did! It hurt. We just had to assume she wanted a clean break.'

'"Had to assume." Well, so far a dead Mary's telling us more than all the living members of the Black Sistahs Book Club.'

Ally grabs her bag, standing up. 'I've got lectures.'

Diana leans in. 'Ally, I have a suspicion that you – or someone in the book club – *knows* who the FGM cutter was. I need you – or them – to come forward. Otherwise, next time I see you, it won't be coffee, cake and a chat. It'll be an arrest for aiding and abetting.'

The door swings. Diana stares at the abandoned carrot cake impaled on the broken plastic fork.

Chapter 36

SATURDAY 30TH OCTOBER, 2010 – DEWBOW

Bruno

Not in mood for dickheads today. So of course they all decide to pay me a visit at the butcher's. This one's moaning about the sausages being twisted funny. I'll twist *his* sausage funny. But I weighed him out his pound of porky flesh. Exactly.

'Where are you from?' he goes.

'Sheffield.' I snip the sausages.

'I mean where are you really from?'

'Sheffield.' I turn around now, look him right in eye. Slam sausages on paper and start wrapping.

He's leaning on counter with his hairy elbows and blobby nose. 'Where do you *originate* from?'

Man. 'Where do *you* originate from?'

He pulls himself up with a smirk. 'I'm British.'

Never mind, mate.

'Same here.'

'No, I mean …'

I Sellotape his sausages. 'You mean my heritage? What's yours?'

'I'm English.'

I mock surprise. 'Me too.'

His eyes narrow.

I say: 'Ohhhh you mean *English*. Invaders, immigrants, pirates, hybrids, slaves and tyrants from what – fifty nations? Which one, mate? Me, I'm green, yellow and black all wrapped up in red, white and blue. More British than this pork chop.'

I slap one on top of his precious sausages. He swallows, frowns, looks about for Mr Samuels.

'Where's proper butcher? Just came in for my sausages not a bloody history lesson …' he mutters.

'One pound fifty-three pence please.'

He puts a fiver on glass counter. I take it with a thumb and finger, go to till to get him his change. I give it him slowly in coins. Man bolts. I go to the door with his sausage parcel. He's already down road.

'Oi.'

He turns, petrified.

'Sausages.'

He snatches parcel.

Prick.

I walk back into shop. Mr Samuels is at the counter. 'What's going on, Bruno?'

Maya's car pulls up and she gets out. Door rings as she enters. That perfume: something rich, earthy, exotic like oranges and woodsmoke. All swag with her designer purse and a wink at me that makes me glad I've got this apron on.

'Mr Wilson looked upset. You short him on his sausage?' Samuels glares at me.

'He wor being rude.'

'*You* were being rude!'

'He's ignorant.'

Maya's looking between us. She gives Samuels hard eye. He tuts, wiping his hands on his apron.

'Yes, lad, he is. But he's also a customer. Look, you've worked hard today and no lunch.' He gives us a side-nod. 'Go on. Get off.'

I go out back, scrub off, put on my hoodie. Sure I see Axmed bobbing about out back. They need to get out of Dewbow. It's stressing me out today. I've seen Axmed and Malco three times and Ryan passing through in his grubby white van like he knows

– no, *owns* – the place. When I go to shop on my break, guys on the street give me the nod like I'm serving.

I walk out front. Mr Samuels hands me my envelope.

'What's this?'

Please not my P45.

He frowns. 'Your wage.'

'Nice one, Mr Samuels.'

'See you next Saturday, Bruno. I might need you for some weekdays as it's peak season. Just be courteous. If customers are rude to you, let me take care of it.'

I jog down the street, hoping to get the 4.30 bus. I hear brakes behind me, a car pulling up. I spin around as an electric window purrs. Maya leans over leather upholstery.

'Samuels said you had a bad day, Bruno?'

'Man.' But now it's my head that's buzzing.

She nods, opens the passenger door.

'Get in. You can have a brew at mine. 4.30 bus has just gone.'

Her car's immaculate. I bet she has it valeted every week. Backseat full of Waitrose bags and bouquets of flowers. Her tanned hands are perfect. Dainty nails. Am sure those rings are diamond. She must have a baller bloke. Gold bracelet banging on the leather headed gear stick. She knows how to live! Maybe she can teach me. Bass speakers bumping Nas's *The World is Yours* in Dewbow. I want to laugh out loud. Window down, staring out the numpties with their baskets and snide looks.

I sigh. 'Sorry – it's just some of the customers ...'

'I know. I'll get Samuels to have a word. Lots of folk in the village appreciate your butchery, Bruno. Samuels himself is well impressed by how fast you're picking up the jointing of larger cuts.'

She turns into the drive of this mansion. *Dewbright Hall.* 'It's not for everyone.'

Is she talking about butchery or ... this? She's talking more, but I don't hear any of it.

'Been shopping?'

Dumb question, Bruno. No, she's just been on a shoplifting spree.

'Yes, doing a big brunch party for my book club tomorrow. You can help me set up if you like.'

If I like? Yes, I like.

I nod, just hearing the roar of trumpets, feeling the bassline, seeing in front of me the biggest Fk Off mansion I have ever seen. A drive as long as my old street. A pond – scratch that. A *lake* that wraps around the side.

'Is this your yard?' I manage.

'Yard?' she says, with a small smile. Her lips red, perfectly lush, anime-style.

'This your gaff?'

She just chuckles. 'Yes, Bruno, this is my gaff. Gaff. I like that. Might change the title deeds.'

She taking the piss now? I feel daft. She parks up on a gravel yard. Pulls up the handbrake. Unclicks her belt and gets out. Bends down to face me.

'Don't worry about the buses. I'll take you back later.'

My pride's about to say 'It dunt matter, I can make my own way back' but I want to know what her life's like. What is it like to live in a place the size of a school? I've never been this close to proper money – not rolls of elastic-banded twennies in socks, but vaults and ponds and title deeds and a front porch with a boot scraper. She shuts the driver door and heads down a flagged path. That arse in those ... what are they? Leggings? Not jeans. You'd never catch her in jeans. That arse in *anything*.

Bruno, stop it. You pervert.

I'm just sitting here like a gormless moron, staring out at windows half the height of lamp posts. I unclick the seat belt, get out. Stare around me. She is marching around the corner. I guess I'm meant to follow. More buildings – all of stone. Proper country manor. Wait till I tell ... who? Who could I tell about this?

I'm telling no one.

I quick jog to catch up with her.

'This where you grew up?'

'No. No. Mostly weekends.'

Weekends? I spent my weekends at bus stops and on street corners. Where did she live in the *week* then? A marquee? A

270

treehouse? I feel ignorant now – just like that bloke in the butcher's. Stupid, small. I want to go home.

No, I don't want to go home at all.

I don't ever want to go home.

At the back door, I stand on the doormat.

'Should I take off my trainers?'

She unlocks the door. 'If you want. Make yourself at home.'

Chapter 37

SUNDAY 31ST OCTOBER, 2010 – DEWBRIGHT HALL, DEWBOW

Bruno

I'm upstairs, showering off. Been up since seven, working on her brunch party thing. Then Maya gives me a very different kind of breakfast in bed. Sex with Maya must be what driving a Ferrari feels like. I'm still feeling dizzy. I told her a lot last night, I think. Maybe too much. About Ryan's dodgy business and what he's doing with Axmed and how I don't want to go back to the Hut. Got the fear a bit today.

Her place is dead modern apart from that creepy stag head. She was asking about my schoolteachers and who was my favourite. That was weird. I don't want to think about school when I'm with her ... Maybe I'll stay and finish off that game on PlayStation.

Bruno, get a grip! It's not your yard.

I can hear women guests screaming, squealing, heels on the gravel drive. Volvos and a beamer and couple of runarounds in the drive; not on her level. I see a bunch of black and brown women get out. Social workers, nurse types. One of them's crippled. One a proper Yard girl. I peek from behind the curtains. That African granny is walking up the drive.

'I'll just tell them you're my private chef!' Winking at me from the bathroom door before she went downstairs.

I can hear her opening the big wooden front door, looking lush, super-groomed, even in her cords and a cashmere polo neck. Reminds me of somebody. JLo? Na. Someone I know … Lickle gold bouncing off her but not flashy. There's more squeals from the sisters. House is *huuuuge*.

I did good with all her Waitrose groceries. Table spread with every cut of cold meat, saltfish and ackee, plantain, fried dumplings, carrot juice and orange juice and pomegranate – pomegranate! – juice. Fresh mango, pineapple. Cinnamon pumpkin muffins. Brioche! She says it's a mix of a croissant and hard dough and challah. Didn't want to tell her I haven't a clue what challah is. Full fat proper Philadelphia cheese. And now I know how to make coffee machine coffee, I could get a job in Starbucks.

The pantry's bigger than Mum's flat. Polished floorboards, big Persian rugs, more wine bottles than an offy. Is that a car or a fridge? Windowsills so deep I'm not sure if it's a floor or a step. I felt so class laying the tables with a right feast: blood oranges, grapes – like those big green Waitrose grapes the size of plums not them withered mouldy ones Mum sometimes gets off Castle market.

'What's that?' I hear a voice. A voice I recognise. I freeze.

'Venison. Smoked. Straight off the estate.' That's Maya.

Estate. Not council either.

'It's deer, my dear.' An African voice.

'They don't have deer burgers in your uni canteen, Al?'

'No, they don't. Great start to my reading week!'

I know that voice. Who is that?

I can hear them cooing over the Bucks Fizz. Orange juice with champagne – Maya says it's a posh breakfast treat. She's got on some 1990s R & B music like what Mum plays.

I need to know who that voice is before I chip. I look out on the back, at frost on dead leaves on the slabs. Flat heavy sky reflected in that pond-lake.

'Are there fish in that?' That voice again.

'My dad put perch in there – I'm not an angler myself. More a hunter.' Maya again.

'Fried fresh fish too!'

273

Fk it. Just go already.

I'm tying up my laces in the back hallway. I hear a thud and scrape across the floor before I realise, too late, someone's in the kitchen. I feel someone staring at me, look up and see a twisted shape leaning against the counter with a coffee cup, holding it funny. She puts her cup down, fist behind her back. Those green eyes, one droopy. A dark line across her top cheek.

Shit.

Maya comes in from behind her. 'Here he is! Ally, meet Bruno, my private chef who helped me prepare ...' She grabs a plate of pancakes and returns to the sunroom and women.

I stand up full height from my squat, stare straight back into those green eyes. The woman is frozen, her eyes begging me: *Please no*. She shakes her head. I nod. My gut a knot. Grab the door handle and bolt.

Ally. Oh my dayz.

Diana

Room two, late Sunday morning, stomach growling. Maybe she should have gone to that brunch with MaMa. Diana sighs, edging her blue overlay down the page, slowly re-reading the diary. Notepad at her elbow. Dates scrawled in red Papermate Tempo.

MONDAY 1st OCTOBER 2007

Sick of Daniels straight up lying to me. Sick of Leroy lying, breaking my heart, breaking my window, nearly breaking my arm. Breaking promises – to the kids, to me, to his WIFE and BAIRN. I'm so stupid. Ally had warned me. It's my own fault.

I'm feeling more and more alone here. Just hedged in with Ofsted looming, parents' evenings, exam result analyses, Governors' reports, trying to explain to my kids and my department why the new curriculum is **not** *the new curriculum after all.*

I keep my head down, somehow get through to the weekend but then at the weekend all I do is think. Even when I try not to think, it creeps into my dreams, my memory brings it up like the bile that keeps creeping up from my gut. This weekend all I'm thinking of is Boshreh Akhtar's Original Writing coursework. That's two years ago; she's left now but I have this horrid feeling ...

I'd used a previous AQA coursework title for them to write about a significant moment in childhood of loss or disappointment. Told them to work on their descriptive and narrative techniques, develop a sense of perspective. Show not tell. I remember being a bit thrown off; Boshreh was an A-grade student. She was always good at description from Key Stage 3. So I thought her choosing a birthday party was a bit lame. And it's likely a birthday party in a Park Hill flat may be disappointing. No birthday presents, no fun, no garden.

But now I think of it, she didn't mention it was a **birthday**. And she kept going on about this pink fizzy liquid they were all drinking and the grumpy witch-like aunties with hairy warts and hard eyes and the smell of bleach and disinfectant. The screams. I didn't get why they'd be screaming and crying at a birthday party unless there was a clown or the adults were telling them off.

And she ended with saying how she hates Tesco Value Victoria sandwich cake now and those jammy donuts. Especially the jammy donuts. If she just sees one, she throws up. How it was the worst day of her eight-year-old life and even now, at sixteen, she still thinks it's her worst day and prob-

ably always will. I thought she was being melodramatic. I mean, I had nothing but disappointing birthdays after mum passed.

I gave her a B- and commented: **This is not a significant moment, Boshreh. This is not a disappointing event – it's a disappointing effort. Try again.**

But I'm sitting here right now, thinking on Aamiina staying here and remembering how I used to get cross with the girls for having 'period' or 'urinary tract infections' all month, every month, going out of class to the toilet or so many 'medical' absences without a doctor's note.

Man. She was an A-grade in all her other English coursework.

'Not a disappointing event'?

No – it was the **worst** *event.*

Aamiina's at King Edward's now so I can't ask her. And the police never got back to me.

I've been trying to tell myself it's OK but—

It's happening here, isn't it? To the girls in my classroom, in my care.

And I can't even stop it.

Diana leans back, rubbing her hands over her eyes. If this comes out, it does not make the police or CSC look good. If this does *not* come out, the criminals get to carry on another day. She can already hear Lawton's dismissive: 'Irrelevant!' and Marchant signing her off for traffic duties in Bolton.

Bruno

Where's this bus? Sunday innit. It's foggy and cold out here. Got one bar of battery. I switched it off last night. Three texts from Axmed yesterday. Ten missed calls. Three off Mum.

AXMED: Bro. WHERE R U? Need 2 talk.

AXMED: Bro, pick up ya fone.

AXMED: Bro! Ansa ya fkin fone.

They're still buzzing through.

AXMED: Bro, r u ded?

He answers on first ring
'Where've you been? Need to talk to you!' He's tearing my ear off.
'You in a car?' I ask.
'Yeah.'
'Who with?'
'Gary.'
'Who's Gary?'
'Gary. He drives for us.'
Who's us?
'Where are you?'
'Where are *you*, bro?'
'You know where I am – Dewbow.'
'The butcher's? On a Sunday?'
'Axmed, where are you?' I keep my voice low, definite.
'Just leavin – what's this Gary?'
Some mumbling. That'll be the Gary.
'Matlock.'

277

'Right. Pick us up,' I say.

'Where, bro?'

'I'll be walking up towards Baslow from Dewbow.'

'Baslow?'

'Hurry up.'

I hang up. Hand shaking. I'm trying to piece together what's happened. What I just saw. Last night was enough, but this morning … Adrenaline thumping in my head, my legs like pistons. I feel sick. My head spins, stomach cracks into my mouth—

I stare down at the pool of bile and coffee and bits of egg. Bitter bile in my mouth.

Get it together, Bruno.

Halfway up the hill, my head's pounding. How did she get like that? Maybe it was a car crash. Yeah, that'll be it.

Shut up, man.

If it was a car crash, she'd not be hiding, not be scared – man, that look on her face. No 'Hiya, Bruno!' Like she used to.

There's a squeal of tyres behind me. A blue Cavalier pulls up onto the kerb.

'Alright?' A whiff of weed from the drawn-down window. Axmed's long arm hanging out the passenger side.

'Took your time.'

I open the back door and get in, shoving a clutter of cartons and pop bottles to the floor. Car's a dump, stinks of old skunk, BO and stale Chinese. Axmed looks at me in the rear-view.

'Bro, you look like you've seen a ghost. For real.'

I look at this Gary fella in the mirror. He's probably in Ryan's back pocket. Just stares at me and says, 'Alright'.

'Yeah. Well, Hallowe'en innit.'

Axmed locks eyes with me. *Shut it. Wait till we out.* Axmed nods, turns up the dial for Giggs' 'Matic'. I lean back, close my eyes and focus on not spewing.

Open them when we out of Totley.

'Drop us off on London Road, mate,' I say.

'Not a taxi service,' he grunts.

Axmed frowns at him. 'Drop me off 'n' all.'

Soon as rear end of the blue Cavalier is beyond the lights,

278

Axmed turns to me. His eyes are sunk in dark, sleepless hollows, some shadow on his upper lip and chin. His jeans look three-day worn.

'Bro, police pulled me in again. I mean CID. This Phillips guy and a Detective Lawton. Right bastard.'

'They've nothing on you. Don't get dramatic.'

I kick a can into the road.

A cab honks. I give him the finger. 'It's nowt.'

'What's up with you? Where've you been? Wait – I need Rizlas.' He steps into a paper shop.

'Get us a juice. My mouth's rank.' I stay outside. Stare at the A-board. *Legley Road PE teacher missing.* On the other side, *Body Parts found in Pastor's garden.*

He comes out, passes me a juice, Rizlas between his teeth and juice for himself in his other hand. He puts Rizlas in his pocket. I walk on to the basketball court to sit down.

'What happened to Miss Matthews?'

'Who? IT lady? Fk her. Bro, I want to know where *you've* been.'

I stare ahead, trying to remember the last time I'd seen her.

'Why'd she leave?'

He shrugs. 'I dunno. New job? Wasn't she your dad's gyal or summat? He'll know.'

I down the juice. Peer over the park at a wino shuffling through a bin. Stare at the demolition site that used to be Legley Road High School.

'They broke up three year back.'

'What we talking about her for?'

I finish my juice, crumple up the carton in my fist. 'I think I just saw her.'

'Where?'

'In Dewbow.'

'What you doing in Dewbow?'

I look down at a scuff on my trainers. 'She was mash up. I mean, deformed. Crippled. Face had a scar across her cheek 'n' eye, finger missing. She were shuffling about with this limp.'

'Bet she's on crack.'

I give him a side look. 'Shut up, man.'

'I dunno, bro. Did you call the ambulance?'

'You dumb, Axmed? No – I mean, it's *happened* to her. Time ago.'

'What?'

I give up.

'Bad luck then. Anyway, what we gonna do about the Feds?'

'What are *you* going to do, you mean. You're the one in Ryan's pocket.'

'So are you.'

'Not like you. I warned you. Been warning you. Since Year 9.'

Axmed looks down at the choddy in tarmac ground. His face twist up.

'Am not going back to Somalia. No way.'

'You'd rather do jail? Or this? Apply for college or summat.'

'It's easy for you.'

I hurl the crumpled carton at the overflowing bin. It misses.

'Nothing's *easy* for me!'

I walk off. Can't deal with this. I can't deal with something edging into my brain. Some toxic reality I don't want to let in. But the foot's in the door.

Axmed calls after me: 'Bro! We need to sort out a plan.'

'Fk a plan!'

Njambi

This food is too rich. I drink the coffee and eat slices of mango and berries only. I sit on the window seat, looking out on the lake. The others are feasting, laughing, eyes greedy for the house and the good things. Maya approaches, smiling and carrying a glass of pomegranate juice.

'I don't want to sound ignorant, Njambi, but what's your case about? Rehema keeps saying you have a case against the British Government. Maybe I can help you get a good solicitor?'

'She has a good solicitor, Maya. Leigh Day,' Rehema calls across the room.

'I can speak for myself, Rehema.'

The music stops. Outside a crow squawks.

There is too much noise in here. I don't want to eat. I want to sit out in the cold air. Look on the trees. I have never seen trees shed leaves like these: gold, red, amber, lifting their skeletons to the sky. Limbs built on faith and deep, deep roots. I get comfort from these bare trees.

I go to stand by the side door, pulling my shawl around me.

'MaMa! What are you doing? Are you OK?'

I look at her and she looks away.

'I'm fine. I just want fresh air.'

'Let her go, Rehema.' Maya waves one hand, the other is on a knife as she slices a pineapple on the sideboard.

'I'll come too, Njambi. I need a smoke. Just put my coat on.'

I don't want company but I don't want to say no to the woman with the limp. She reminds me of Tanika from the camp.

Outside fog pools around the lake. My breath too forms small clouds. The cold is like the uplands, mornings with my father.

'If I don't move, I get stiff,' Ally says. 'I've eaten so much I'll fall asleep. Plus, I need a cig.'

She sits on a low stone wall. I walk around the large pond. There are lilies at one end. I can see flashes of grey fish. But it's black in there. I look at the land, the house and the trees. I try to remember what it felt like to own the air that I breathe.

But the air is heavy here, pulling down to the ground. Not like the air of the uplands, rising to the skies.

My eyes are not good for far away, but I see the limping girl watch me, pulling on her homemade cigarette, small puffs rising up. Her other hand, the one like a paw, grips the stone wall. Then she takes a long pull, flicks the last of it into the lake where it bobs on the surface. We both watch as a shape from beneath emerges, a grey spotty skin underwater. Bubbles appear and a pink open fish grin grasps at the bait before spitting it out, returning to the depths.

Ally stands up. I walk around to her.

'Let's go back in.'

Ally leads me back to the window seat, sitting down. The music is low. Rehema stands by the far window, looking out at the lake still. She must have been watching us.

281

'Who's this Hulda Stump woman, Ma? Diana said ...' Rehema says.

'Stumpf. Hulda Stumpf. She raised me after my father left. Before the school.' I sit down.

Lubanzi, the church lady, looks up from her plate. 'Hulda? She was the prophetess in King Josiah's reign.'

The others say nothing but I know Miss Hulda *was* a prophetess. She warned them. They didn't listen.

'What was it like, Kenya back then?' Shola asks, sipping pomegranate juice from a glass.

Ally mutters: 'Sake, Shola. Leave her be.'

'It is fine,' I say.

They want truth to give them some root. I'll give them some. But they will spit it straight out. Swallow instead the fake bait.

Pauline piles slices of venison, potato salad, tomato salad on her plate. Shola gnaws on a rib. Rehema cracks pistachios. Maya pours wine into glasses. I stare out at the trees. I tell it to them.

'We were put in camps. "Protected villages". But we were not the ones protected. We were from different Kenyan communities. I saw things I cannot unsee.'

'Like what?'

I shake my head. 'I can speak of it. It is not *my* shame – it's the shame of the violators.'

I see Pauline put her plate down. Maya sits cross-legged on the floor. Ally reaches over and holds my hand with three fingers. Rehema only stares, her face taut, framed against the window.

'Many died in the camps. Sometimes we got bad food, sometimes none. Sometimes water, sometimes none. Often they whip or beat us with nails in sticks.'

I roll up my sleeve and they gasp at the white smooth scar like a flat egg above my elbow.

'Many died – from injuries, disease or starvation. Those of us who dared to survive ... we had our sex ripped out of us. I see men castrated ... I see ...'

I am not here. They cannot see me.

'My friend, Jane. Two men each hold an arm, one man he prise her thighs apart like a clam. White man sit on a chair in front as they inset the bottle of boiling water and he force it in

282

with the sole of his foot, push, push while the Kenyan looked on, directed him. She had not taken the oath. Neither me. I still hear her screams. Buried deep inside me.'

'You told your solicitor all this?'

I don't know how you show a solicitor these scars.

Rehema stares out at the lake, her back to the room, gripping the window frame, her shoulders up and down like pistons. Ally's eyes shine. Maya looks up at me like I am some goddess, sitting bare-soled, cross-legged at my feet.

Bruno

I get back to the streets in the sky. Streets in the sky. Streets in hell more like – where *every* day is Hallowe'en. Park Hill walkways always have ghouls and ghosts. Kids in mash-up tacky outfits with old man eyes and real knives. Blood on the piss-drenched concrete stairs and it's not fake. Real live rats in the lifts, in the walkways rummaging in overflowing shitty nappies, their heads in value bean cans, tails in yellow polystyrene takeaway cartons. Filter tips, screwed-up foil balls, bent needles tossed next to a baby's mitten next to a random buckled buggy. Nowt more scary than home sweet home. Bins bin liners screams bags of more nappies and shit shit everywhere tags telling me someone WOZ ERE just to prove he's not a ghost but he's fooling no one he *is* a ghost because no one sees him *ever* even if he leaves blood sweat tears 'n' shit. Shit.

They might remember the shit.

This is where I grew up. But not my home. Used to be safe when Nan lived at number fifty-four. That is for sure. I know Nan loved me. That's real.

I unlock the front door. Telly's on. Mum's on phone, moaning about summat to someone. I run straight upstairs. Need a piss.

Hear her yelling: 'Bruno? Come here!'

I slam and lock bathroom door.

Her thumping it. 'Where were you last night? Why ent you answered your phone?'

283

Go to the sink. Wash me hands in a sliver of grey soap. Keep cold water running. Splash cold water on my face, looking in the soap-splattered mirror.

I want to spit at my reflection, break the glass, smash anything that may look like *him*.

'Bruno! Bruno! Open this door now.'

I'm about to rip off my hoodie. Then stop. I still smell of Maya. Not going in shower. I want to own this stink. I want to stink of her. I want to smell strange. I am strange. Strange to myself. I bust out the door. Mum is right in front of me. Full make-up doesn't hide her knackered face.

'What's up with you? Where've you been?'

'Not your business.'

I go in my room to pick up my phone charger.

'Er – it *is* my business. I'm your mother!'

'Are you?' I mutter.

'What did you say?' Her face in shock. I nudge past her, run down the stairs. She follows me.

'You been with your dad?'

I'm in the kitchen, which is in a right state. Sink full of unwashed dishes. I pick out a mug, rinse it through, fill it with water.

'"Dad"?' I gulp water.

She comes in, staring like a zombie. I look at her, over the rim of the mug.

'Is he? Is *he* my dad?'

She just stares, mouth drooping open like a long O in those scream masks. 'You what?'

'So, I can get a paternity test done and it'll come out positive? Do you want me to do that? I will, you know.'

She's frozen, a Hallowe'en victim.

'He's not my dad, is he? Look me in the eye and tell me he's my dad.'

I walk forward. She backs up against the wall, her mouth still an oval, palms on the broken storage heater.

'Look me in the eye.'

I know she can smell me. Smell difference.

'You are my mum, aren't you? So, you should know.' She looks beyond my ear.

'Bruno,' she whispers. 'I don't know you right now.'

I back off. 'No, you don't know me. You don't even know who my dad is.'

I nudge past her shoulder, head towards front door, her voice behind me.

'Bruno! You ungrateful bastard. I gave birth to …'

I spin around. 'A bastard!'

She stares.

'You just called me one. *Why've* you been raising me? Not exactly had empty pockets because of it, have you?'

Slaps me right on the jaw, door slamming after me.

At the Ryano Hut, dickhead comes into the kitchen, squeezing past, looking me up and down.

'Y Pree, yout.'

Don't Y pree me, you muppet.

'Look at the state of you,' he says.

Good.

'You're not going out front looking like that! Where've you been anyroad?'

I wash my hands, pick up the knife, sharpen it on the block. Once, twice. Take out the first carcass from fridge.

Knobhead's staring at me. 'Oi. You're mucky.'

'I had a shower this morning.'

And the rest.

'Where? Where'd you have your shower?'

'You want to know where I take a shit too?'

He steps closer. I slice under the carcass's pimply skin. 'What happened to Ally?'

'You what?' His face grey. 'What you mean? Why? Have you seen her?'

'Just saying. She just disappeared.'

'We split up.' But he's not looking at me, faffing about with the bins.

'Just left? Like Miss Calley? Like my English teacher left town? The one found dead in a …'

He stands up. Those red-lidded eyes, jowly chin, faded tattoos. Old man. He does a dirty chuckle.

285

'Oh, I get it. You've got a lickle girlfriend in Dewbow? Suddenly think you're cock o' England. Axmed said ...'

'Axmed said what?' He best not have mentioned me seeing Ally. I spin around, still holding the knife. He backs off, lifts his palm.

'Alright, alright, calm down. It's just a bird.'

I start laying the chicken flat on the chopping block.

'I'm your dad. Worried about you.'

Eyes to the board. Peel back the pimply skin.

'You're not though, are you? You're not my dad.'

'You what?' He looks puzzled, like I'm drunk.

'So, you'd take a paternity test?'

'I'll take a paternity test. And I'll tell you this for nowt: I'm the one who's looked after you all these years. Gave you a job when you'd be doing what Axmed's doing or worse.'

'You've not *given* me a job. Just made me a slave. A complete stranger has given me a *job*.'

He grabs me by the front of my hoodie: 'Shut it, you cheeky bastard.'

'Bastard. Yeah. I am. Gerroff me.'

The knife hits his belt buckle. He pushes me back.

'What's your mother been saying?'

He can't even hide the menace, the fear in his voice.

'Been saying nowt. Like you.'

I separate the thighs. Cut along the joint, crack bones open. The only sound: the blade ripping flesh, hitting the board. Repeat. Slap, split, crunch, crack. Slap, split, crunch, crack.

'Watch it, son.' He swallows, moves off, turning at the door. 'Hurry up with that chicken. We've a right queue out here.'

I focus on cracking joints open, pulling sinew from muscle, trying to work out what to do.

My phone's buzzing. Axmed.

I look.

It's not.

Where'd u go? Want a re-run? Call of Duty?

...

U no u want 2.

* * *

286

Diana

Even though it's been a long, tedious day, getting her facts and warrants together, Diana knows she has to call in at her mum's. Clear the air. She doesn't feel good about how they parted the other night.

As soon as Diana pulls up outside, she senses something's off. She parks up and walks slowly along the path, frowning, getting her apology ready. She knocks. The light's on, radio's on. Even after the third attempt, two minutes waiting.

Diana pushes the letter box. 'Ma? It's me. Look, I'm sorry. Ma?'

Diana steps back, looking up at the top lit window, MaMa's old room. She's sure she sees a shadow move. Silently, she edges around the front, over the wall and jogs down, knocking loudly on the back window. Rehema, head in hands, jumps from her slumped position at the table. The terror on her face tells Diana something's seriously off.

'Mum! Open door!'

Rehema staggers up, unlocking and unbolting the door. As Diana enters, she sees her mum's hand shaking. She looks around the orderly kitchen, back to her mum, shiny-eyed, crumpling back into the chair.

'What's happened? Ma?'

Rehema says nothing, just shakes her head. There's a thud and thump upstairs. Diana looks at Rehema, frowning.

'Did you bring MaMa back?'

'No – she's at yours.'

'Then …'

'Ally's up here for reading week.'

Diana's eyes narrow.

'Ma, you best tell me why you're sitting here trembling like you're having a stroke.'

Rehema's voice is low, she stares at the table.

'Ryan Pierce just knocked on my front door. Asked if Ally was here. I said no.'

'And …?'

287

'He gave me a filthy look, pointed at me and stood back down the steps. Then he shouts: "Ally! It's Ryan, love. Just come to say hello." He just stands there and then he says to me: "Tell her I'll catch her later." And then he walks off and gets into a white van.'

Diana's head implodes. There's ten million things she wants to blurt out right now, five she wants to do. There's a thud on the stairs and Diana looks up as a familiar silhouette hobbles into the light of the kitchen. She can't see Diana, standing behind Rehema's chair but Diana can see her.

'Rehema?' Ally asks. Then she gasps, stepping back, seeing Diana.

She doesn't know.

Ally stares at Diana and then at Rehema. Diana shrugs. So, Ma hasn't even told Ally the detective 'stalking' her is her own daughter …

Diana breaks the silence: 'She's just had a bad shock. Did you see or hear anything?'

'I-I …' Ally looks at Rehema helplessly, but Rehema continues to stare at the table.

'Recognised a familiar voice?'

'You call the police, Rehema?' Ally whispers.

'I came to see my mum, who's in a state of shock having had your ex at her front door.'

'Your *mum*?'

'Yes, Ally. My mum. Even police officers have them.'

In the car, her heart's still thudding, a scream stuck somewhere under her ribs as she clicks in her seat belt. *Her mum.* Pierce came to her mum's house, intimidated her, and Rehema still won't call the police. As she turns the key, Diana winces.

So much for Phillips' physical surveillance. If *she* calls it in, she's compromising her place on the investigation.

And her mum will never call it in.

How did Ryan find out Ally was back in town?

CHAPTER 38

Monday 1st November, 2010 – Sheffield HQ

Diana jog-hops with her double espresso from a parking space so tight she'll need a tin opener to get out. She shoulders doors, taking stairs two at a time, splashing scalding black coffee over her hands.

Robertson gets up from his desk, clutching another of his manilla folders. Spick and span, crisp white shirt, tie so square you could cut corners with it. Colgate grin, gelled-back hair with the irrepressible cowlick. She gives a wry smile, following him into the briefing room.

Neville, Khan, O'Malley and Lawton are already inside, Lawton sipping a milky brew from a giant Sheffield Wednesday mug. He looks pointedly at his watch. She leans against the back wall while Robertson sits on a chair, his folder in front of him on the chipped veneer of a desk.

'Right. Let's make a start. Lots of new intel and we need to get pulling some of these POIs in. I've asked DI Phillips to join us after I've updated you all.'

He flicks out an envelope, brandishing it like a magician.

'Following surveillance on the Manchester OCG and Pierce's crew including his son Bruno, and Axmed Ahmed, we have evidence they're running lines into Dewbow, north Derbyshire.'

Some surveillance. They obviously hadn't surveyed him at her mum's last night …

Robertson mouths: 'Dewbow, Boss?'

Diana just raises her eyebrows, fixes her deadpan look on Lawton. She really wants to insist on an arrest – especially since he's called at Rehema's. But, without Ally making a formal complaint, it's hard to make a case for it. Calling around to ask to see an ex-girlfriend is scraping at harassment with no history.

Lawton opens the envelope, sticking telephoto shots on the board with Blu-Tack.

'Possibly using the front of Bruno who appears to be working at the butcher's. Interesting skill considering the method of mutilation …'

'Wow!' says O'Malley.

Lawton nods. 'Yes, our Bruno is there every Saturday, slicing and dicing, serving the good folk of Dewbow. Maybe not just bacon and rump steak either …'

Neville chuckles. 'Bit of scrotum with your sausage, ma'am?'

Diana pulls up a seat next to Robertson.

Lawton sticks close-up photos of Axmed and Bruno face-to-face down the alley

behind the butcher's. Bruno looks angry, raising his hands. Axmed, hood up but face clear, seems to be trying to placate him, an open palm out. Diana notes the orange poster in the window promoting the Bakewell Autumn Festival on Saturday 23rd September. That pic is old. Must have been when Bruno'd just started.

Robertson frowns and mutters to Diana.

Lawton glares at them both. 'Care to share, Robertson?'

Robertson clears his throat. 'I was just saying to DI Walker, sir, that Bruno was always so anti drugs when I was at Legley Road.'

'He doesn't appear to be now.'

Diana says: 'Two friends having a disagreement down an alley is hardly critical evidence. And it was taken ages ago – all the posters for the autumn festival were taken down first week in October.'

Lawton scowls. 'Yes, but why are they in Dewbow?'

'Because Bruno works there?'

'But Axmed never takes the bus there. And what about these?'

290

Lawton pastes up more photos showing Ryan's white van, Axmed jumping in, out, two white youths in hoodies, one in a plaid shirt. Axmed in a park talking to a well-dressed youth. Another photo of a youth in the Chinese takeaway. One of him coming out empty-handed, getting into a red Ford Mondeo.

'Whose is the Mondeo?' asks Diana.

'Licensed to an Omear Rajib, but he's not driving.'

DI Phillips walks in. Diana doesn't need to turn around. The same Imperial Leather soap smell, his particular stench of sweat masked with several layers of Joop! She buries her nose in the Styrofoam cup to mask her nausea.

Lawton smiles broadly at him. 'Morning, Phillips! Want to update them on how this links with your operation and the OCG?'

Phillips strides forward, both hands in his pockets. He sweeps the room, eyes over Diana's head. Behind her, Marchant's cough.

'We've had surveillance on Ryan Pierce—'

Diana snorts. He glares at her.

'—and his trans-Pennine express to a cash and carry in Newton Heath, Manchester for almost a year now. We know he's distributing – but small time. Just MDMA and marijuana. And just to kids.'

'Just to kids?'

'I mean, not volumes. No Class A – yet. The network's there though, and his chicken shop's never going to bank much. He's got several youths delivering for him.'

'Including Bruno?'

Phillips stares at DC Khan like he's just farted.

'Not Bruno. We've had eyes on him for some time, but nothing doing. As yet. But these guys – the Liverpool crew – are trying to get into Derbyshire and go through the back roads into Staffordshire too. We've got covert surveillance in both Liverpool and Manchester but just us CID working Sheffield.'

Diana frowns. 'There are plenty of dealers in Sheffield! Why focus on Pierce, especially if he's not shifting heavy volumes and Class As?'

'Pierce is the only one dealing with this cut-throat lot – code name Ting X – operating out of Manchester. They don't mess with any established gangs; they're wanting to undercut them in every way, but when they sting, they're brutal. Not a nice bunch.'

Robertson asks: 'So how's Pierce involved?'

'It may have something to do with the fact he's been a regular at the cash and carry for a decade, knows the scene. No record as such. We want to keep it that way for now. We risk ruining a major complex case if we shift Pierce and literally give the reins of power to a deadly gang,' Lawton says.

'Yeah, OK, but what's all that got to do with this homicide case?' Diana folds her arms. This is not adding up.

Phillips sighs like he's explaining something to a ten-year-old. 'Because Daniels may have threatened—'

'May have?'

'Can I finish? Thank you. May have threatened to tell on Pierce's distributing if he didn't pay him a tax for the privilege.'

'And the Ting X crew did not like that risk. So they took care of it,' Lawton adds.

Diana scowls at the carpet. *Took care of it.* These guys watch too much TV.

'Sir, we need to pull Ryan Pierce in for an intelligence interview. Or go to his place ...'

Phillips snaps. 'No! You shouldn't even have gone to interview his son there.'

'Bruno? Why?'

'We don't want to spook the OCG.'

'Spook? How exactly?'

'You don't need to know.'

'Well, I probably do, if this is such a major op.'

Phillips closes his eyes, exhales. 'Look, if Pierce *is* your man, it will be linked to the OCG op, so your little fishing expedition may well cost us a two-year op and our undy's cover.'

Marchant clears his throat. They turn to see him standing at the door.

'Walker, do you have enough evidence for an arrest?'

Diana frowns. 'For Pierce? No. But we do need an interview for intelligence or elimination.'

Marchant shakes his head. 'He's probably not going to tell you owt and you're chancing your arm.'

292

Phillips addresses Marchant only. 'Until we've got hard evidence Pierce is holding guns and setting up the county line network, sir, bringing him in prior to a full-on arrest is jeopardising the whole op.'

'We have no evidence that Pierce was blackmailing Daniels though. Robertson and I went through Daniels' bank account and the school finances and ...' Diana says.

'Pierce operates in cash. Daniels cleared his debts with cash payments.'

'That was through re-appropriating Mary Calley's new curriculum money,' Diana says.

'It was cash he deposited, Walker.' Lawton dismisses Robertson with an eyeroll. 'Axmed Ahmed, who runs drugs for Pierce, was also the tagger at Legley Road High School. He could have been indicating the site or sending a message to someone. For someone.'

'And Bruno Pierce was there too,' Phillips says.

Diana stares into her empty cup. 'None of this will stand in court.'

Marchant barks: 'Enough. Walker, no more interfering with Pierce.'

Diana closes her eyes. *Interfering with Pierce.*

He continues: 'But, Phillips, pull your finger out and get some evidence fast for this OCG wrap-up. If he's running guns, I want him in. Then we can square him with this homicide. Let's see if we can kill two birds with one stone.'

As they exit, Diana throws her crumpled cup in the bin.

Like we need any more birds killed.

Bird ...

Diana swallows her bile and fills the kettle. Sits back at her desk and reaches for the transcripts taken from Mary's phone. There was something that bothered her when she first looked through these ... what? The language and phonetics are starkly different to Young's gaslighting. *The c-word.* The explicit threat of brutality and face-slicing. *Who was this?* Not a number stored on Mary's phone. And no one on their TIE list. Maybe there is something in Lawton's OCG theory. Maybe Mary knew more than was good for her.

293

Who was 0039?
My bird.
Ally.

Diana looks up. Robertson is standing, breathless, a bit flushed, grim-faced, shirt crumpled.

'What've you been doing? Running up and down stairs? I know I told you to get fit, but not when there's things to ...'

Robertson avoids her eyes, straightens his tie.

'Just went to the gents.'

'Right.' She's about to drop a witty quip about tussles with the toilet roll holder but then holds it. She sees Phillips and Lawton walk in, laughing, Lawton sorting out his tie. She leans back, swings on her chair and sees the gents door closing. Robertson's chewing on a Bic biro, head buried in a manilla folder.

'Fancy going to do some sur-veill-ance? My coffee was DOA so I'll get us both a new one.'

'Kettle's just boiled.'

'Can't do instant.'

He nods, avoiding her eyes.

At the door, Diana turns as she pushes it with her back, facing his chest squarely. Second shirt button is hanging by a thread, collar askew. He was pristine half an hour back.

'How'd that happen?'

He blushes, looks down.

'I-I'll sew it back on tonight.'

Bloody bullies.

Diana shifts gear out of the petrol station, pulling out after Pierce's van is two hundred yards down the road.

'CID can take over from here. I'm more fussed about Axmed and Bruno. There's a lot not making sense.'

Robertson is quiet, looking sideways at the wing mirror. 'Lawton says I'm better fitted for analyst work.'

Diana screws up her face. 'Because you're thorough with your evidence checking?' She snorts. 'You're invaluable on the frontline.'

Robertson is grinning like a kid at Christmas, making Diana feel bad. She really should big him up more. 'You think so, Boss?'

'I know so. What's he say that for any road? He's not said it while I'm around.'

Robertson looks away. He can never lie. 'In bogs earlier.'

'I knew it. You eat too many apples to be constipated. Don't listen to their bullshit, Carl. They're not top dog.'

'Mmm … they kind of are.'

Diana snorts. 'It ain't over till the critical evidence sings. They haven't got enough on Pierce. And Leroy Young's still AWOL. I'm getting a bad gut feeling our killer's not finished. We haven't got the message yet.'

'What message?'

'Exactly.'

Robertson frowns. The traffic is solid since the roadworks started up again on London Road.

'I saw Geoff Thomlins with Phillips, Neville and Lawton last Wednesday.'

'Doing what? Where?' Diana's neck rolls.

'Just in pub. Hare & Hounds. Having a laugh and a pint.'

'Aye rate. A laugh and a pint when we've got a murder investigation and crime scene on Thomlins' site?'

Robertson swallows, stares at Diana. 'You don't think—'

She doesn't think; she *knows*, but …

Diana shrugs. 'No evidence.'

'I mean, they were just having a drink.' Even Robertson doesn't sound convinced.

'Your coffee.' She nods at a fiver nestled in the cup rest. He picks it up. 'How's about checking in with Mrs Thompson this afternoon? See how Pastor Calley is doing …'

Robertson looks at her.

'He's not doing anything, Boss. He's had a stroke.'

'I know that, but you can ask. Probe for more detail about Mary's alleged affair with a married man.'

Robertson stares through the windscreen at a pigeon the size of a dog pecking at a plastic egg carton.

Diana sighs. 'Or just get her ginger cake recipe. Just come back with something. I've a feeling our Mrs Thompson is the only link we have to Mary's past and, potentially, the mystery of her strange demise.'

'You know, Boss, sometimes you do sound *a bit* obsessed by Mary Calley.'

Diana starts the car.

'Well, if police aren't obsessive about their victims, heaven help the poor souls.'

'Isn't Daniels our victim?'

Diana nods. 'He is. But the clues are stacked oblique so we have to think the same way, Robertson.'

He stares at her. 'Oblique. Is that like a triangle?'

Diana frowns. 'Coffee.'

'Oh, yeah. Right-o, Boss.'

Opening the car door, he lumbers out to join a queue of three outside the deli. Diana checks her phone; it had rung earlier when she was filling up at the petrol station. She'd sent Michael a text after the briefing. She's no time free to promise a date. She's not even sure what to say. But she wants to hear his voice.

She's still on the phone when Robertson comes out of the deli carrying two plastic-lidded cups.

That gravelly voice: 'Cool. How's seven sound?'

Diana leans over, phone under chin, opening the passenger door for Robertson.

'I may cancel suddenly,' Diana says. Robertson looks confused. She reaches out for her cup, smiling at Michael's sign-off.

Robertson squashes himself into the passenger seat, spilling flat white over his buttonless shirt.

'You too. Bye.'

'Some new lead, Boss?' Robertson belts up.

'No button and a coffee stain. What will our Doris think?'

She starts the engine. She's holding onto this case – the real one, not the fake fit-up one, by her fingernails.

Finger. Nails.

Fingernail.

'Robertson, did we ever get any DNA from that fingernail found on the site?'

'Yeah. Doesn't fit with any on the database or our POIs. Should we look at the manicurists in Sheff or the nail bars?' he asks, sipping in short bursts.

296

Diana slaps the steering wheel. 'Mrs Young! She even gave me her card.'

She looks down at her dried flaking nails, cuticles peeling off in shreds.

'My hands are *not* sexy. Need a manicure before my date.'

'Date?'

'I've got a date tomorrow.'

Robertson smiles. 'Right, the mystery phone call. Go for it. Daphne always feels better after she's had her nails done.'

Diana changes gear. 'You see our Doris for tea and cake. I'll get a manicure.'

'Deal.'

Mrs Young opens the door, eyebrows raised.

'Afternoon, Mrs Young.' Diana smiles.

'Gel tips for police. That's a new one.'

'Have you seen the state of mine?'

'Yeah.'

She leads the way into the lounge, to a stool in front of a nail table.

'Have to be quick. Got to pick Maisy up from my mum's.'

Diana sits down. Julie Young pulls her stool in and taps the table.

'Do you have some styles I can see?'

Julie looks at her blankly.

'Styles? Are you joking, love? I'm an elite manicurist. Just do French tip manicures for the top brass. If you want some flashy ghetto talons, go down London Road.'

Diana takes a photo out of her bag. 'Is that a French tip? I'd like my nails done like that.'

Mrs Young looks at the photo. Raises her eyebrows.

'Usually, it's a full hand pic not a random nail. OK. Square-tip French. I usually do oval, but got a couple of clients who like the square …'

Diana stares at her. 'I like them. Very cute. No talons for me please.'

'Give us your left hand.'

As she does, she also lays down the photo.

Diana puts her left hand dutifully in the bowl of soapy water.

'What kind of clients usually go for them?' asks Diana as nonchalantly as she can.

Mrs Young screws up her face, towelling Diana's hand.

'It's not cheap. Right hand.'

Diana obediently swaps, dipping it in the soapy water.

'I'm sure. By the way, does Leroy smoke?'

'Smoke? Funny you should ask – found a lighter in his sock drawer today.'

She shakes her head.

'Only when he's stressed. He never buys them and hates that I smoke. But he'll tax a cig off me, won't he? Hypocrite.'

She files Diana's nails vigorously, yanking at the fingers.

'Who else?' Diana says.

'Who else what? Smokes?'

'No – who else likes French square-tips?'

'A couple of lawyers. This posh lady accountant. Drives an Audi TT. She has hers done every other week.'

Diana's about to ask her name but holds back. Instead, she looks critically at her own nails.

'You think they'll stick on mine? My nails are a right state, very brittle. Do fakes fall off easy?'

'Rarely, but I don't use that cheap MMA tooth enamel shit which makes your real nail snap. Nails should stay flexible.'

Her lips tighten as Mrs Young cuts into the cuticles.

'The tips *can* fall off, but you still need to get them removed professionally. It's only happened to one of my customers,' she announces proudly. 'The accountant lady lost her index nail over Bank Holiday. Said she'd been gardening. Came to me day after for a replacement. Did it free of charge as she's a regular and always tips. Do you want to pay now – before your nails are done?'

'Sure.'

Diana stands up, admiring her creamed and glistening hands. Mrs Young stands up too.

'Oh. What's the name of this accountant lady who lost her nail?' Diana asks.

Mrs Young stiffens. 'I don't give out customers' details.'

Diana zips up her Berghaus. The manicurist's eyes narrow.

'As an investigating detective, I need her full name and contact details and all the times she's had her nails done here.'

After several hours in the office, Diana, squint-eyed, is feeling less glamorous and successful, poring over blue-screened transcripts, analyst reports of countless spreadsheets. Not for the first time, she wants to raise a complaint about paperwork but daren't in case her dyslexia is brought up as being the reason why she 'can't do her job'. Surely every DCI has to do this. Yet Diana can honestly say she's not seen them do it.

She hears the door swing behind her and a fresh waft of cold November air blows in, cutting through the overheated, stale, stinky office. A large Queen's Silver Jubilee cake tin, red and white worn and faded in rust-crusted corners, is plonked on her desk with a dull thud and clang.

She looks up at Robertson's beaming ruddy face as he pulls off a soaking wet anorak, his cowlick dripping water onto her desk.

'Fancy a brew, Boss? Have some of Mrs T's ginger cake 'n' all.'

Diana nods slowly, speechless. Robertson's back is to her as he switches on the kettle.

'You got the actual cake?' she asks, incredulous. He sniffs at the semi-skimmed milk carton.

'And the rest.'

Diana leans back in her chair, her crumbs of Jamaican ginger cake on a chipped enamel plate.

'Mrs Thompson says it's unlikely Pastor Calley's going to be talking soon. They say he's got a good six month of post-stroke rehab ahead of him. *If* he makes that. She's just keeping house for him until … well, she doesn't think he'll be coming back.'

He hands her a couple of old photos, in faded colour film. One's a Polaroid.

'Here's Sunita Calley at her wedding to Pastor Calley in 1968 and with a newborn Mary in 1972.'

1968: A happy radiant young woman, hints of Indian cheekbones, the firm jaw, snubby nose. The eyes – Mary definitely got her eyes. Diana searches but can find nothing of Pastor Calley's doughy features in there. Sunita reminds her of someone else too … who? The 1972 photo shows a grey, drawn woman, who has aged ten years in four. She looks bereft, dressed in dowdy brown and maroon.

Diana wonders aloud: 'Most women are glowing after their firstborn. Did Sunita have postnatal depression?'

Pastor Calley doesn't look that thrilled, not touching the child. His hand on Sunita's shoulder looks oppressive, as if he's holding her back or down – not the affectionate gesture of a husband to the mother of his firstborn.

'Something a bit off here. I know it's the seventies, but still, folk had fun.'

'I thought so too, Boss. I mentioned it. Mrs Thompson became very agitated, saying, "Those poor little girls, those poor little babies. Lord, have mercy on Sunita's soul."'

Diana looks at him. 'And …?'

He drains his coffee mug. 'Turns out …' He rolls his eyes, blows out his cheeks. 'Sunita gave birth to non-identical twins.'

Diana's brain fizzes.

'Mary never knew,' continues Robertson. 'No one knew. Sunita was sworn to secrecy, but she told Mrs Thompson. Mrs Thompson knew her job depended on it, and also – you know, not good for the church. She kept saying, "He's a good pastor, you know. A good man to work for. They tried for kids but he never – he couldn't."'

Diana leans back. 'What would Mary Calley's twin look like today?'

Robertson passes her another photo.

She starts to sip from her mug of strong tea and then freezes, mouth pursed, staring down at a yellow-toned Technicolor photo of a beaming Indian woman in a floral nighty holding two babies in her arms on a bare hospital bed. The nurse in the background looks like she's just dropped out of the TV programme *Angels* Rehema used to watch religiously.

'It was Doris who took Sunita to hospital and sat with her through labour. It was Doris who took her husband Walter's camera with her. That's the first – and probably last – photo of Mary and her twin,' says Robertson, tapping the papers back into the file.

'Brother? Sister?'

'Sister. Two girls, Doris said. But not identical. Look, you can tell.'

Diana frowns. She wasn't very good with babies. They did look more or less the same, but yes, one was slightly thinner, larger eyes.

'That were the second 'un. The one that looked like the father. That was the one given up.'

'Pardon?'

'Mr Calley was impotent or too old – can't remember which. Anyhow, Sunita was twenty-odd year younger. Had a fling with a young Irish doc called Frankie Smith doing some training at the hospital. Attended Legley Road Baptist. Sang in choir with Sunita. Pastor sent him packing back to Ireland when he found out he'd been knocking off his missus. Then he found out she was knocked *up* 'n' all and went nuts. Mrs T said he were so worried about his reputation. And then when he found out it were twins, that were it. He sorted out a private adoption pronto.'

Diana frowns, shaking her head. 'Poor bairns.'

'I know. Doris said it broke Sunita's heart. And her health. She never recovered fully. Always loved Mary, but felt guilty and sad – either for Mary or herself or the other baby she didn't even get to name and couldn't even tell Mary about. She kept saying to Doris the other bairn would have a better life, but in her darkest moments, she would confide to Doris she wished Pastor had put her and Mary up for adoption 'n' all – or out of their misery.'

'I'm just amazed Doris could keep working for him, knowing what he'd done.'

Robertson puts his mug down, picks up his biro just to click.

'She needed the job, the security. She said Mary and Sunita were like her own daughter and grandchild, as her and Mr T never had kids. Then he died. Pastor paid her well—'

'Paid for her silence more like. But aren't pastors poor?'

Robertson chuckles and cuts himself another slice of cake.

'Don't know much about churches, do you, Boss? The good

301

ones give it away. They're always poor and running on grace. The not-so-good ones invest.'

Diana inhales, leaning back on her chair, holding up the photo for a better look under the light.

'Why didn't Doris tell us all this before?'

Robertson shrugs. 'She said she'd promised Pastor never to breathe a word. She started crying, said she felt so bad for poor lickle Mary and Sunita. Always felt so helpless. Now at night she stays awake, wishes she could've done more.'

He puts half a slice in his mouth and chews with relish.

'She puts real stem ginger in, you know.'

Diana rolls her eyes. 'Don't let your Daphne know you've been eating another yardgirl's cake. Now to find the other twin.'

'No offence, Boss, but why? I mean, Mary's dead and so's her mum – it's only going to upset her if—'

'Because until I've eliminated her, she's the only person I can think of with a motive to avenge Mary's death.'

Robertson's face whitens. The door slams and a waft of cigarette smoke and two-day-old gym sweat enters.

'Hey up! Thur sitting up in here having high tea and crumpet while we're out slaving!' remarks Lawton, only with a tinge of humour.

Diana narrows her eyes.

'Slaving to what end?'

Lawton tilts up his chin.

'Plenty. Briefing in ten, so clear up them cake crumbs and get in there.'

For yet another nail-chewing episode of the OCG Drama Cops R Us scripted by real live police officers for BBC1.

Chapter 39

WEDNESDAY 3RD NOVEMBER, 2010 – REHEMA'S HOUSE, SHEFFIELD

Njambi

My eyes are failing me. I don't need to read to know what time this is. Rehema brings me back to hers after we collect my new glasses from the optician.

'You need to use them, MaMa, so your eyes get used to them.'

I don't want to get used to decaying. But she is not listening; she is getting ready for book club. My left eye flickers and twitches still. Two months ago, I notice the lid is drooping. I do not like this shutting down.

'Tea?'

Her doorbell makes a clang and her book club friends enter one by one with their different scents and colours, walking-talking flowers. I smile. It is this that gives me pleasure. Their different smells and voices layering over each other. Till it gets too much. I excuse myself to sit in the garden.

'It's cold, MaMa,' Rehema calls, closing the window to two inches. 'And dark.'

'Your pots need sorting. You can put on the yard light.'

I busy myself with sorting out her terracotta, scattered like abandoned children over weedy flagstones. I get the broom and sweep up brittle leaves. Pull up weeds from the cracks. I need air, wind; not the confinement of rooms and words-words-words that wake in me pains I want to lose. I get a bucket and nail brush, sit on the step, scrub plant pots till all the mould, cobweb and dust is gone.

Behind me, I hear the kitchen door squeak open and two voices: one is Anoona, the other – the lady with the limp. Aaliyah? Ally? The smoker. Her voice low and heavy.

'That's two herb teas, two coffees with milk, one black, one tea with soya milk … what did Maya want?'

'She's in toilet. Ask her when she comes out.'

'Did you make flapjacks?'

'Of course.'

'Yesss!'

'How long are you staying at Rehema's?'

'Just Reading Week. Go back tomorrow.'

I hear tins opening, kettle filling, china clinking, a foot dragging. A roar rising.

'Anoona, I've decided. I'm going to report Ryan Pierce for … what happened. You know, the rape, the attack. I promise I won't get you all in trouble, but … I've got to. He came around here last night. Knocking on the door, threatening Rehema. I'm not having that.'

'Are you sure? Rehema can handle it. There's no evidence now, and …'

'I am the evidence! Me. This.'

There is a space filled with pain. I know those spaces.

'I am a living, breathing box of bloody evidence, Anoona. I don't see why I should be the one living in hiding. I might *as well* be dead.'

'When?'

'When what?'

'Are you going to report …'

'Not sure. Before I go back down Wolverhampton. When I'm ready for Rehema's detective daughter. She interview you 'n' all, Anoona?'

304

'Yes.'

'Me too. Too many times. She's on about FGM and the attack on Mary. She thinks we know 'n' all ... Do we? Do *you*?'

Kettle boiling.

'Anoona? I'm not doing time here for something I don't know. I know you know. All Somali women go to you at the library for help filling the forms ...'

I watch the dark sky and two sparrows on the wall. Waiting for dawn; weeded flags mean more worm.

'Know what?'

Ally snarls. 'Don't lie, Anoona. Just before Mary left us, when she got beat up and stayed at mine ... you said a name. I just can't remember it.'

Silence cracking like these old pots and flags. One tap and it'll shatter.

'Anoona, this is the kindest thing I will ever do for you. That detective's not like other police: she's a ferret after a finger. She does not give a *fk*. She'd lock up her own mother if she had to.'

My seed. She would.

Anoona sighs. 'I know.'

'Well, she's got me under the kosh with the FGM link to Mary. Who was it ... Hassan?'

Anoona sounds tired, sad. 'Not sure, Ally.'

'Well, you best *be* sure, because this detective is convinced we *all* know.'

Water pours. 'Ifrah Hussein? I know she was living up Pitsmoor.'

'Ifrah Hussein? Never heard of her. Ifrah. How do you know it was Pitsmoor?'

'Because I work at the library there? She was always coming in for help with her forms. I'd hear her talking with the other women.'

'OK, well. Just make an anonymous call, send in a note or something. Don't want that bitch down Wolverhampton again. And I don't want any of us in jail.'

The downstairs toilet flushes. A bolt unlocks. A whiff of that strong musk scent. I know that smell.

The older library lady asks the musk smell: 'Maya, what you want to drink?'

'I'm fine, Anoona. Got to shoot off. See you next week.'

'OK. Bye.'

'Nice meeting you, Ally.' That's Maya.

'Yeah. Thanks for the brunch.'

Click-clack-click. The front door closes behind her.

'Or was it Irfrah …?' Unsure older voice.

'Well, get it right and let her know for all our sakes. Did Rehema take flapjacks in?'

They clatter out of the kitchen.

I sit on cold stone, watching sky bleed.

Chapter 40

THURSDAY 4TH NOVEMBER, 2010 – DEWBOW

'Why is your car lopsided, Diana?'

MaMa is squinting through the lounge bay window at Diana's car. It's a grey, dark morning.

Diana doesn't feel grey though. Her date with Michael, a brief hour in Henry's bar, gave her cause to wake with a smile this morning. She'd picked up a thoughtful MaMa from Rehema's afterwards and she'd gone straight to bed. That must be why she's up, alert as ever, before Diana's out the door.

'Not sure, MaMa. Where's your glasses?'

Maybe she's got cataracts.

MaMa remains standing, frowning out of the window. Diana kisses her cheek, grabs her keys and heads out.

Halfway down the path, she stops dead, staring at her car leaning on two neatly slashed flat tyres.

Two hours and two new tyres later, a slow persistent drizzle bores down on Diana as she scutters into the car park at HQ. Her heartbeat seems to have become the clock, ticking ever louder and faster today. And she's till trying to work out who would slash tyres in Dewbow.

A couple of plain-clothed, Toby-jug faced CID sergeants swing through the door, laughing.

One yells: 'Going wrong way, lass. Job Centre's down road!' but she's already one flight up.

She shoulders the door into the office.

Lawton looks up from his desk, scowls and taps his watch.

'Late again, Walker.'

Phillips, standing over him, raises his eyebrows, shaking his head.

Diana starts an explanation: 'My front tyres were—'

'I don't want to know, Walker. There's work to be done!' barks Lawton.

Diana rolls her eyes and walks back to her desk. Robertson scoots over on his roller chair, making sly moves with his head, which, coupled with him rolling on his chair, has the effect of making him look as though he's having spasms.

'You alright, sergeant?' frowns Diana.

Robertson pulls up his sheaf of papers.

He hisses: 'Boss, I've gone through everything. It was a private adoption. The child was in Social Services' care barely a month before a local wealthy white couple took it.'

'It?'

'Sorry. Her.'

'What's *her* name?'

'I don't know. The couple were called Johnson. Wealthy couple in industry. Lived at Nether Edge. He was a Master Cutler.'

Diana needs to hear Robertson reach the same conclusion as she has.

He passes her the papers. She looks at them. 'So the two girls never met? Never knew of each other?'

Robertson shakes his head. 'Sunita was told she'd be kicked out if she said anything. Mrs Thompson reckons she died slowly and miserably of a broken heart.'

'Where are the adoptive parents?'

'Mr Johnson died of pancreatic cancer late 2007. Mrs Johnson is in a Matlock nursing home.'

'So, the daughter must be responsible for her care – unless they have other children?'

'No other children. There seems to be a trust that deals with her care. I can't get any link back to the daughter, even her name.'

Diana looks up at dead flies caught in the flickering fluorescent light strip.

'And Sunita never met her other child? You sure of that?'

Robertson looks down, flicks through his papers. 'I asked. Mrs Thompson said only once, just before Easter in 1978 when Sunita told Pastor Calley she was going to look after a sick cousin out of town. She took Mary with her. Mrs Thompson saw her in Castle Street Market and Sunita begged her not to tell Pastor Calley she was in Sheffield and that she'd be back soon. She never told her why. But Mary wasn't with her.'

'When was that? March, April 1978?'

He nods.

Neville comes through the door, sees Diana. He stands, grinning, hands in pockets. 'We've had Axmed Ahmed in. Pulling in Bruno Pierce next ...'

Diana nods, without looking up. Picks up her keys.

'Where you off?'

'Matlock.'

'What?' Neville asks, as Robertson shrugs, turning back to face his monitor.

'Critical evidence,' says Diana as she strides past him.

'In Matlock? Have you told DI Phillips? His team have probably ...'

The door swings.

Sky splits above her and a shaft of yellow gold shoots out over the moors. Diana leaves the grey clouds over Sheffield and enjoys the rare moment of a lorry-free stretch before dipping down to Baslow. She wonders what MaMa's doing. She says she goes out walking. Diana worries she might intercept a horny stag or worse – be shot by a hunter. Every time Diana expresses her concern for her wanderings, MaMa's thousand-yard stare shuts her up.

She drives past her cottage, but it looks empty. Past Dewbright Hall. No cars out front today. Just the interminable chainsaw going, the gardener's van parked out front.

The low winter light exposes the last bits of ragged leaves and berries on bare branches, the grey now surrendered to a lilac blue sky. Matlock in thirty-five minutes. Not bad. She drives down the steep hill into the sweeping drive of another old building – an ancient disapproving aunt standing amidst a series of low-level huts, scattered haphazardly like a petulant five-year-old's Lego diorama.

Diana parks up on the gravel and enters the ancient aunt building. Waiting in the foyer, she tries not to inhale the smell of bleach, boiled cabbage and stale urine. The décor's 1980s, cherry-red upholstery, faded Monet prints hanging off magnolia walls. Five stars on its website recommendations. Still, she'd never bring MaMa to one of these places.

Ever.

MaMa'd burn it down. Or just bolt.

Diana rings the bell, writing her name in the visitors' book. She flicks through 'Visitors' for Muriel Johnson. No one. She looks up at the plastic roses on the windowsill while a harassed nurse bustles off to fetch Mrs Davis, the care home manager. In the distance, Diana can hear patronising cajoles, cheery 'Good morning!'s 'Oh, *what* have you done now?'s. Clangs and squeaks, whimpers, screams, otherworldly noises. She tries not to imagine Marchant's response to her questioning someone with possible dementia.

A broad-shouldered, wide-hipped block of a woman in a trouser suit appears, giving her best brochure-smile beneath heavy make-up.

'Good morning, detective …' she says.

'Walker.' Diana pushes out her hand, which Mrs Davis holds like a soiled cloth.

'Don't generally have police interviewing any of our residents. As you know, we specialise in caring for those with Alzheimer's and dementia, so …'

'I understand.'

Diana follows her down a maze of corridors, dodging tea trolleys and exhausted grey faces carrying bedpans out of rooms.

'She'd normally be in the day room, but I thought you might need quiet.' As if on cue, there are yelps and screams from down the corridor. 'Don't upset her please. She doesn't get many – well, any – visitors, so may get a bit excited.'

'Not even her daughter?'

Mrs Davis frowns. 'She has a daughter?'

'Yes.'

'Well, she never visits. Her fees are paid by a trust. Carte blanche, so we've no complaints.'

Jail at least allows you visiting orders.

Mrs Davis looks at her watch.

'The doctor comes round at two.'

She opens a door to a long room, a bed and high-backed chair by the window, looking out on a paved garden. Chintzy curtains, polyester floral bedspread, limp pillows. A room to be wheeled into and wheeled out of. In the cherry red armchair in the corner, a bodiless face floats. Diana does a double blink. The shrunken woman with straight white hair wears a crimson button-down dress – hence the floating illusion, stroking her teacup as if it's a small animal. Her blue eyes look up at Diana and spark.

'Ah! There you are!' she says.

From the door, Mrs Davis turns to Diana. 'I'll leave you to your business, detective. Be gentle please.'

Diana gives a small smile and pulls up a vinyl chair to face the Shackleton high-back.

'Good morning, Mrs Johnson. My name's Detective Walker.'

'The tea is quite gin and tonic at this time of cutlery.'

Unsure how to respond, Diana tries: 'Yes.'

Mrs Johnson beams. 'I was waiting for you. I took the taxi.'

'I'm here to ask some questions about your daughter.'

'We're so very grateful.'

'How is your daughter?'

Mrs Johnson's face falls. 'She's not been well, you know. The bruises. The poor thing. No hope. Doctor says.'

Her eyes brim. Diana reaches for the Kleenex box.

Mrs Johnson takes one, crumpling it into a ball, rolling it around the tray and teacup.

'Thank you so much for bringing your angel.'

Diana smiles. *Angel?*

'What's your daughter's name, Mrs Johnson?'

'She'll get better soon. Because of your angel. Doctor says.'

Then she puts her finger to her lips.

'Sssshhh. Ssshhh. Don't tell anyone. He might find out. It's our secret, isn't it?'

'What, Mrs Johnson?'

'Exactly! Ssshhh. No, no. Nothing happened. She's all better now. She'll soon be so much better. She'll come home soon.'

'Who will, Mrs Johnson?'

Diana looks around the room. Surely there'll be a photo or something to help her out here. An old mad woman in a sterile room. This was a waste of …

'Did you bring a bucket for the jigsaw? How is your angel? You understand, don't you?'

Not quite.

'Where's your daughter, Mrs Johnson?'

Tears stream down her wrinkled white cavernous cheeks. 'In surgery. In the special hospital.'

'Which hospital?'

'Claremont.'

'What's her name, Mrs Johnson?'

The old woman stoops forward, finger to lips, eyes fierce. '*Ssshhh*! He can't find out. He punishes you.'

'Me?' Diana pulls her chair in.

'Yes, Sunita. You and the child.'

Sunita! She thinks I'm Sunita.

'Who punishes me?'

Mrs Johnson bends forward, whispering.

'The Cornish Pasty.'

Mrs Davis knocks on the door. 'Sorry, detective. The doctor's here early.'

'Five minutes.' Diana is desperate. The door closes.

'Well, Mrs Johnson, it's been lovely speaking to you.'

Mrs Johnson sits upright, hands shaking in front of her, hovering over the tray.

'You can't go! You must stay in case she needs more!'

'More what?'

Diana stands. She had her and now she's gone back to la-la land.

312

'Marrow. Stuffed marrow with no bones!' yells Mrs Johnson, hurling the balled tissue at the window. Then, in one fierce, violent movement, she hurls the teacup against the wall. Bone china fragments scatter over the bedside table. Diana is at the door, looking left and right. Mrs Johnson stares mournfully at the broken china.

'All the bones, broken. She needs the marrow. For her blood.'

'Hello?' Diana calls down the corridor.

Mrs Johnson is hissing, trying to get up out of her seat, but her emaciated limbs won't hold her. Her face contorts. 'Her bones! Save her blood. She needs blood.'

Diana turns around. Mrs Johnson is scratching nails on the table, trying to get up out of her chair.

'What did you say? Her blood? Whose blood?'

'Pedigree chum! The marrowbone. We need the marrow for the blood.'

Mrs Davis rushes in, frowning.

Diana stands helpless in the doorway. 'I'm sorry, I—'

'OK. I've got her, detective. It's alright, Muriel. No one's taking the Pedigree Chum. Doctor Lyons is here now. You like him, don't you?'

Two nurses rush in, glaring at Diana as they pass her. Diana walks swiftly out, past a bored, balding doctor, swinging his stethoscope like a slingshot.

Inside her car, she makes two phone calls. Gets back to HQ within the half hour. Needs her notebook of dates. She runs up the stairs, hearing sniggers in the corner as she opens her top drawer.

On top of it, an unlabelled Jiffy bag. Frowning, she rips it open.

A purple rubber – truncheon?

With a switch at the end and a pack of AAA batteries.

313

Chapter 41

FRIDAY 5TH NOVEMBER, 2010 – SHEFFIELD HQ

In a deserted, stale office, Diana rubs her dry eyes. The door swings. As if on cue, Robertson is at her elbow with a steaming Styrofoam cup of black hot stuff. She smiles up at him.

'Your missus, Daphne, trains you well.'

'Morning, Boss. Actually, it's my mum. But I let Daphne think it's her.'

'Smart man.' She sips. 'Can you just run Rob Samuels' interview past me again? And all the other TIEs around the Dewbow summer fete. Any photos of Daniels there?'

He shakes his head and pulls out a manilla folder.

'Not found any photo evidence yet, Boss. Although Mrs Daniels' friend was right: he *was* invited and Samuels confirms he *was* on the guest list. Had a place card in the banquet hall. He remembers, as Mrs Gascoigne was arguing to get a discount price for it. Late sale and that.'

'All for a bit of deer pie and chips.'

'Roast venison and dauphinoise potatoes.'

Diana shakes her head. *Love it.* Robertson and his details. She flicks through the papers he hands her.

'What was he saying when you interviewed him? Did he seem anxious?'

Robertson pushes out his bottom lip, opening up his Egg McMuffin.

'No, Boss. He thinks it's quite standard procedure. He's known Maya all her life. His parents were good friends with hers too. He said Maya arrived around five, which was late, but in time for the banquet, speeches and dance. She helped clear up before dropping him and his wife home at two in the morning. Said he met Bruno for the first time in September at the Ryano Hut, but Maya had been talking about him for several weeks. Told me the board at Shining Light Trust had been looking to set up apprenticeships with inner city Sheffield multicultural youth since Easter this year. Bruno was the first.'

'Very noble of them. I made a log of when Bruno's worked at the butcher's according to Bruno – does it tally with Samuels?'

Robertson shows her his notes. She nods.

'So when did he ask him to start doing some weekdays?'

'The last week in October. He wanted to make him more official as there'd been some racist comments. Maya said it defeated the object of the exercise. They offered him extra hours to prepare the surplus game in peak season.'

'Even though he knew Bruno had another job in Sheffield?'

Robertson points at the final line. Diana reads it slowly: 'Samuels said Ms Smith had told him he wanted to get away from working at the Ryano Hut. Ryan Pierce was always calling by in Dewbow, and Bruno seemed to dislike this.' Robertson coughs. 'He did mention one thing I thought a bit weird. Said Maya was a very generous lady, that she'd just signed over the title deeds of Dewbright Hall to the Trust as she plans on moving to an apartment in Nottingham.'

Diana frowns. 'Why would she sign over the deeds? She's on the board of trustees … why Nottingham, if her offices are in Sheff?'

She pushes the file from her, spinning on her chair.

'A tax dodge?'

'Maybe. Or maybe Bonnie met her Clyde …'

'Isn't it Clyde met Bonnie? What you mean, Boss?'

Diana pushes back her chair. 'Meet me in the car park in ten.'

She marches to the super's office.

'Sir?'

An irritated Marchant looks up from his phone.

315

Diana says, 'Sir, can I have a copy of the C & AG Compliance Police Audit 2009?'

'Why?'

'The one where we failed on compliance?' Diana asks.

He winces. 'I'll email Tracy in HR.'

'Was it our failure to comply with regulations for logging our sexual assault stats? How come no one brought it up with the IPCC?'

He reddens. Looks at her fiercely. He's still not on the keyboard, still not sending that email to HR. 'I hope this is all relevant to the case in hand, Walker?' Marchant says.

Phillips walks in. Diana turns to him.

'If you won't let me bring in Pierce, at least let us have some of the camera reconnaissance. It may be relevant to this homicide.'

Phillips snorts. 'No chance, Walker. You're not having any of our surveillance product. It's sensitive, not relevant to your investigation. You're not having it.'

Marchant looks at the pigeons for support.

Diana folds her arms. 'It is relevant. It's his movements and potentially the movements of a weapon. We're investigating a homicide by a marksman.'

Phillips shakes his head. Marchant's phone rings and he practically leaps on it to answer.

'If you hide it, the defence will claim unused material or evidence has not been shared with them, and a guilty man will walk free.'

'Then you should've got better forensic evidence, shouldn't you, Walker?'

Marchant puts down the phone and sits, resting his chin on his palm to watch the two spat.

'I need the tracking of the guns at least.'

Marchant sighs. 'Let her have it, Phillips.'

Phillips narrows his eyes, muttering, 'It'll take some time ...' as he turns for the door.

'Today.'

Diana waits till she sees Phillips grab his coat, smacking the door open at the back.

'Thanks, sir. There's something else ...'

Something else. The two words Marchant dreads the most.

'What now, Walker?'

She closes the door and approaches his desk.

'I'm concerned for DI Lawton's and DS Neville's safety. I think either or both of them could be a potential target according to my line of inquiry.'

'How do you work that out?'

'Sir, the one thing the murderer has had access to that a member of the public wouldn't is confidential data. Including emergency services and police reports.'

Marchant looks out of the window at three pigeons dead-eyeing him from the top of a rusty drainpipe.

'And?'

'I think the murderer has a grudge. And is targeting specific individuals.'

'Where's your evidence? Who do you have in mind?'

'Give me a couple of hours, sir. But please don't put Lawton or Neville out there alone.'

Returning to her desk, she sees him pump his biro and shake his head at the pigeons. *He is never going to send that email to Human Resources.*

In eighteen years, Diana's only been to Human Resources three times: once to give them her NI number, another time to check on her pension, and then when Marchant forgot to sign off on two months' of overtime. She can never find the place down so many corridors and she's in a rush. She turns her march into a quick jog. Finally, a labelled grilled window 'Human Resources'. She knocks. Knocks again. A ginger-bobbed woman with Deirdre glasses comes to the window, unlocking the door.

'Hello, can I help you?'

'Morning, I'm DI Walker, working on the headmaster homicide. I just need a printout of the C & AG Compliance Audit for the SYPD 2009, and the recommendations.'

Blunt-bob-Deirdre looks over her shoulder and says something to someone.

'When for?'

'Now.'

317

The door closes in her face. Diana leans back against the wall. She feels sick and giddy, as if she's on the edge of a cliff. She sees the fire exit door at the end. May be faster to go down those stairs to the car park, the Smoker Stairs – the stairwell smokers use now they can't officially smoke inside.

The door opens. Blunt-bob-Deirdre hands her a printout. Diana looks at the name of the company.

'Thank you so much. Oh!' From her pocket, she pulls out the long blank envelope, now labelled *Confidential to Personnel*. 'Can I leave this with you please?'

She turns and marches down the corridor, pushing the fire exit door, rolling the document into a tube. Two flights down and she smells cigarette. A familiar broad back turns from the open fire exit door, the smile twisting into a sneer.

'What you doing down here? Only real cops smoke, Walker.'

'Excuse me, detective.'

Phillips stays where he is. He points at her chest.

'Lawton wants you off the case.'

'Good luck with that.'

Phillips leans back against the wall. His sweat-stink is creeping into her skin, into her breath. The ceiling and floor are closing in.

'You were a good sergeant, Diana. You should have stayed in post. Now, you're out of your depth and clutching at straws, mate. Let the Big Boys handle this. Leave Pierce alone. And that up there – that was all for Marchant's benefit. You're getting fk-all product from me.'

'I need to bring Pierce in!'

His eyes bore into her, mouth a grim line. Voice lower.

'Leave him alone. You've no evidence he's involved in this murder.'

'That's why I need to do an intelligence/elimination interview.'

'This is far too complex and sensitive a case to scare our main man on *your* speculation.'

'This is a homicide, detective, and it's not a speculation.'

His eyes narrow. 'We are this close—' He pinches his thumb and index finger close together, bringing them towards Diana's nose. She pulls back against the wall.

'—this close to wrapping up this multinational OCG case. I've warned you – leave it.'

'Or what? You'll run me off the road, slash my tyres again? Leave a vibrator in my drawer?' She knows it now, in her bones. No roadman was tailing her with TPAC manoeuvres.

He pulls back, laughing. 'You really have lost the plot. What the fk are you on about?'

'My gran is a light sleeper. She saw the creeper around my car.'

He shakes his head, snorting at the fire exit door as if for support.

'Sounds like you could both do with some Valium. Like I've time to go scooting over to Dewbow after a fourteen-hour shift.'

'Who told you I lived in Dewbow?'

He points at her chest. 'Your fabricated nonsense is a pointless irritation when we're about to wrap up over two years of covert surveillance.'

'Amazing.' But Diana reels back.

Phillips pulls back, laughing, looking her up and down, shaking his head. 'Silly bitch. You haven't a clue how real policing works. Got yourself in deep now, love.' He winks at her. 'But cred-it's due – you are good at one thing.'

Diana's right fist tightens. The left one holds the rolled-up HR document like a taser.

'Yeahhhh.' He continues, looking her up and down. 'You're good at that, aren't you? Bet you miss that, now you're alone in your little Derbyshire cottage, flicking your bean. Don't worry – there'll be plenty of time for you to develop your repertoire now that your career's finished.'

A strange calm overwhelms her. She exhales, tapping the document against her other palm.

The rant continues: 'We're still going to pick up both father and his butcher son, Bruno. Get that little asylum seeker Ahmed to squeak. They're running guns and county lines into Derbyshire. I'll get the credit for solving this homicide *and* the OCG case. Make DCI and push you in the bin for good. The cherry on the top will be seeing you packed off to Oughtibridge Traffic Police.'

Diana sighs. 'Excuse me, detective.'

He moves instead to block her exit. Hands on hips. He slowly raises his hands. Diana's stomach is in her throat, but she continues to breathe slowly, deeply. His hands raised, Phillips moves to the side, but there's still no space for Diana to pass without brushing against him. She won't even approach the odour of his stink. She turns, keeps walking to the stairwell, to the CCTV. Away from the sweat, the cigs, his accelerating chuckle like sludge down a blocked plughole.

'Be careful, detective. This OCG may not stop at slashing tyres next time …'

His dirty plughole chuckle echoes up the stairwell.

When she gets outside, she is shaking. Robertson is at the car. Diana exhales.

'You OK, Boss?'

'Fine.' She taps the document against her hand. 'Got a bit lost and the fire exit was blocked by a smoker.'

Robertson looks puzzled.

'Come on, Robertson. We've a lot to do.'

Her heart's still pounding. Ten thousand screams in her head and not a second for one of them.

An hour later, they return to HQ, Diana still clutching the Police Audit 2009. Diana turns to Robertson. 'Have you got the transcripts of Mary Calley's texts, emails and diaries?'

'Boss.' Robertson hands over a sheaf of papers.

She nods her gratitude. 'Right.' She looks at the clock. Then she looks at Marchant's office. DI Phillips is back in there, hand on the door speaking vehemently to Marchant, who keeps looking over at Diana and back at Phillips with raised eyebrows.

'So, can we pull Ryan Pierce in now, Boss?' Robertson asks.

She shrugs on her coat. 'I'm going to Claremont Hospital, Robertson. I need one more piece of info before I apply for a search warrant.'

She shoves the sheaf of transcripts into a folder and heads for the door.

An hour later, she's sitting in the small back office of the old end of the private Claremont Hospital, raking through files. It smells of dust and disinfectant, the fluorescent light above her flickering on and off. A squat woman with a silver mullet enters hugging a stack of enveloped black vinyl squares. With a grunt, she plonks them down on the table next to Diana, a cloud of dust rising to sting her eyes.

'Most of the files from the seventies were put on microfiche in the late eighties,' she states. 'You don't know the consultant's name?'

Lady, I don't even know the patient's name.

Diana looks up. 'It may have involved a blood transfusion or bone marrow transplant? What would that be for? From a six-year-old girl?'

The woman peers at Diana over her frameless specs.

'Hmmm. Maybe something to do with leukaemia or cancer. Try the microfiches. Look under Winthrop; he was the only hae-matologist-oncologist working out of here then. Got a whole army of them now.'

She leaves, closing the door behind her. Diana grits her teeth and starts peeling through the microfiches, scrolling through the tiny screen in the damp room. Is it really worth it? She thinks of Lawton's sneers and Marchant's threats. Phillips' – *Don't go there now.* She can do this, but she needs evidence. Fast.

Her eyes are burning, dry, tired, aggravated by the dust. She blinks furiously. *Focus, Di.* She frowns. A name redacted out on the screen. Two, three pages. The name replaced with Patient X. But one familiar name there.

The cogs connect. The engine breathes into life: a motive.

A fury burns in Diana's chest and it's not hunger. It's not rage. It's—

Time.

Four hours later, Diana drives home, her brain still trying to jump over blockages, her nerves roaring with exhaustion. She doesn't want to admit defeat, but Marchant's repeated dismissal is begin-ning to wear on her; he keeps maintaining there's more of a threat to life through the OCG than this 'speculative' raging psychopath. What's speculative about a mutilated body? All she's asking for is an intelligence interview with Pierce.

321

As she clears the last bend in the road, she changes up a gear and her brain exhales. Stuff the whole lot of them. If they had done their jobs, none of this would be happening. The realisation cuts like a cold blade.

None of this.

It's alright her urging Ally, the book club and her mum to speak up, but, seriously, what's the point? And what has she gained for her efforts? An effective demotion, sexual assault and harassment, major fall-outs with her mum, a dissatisfied public, and irate victims.

Face it, they're right, Diana.

She pulls up on her street just after 11 p.m. As she locks her door, she thinks she hears a step behind her. She's parked her car under a street light this time. Keys grasped in her hand like a knife, the other clenched in a fist. Ready.

She scans the whole street. A cat leaps off a wall.

There's no one out here. Get some kip, Diana.

In the moonlight, she pulls off her shoes, wraps the duvet around her. Curtains open so she'll see any shadows near her car. MaMa shouldn't be down here on her own. She's not seen her even to say good morning, goodnight to.

Diana curls up, grateful for sleep's black oblivion.

The roar. Bearing down on her, the stag's head about to fall on her morphing into Daniels' head, antlers tangled in her hair, maggots crawling on her. Red flashing eyes, the mist. Her hands are sore, her shoulder aches.

The roar. More like broken barking, louder than a dog's. Desperate.

Diana blinks into the greyness. The red light of her BlackBerry flashes and MaMa's shadow stands over her, a steaming cup of ginger and cinnamon black tea in her hands.

'You got a cough, MaMa?'

'No. Drink some tea.'

'What time is it?'

'Nine ... thirty ...'

'What?!'

Duvet thrown back, BlackBerry grabbed.

322

Chapter 42

Saturday 6th November, 2010 – Sheffield HQ

Diana arrives at HQ in a hurry. She needs to work through this fresh evidence from Claremont. If Mary Calley *did* have a twin sister, there is a chance she is still alive and incognito. She would be the one person invested enough to have a motive to kill. Diana's got one shot to convince Marchant. One shot and a very strong likelihood she will be packed off to Blackburn or deepest Goole if she fails.

Her desk phone rings.

'Hello?'

'Morning, detective. It's PC Rowlands on Reception. We've got this woman here won't leave till she's spoken to you. Been here since eight-thirty.'

Two hours.

'What's her name?'

'Aaliyah Matthews.'

'I'll be right down.'

Yes. The name of the FGM cutter.

Reception is full of whining, stressed revellers in various states of intoxication and outrage. Ally sits upright in her anorak, an alarmed doe amidst a feral melee of cursing shell suits and stilettos.

'Morning, Ally. Sorry you've been kept waiting – I wasn't told.'

Diana glares at the bulky receptionist trying to deal with a boisterous drunk.

'My train's at twelve …' Ally mutters.

'Where's our Bruce?' slurs one woman, slouching on the same vinyl bench.

Diana nods at Ally.

'Follow me.'

She holds the door for her to hobble through, firmly closing it on the drunk woman.

Diana chooses the far interview room. It's quieter than the ones closer to reception. She indicates for Ally to sit.

'Where's your bags if you're going back?'

'Rehema – your mum—'

'Rehema,' Diana says shortly.

'Rehema's taking me to the station at twelve.'

Rehema's never seen her own daughter off on a train.

Stop it, Diana.

'What brought you in here today? Something to tell me?'

Ally pulls her chair in, looks down at her hands. Up at the ceiling. At the four walls.

'Is it to do with the FGM we mentioned?'

'*You* mentioned.'

She shakes her head.

Ally's hand trembles.

'I've told them to tell you if they know.'

What then?

'It's – it's about me.'

Diana waits. Ally looks down at her stumped pinky, inspecting it. Then up at Diana, her eyes shining, her mouth a line.

'I want to report a rape.'

Marchant sighs, his eyes closed.

'Nicely engineered, Walker.'

Opening his eyes, glaring at her.

'Sir, the woman's reported a rape. We need to bring Ryan Pierce in for questioning immediately …'

He gets up, keeping his back to her.

'Phillips is not going to be happy. If it's historical, surely it can wait?'

'Wait, sir? It's a *rape*. We need to bring him in, we need to question him today, he should be—'

Marchant sits back down on his swivel chair.

'I know what we need, Walker!' he roars.

'I also need two search warrants, sir.'

She pushes the evidence log towards him.

He gives it a cursory scan. Squints. Looks closer.

Finally, he pushes it away on the desk.

'Well, if the courts sign it off, you best get on with it, Walker.'

Time has become a sludge while the clock tells Diana it's now Sunday 11.30 p.m. Waxed jacket half on, about to leave, she stands behind Lawton, frowning at the paperwork. She's tired – and it's not because she's been here over fourteen hours.

'Have we picked up Ryan Pierce yet?'

'No. Been busy.'

It's been two days now, going into three. Diana glares at his back, about to launch into one, but then shakes her head.

'So, why've we got Axmed in?'

Lawton, head down, taps his file on the desk.

'For questioning. He wor picked up at Pond Street bus station – got the last bus from Dewbow. Tip-off.'

'What about Pierce?'

'He's been in Derby. Passed it on to police there.'

Lawton sweeps his jacket off the back of his chair onto his shoulders.

'Walker, interview Axmed.' Lawton points at her. 'But keep to the script. This guy was at the Legley Road crime scene *and* from a country where decapitating traitors is the norm. Don't go all social worker on this one!'

Diana slowly takes off her jacket.

Chapter 43

Monday 8th November, 2010 – Sheffield HQ

12.10 a.m. Diana steps into the interview room with two small bottles of water. The room's damp, smelling of piss and BO. Axmed is slumped in a chair next to a bald, short man in a grey suit two sizes too small. The kid's wearing a navy waterproof Nike raincoat, his Air Force 1s scuffed with mud, legs straight out under the table, long brown fingers tapping the edge of the Formica. He looks up as she enters, narrows his eyes and looks back down at his hands. His face looks drawn, exhausted. Dark circles under bloodshot eyes, a smudge of a moustache and beard. His fingers ashy, dry. Fingernails grubby, bitten.

'Where's *he* gone?'

'DI Lawton? He was called out so I'll finish up, Axmed.'

She passes a bottle of water over to him.

'Why am I here?' He looks at her from half-closed lids, but his hands slide over the water bottle. He inspects the seal before snapping it open. Swigs.

Diana looks at him. 'Long day? Me too.' She unscrews her bottle, sips. 'We just need to clarify some details.'

'I've nowt on me. Weren't doing owt either, so you best let me go.'

'Axmed, I need to talk to you about Ms Calley.'

The lawyer frowns.

Axmed inhales, rolls his head back. 'She's dead.'

Diana nods. 'I know that. But I want to ask about an incident in the summer of 2007. You and Bruno got into some fights, got excluded until the end of term, right?'

He shrugs, eyes wide. 'Clueless teachers freaking out.'

'Can you remember what the fights were about?'

He pushes out his bottom lip. 'I don't keep a diary.'

'Yeah, but others might. Certainly, the school logged it – or rather Mr Young did.'

She pulls out her notepad.

'He said it was between you and some Somali boys in Year 10, and Bruno joined in.'

She watches Axmed's face. A brief flash. He remembers *exactly* what it was about. The lawyer keeps tapping his pen, looking sideways, with brief coughs.

Axmed shrugs.

'I can get you a Somali-speaking solicitor if you'd prefer?'

The solicitor glares.

'I can speak English. And Italian too. Why not an Italian solicitor?' Axmed leans back in his chair.

'Really? So, what's a multilingual guy doing with Ryan Pierce?'

He swigs from the bottle.

Diana perseveres. '"*Ka daa*". What does it mean?'

'*Ka daa*,' he repeats, slowly.

'Yes – *ka daa*.'

'No – I'm telling *you*.'

Diana looks confused. Axmed tilts up his chin defiantly. 'Leave it alone.'

Is he being rude? Diana lifts up her palms.

'That's what it means – leave it alone. Let it go, mate. And that's what *you* should do.'

'Leave *what* alone, Axmed? What was Bruno telling that woman to leave alone?'

Axmed sighs, looking to his right at an invisible ally, shaking his head. The lawyer chews his lip.

'It's our culture, innit. You don't understand.'

'Bruno is not Somali. Why's Bruno yelling "Leave it alone!" in Somali at a Somali woman?'

Axmed looks at his palms.

'You know why I'm bothered, Axmed? If there was nothing wrong, you'd be working at your brother's shop, your family would still be as respected at mosque, your sister wouldn't get chatted about in the schoolyard, on the street ...'

In one flash and arc of his arm, Axmed flings the water bottle against the wall, spraying all over the lawyer.

'Leave my sister out of it! Where's that other detective? I'll answer his questions – not this bullshit!'

Diana looks calmly at him as if nothing's happened.

'... and you wouldn't have to run lines for Ryan Pierce and some very dangerous men in Manchester.'

The lawyer gets out a pack of tissues and starts dabbing his brow and glasses, frowning.

'You know nothing!' Axmed hisses. Diana lets the rage fizz out of him.

'I know *little*, but I wouldn't say I know nothing. I know an uncut sister can lead to some serious consequences and a schoolyard scrap is the least of them.'

'*Ka daa*!' Axmed mutters. Diana shakes her head.

'See, Axmed, I can't. I can't because I don't think you or Bruno or Ryan *are* to blame for these homicides. And, if you're not, that means the killer is out there right now.'

A shadow passes over Axmed's drawn face.

'What's this got to do with my family? With Aamiina?'

'That's what I'm trying to find out. But no one's talking. Everything keeps coming back to Ms Calley and what Legley Road High School's senior management did or didn't do. I've already spoken with Aamiina and with your parents. Maybe I should return, see if ...'

'No!' Axmed shouts, but it's more of a plea. 'Please, I'm serious. Don't talk to them about this. They've been through enough. My dad's about to send me back to Mogadishu. I'd rather them just think I'm a drug dealer. I'm not grassing on my community. You really don't understand!'

Diana looks at him evenly.

'Axmed, if you don't tell me who the cutters are in your community, someone else is going to take the law into their own hands and the outcome won't be a fine or jail.'

'What you mean?'

Diana raises her eyebrows.

'What? They're killing cutters?' He frowns. 'Daniels weren't no cutter.'

'My job is to make sure it doesn't happen, and I'm not about to allow you to play Russian roulette with someone else's life.'

Axmed puts his head in his hands.

'Man, I don't know! The women – it's nowt to do with me. My mum and dad are proud of Aamiina, but not me. I'm fked.'

'You want to protect her though?'

Axmed nods.

'Does Bruno know who—'

Axmed breaks in: 'Bruno knows as much as me. Aamiina knows even less.'

'So who's protecting you all?'

Axmed puffs out his chest. 'I am. I will.'

'Axmed, you can't even protect yourself. You're in a police interview room being interrogated for a homicide ...'

He screws up his face. 'Look! Cutters, they move about. Bounce between cities, sometimes countries.'

Rent-a-cutter.

'You do know why Female Genital Mutilation is a crime, Axmed?'

He nods vigorously. The lawyer pales. The kid *wants* to talk about this. 'My mum, my cousins, my brother's wife ... they always at hospital. Lots of problems. My brother was mad as his wife had one son born dead, his first son's got brain damage, and so he got another wife. My mum had to be cut open for me and Aamiina, and she's not well now. You can't ask them. Please.'

'Just give me a name, Axmed.'

He shakes his head. 'I don't know a name.'

'But you do know knowledge about FGM carries a four-teen-year jail sentence, right? No worries, I'll ask Bruno. He knew who he was shouting *ka daa* at.'

Axmed looks up sharply. 'No, he didn't. He thought he was helping, but he weren't and it caused a fight.'

'Why were you travelling back from Dewbow tonight? Alone?'

Axmed shrugs, looking away. 'I went to see Bruno and we had a falling out. It's nowt. We fight a lot.'

'What happened, Axmed?'

He glares at her. She waits. Finally, he crumples forward, rolling his eyes.

'Rich bitch wants to do business with Ryan, get him to take some of her game meat or summat. Me and Bruno go upstairs to play on the PS3. I want to check my Facebook on the computer but Bruno says we can't go on. I say I need to as my cousin's been messaging me and he gets mad and we both hear van drive off. That woman not there so Bruno says she's gone with Ryan. Bruno and I row after a second game and he tells me to get bus. I'm right with that; don't want to stay in that big spooky yard. I reckon Ryan'll come and get me but he never did, the prick. So I end up freezing cold, getting the late bus. You lot waiting for me at bus station. Bet some curtain-twitcher reported a black man in a bus shelter.'

Diana looks at Lawton's paperwork. Axmed's not far off – Miss Rawlins, no less.

'Alright, Axmed. I'll have to keep you in—'

For his own safety.

He starts up, indignant. 'You can't do that! Thought you said it was just Mary Calley – you weren't dealing with …'

Diana puts down her pen. The solicitor's face falls.

'With what, Axmed?'

He closes his eyes, the curse spat out without a vowel. Diana leans forward.

'What was the business Maya wanted with Ryan, Axmed? Surely she could do that over the phone?'

He shrugs.

'In fact, how did you even know they had business?'

'Bruno called me, innit.'

'Bruno? When?'

He glares. 'If I had my phone, I could tell you. This afternoon …'

'It's Monday now. Just gone one in the morning.'

He rolls his eyes. 'Yesterday then. He said Ryan had to come to Dewbright Hall. Maya had some business.'

'Ryan didn't ask what business?'

'No. He seemed to know.'

Diana frowns. 'Why didn't Bruno call Ryan directly?'

'What you asking me for? All I know is Bruno can't stand Ryan.'

'Why's that?'

Axmed shrugs. Diana taps the tape recorder. 'You're Bruno's best mate, right?'

'Yeah.'

'So he can't be too thrilled about you running drugs for Ryan?'

The brief starts to bluster. Axmed says, 'No comment.'

Diana ignores both. 'So Maya doesn't want a phone trace to her … was she buying drugs?'

'No comment.'

'You seem very definite about that, Axmed. How are you so sure if you don't know what business she wanted with Ryan?'

'It wornt drugs. Told you. Deer meat.'

'Then why wouldn't she call him direct?'

'I don't know!' Axmed shouts. Diana leans back, lets him calm down, focus on the cuff of his hoodie.

'How many times you been over to Manchester with Ryan, Axmed?'

'No comment.' Eyes still on cuff.

'Twice a week. Three? More than the thirty we've photos of?'

Axmed pulls at a thread.

'To Donny's Cash and Carry?' Diana keeps staring at him. He tries to snap the thread. 'Axmed, give me one good reason I shouldn't tell DI Lawton to pull you into the OCG investigation.'

Axmed snaps the thread.

'See, I know you've had a rough time, Axmed. But things can always get rougher, and right now we've got a killer on the loose and far too many loose ends – you being one of them. So, I'll ask you again: what was the business Maya had with Ryan?'

Axmed slowly shakes his head.

'For the tape, Axmed. How much was that business worth? You said Ryan was expecting the call, he was ready.'

Axmed mutters: 'He said it was the Manchester ting.'

'Ting?' Diana raises her eyebrows. 'A hand ting he got from Manchester?'

The lawyer swallows. Axmed notes it, rolls his eyes.

'A brown paper bag from a box of vegetable oil in the back. He put it in his jacket pocket.'

Diana nods slowly. 'So, it could fit in a pocket? A big pocket?'

'Yeah.'

'But not that big if it's in a jacket ... an inside pocket?'

'Yeah.'

'So it was a handheld item?'

'Just something in a brown paper bag.'

Diana pulls her chair forward. 'What made you think it was a handgun?'

'Wait a minute! I need five minutes to talk to my ...' squeaks the lawyer.

'Why would you protect Ryan Pierce? Is he going to do the same for you?' she asks.

Axmed's eyes narrow. He sighs.

'Look, I didn't see it. It was about that size and weight.'

Diana sighs. Eyes closed. *Please no. Don't let DI Phillips have his day made.* She taps her pen. 'Axmed, when was the last time you saw Ryan Pierce?'

'In the hallway at Maya's house. She told Ryan the meat was in her outhouse and he followed her. Bruno asked me upstairs for a game of *Call of Duty* so I went straight up.'

'You didn't see where Ryan Pierce or Maya went?'

He shakes his head. Diana taps the tape recorder.

'No,' he sighs.

'Did you see him leave?'

'I saw van leave.' Axmed looks tired, worn down, his lawyer deflated.

'Have you spoken to him since then?'

'No! That's why I'm sat in here with you lot! He's not answered my calls since he left Dewbow. Dickhead.'

'Indeed. Oh, one more thing. Nadhiya's aunt. Do you know her?'

Axmed's face screws up in confusion. 'Who's Nadhiya?'

'I was hoping you could tell me. Year 8? Ms Calley certainly knew, and you did know when you were in Year 10. It got you excluded. Something to do with Aamiina?'

332

Axmed's eyes are slits. 'I told you – leave it!'

His solicitor coughs. Diana waits, looks at her watch.

Finally, he sighs, looks at his fingers, mutters: 'Nadhiya Mahmood … dunno her mum's name.'

'Where is the mother of Nadhiya?'

'How should I know? Try Europe or Africa.'

Diana and Axmed glare at each other. The solicitor swallows.

'Axmed, let us deal with it. Do you understand what I'm saying?'

'Not really but … whatever.'

'Interview terminated …' she looks at her watch. 'One-thirty-eight a.m., Monday 8th November.'

Diana marches over to Lawton. Twenty-four hours in and out of HQ, no sleep, scrabbling for paperwork. Her emotions are fit to tip.

'Lawton, where's Pierce? I thought you said you had surveillance on him?'

Lawton looks up from his desk. Clean-shaven, reeking of Lynx. A fresh latte in front of him.

You went home for a sleep, a shave and a shower and left me with your dirty overnight clean-up. I may have saved yours and Neville's scalps and you have no idea …

'Morning, Walker. We do. We have. It went cold Sunday night.'

Diana nearly pops.

'Detective, a rape was reported Saturday morning. He needed to be brought in then. Why is it Monday and still no sign of him? Do you know where he was Saturday?'

'He was on a run from Manny to Derby with that Axmed kid.'

Phillips walks in, puts his hand on Lawton's shoulder.

Lawton looks up, worried. 'Well, he was.'

Diana glares at them both. 'So, you knew where he was but didn't bring him in?'

Phillips stares at her with lead eyes. 'He was running guns, Walker. Out of our jurisdiction, so I passed it on to Derby police. It was too dangerous to intervene. The tracker was on.'

'Is it on now? We need Pierce in – like yesterday!'

Marchant comes out of his office.

'Phillips, just bring him in. I am so tired of this.'

Phillips looks sheepish.

'Sir, I would, but – we can't find him. Got a visual of the van in Pitsmoor, but no Pierce.'

'And the guns?'

'Gun.' Phillips looks out of the window. 'Tracker's off.'

'You mean you don't know where Pierce is? *Or* the gun?'

Diana swivels. She needs air to scream into.

Outside, she inhales the arctic November air. The first flakes of snow in November? The world's changed while she'd spent the hours after Axmed's arrest searching for an FGM database. Somewhere. Anywhere. But it's nowhere. She gets a double espresso from the sandwich shop and leans against the doorway, looking up into the huge grey sky. Thick white flakes fall on her lashes, on her tongue.

Two missing men. One dead. Quite a few common factors – including their last destination.

Back in the office, on the phone to Records: 'What do you mean, there isn't a register for FGM cutters?' She puts the phone down, rubs her forehead, yawns. She stares outside at the falling fat flakes of untimely snow. Something hits her on the shoulder. It's a screwed-up paper ball. She looks up in annoyance as Neville paper-flies a brown sealed envelope across her desk.

'Wakey-wakey, Walker. This came in on Friday when you were out. Forgot to pass it on!' he yells.

Diana glares at him but inspects the envelope. First class stamp. Sheffield postmark. A printed blue biro copperplated address: *DI Diana Walker. Major Crimes.* Familiar handwriting … Instinctively, Diana pulls on her gloves, her ruler serving as letter-opener.

One sheet of lined airmail notepaper, folded. On the top half: *Ifrah* crossed out and then *Irfrah Hussein, Pitsmoor.* On the bottom half: *FGM Cutter.*

Diana's stomach drops.

Marchant wrinkles his nose as if she's just handed him a part of Daniels' anatomy.

'Who wrote this?'

A flash in her head of the book club list stuck on the side of Ma's fridge with a strawberry fridge magnet. Mary Calley's name. Anoona's handwriting.

'No one on our database, sir.'

Marchant pushes the note away from him as if it's contagious. 'Someone who can't spell or isn't sure who they're talking about.'

Possibly.

Diana shrugs. Marchant sighs.

'So, I guess you're suggesting we go visit every Irfrah Hussein in the City of Sheffield? Which, at a rough guess, would be around two hundred.'

'It says Pitsmoor, sir. There's twenty-seven if you also include Ifrahs.'

His mouth drops. 'And this has *what* exactly to do with the case you're assigned to?'

'Sir, I have a ...'

'Strong suspicion? Yeah, I have a strong suspicion too, Walker, that you are about to waste my resources again leading my officers down the garden paths of Husseins and starting countless harassment suits which I can do without. Pass it on to CSC.'

'Sir, I believe the killer is going to target this woman.'

'Give me strength.' He sighs. 'Based on what evidence?'

'She delivered a fatal punch to Ms Calley in November 2007. Both Daniels and Young are people who did wrong to Ms Calley and got away with it. It's the only connection factor I can find. The drugs really don't work, sir. I need to trace, interview ...'

He glares at her – but then he always gets frustrated by any cultural reference after 1985. Marchant closes his eyes, inhaling slowly.

'Sake. Take Khan, O'Malley and Robertson, as Lawton seems to be closing in on Pierce and the OCG. And put some pressure on Axmed Ahmed. He'll crack soon. Bring in the other kid – Pierce Junior.'

'Sir, they've already been interviewed twice. If I bring them in again with no ...'

'Then arrest them! You already know Axmed's dealing. Stop fannying about.'

'Sir.'

She leaves Marchant muttering at the window.

Robertson hands out the list of the Ifrah and Irfrah Husseins on the electoral roll.

'Twenty-*seven*!' groans O'Malley over his shoulder.

'You having a laugh?' spits Khan.

'No, Khan. No one is laughing here. Just count your lucky stars it's not Kylie Jones or Liam Smith,' Diana says.

'Why Ifrah *and* Irfrah? What's the difference?'

'The letter r.'

O'Malley looks as if his car's just failed its MOT.

'A typo or a mistake might cost a life. So yes, Khan, we're doing Ifrahs too,' Diana says.

Robertson pulls on his coat. Diana's already at the door. 'I'll pay Ms Shanda another visit. Catch up with you in Pitsmoor.'

Outside the dilapidated house on Rock Street, Diana blows on her hands, as she walks up the concrete path towards Robertson. The snow is starting to lie like icing sugar across the broken flags.

'Nippy this morning. How'd you get on, Boss?' says Robertson. Diana nods.

'Ms Shanda finally admitted she sent the note and *thought* she knew who the cutter was. An Irfrah Hussein.'

Diana stares at a crisp packet poking out of a white-crusted mound, the snow trying to cover the ugliness of neglect, the crumbling pathway that last saw a landlord's care a decade ago. Even weeds hesitate to grow here. The windows' grime renders them useless. The door has one panel boarded up. Ragged grey nets stick forlornly to the condensation. A small, sallow face appears, waving a clawed fist before being snatched back. Thumps and indignant wailing is heard, followed by fierce Arabic.

Robertson stoops to the letter box.

'Hello? Mrs Hussein? It's the police. We were just …'

'Police?'

'… a word please. We need to make sure … Mrs Hussein?'

The sound of a key turning. A thin elegant Somali face, thick-lashed, headscarved peers out from the darkness.

'Mrs Hussein?'

'What want?'

'Can we come in please? It's about a …'

Diana's phone rings. She looks down.

HQ.

'Excuse me.' She turns to the side.

The confused woman half closes the door, but Robertson holds it. 'Sorry, Mrs Hussein – one minute.'

'Sir?' Diana says, watching a woman scream in the road further down. A siren wails and a uniform is taping round a house. Probably another drugs bust.

'Walker, get down to Catherine Street now.'

'Sir? I'm on Rock Street with the Husseins.'

'Wrong one. Refuse collection just called in a body found behind bins on Catherine Street. Lawton's gone up to deal with it. CSI en route. You, get back to HQ. I think we need to reconfigure.'

You reckon?

'Shouldn't I just pop down while I'm here and…'

'Now!'

'On my way, sir.'

She hangs up. The V over Robertson's nose creases.

'What's up, Boss?'

Diana raises her eyebrows at the woman now standing indignantly in the doorway.

'Must be your *very* lucky day, Mrs Hussein.'

'Huh?'

Diana turns down the path, Robertson behind her: 'So sorry for disturbing you.'

In the briefing room, Lawton is pacing, popping his knuckles. O'Malley and Khan look relieved to be off Ifrah/Irfrah Hussein duty. Neville looks as if he's just swallowed a bluebottle.

'So, we have a woman found shot behind the bins at 35 Catherine Street, Pitsmoor this morning. Ryan Pierce's van was seen near the premises around 11.30 p.m. last night. His van is now parked up outside the Ryano Hut, but no Pierce to be found. Nor is he answering his phone, which we found in the glove compartment. Along with the weapon …'

337

He sticks a Polaroid photo of a 9 mm handgun on the wall. There is an audible gasp around the room.

'Two bullets missing out of the fifteen– one found in the Pitsmoor victim.'

'What's her name?' asks Diana, nursing a cup of hot water. Lawton glares at her briefly.

'Ifrah Hussein. Forty-two. Mother of three. Husband a night porter at Northern General.'

'*Ifrah? Ifrah* Hussein?' Diana asks.

Please no.

'Yes, Walker. *Ifrah* not Saddam.'

Marchant, standing in the doorway, avoids her eyes.

'How did no one hear anything?' frowns Neville.

'Not sure,' says Lawton. 'A neighbour says he saw a flash or flame. Thought it was a firework or camera.'

'A silencer,' mutters Diana.

Lawton puffs out his chest. 'Typical OCG method. A professional hit.'

Marchant clears his throat. 'Lawton, I want you to find out where this gun came from and to find Pierce. And the real Irfrah Hussain. Bring Pierce in regardless. I'll handle Phillips. But Walker you're the SIO from now on with this homicide.'

Lawton's head rears up indignantly before being met by Marchant's icy glare.

'Walker's presented sufficient evidence for warrants. All three men had their last rendezvous at Dewbow so we'll need to liaise with Derbyshire police too.'

'Sir. What about Axmed?' nods Diana.

'Let him go.' Marchant leaves the room. Lawton gives Diana a sour glance before striding out. O'Malley and Khan look desperately up at her.

'So, if she's dead, we don't need to find and interview …'

'All the other Ifrahs? Yes, we do. Our killer may attack again if they know they got the wrong one.'

An eye roll, neck back, hands in pocket.

'And the Irfrahs?'

'Yes! And if they've left country, find where they've gone!' She looks out of the window. 'Find the second bullet 'n' all.'

'What?'

'We'll have to wait on ballistics to find out whether the bullet Ifrah caught was the first or second. If so, there's a bullet – and possibly another body – to be found.'

Chapter 44

WEDNESDAY 10TH NOVEMBER, 2010 – DEWBOW

Diana

It has to be a pre-dawn raid. This woman gets up early, thinks and acts fast. Nothing's beyond her. Diana's got one shot at this and no room for doubt.

Robertson, O'Malley and their team flank up the woodland end and road to the hilltop. Herself, Khan, Neville and the SWAT team head up the long drive as fast as the gravel and November fog allows.

Lights go on. A shape at the window.

Car doors slam.

Khan knocks on the wooden twin doors.

'Police! Open up!' yells Khan.

Diana steps back, squinting up at the windows and then around the side towards the back door. She can hear the sound of footsteps on the stairs, deadbolts scraping back. She returns to the porch as the door opens.

Maya stands there, still glistening from a shower, in her white robe, hair in wet ringlets against her flushed cheeks. But no surprise in her eyes. Just an unnerving calmness.

'Maya Smith, I've a warrant to search your property. I'm

arresting you for the murder of John Daniels and Ifrah Hussein. You do not have to say anything. But it may harm your defence if you do not mention when questioned something that you later rely on in Court. Anything you do say may be given in evidence.'

Maya sighs. 'I need to put some clothes on, detective, unless you want me naked?'

Diana follows her upstairs.

In the bedroom, Diana looks at the tussled emperor bed, two sets of double pillows slept on, duvet kicked way back.

'Can I have some privacy please?'

'No.'

Maya shakes her head, eyebrows raised. Diana's eyes remain fixed on Maya as she pulls off her towelling robe. Her body is Amazonian, bronzed, muscled, full of vigour. She pulls on black lacy panties, clips a bra on. Slowly.

'Hurry up. You're not dressing to impress.'

Maya drops the pair of tights back into her tall dresser. Opens a drawer, pulls out socks. Jumps into brown cords and a camel cashmere sweater. Diana pushes down her memory of when she was last here, downstairs, shaking, concussed after this woman had saved her life. Maya ties her springy curls into a loose bun, pulls on her Rolex watch. She looks up at Diana, who shakes her head.

'It'll just be handed in.'

Maya takes it off, putting it on the dressing table. She picks up a Chanel lipstick.

'Won't be needing that either.'

The lipstick rolls on the table top.

As they leave the bedroom, the toilet flushes.

Diana looks at Maya, who looks at the en suite bathroom door as it opens.

'What's going on?' says Bruno, standing in the doorway, clad only in white boxers.

'I'm about to find out. Get dressed. Bruno Pierce, I'm arresting you for the murder of John Daniels and Ifrah Hussein. You do not have to say anything. But it may harm your defence if you do not mention when questioned something that you later rely on in Court. Anything you do say may be given in evidence.'

At the foot of the stairs, Khan waits with two pairs of handcuffs.

'Hands out.'

'This is some bullshit!' mutters Bruno, slowly raising his wrists.

O'Malley snaps cuffs on Maya and then Bruno. They are taken out into the November fog where Khan and Neville take them to separate cars, pushing down gently on Maya's springy curls, Bruno frowning, bobbing away from Neville's hand.

Once the cars have disappeared onto the road, Diana turns back to the house, DCs Khan and O'Malley.

'You have the keys. Do the house and outbuildings first. By daylight, the frogmen will be down to drag the pond.'

Diana clicks on her radio. 'Robertson? All clear. You can come down here now. Neville will process them.'

Diana makes her way to an outbuilding on the far side of the house. With a grunt, she manages to open the heavy doors with the deadlock. Inside, dark shadows, and an earthy pungent smell. No windows. Groping on the wall, she flicks a light switch and a blinking whizzing white tube stutters and growls. Diana strokes the soundproofed door. In the centre of the room, a long, large stainless-steel table, waist height. Shelves around her, stacked neatly with labelled cans and hooks for clean instruments. Solvents and a large deep sink. Robertson, now in a white suit, appears at the door, Diana turns.

'I want this place peeled apart. I reckon this is where the butchery took place.'

A sudden gust of wind rushes through the door. There's a squeak above her. She looks up at a deer carcass swinging from a pulley.

'You alright, Boss?'

'I think that's the stag who would have gored me if Maya hadn't shot it.'

They both look up at the stiff, dry legs.

He snorts. 'Save your life? That's enough meat to last all year.'

Diana looks around the well-equipped room. With her gloved hands, she opens a locked cupboard with another key revealing a wall of shining blades, cleavers, machetes, knives. She picks up a boning knife, sees a motorised saw in the corner, a handsaw big as a bow.

'That would cut through a human spine like butter.'

By eight o'clock, a wet mist falls over the white tent by the pond. Daylight, but the sky is closing down, a strange wind blowing over the tent. White-suited men carry out items from the outbuilding. Diana walks around the edge of the pond, pacing out to the woodland and back, watching the house, crouched low and black in the fog. Men in rubber suits with masks bob up from the water like seals. One nods his head, raises his arm. Slowly the truck reverses and the crane is positioned over the pond, the pulley wound by a man not in a suit. The seal man takes the cage and pulls it down.

Ten minutes later, the pulley starts creaking and cranking up. Diana's heart pounds in her chest. The cage bursts out, dripping in pond weed and slime, but it is not empty. Inside there is a big grey eel with slimy trousers and muddy shoes, blue stripes just visible. Another seal man pops up and the two guide the cage closer to the edge. It lifts up clear in the air. A rank stench, swamp water and rotten meat, fills Diana's nose. Robertson gasps, holding a forearm against his mask. One arm of the grey eel drops out of the cage.

'Careful!' shouts Diana. The winch-man yells at the driver.

The hand of the arm is clawed up, the arm itself in a red nylon sleeve, netted with strings of weed.

'Did Daniels' neighbour specify what Daniels' driver was wearing on Saturday 28th August? The mysterious black man?'

Robertson says: 'A red tracksuit top.'

Diana sighs. 'I think we may have just found Leroy Young.'

Njambi

I see from my window the cars come before dawn. At daylight, I have breakfasted on egg and go down to stand under the trees. The rain doesn't touch me here but the mist and smell does. It smells like the pit where they threw the dead from the camp.

I see the grey man come up out of the pond. In the fog, I see shadows. Hear the yell. A monster from the deep. The frogmen will never find the bones in Kenya though. They will be eggshell now. Not even eggshell. Even so, they will grow truth.

A man in a white suit comes from the outbuilding. He carries a plastic bag. Inside is a black oblong the size of my purse. Two frogmen pull up onto the wall from the pond, next to where Ally stood smoking. They hold a large machete – like the one they used on Gituku when they took his manhood. The other man holds a hacksaw, like the one we used to chop up buffalo bone. They place them in large transparent sacks.

I see Diana, in a white suit. She points to the house, starts walking fast. She knows what needs to be done.

I return to the cottage. I am tired now.

Chapter 45

Wednesday 10th November, 2010 – Sheffield HQ

Bruno

This is not a room. Not a cell. It's a concrete refrigerator with a grilled letter box of wired glass eleven feet from floor. Why've they brought me here? Again. I've done nowt wrong.

Except exist. Try to get a job. Try to get out of hell.

And I *still* end up in a cell.

One Formica table, like one at the Hut. Two chairs. Tape recorder. Notepad. Two paper cups of water. It smells of shit and disinfectant in here. Across table, that weird detective, again. She *looks* like shit. Like she's not slept for a week. She switches on the tape machine.

I lean back in the chair.

'You sure you don't want to have the duty solicitor present?'

'Yes.'

'For the tape, state your name, date of birth and current address.'

'Bruno Pierce, date of birth twenty-second of the ninth, nineteen ninety-two. 25b Park Hill, Sheffield S2 1XL.'

'Thank you. Are you sure that's your address?'

'Yes.'

'Not Dewbright Hall? If so, you weren't at home this morning.'

'I know.'

She's looking at me like *Stop fartarsing about.*

'Why not?'

'I'm not …' Can't say I'm not living there as they'll put me down as no known address.

'I stay over in Dewbow when working at butcher's.'

She just raises her eyebrows. 'Interesting. Didn't know Dewbright Hall was a hostel for apprentices.'

She being funny?

'Hostel? I've been helping my sponsor and Mr Samuels. Peak season, innit.'

Stop staring at me.

'Sponsor? Can you explain your relationship with Maya Smith?'

'I just have. Apprenticeship in butchery.'

She steeples her hands. I hate it when people do that – like they're the Pope or something.

'How did you meet Maya?'

'She wor a regular at the Ryano Hut where I used to work. You came there with Carl – that Detective Robertson.'

'Best steamed vegetable and dumplings. Your carrot juice has a nice lot of ginger.'

Yeah – my touch that ginger.

'I do the meat. She brought Samuels to see me quart a chicken and he offered me the apprenticeship.'

She raises her eyebrows. Like *Yeah right.*

Diana

Diana stares at the chisel-chinned youth before her. Bruno Pierce. What an enigma. What a mess. He's in a fair sulk too.

'It's not me should be here; it's Ryan.'

'Why Ryan?'

'He's not paid me and I don't like what he's doing with Axmed.'

'What's he doing with Axmed?'

'You know what he's doing. Undys been watching them years. You still not done owt though, ev you? Axmed's going to end up dead, in jail or back in some burnt-out hole in Africa.'

'Fair point.' Diana puts her head on one side. 'But let's talk about you first. How long have you been sleeping with Maya?'

Bruno snorts, shakes his head.

'Two months. Six?' Diana tries.

He glares.

'Three?'

She waits.

'I'm eighteen!' he starts. 'Who I sleep with is none of your business.'

'Which is why I asked how *long*, because if it was three months or more – it *is* our business.'

'Well, it isn't.' He closes his eyes in frustration.

'So,' Diana persists. 'Just to confirm, you *are* sleeping with her?'

That glare again.

'Do you feel obliged?'

'What you mean?'

'Well, here she is, your fairy godmother – sorry, sponsor – saving you from skinning chicken for four quid an hour, giving you a way out of Sheffield, a chance to get your academic act together. You may feel it's rude to say no.'

Bruno rubs his temples and squints at Diana between his knuckles.

'No comment.'

'How long have you been staying over?'

Bruno wrinkles his nose.

'Just said – when I'm working. Samuels gave me more hours as it's peak season and Ryan's being a knob. Had a row with me mum 'n' all.'

'What about?'

'She *thinks* I'm informing. She *thinks* I'm in trouble with you lot because *you* tipped her yard upside down twice and like to drop in for uninvited chats.'

'Is that all?'

'That all? Are you for real?' His brow is sweating and he clamps his jaw. Diana calmly places her pen on the table. Watches it roll. Bruno watches it too.

Finally, he mutters: 'I asked her if Ryan were my real dad. She wouldn't say.'

'And Ryan?'

'He's a maggot. Just uses people, poisons their lives.'

'I see.'

'So, I've been down Dewbow, but you lot keep popping up like mushrooms.'

'Planning a new life with a forty-two-year-old auditor?'

'I'm not planning owt.'

Isn't that the truth. He looks tired. Alone. Frightened. A kid in the wind.

'I get that, Bruno. My concern is: has *she* got plans on *you*?'

He shakes his head, leaning back in the chair, muttering to the chipped ceiling.

Diana continues: 'And then ... your problem arrives back on your doorstep Sunday night.'

'What you mean?'

'Well, Ryan drives up to Dewbright Hall in his van with Axmed. He drives off with your lover. Poor Axmed has to get bus home.'

Bruno, swinging on his chair, suddenly catapults himself forward onto the table, gripping it, eyes level with Diana's.

'Poor Axmed? Wish I'd got the bus 'n' all.'

'Why didn't you?'

Bruno shrugs.

'She said I could stop. She had more game to cut.'

'Game to cut.' Diana looks at her notepad. 'So did you?'

'What?'

'Cut game?'

'No.' He looks sideways, frowning. 'No, I didn't as it happens.'

'You didn't think that a bit odd?'

'Odd? How do I know what's *odd* for an accountant deer-stalker? I was just "Sweet! I can play PS3 after work."'

Diana is writing numbers on her notepad, frowning.

'What time did Ryan and Axmed arrive?'

'Dunno. Eight-thirty, maybe.'

'And you don't know why Ryan came?'

'No, detective, I do not.'

'I'm just confused, because Maya didn't call Ryan ...'

'He was probably just being nosey then.'

Diana blinks and shakes her head.

'Bruno, Axmed already told me it was *you* who called him, and your phone backs that up. Axmed said you called him, said Maya wanted to see Ryan.'

Bruno shrugs.

'OK. Whatever. Same difference. I don't know what that business was, just that she didn't want Ryan having her number.'

He stares evenly at her. Diana sighs.

'OK. Ryan arrives – what happened then?'

'Maya suggests I have a game of *Call of Duty* with Axmed while she discussed some business with Ryan. So, I go upstairs with Axmed. Next I know van's off down drive.'

'What time?'

'We'd just had one game – about nine-thirty maybe. No, hang on, it were two – maybe ten-thirty?' He squints. 'I don't know!'

'So, the van drives off – neither of them say bye?'

Bruno looks puzzled. 'No. She calls me about five–ten minutes later though. Says Axmed can stay if he wants. That Ryan was giving her a lift to her office as she had some paperwork to do and an early train to catch.' He pauses. 'I was a bit pissed off, to be honest. Took it out on Axmed. We had a row and he left, got bus.'

'Bit late for buses.'

He shrugs.

'Did Ryan explain to you – or Axmed?'

Bruno snorts. 'That dickhead's running from us both. Owes wages.'

'So ... why did Maya want to speak to Ryan?'

Again, he shrugs.

'Does she fancy him?'

Bruno's face contorts.

'You seem pretty sure about that,' Diana says.

'Just selling him wholesale venison.'

Diana frowns. 'She could have just called.'

'She didn't want him to have her number.' He glares at her.

OK.

Diana leans back. 'If you care about Axmed so much, why tell him to get the bus at ten-thirty at night?'

Bruno swallows. 'He were doing my head in. He beat me at

349

Call of Duty and was goofing about the room, on at me to use her computer for his Facebook. That's a defo off-limits. He said some stuff about Maya so I told him to do one.'

'Maya must really trust you.'

Bruno stares at her.

'Enough to leave you alone in her house overnight.'

'I was knackered. Went to bed. Had to be at butcher's for seven-thirty.'

'For the tape, Bruno.'

'Yes, I was on my own at Dewbright Hall!' he spits.

Finally.

This second interview room is a dungeon with letter box windows at street level near the ceiling. Metal chairs scrape against the floor. Diana stares at Maya, her defiant halo of free curl, the cashmere jumper. Immaculate nails. Ready for the office. Ready for success. Ready for this? Diana stares down at her battered hands, at odds with the acrylic tips. Next to Maya, her solicitor, a slender balding Asian whose wire-rimmed glasses keep sliding down his oily pointed nose. He repeatedly clicks his silver Parker ballpoint.

'Can you not click please – for the tape?' says Diana.

He puts the pen down. Maya gives a small smile.

'So, Maya, can you start by telling me where you were this August Bank Holiday?'

'I had a three-day charity function going off in Dewbow.'

'Which charity would that be then? You're on the board of quite a few,' Diana asks.

Maya pushes out her bottom lip, head nodding. 'Yes, I am. This one was the Dewbow Shining Light Trust.'

Diana tries to find Mary in Maya's features. Maybe the shape of the eyes? Almond, cat-like? A similar snub nose, full lips. Soup-cooler lips. Maya's eyes are almost green; Mary's seemed darker in the photos. Mary was a slip of a thing; Maya looks like a tri-athlete. Her forehead is large, smooth, framed by the glossy curls. Her wrists thick. Better genes or just better fed?

There were insufficient photos of Mary for her to check against Maya.

350

Is she wrong?

'The Dewbow Shining Light Trust. We raise funds for the youth in the area and for inner city youth in south-west Sheffield and Derby.' Maya pauses. 'We had a barbecue on Saturday evening.'

'Where was that?'

'Dewbow recreation grounds'

Diana lifts her palms from the table, sticky with neglected spilled tea. 'And you were there how long?'

Maya shrugs. 'I was late Saturday as had paperwork to finish at home. Got there around five p.m. to help with the banquet and drive home board members who were …'

'Drunk?'

Maya smiles. 'Not legal to drive anyway. I was there all of Sunday helping set up the contests and the Sunday sit-down banquet. The Summer Ball Dinner. Monday there was a Fun Day for families and kids. Just wandered about, drinking prosecco, chatted with the local landowners.'

She fixes Diana with a cold green stare.

'Who can vouch for you?'

Maya raises her thick arched eyebrows. 'Most of Dewbow. Mr Samuels, Harry, Wes …'

'I'll need their details.'

'No problem.'

Maya spells out their names, contact details. *She's too smooth. Just like those nails. That make-up. It's all make-up.* The solicitor clicks his Parker. Diana looks at him. Maya gives a swift glance. He stops, mid-click.

'You take the charity work very seriously.'

Maya flicks her hair. 'Of course.'

'I'm surprised you're so focused on inner city issues. Why not conservation or environmental problems? A new cricket ground? Help with the upkeep of the churchyard—'

'This question is not relevant,' butts in the solicitor.

Maya smiles, ignoring him. 'You've noticed they're in a bit of a pickle? We do our bit there too. But we like to give back to those who don't have the same privileges of country life.'

'Who's we?'

'The board of directors. Members of the trust.'

Diana sees Phillips' sour face at the window. Her stomach tightens. He slowly shakes his head, pushing out his bottom lip. Still trying to get her to doubt herself, undermine her. She sees Maya clock her shaky glance. Last thing she needs: Maya working out she's standing on a cliff edge. A wave of vertigo overwhelms Diana; a moment ago, it was all clear in her head, but now she's unravelling. And Maya's a neighbour who probably saved her life. If she is a killer, surely she's had opportunities to 'accidentally' kill an investigating officer?

Diana closes her eyes. She sees Daniels' head. The tick on his cheek. Maisy Young playing with her dolls. The mould in Mary's bedsit. *Let sleeping dogs lie …* She opens her eyes.

So, where's letting dogs lie got you?

'How did you know John Daniels?'

Maya shrugs. 'Charity do. A couple of functions. Scrounging money for his new curriculum.'

His?

'And the Legley Road High School audit? Bracewell Smith were contracted by C & AG to help with that, correct?'

The solicitor frowns and pushes his tailored white cuff across the table.

'What has this got to do with the charge you're bringing against my client?'

'Plenty. Bracewell Smith did the audit on Legley Road High School.'

Maya pulls back from the table. 'I'm a professional, detective. I'm sure you of all people understand.' She narrows her cat eyes.

'Yes. A professional. Miss Certificates.'

Diana pats a large brown envelope in front of her.

'In fact, Maya, you are more than a professional; you're a Responsible Individual. For the sake of the tape, can you explain what that is.'

'Only a Responsible Individual – a certificated, audit-qualified person, can sign off the audit report of the financial statements of a market-traded or designated company or authority.'

'It takes a lot of hard graft and good references to get that title.'

'It does.'

'Ambitious *and* talented.'

Maya shrugs. 'Jealous, detective? I work hard. I'm up long before your jog.'

The solicitor looks from Diana to Maya – as if she's just appeared out of a cloud. Maya waves her hand dismissively.

'We live in the same village.'

Diana continues with her point. 'Bracewell Smith is the most reputable auditing firm in South Yorkshire.'

'And north Derbyshire.'

Diana leans her elbows on the table. 'Did you find something interesting on DS Neville and DI Lawton?'

Maya shrugs, looking at her nails. 'If I did, it would have gone in the report on the Compliance Audit for SYPD.'

Diana says: 'All I recall is a general comment about the disparity between reported cases of assault and domestic violence and prosecution. Unreliable crime logging and follow-through.'

'Just doing my professional duty.'

'Indeed. You are an RI, so would have had access to police files up to that period.'

The solicitor frowns and taps his pen on the table.

'I'm sorry, detective – how is this relevant?'

Diana sits back. 'It's just whoever is behind the murder of Daniels and Young had intimate knowledge of Legley Road's finances and staff management *and* police files. I have been trying to work out who on earth could have an Access All Areas pass.' Diana nods towards Maya. 'Your client seems to be the only one.'

Maya snorts. 'Rather circumstantial, detective. Sorry for being good at my job.'

Diana leans forward. 'So why risk it all? Throw it away?'

Maya leans back in her chair with an incredulous grin. 'Didn't know I had!'

'Maya, you've been arrested on suspicion of two murders.'

Maya raises her palms. 'Good luck proving that.'

'No need for luck when you've got evidence.'

'What's the evidence?' asks the solicitor, daring to look at Maya, who blanks him again, eyes screwed on Diana. 'You have less than …'

He looks at his chunky silver watch.

'Thirteen hours thirty-five minutes and forty-six seconds,' says Diana, staring ahead at the smirking Maya. 'The evidence includes: connections with all of the deceased, the body of Leroy Young found on your premises, access to restricted data and documents, auditing Mary Calley's inquest, use of a black jeep registration number MY1 N0W seen driving down the A621 at significant times ... shall I continue? There's more – just waiting on forensics and matching ballistics from a .308 WIN rifle.'

Maya's face flashes – either with fury or pride, Diana can't quite tell. The brief's forefinger trembles over the Parker.

'Largely circumstantial,' he mutters.

Diana pushes forward a birth certificate. 'You already explained about your name change. The Irish surgeon, Frank Smith, now deceased, was your biological father, correct?'

Maya doesn't look at the birth certificate, but the solicitor picks it up.

'And Sunita Calley was your biological mother?'

'It's not a crime to want to find your real parents.'

'No, it's not a crime. Nor is it a crime to trace your twin sister.' Maya doesn't blink.

'Did you believe Mary Calley to be your twin sister, Maya?'

Diana looks up at the slashing rain, the floating crisp packets in the gutter.

Over her head.

'You've no right to rake through my personal medical history ... You have no idea, with your neat tidy little family, your heritage all justified and righteous ...'

You have no idea.

Diana continues: 'And then there's your butchery certificate. Takes some skill to get that.'

'My client's achievements are not evidence, detective.'

Diana's eyes remain on Maya, who glares back at her.

'No, they're not, but you have enjoyed a very privileged life, Maya. Not like Mary Calley.'

'What has that to do with my client?' The solicitor takes a deep breath.

This guy.

'Let's take a break, shall we? Ten minutes.'

Diana glares at him, stops the tape.

She leans back against the toilet cubicle, eyes closed. Forensics haven't texted her yet with the results from Maya's swabs to run against the fingernail – or any particulars of Daniels and Young that could be found in her butchery room. Diana gets out her BlackBerry, texts Robertson.

DNA back yet? Firearms checked?

She stares at her screen, willing for an answer. Nothing. She pushes the door of the toilets, stares at herself in the mirror. These basement loos are badly ventilated, rarely cleaned. She can't remember when she last slept – even on her sofa. Two mornings of cat licks. Her skin a dull green-brown, grey shadows under her eyes, hair a wiry, wild nest.

But Maya is cracking. She can feel it.

Diana's BlackBerry vibrates in her pocket. Its red light's been flashing every time she's checked it on a break. No time to look or think outside of this. *Yes, Robertson! Let this be good news.* Sees the name.

A butterfly flip in her stomach.

'Michael.' Her voice echoes off the ancient, cracked porcelain and lead piping.

'Y'alright? Where are you – in a sewer?'

'Don't ask. How are you? I am so sorry – I never …'

Diana leaves the cubicle, smiles at the refection in the cracked, pitted mirror. Like he can see her.

'You're busy, I can hear it. Interviewing crackheads and knobheads. Bet you wish it was that headmaster killer.'

'Yeah. That would be great.'

'Well … just checking in to remind you.'

Diana hears footsteps in the corridor and turns to the door.

'Remind me what?' she asks.

'You owe me a drink.'

'Do I? I can't have outstanding debts.'

Can he hear her smile? He laughs.

355

Yes, he can.

'Shout us when you're free. Take it easy, Diana.'

'You too. Thanks for …' She grins at the grim face in the mirror. 'Reminding me.'

'Anytime. See you later.'

'You will. Bye.'

BlackBerry in pocket. It vibrates again. She answers on first bell, still smiling.

'Michael?'

'Boss?'

'Robertson … Any news?' she asks.

'Match on ballistics from the rifle. No prints.'

Hallelujah.

'Handgun that shot Hussein is covered in Ryan's prints. Phillips is well excited. It's an erased serial number, but they think it's Manchester-linked.'

Course they do.

'So, Pierce is just randomly shooting Muslim women putting out the bin?'

'No DNA back yet from Maya's swabs …' he says.

'Robertson, I need it now. Blood group 'n' all.'

Hanging by the thinnest of threads.

With a fake fingernail.

Jams the BlackBerry into her pocket, grips the basin, runs the hot tap over her fingers.

Shakes her head, raking wet hands through limp locks.

Slaps her cheeks.

Round two.

Diana pulls her chair in close. The brief looks up from his papers as if she is a minor interruption. Maya is calmly perusing her nails. Diana clicks on the tape.

'You're right, Maya. I *am* jealous. Jealous of your hair, your ability, your wealth, just how *easy* life is for you. Because it *is* easy being Maya Smith Johnson, isn't it? Bet your dad raised you like a son, right? Encouraged you to be the best? Your school too. All those motivational speeches. All that private tuition. You could have been an Olympian – three years running county champion

356

at javelin and shotput. Winner of athletics award 1984, hurdling finalist for Yorkshire 1985. Me: I'm dyslexic. Did well to get to uni.'

The solicitor scowls. 'This is not appropriate.'

Diana places her hands flat on the table.

'Raynaud's, you know. Kicked in three years ago. Wish I could have lovely nails like you.'

Diana waves her black-tipped fingers in the air, head to one side. Maya follows them, as if looking at an exotic horror. The solicitor tugs his cuff off his watch.

Maya's lips curl. She shakes her head. 'More like chronic anaemia. Told you to eat some venison.'

Maya's smirk disappears.

'Well, you'd know.' Diana puts her elbows on the table. 'But it was a different kind of anaemia you had, wasn't it?'

'How is this relevant?' the solicitor says. Diana lifts one finger.

'Aplastic anaemia. It's not anaemia – it's a cancer of the blood, isn't it, Maya? You needed a bone marrow donor. And you have a rare blood group. Your adoptive parents had to locate your biological twin. And neither of you knew. Poor Mary believed *she* was the patient. Your adoptive parents ensured she could never be identified; ordered her to be referred to as Patient X or blanked out. Except one night nurse didn't get the memo. Nurse Susan Bedford, bless her cotton socks, handwrote on the ward notes: 'Mary had been without food for twenty-four hours and threw up when given some soup.' And in the following night's report: 'Mrs Calley sat with Mary all through the night.' But Mary never knew the sick girl in the bed next door was her twin sister. Or that she was saving your life.'

The solicitor freezes, staring at Maya, who tilts her chin to the ceiling.

'You made one great recovery!' continues Diana. 'Must have been all those venison burgers and Mary's blood. Look at you – an outdoor girl in the cells and still pure boujee glamour. That white tip – what you call it? French manicure?'

Maya stiffens, takes her hands off the table.

'Fancied some myself,' says Diana. 'I tried everywhere. Finally found someone local ...'

Maya stares at the wall to the side.

'… formerly Psalter Lane. *Clous pour tu? Oui?* Does *beautiful* French-tip manicures. Not many in Sheff do these classy ones. Like yours. Like …' Diana opens the manilla folder, takes out the photo of the acrylic nail found at the Legley Road site. Pushes it towards Maya. 'Like this.'

Maya shakes her head. Her brief looks at her sideways. He taps his pen impatiently.

'I'm sorry – a random acrylic nail proves – what?' snorts Maya.

'Next to the filing cabinet that contained John Daniels' head?' Diana keeps pushing in. 'Take another look.'

'I've looked!' says Maya. 'A nail. I don't lose nails. I can't go to meetings with shoddy hands, detective. It's unprofessional.'

'So, you definitely never went anywhere near Legley Road High School?'

'I was there as part of the audit of the LEA's management of the school closure.'

'Ah. When was that?'

'Some time in the summer.'

Diana flicks through her papers.

'July 30th was the last day you attended? Did you take the filing cabinet key then or later? Recommended CCTV be removed. Correct?'

'If you say so. Yeah.' Maya shrugs.

'There was no reason for you to be there thereafter. The report was completed and filed August 24th 2010.'

Maya nods. The brief looks irritated. 'This has nothing to do with the charge.'

'I beg to differ.' Diana tugs at her uncombed wiry locks. 'Your client's manicurist seems to have a more specific memory.'

Maya stares, impressed. The solicitor's Adam's apple is going up and down like a bobbin.

'It could have been there from when I did the audit,' says Maya.

Diana shakes her head.

'No. The rubble is from after the demolition. I did ask, did everything I could to find a possible explanation that it was older debris.'

She tucks the photo back in the folder.

'But it wasn't. It's *your* nail, Maya.'

'No, it's not. It's a fake, acrylic nail Applied by a manicurist.'

'Julie Young, right? She keeps her customer notes. You came for a replacement Wednesday 1st September. She always takes care to attach her nails securely. You are a good regular customer so she's happy to oblige. They would have stayed on if you hadn't been shifting a heavy filing cabinet. Maybe you pulled your gloves off too early? Stripped off a wee bit of your DNA though.'

Maya exhales. Her brief looks at her desperately, pushing his glasses up his beaky nose.

Maya leans back, glaring at both hands in her lap.

'Seriously, detective. Nails. Certificates. Filing cabinet keys.'

Come on, Robertson. Where are the forensics?

'You're right. Maybe nothing.'

The solicitor scribbles furiously, getting ready for a juicy case of bias and prejudice. Maya inhales, stares. 'Bravo, Diana. An entire case, hanging by your fingernails. Literally. You *are* jealous. Now, if you don't mind, I want a bottle of water and a private talk with my solicitor.'

Bottled water days are over, love. She'll get a plastic cup of chlorinated tap.

'See what I can do,' says Diana as she stops the tape, pushes her chair back and leaves the room.

Outside, she leans against the wall, closes her eyes. Exhales.

Her BlackBerry buzzes. She looks down.

Yes.

It's 9 p.m. and Maya's not looking as magnificent as she did this morning. Lost that post-coital glow, the cashmere crumpled. The solicitor looks desperate to click his Parker.

'Where was it you said you needed to be today?'

'Nottingham. I have…'

'A lot of business in Nottingham, I know. In fact, it was Bracewell Smith who audited Nottingham City Council's council tax department from 2007. You used your powers and access to private data to locate Mary.'

'I most certainly did not. It's not worth my job.' Maya stiffens, her eyes glaring furiously at Diana.

'No, it's not. But it's worth discovering your sister. You accidentally discovered a Mary Calley in the records with the same birth date as you who had recently relocated there from Sheffield and was claiming housing benefit and a twenty-five per cent single person council tax discount.'

'I could have but I didn't.'

'No worries. I guess your own meticulous records will vouch for us in court though. We got a search warrant for your offices, by the way.'

Maya glares at her solicitor who is looking at his pen with intense concentration.

'You have no—'

'Unfortunately I do. Although I appreciate it must have broken your heart – knowing your own flesh and blood, the sister who had given up her own to help you survive, was abandoned and treated as vilely as she was. Left to rot in a Housing Association bedsit while you enjoyed skiing in Switzerland and a privileged life.'

'My lifestyle is not a crime, detective.'

'No, it's not. But even a hard nut like you may have a *bit* of guilt.'

Maya shakes her head.

'How about survivor's guilt?'

Maya exhales slowly.

Diana shakes her head, taps her papers together.

'OK, well, we'll just have to find some other explanation for the coincidence of Bracewell Smith being the auditing company of Nottingham Council and Mary Calley's details being on their database. And you being the lead RI in the case from 2007-2010. I am pretty sure if Pastor Calley could talk, he'd tell me he gave you the Grant of Representation – just to shut you up and get you away. Is that why you went to church again?'

'No comment, detective. Can I go now please?'

Diana pulls up her chair. 'You seen Leroy recently? Your manicurist's hubby?'

Maya exhales, rolls her eyes.

'No? Good news then – we found him at last!'

Maya looks up sharply.

360

'This morning, feeding your carp. He's a bit worse for wear having been *in* the water for two months. But he's the one who really screwed up Mary, isn't he?'

The brief blanches. Puts his pen down.

Diana looks through her file, pulling out a photograph of the gold torpedo bullet. 'Same one as found in your shooting rifle. Weird coincidence that, eh? Did you miss first time? Was he snooping, after dropping off Daniels? Or part of your original plan?'

Maya sighs. 'From what his wife told me, he had a lot of enemies ... including her. Maybe you should be looking there.'

'Don't worry. We looked. No love lost, but no evidence for murder either. Yes, Leroy Young ruined a few people's lives. Bruno's. His wife and kids. Mary's. He's the one who messed with her head, not to mention the domestic violence. You've seen the texts, the emails, the diaries, haven't you?'

Maya's Sphinx-like face. 'I've reviewed them professionally, detective. Legley Road and your police force failed in many areas, which I duly reported on.'

'Agreed. Yes, the police were worse. The one institution Mary should have got protection from. She called the police four times. *Four times.*' Diana hits the table four times. 'And four times it was the same duty officer. He never even called back, turned up, posted a card through a letter box. Didn't even give her a crime number. Nothing logged. I get it. Colleagues of mine. We came up through the ranks together. But they are bang out of order for what they didn't do. I am so sorry. If I'd been on duty, she'd have got a crime number and a visit.'

Maya looks up, eyes narrowed.

'Mary trusted the police. She was a tax-paying professional. She had called them as a vulnerable single woman in danger. Alone. Her health started to suffer, just like your birth mother's, from this chronic undermining. She had, according to her medical records, gastric reflux, anxiety, mild depression, stress, self-neglect due to domestic abuse and prioritising teaching over self-care. Developed a stomach ulcer. On top of that, a strange guy – not Leroy – sent malicious communications threatening her. But she did have the book club, didn't she? That was good for her ... up to a point. But I don't think they listened to her enough. She became more irregular in attendance, isolated herself. Maybe they got fed up of her always making "bad choices in men". Whatever. Mary slips through *their* fingers too.'

Maya looks up at the clock. Diana flicks through her papers.

'I started thinking: what would I do in Maya's position? Who wouldn't want to be Maya Smith? You just move seamlessly in and out. You get your hands on data easier than I do, and I'm a police officer! A better detective than all of us ...' She pauses. 'To start with.'

The brief looks at his watch.

'Why's Pastor Calley still alive?' Diana asks.

A flicker of rage across Maya's eyes.

'Because he *is* suffering, just the way you wanted him to. He can't speak any more – just like Mary and Sunita – lost *their* voices. He's just got to sit and wait till his body gives up and the maggots claim him. And who's going to mourn him? Mrs Thompson? The body behind his beloved greenhouse – that was a clever touch. You must have spoken to him. I saw your name in the visitors' book at church – or rather the name he would recognise: M Johnson. I guess you didn't go to repent. What *did* you say to him? Did you taunt him about your real biological father?'

'No comment.'

'See, Mrs Thompson who cleans for him also knew your mother well. And it was she who remembered he set up a private adoption with the Johnsons after hearing through a charity of their desire for an *exotic* baby. She remembers because it broke your mother – Sunita's – heart.'

Maya's face still flint, but Diana watches her neck muscles tighten with the swallow of that pain.

Diana sighs. 'But then, you did save *my* life. If you had known I was the SIO, would you have?'

There's a pause. Diana looks at Maya, who stares blankly back. Diana shrugs. 'Or maybe you wanted me to find you. Because the others wouldn't have. DI Phillips wants to make it into his OCG case, and DI Lawton believes it too. They would never have got you because, in their minds, you aren't a predator, not someone who's capable of pulling off something this devious, this confident, this clean. Because they don't *see* you, Maya, do they?

'But you still couldn't work out what finally killed Mary. Who was this mysterious black woman? Someone from book club? No name. Nothing on record. No measurement. Your one tool blunted. The only way you'd find out was by getting into the book club. And, hey presto – Ally shows up. You're able to join the final dots – so you think.

'Who would be next on your list? The negligent police officers? You knew no one would ever suspect you unless they found Mary, unless they cared about Mary.

'And the fact is *nobody* cares about Mary or the hundreds of thousands of women like Mary, like Sunita, like Ally. Most folk don't even see them. They are ghosts. But, see, there's one thing I don't understand: you being a woman so clued up on procedure, on legislation, with your power and privilege – why didn't you bring Mary's case to the attention of the IPCC? Then the negligent officers would be appropriately punished, some justice would be served for their failure to protect the victim after domestic abuse had been reported. If Mary had lived, she could have done that. But she didn't. And no one did it for her – not even you. The road to justice is harder and longer; you just chose the shortcut. But there isn't one.'

Maya is stabbing her nails into her palms. 'That bang on the head's affected your judgement, detective.'

Diana inhales. The brief shuffles his papers. Robertson appears at the door, wearing latex gloves, holding a small plastic evidence bag and two unsealed cream envelopes up to the window.

Diana pauses the tape and gets up to open the door.

'Boss, we found these. In one of her dresser drawers. CSI unsealed the envelopes. Looks like those two missing letters from the Nottingham box.'

He passes two sheets of cream notepaper over. Diana flicks her eyes over them.

'Perfect timing. Thanks, Robertson.'

'Oh, and with them we also found Young's wallet and both his and Daniels' driving licences.'

'A proper little collector.'

He flourishes a small plastic bag with a tangled chain at the bottom. Maya freezes.

'But this is what you were really looking for ...'

363

Diana empties the contents onto the table and holds up the silver chain. On it swings a tiny key.

'Wow!'

'Found in her jewellery box. Gorman tried it – it fits the same filing cabinet that contained Daniels' head.'

Diana looks at the grey-faced Maya.

'Another trophy to add to your wall-hangings? Or a cool piece of costume jewellery?'

She carefully bags up the chain again, hands it back to Robertson who leaves, closing the door after him. Maya stares at the sheets in Diana's hands.

Diana says: 'I was wondering where those two extra letters went – maybe have to get you for tampering with police evidence as well, eh, Maya?'

Maya looks desperately at her brief, but his eyes are on the letters.

'You've no right.'

The brief shakes his head. Maya's eyes widen.

'No – Maya. This time, I *do* have the right. And you don't.' Diana turns to the solicitor. 'These are the letters Maya wrote to Mary after she discovered she had a twin sister. You have exquisite handwriting, by the way, and such elegant stationery. If only Mary had received them. Just to remind you of their contents ...'

Diana reads them aloud:

Dewbright Hall,
Dewbow
Derbyshire
078964321
msmith@bracewellsmith.co.uk
28.1.2008

Hello Mary

Happy new year and happy new everything! You don't know me and I don't know you but we shared the same womb, if not the same egg. I am your other half. Your non-identical twin sister. Pastor Calley made our mum, Sunita, give me up because I resembled our birth father. I was adopted and raised in Sheffield. We met without being introduced briefly when I was seriously ill. We were six and I had aplastic anaemia. You donated bone marrow and helped save my life at Claremont Hospital. I only found out I had a twin when my adoptive father was dying last year.

Hope you don't mind but I was doing an audit on the council tax department at Nottingham City Council, came across your name as a new tenant at number 43 Ivy Way in receipt of single person discount and housing benefit. I'm risking my job in contacting you like this but there just can't be many Mary Calleys with the same birthday as me who also previously lived at 112b Rainwalk Terrace, Sheffield. I believe this is you and you are my twin sister. I work a lot in Nottingham so please contact me if you'd like to meet up. I really want to help you. If it's not you, please ignore this letter and I'll accept whatever consequences; I'm just desperate to find my sister. Hope you understand.

Our birthday is in two weeks and I'd so like to celebrate with you.

I can drive down and meet you in Nottingham. I really want to meet you, Mary. I do owe you my life and you now are the only real family I have.

Please write back. Or call. Or email. Anything.

Love you already and always

Your sister
Maya xxx

Maya has turned her face to the side, but Diana sees her eyes glisten – in fury or pain? In rage?

'And the second one dated 6th June 2008 ...'

Dear Mary

I've not heard from you. I keep thinking maybe you moved or didn't get the letter? Hope you get this one.

I've really tried everything to find you, but you've disappeared into thin air. Maybe you've gone travelling? Maybe you have moved on and don't want to pull up the pain of the past.

Even if you don't want to be connected, please let me know you are OK and well. I feel concerned. I always love you and am grateful forever.

Your sister
Maya xxxx

Maya glances at her solicitor whose mouth is open, catching flies. She shakes her head with a small smile.

'It must have been a disappointment when Mary didn't reply to your letters. You must almost have been relieved to realise the reason she didn't *wasn't* because she didn't want anything to do with you – but because she was dead.'

'No comment. Seriously, are you done now? I really need to go and you can't keep me.'

Diana sighs. 'You think it won't make CPS. Not enough evidence, a detective with a bee in her bonnet about an unrelated case. Too much evidence to suggest an OCG was responsible. I'm sure your brief will have a field day. I'm hanging on by my fingernail, a bullet, a filing cabinet key and some blood. Oh, and Bruno.'

Maya looks up sharply.

'Leave Bruno out of it.'

'Maya, it's *you* who involved Bruno. There's more than a suggestion you exploited him for both criminal *and* sexual purposes.'

Maya throws her head back, laughing loudly. 'Detective, you really need to start dating instead of tying your knickers in a twist over an unsolved case. Bruno's a young man, his own man.'

'Barely, Maya. You were scoping him long before he turned eighteen, grooming him.'

'Grooming!' Maya snorts indignantly.

'Anyway, he's had his swabs taken and is being investigated. If he's clean, he'll walk free, don't worry.'

Maya rolls her eyes.

'When can my client leave?' asks the brief.

'I've still got some time. And some questions.'

Maya shakes her head. 'I'm cold, bored and have clients waiting for their work.'

'No doubt. You were almost through your to-do list too. Of course, there was Aaliyah – or rather Ally. That was confusing. What happened to Ally? She used to be such a stunner, according to the photos. Both her and Mary. She's a scarred cripple now. Lives out of Sheffield. Oh, I know she's at uni, but how come both her and Mary left? Did the book club let you into the secret – or did you work it out yourself?'

Maya shivers, pulls her jacket around her, hands on her shoulders, eyes half closed.

'The reason I ask is we've not been able to find and arrest Ryan Pierce since Ally came in to report the crime this weekend. And it seems you were the last person to see him. Do you know where Ryan is, Maya?'

Maya rolls her eyes.

'Sure? OK, well, I'm sure he'll turn up. I think you were more concerned about an enemy of Mary's not to be found on any of your databases. Did you discover the most possible cause of Mary's death – a ruptured spleen, haemorrhage, ripped ulcer, caused by a blunt force trauma? There was no autopsy done on Mary, but a ruptured spleen or gastric haemorrhage might explain why she didn't last long at the Nottingham bedsit. She wouldn't have had access to a GP over the Christmas/New Year period. There's no evidence Young, Daniels or our 0039 texter knew where she was. Maybe the assailant was linked to her report of FGM. There is no database for FGM cutters in Sheff. Probably not in the UK. So being an RI is not going to help you there.'

Maya sighs deeply, looking sideways at the wall.

'Somehow you found out the name of who they *believed* was responsible for Mary's fatal injury.'

Maya starts tapping the underside of the table.

'Ifrah Hussain.'

'Only it wasn't Ifrah. It was *Irfrah*. Irfrah Hussein.'

Maya stops tapping.

'What happened next, Maya? Did you hear the name and Pitsmoor? For once, your emotions overtook your professionalism. Did you plan on knocking out all twenty-seven Ifrahs and Irfrahs in Pitsmoor? While you feel your vigilante murders are warranted, where do you stop and why would you, when you can get away with it? When you can justify it? After all, isn't one Ifrah as good – or as bad – as another? See – you're no different than the racist institutions you hate.'

Maya looks up, frowning. Diana shrugs.

'Yet – what *could* you have done? Google FGM cutters in Sheffield?'

Maya shifts in her seat. She's looking at her nails, but Diana sees her thumb is shaking.

'Even if you had, you'd still have been wrong. We'll find the right Irfrah and she will be investigated. Thoroughly – for both FGM and the assault. But she won't be executed behind a wheelie bin without a fair trial, that's for sure. Killed with a silenced nine-millimetre a couple of hours before the bin men came.

'DS Robertson had to tell her husband, a cleaner at Northern General Hospital, that he's now a widower with a family to raise on his own.'

Maya keeps her head down. The brief clears his throat.

'Or did you get Ryan Pierce to do that? His fingerprints are all over the gun, so Suspect Number One should be him – not you. No one's heard or seen him since you left yours together on Sunday.'

Maya shakes her head, eyes to the ceiling. 'He dropped me at my office around eleven Sunday night. I sleep on my couch when I have an early train and an important case.'

To get to a ten-thirty appointment that you cancelled.

Diana continues: 'And then his van was seen parked up at Pitsmoor down the road from the wrong Ifrah. Sorry – Irfrah.'

Maya shrugs. 'Sure he'll turn up soon, detective.'

'Bad pennies usually do, eh, Maya? Like old phone numbers on his son's phone ending in 0039 under "Ryan". Not "Dad".'

Diana collects up her papers. 'So, Maya Smith, I am charging you with the murder of John Daniels, Leroy Young and *possibly* Ifrah Hussein – although maybe you got Ryan to do that? Hopefully he'll set us straight soon.'

Maya's thumb is still trembling.

'How do you plead?'

'Not guilty.' Maya shakes her head. 'This is what my high taxes get me: false accusations. My brief will definitely be in touch.'

She looks at him. He is now loudly clicking his Parker, staring at the table.

Diana gets up, makes her way to the door.

'But, in answer to your question, no.'

'Which question?' Diana turns.

'No, I don't regret killing that stag before it killed you.'

They stare at each other. Diana has goosebumps. She nods.

'The officers will take you back to your cell.'

Back upstairs, she asks Lawton: 'Do you have the surveillance product of the last sighting of Pierce?'

Lawton sighs, barely turning his head to answer: 'Walker, I've already told you. The van's up at Pitsmoor.'

'Not the van – Pierce himself.'

Lawton groans but brings up images on his screen.

He points to one of Pierce and Axmed getting out of the van at Dewbright Hall. 20:08 07/11/2010. Diana frowns.

'And leaving?'

The picture is dark, grainy with the fog and no downstairs lights coming from the hall. Footage of the van reversing and coming down the drive at speed. Diana points.

'Zoom in there. Stop at zero six.' Lawton, frowning, presses the arrow. The images are blurry, but one thing is clear.

'There's no one in the passenger seat. I can see the headrest.'

369

Lawton gasps. Leans back. He says: 'Driver's wearing a blue boiler suit – Ryan got out wearing a black North Face jacket and jeans.'

Diana enters the lab where Gorman is waiting. The barely-there grey matter of mangled Young lies on the slab.

'She must keep some hungry perch in there.'

Suddenly, Diana feels ravenous; she could murder a plate of rice and beans, some jerk jackfruit. She nods at the mass of grey.

Gorman inhales. 'Water will do that. Fish will make it worse, but he went in fully clothed. Look here ...'

He points to the front of a partially exposed upper back.

'Shot in the back of the lower neck with a .308 rifle.'

'Like Daniels.'

'Like Daniels.'

Diana turns from the corpse.

'How long you think?'

'Hard to be bang on, but at least ten weeks.'

'August Bank Holiday?'

'Most likely.'

'What about the machete in the pond?'

He shakes his head. 'Clean.'

Her shoulders drop.

'The hacksaw?'

'More luck there. Bits of bone, tissue, even blood in its teeth.'

'Daniels?'

He nods.

'Yes! Great work, Will.'

He takes the reports, moves around the table towards her. Diana's already heading for the door, hand out for the folder.

He holds onto it a moment. 'And someone else's who *is* on our DNA database.'

She stares.

He nods.

Chapter 46

SUNDAY 14TH NOVEMBER, 2010 – DEWBOW

After three more days of yet more paperwork, evidence-checking and ballistics results, Diana is shattered. Driving home, the sky is low, dark, a grey-purple sundown. Yellow blinks of the farm above her. Headlights on into a tunnel of black-armed branches, a funnel of needled hail her wipers can't erase fast enough, branches arching over her like some Gothic cathedral. Racket on her roof. Out from the pews of trees, a brown form staggers.

Stops.

Stares.

Diana freezes, slams on the brakes. The *thud-thud-thud* of the wiper on windowpane. *Thud-thud-thud*. Five feet from her. Red-rimmed dark eyes, thick red-brown neck, blood on its shaggy chest, thorns tangled in its mighty antlers, one broken. The stag stares, daring her. But Diana's stopped.

The stag limps off into the dark.

Her headlights bore into the black hole beyond.

And that's when she knows where Ryan is.

In the tunnel of trees, she does a three-point turn.

Chapter 47

MONDAY 15TH NOVEMBER, 2010 – THE RYANO HUT, SHEFFIELD

It's banging it down, hail like nails, hitting the car roof, slicing murky puddles. A huddled figure, bunched up like a round parcel in a black puffa jacket and fake Ugg boots stands in the doorway of the shuttered Ryano Hut. She clutches a red and black brolly whose broken spike hangs down, a ripped raven's wing. Robertson struggles to lock the car door while Diana hopscotches puddles, hood up.

'Tasha? Detective Walker.'

The figure grunts, showering Diana with the pooled contents of the broken brolly.

'Been out here ten minutes.'

Behind her, Diana hears O'Malley and Khan's car pull up. She jumps into the doorway to avoid the splash-back.

'Why didn't you open up before?' she asks as Tasha hands her the mangled brolly and struggles to open the shutters. But she knows why. She can tell from the look of fear in Tasha's eyes. With a shove at the door, it opens. *Beep-beep-beep*. Tasha inputs digits. The red light stops flashing. Blue lights outside start flashing.

Diana steps into the grey, shabby shop front that stinks of stale fried food. She looks around, nodding at O'Malley and Khan as they shake themselves off at the door.

'When were you last open?'

'Sunday – not yesterday. Week before.'

'Sunday 7th November?'

'Yeah. It's not like him to just – not even answer his phone. Bruno's been calling me. Wants his wage. Everyone calling me like I'm his gyal. I got bad men calling me. I don't want to be here when they roll up.'

Diana looks at the sodden Robertson, dripping cowlick, pen out already.

'Miss Taylor, do you mind giving a statement for Detective Sergeant Robertson? The constables and I will go through to the kitchen. Anyone but you and Ryan know the code to the Ryano Hut?'

Tasha shakes her head.

'Bruno might. But if he does, he never uses it. Just waits outside getting mardy.'

Diana goes into the dark kitchen. It's cold as a morgue, smelling of bleach, raw meat and earthy potatoes. Immaculate surfaces, scrubbed to show every scratch and peel of the Formica, not like when she was here before. Even the sink's spotless. She looks out at the closed backyard. Nothing overlooks it.

'Fingerprint every surface,' she says to O'Malley and Khan, pulling on her own gloves. She switches on the fluorescent light. It buzzes like some trapped giant mosquito. She stoops under the sinks, in the cold store, opens the fridge: stocked with blackening cabbage, carrots, blue-green ginger root. Rank, soaked salt-fish. Opens the chest freezer. Pulls out bags of carved-up chicken legs, thighs, breast …

Stops.

Stares.

Ice crystals on grisly brows.

Neck tattoo purpling in wrinkles around a smooth bullet hole.

Blue flaccid lips.

Her own frozen fingers fumble for her phone.

She presses last dialled.

'I think we found Ryan Pierce.'

Marchant barks: 'Where?'

'Next to the frozen peas.'

Marchant's expletives.

'The Ryano Hut, sir.'

373

Chapter 48

Monday 29th November, 2010 – Dewbow

The letter box clatters.

Diana is making coffee, watching the flurry of snowflakes fall over the white blanket in the back. MaMa is arranging her bowl of porridge on the kitchen table.

'What's up with this weather? It's only November. Santa's not even got his sleigh serviced. You ever seen snow, MaMa?'

MaMa's head is turned towards the window, watching the postman walk past.

'The world is reversing, *mwana*. The time has come.'

MaMa scrapes her chair back and walks to the hall. Returning, she holds a stack of various envelopes in one hand, a long cream envelope in the other. She adds the varied envelopes to Diana's unopened pile on the coffee table. Then takes her own letter with her to the kitchen.

Diana turns from the counter.

She groans. 'I'll deal with my post today. Or tomorrow.'

MaMa shakes her head. 'Today, *mwana*.'

'I know. I've just not had ...'

Time. Headspace. Courage. I used it all up.

Diana brings two mugs of steaming coffee to the table, kicking the chair leg to the side so she can sit down. MaMa carefully puts on her glasses, pulling out the double scored letter and reading its contents. It's thick cream paper, but Diana can see it's at least three paragraphs long. MaMa reads it slowly, her hands trembling. Diana sips her coffee, her eyes glued to MaMa's face. Finally, MaMa puts the paper down, removing her glasses. She picks up her mug of coffee.

'That from your solicitors?'

MaMa nods.

'The Royal High Court of Justice will be reviewing our case.'

'Woh.' Diana stares. 'So, potentially, the British Government may be liable for the abuse and suffering?'

MaMa sips coffee. 'The chances are slim, but Mr Day is hoping to gain access to some detailed records the British Government hid away all those years ago.'

'Where are they?'

'Here – in this country. Hanslope Park.'

Of course they are.

'Never heard of the place.' Diana raises her eyebrows. 'So – we see ... and wait?'

MaMa nods. 'And pray.'

An hour later, having de-iced the car, she sits in the front, snow falling in heavy soft flakes over the whitened street. With the heater blowing, her gloved hands slowly open her own envelope, the one franked from South Yorkshire Police Department.

She reads it.

Reads it again.

DI Phillips is going to be suspended from duty pending an investigation into allegations of sexual assault.

Her sobs break the silence of snow.

Silence speaks back to her, its only child.

And when silence speaks, it roars.

Epilogue

FRIDAY 16TH JULY, 2011

Sheffield Serial Killer Sentenced

A top auditor was convicted and sentenced today at Sheffield Crown Court for the murders of three men and one woman and the obstruction of justice between August and November last year. The murders of John Daniels, Leroy Young, Ifrah Hussein and Ryan Pierce shook Sheffield to its core.

The heavily pregnant defendant pleaded not guilty to all charges, but a unanimous jury found her guilty on all counts of pre-meditated murder in a spree that terrorised Sheffield following the demolition of Legley Road High School.

Defence solicitors claimed Maya Smith, director and former partner of Sheffield's top auditing firm, Bracewell & Smith, had suffered an acute psychological trauma in the wake of the death of her adoptive father, top industrialist and Master Cutler Tom Johnson, in 2007. She had discovered she had a birth twin sister, Mary. When she tried to trace her twin, she found the former Legley Road High School teacher, Mary Calley, had been dead for at least two years, undiscovered in a bedsit in Nottingham until March 2010. This, the defence solicitor claimed, triggered a dormant rage directed towards the people and systems Smith believed culpable for her twin's death.

In sentencing Smith to four consecutive life sentences today, Judge Brewer said: 'While I have the deepest sympathy for the way you discovered your twin's death, this does not exonerate you from the cold-blooded meticulous planning of the murder of four people nor the abuse of your powers and the public's trust in your position. Ifrah Hussein was an entirely innocent woman who came to this country seeking refuge from violence. You planned on using Ryan Pierce as a subterfuge for gaining access to a handgun and framing him for Hussein's murder – even though he was dead before she was – thus misleading police into suspecting an OCG element.

'You have left the families of John Daniels, Leroy Young, Ryan Pierce and Ifrah Hussein permanently scarred and devastated. What I have found most bewildering in this case is why an educated, privileged and talented woman such as yourself, with full recourse to the law and the ability to see justice done in the wider community, should choose such a barbaric method of revenge. Revenge is not justice, Ms Smith. Your twin's death, by natural causes, according to the coroner's report, could never be righted through your vengeance.'

Apart from pleading 'Not Guilty', Smith remained silent and impassive throughout the trial. The identity of the father of the child she is carrying is unknown, but the child will immediately be placed in the care of the authorities once it is born.

Arresting officer and SIO of the case, DCI Diana Walker said: 'This case has been particularly difficult as it dealt with a very traumatised and powerful woman as well as undocumented domestic abuse and FGM. These murders have had a seismic effect on our community, but also highlighted the desperate consequences of unreported, unresolved domestic violence and the norm of men evading the arm of justice.'

Mrs Young's family came to the trial as did Mr Daniels' ex-wife and Mrs Hussein's husband. Mrs Young, wife of one of Smith's victims, PE teacher Leroy Young, said: 'Ms Smith betrayed my trust in her as my client and has stolen my child's father and future security. I hope she rots in hell.'

Bracewell and Smith is now known only as Bracewell. Smith's property is now understood to be managed by the

Dewbow Shining Light Trust as a retreat and conservation lodge.

Ex-staff and students from Legley Road High School have said they have mixed feelings regarding the sentencing. 'Ms Calley was a much-loved teacher who longed for a family. To think she had a twin but didn't know and how she died alone is heart-breaking,' said Willeta Muhammed, a former student of Legley Road High School.

The prosecuting counsel claimed Smith had access to Mary's private papers and documents and was able to discover Mary had reported several incidents of sexual assault, intimidation and menacing communications to the police but none had been either logged or followed up. 'When Smith discovered the institutional fraud regarding the award her sister had won for her students, she took it personally. It was then she decided to take matters into her own hands and use her prowess as a country sportswoman and game butcher for the murder and mutilation of these men.'

SATURDAY 30TH OCTOBER, 2011 – DEWBOW

Diana gets out of her car, stepping into two inches of amber beech leaves. The chill of November is already in the air, along with the smell of woodsmoke. Her neighbour's windows parade glowing jack-o'-lantern pumpkins. She must tell MaMa to get ready for the trick or treaters tomorrow night; last year, MaMa had asked for tricks, thinking that they were *offering* tricks or treats, which confused most of the local kids – and their parents. The sky is already a muddy grey, a reminder that this is the last night before winter time kicks in.

Tucking the copy of the *Sheffield Star* under her arm, she unlocks the front door, wondering why the lights are off.

'MaMa?'

No answer. The house is in darkness, but there's flashes of light coming from the kitchen which sends her pulse racing. Flipping fireworks – they'll have sparked the pile of wood chippings and garden rubbish Michael had cleared last weekend. Yanking the back door open, she rushes out.

A tall, broad-shouldered silhouette steps out, carrying a pile of hawthorn sticks in elbow-deep gloves, his locks up in a ponytail. In the shadows, Diana sees MaMa's face looking up from where she sits on an upturned crate, a mug of tea in her ungloved hands. Her face is radiant, reflecting light off the flames.

'There you are! Just in time for our fire.'

Diana's fingers brush Michael's neck as he puts the sticks down.

'Michael, you never said you were coming down!'

379

'Louise wanted to take the boys to some Hallowe'en party so ...' He shrugs, smiling. 'Thought I'd get this shifted. It's going to rain this week.'

Diana hugs him. 'Gave me a fright. Thought MaMa was burning the house down!'

MaMa snorts. 'If I was burning a house down, it would be a furnace not a campfire.'

'It's good tinder though, MaMa,' Michael says, snapping the branches into fragments.

'Here – *I've* got some tinder for you.'

Diana holds out the *Sheffield Star*, but the shadows obscure the lettering. Michael frowns.

'What's that?'

'Look – the headline!'

MaMa looks up at Diana.

'Here. Sit down and read it aloud, *mwana*. I don't have my glasses.'

Diana sits down next to MaMa.

'"CID Detective sentenced to five years in prison. A former detective inspector, Keith Phillips, was today charged for sexual assault, harassment and corruption following his suspension and a lengthy investigation. Sentencing him today at Sheffield Crown Court, Judge Laverty said: 'Your behaviour, sustained over years, was not only an assault against a fellow police officer but against the reputation of the police and the rule of law itself. Even allowing for your pristine career, I have no option but to give a custodial sentence of five years.'"'

'Don't speak his name!' hisses MaMa. Michael glares into the fire, unblinking, throwing in sticks.

'Pristine career...!' Diana mutters.

'Give me that!' MaMa grabs the paper from Diana's lap and slowly, methodically tears it into strips. Rolls the strips into balls. Hurls the balls into the flames.

'Hey!' Diana watches the process. 'Hey, I've not read it all yet ...'

She watches the balls disintegrate into yellow and then nothing. MaMa does the whole paper, strip by strip. Michael snaps twigs, stick by stick before throwing on the birch stump. The hungry fire consumes the offerings, its crackle now a roar.

MaMa smiles with satisfaction. Diana looks up into the darkening sky.

'We turn the clocks back tonight.'

'Good!' says Michael, winking at her. 'I get an extra hour with you.'

Diana beams up at him.

MaMa is elsewhere, staring into the flames. She mutters: 'The clock goes back but fire cleans the soil.'

Acknowledgements

I would like to thank Dr Ngozika Jane Hemuka for sharing her expertise on FGM in Africa, her PhD: 'The Continuation of Female Genital Mutilation in Nigeria: A Mixed Methods Study of Igbo Men's Views and Perpetuating Factors' and her continued work in public health, internationally raising awareness and understanding of this extreme form of violence against girls and women. My friend, Mercy Anne Salipu, and other women who have first-hand experience of the culture and the act itself. All the students of Abbeydale Grange School (Sheffield) circa 2005-2007 when I taught there, St Matthew's Roman Catholic High School (Moston, Manchester), Crown Woods College (Eltham, South East London) and Hampstead School (Camden, London). My landladies, Barbara and Shaz, and their Book Club – which I never attended! The faithful transcripts of UK parliamentary debate in the House of Lords 1952-1955 regarding Kenya and the alleged 'Mau Mau uprising'. Hulda Stumpf – who became a heroine of mine for her courage in standing against FGM and the guise of the 'unification of African churches', and even her own institution, the African Inland Mission. The various myths and legends surrounding her murder and the impact she had on the women and young orphan girls in her care was pivotal to understanding this dark period in history. Stumpf herself was marginalised, labelled a secretary and administrator when she did so much more. Her reports in *The Indiana Progress* from 1909 onwards gave me an insight into her world. I loved everything about this contrary, awkward woman who stood against all of the horrific hypocrisy and politics of the time and stood for the real gospel for women. Like Mary, no strong conclusions could be drawn about her death. She was a writer and chronicler and provided me with the sense of local scrutiny and the local democracy of Kijabe.

I would also like to thank the Kenyan Human Rights Commission. I am indebted to the laborious work, the testimonies of the survivors of the atrocities, and the tenacity of George Morara and Leigh Day lawyers when met with a government unwilling to fulfil its responsibility, determined still to diminish and delete such a seismic fault in British history.

The University of East Anglia, particularly the MA in Crime Fiction's Henry Sutton (who told me to write about education and was cheering for Diana long before I was); Tom Benn, my second-year tutor who introduced me to the novels of David Peace and Pat Barker, a fellow writer (but far more brilliant) in dialect, whose passion for all things historical and northern made me feel slightly less irrelevant. He tirelessly egged me on through my arduous edit of 154,000 words down to 90,000; the erudite Dr Nathan Ashman for giving a cheap and not-so-cheerful mongrel an academic chance and introducing me to the wider world of crime fiction.

My fellow crime writers on the course: Helen, Jo, Mark, Danny, Bex, Kat, Cathy, Asun, Tamsin, Julia and their invaluable critical feedback on the novel in its early stages. Little Brown for awarding me the Crime Fiction prize.

Ed Wood for his generosity of spirit and genuine passion for crime procedural.

Caroline Wood of Felicity Bryan Associates for being a dynamic whirlwind of a reader, agent and cheerleader, who worked tirelessly over Christmas 2022 to get my novel read by publishers and then negotiated like a shark.

Julia Wisdom for being a meticulous, elegant editor and a fearsome warrior for women's voices in crime fiction. Lots of people talk about diversity in publishing; Julia walks the walk. Thank you for really getting MaMa, Diana and Rehema from the start, for asking me the kind of questions that pulled them out of their dark corners.

Elizabeth Burrell for being so thorough, and going through every nuance, nook and cranny of my edits.

Charlotte Webb, the copyeditor, for spotting my mistakes so swiftly and not saying unkind things when I repeatedly made stupid ones.

The entire HarperCollins team for getting behind the novel as one mighty tsunami.

Graham Bartlett for helping me navigate the SIO/Detective Inspector transitions and confrontations.

Grace, the woodland: a place of healing and refuge – not just for me but for the deer. The massive stags, the shy does and the spring fawn. You all breathed your magic on me – although I am guessing you won't read this and could care even less.

Heather Nova for rooting for me and providing me with inspiration since those frozen peas on a North Kensington balcony squat in 1988.

Maria Doctor for friendship and prayers.

Tupac Shakur for being my first reader and writing compadre. Nobody else heard my voice; you did.

Regina King for being my co-writer 1995-1998 and critiquing endless comedy skits and dialogue.

Lockdown 2020-2021, without which I probably wouldn't have spent an entire year listening to my characters until I understood their story.

The cat.

And, yes, I *do* want to thank God, without whom absolutely none of this would be possible.

There are so many people I need to thank but some of the most significant are now lost to me or were former students of mine, old housemates, and fellow refugees in hostels for the marginalised and forgotten. I do believe the more neglected and unknown a woman is, the stronger her myth, her power and her voice for blood *will* speak.

In memory of Cameron Reece Mohammed Wilson aka Speedy. May your voice and story live on.